Paul William

The Rose Garden

Division I + II,

Paul William

The Rose Garden
Division I + II,

ISBN/EAN: 9783337413927

Printed in Europe, USA, Canada, Australia, Japan

Cover: Foto ©Andreas Hilbeck / pixelio.de

More available books at **www.hansebooks.com**

THE

ROSE GARDEN.

IN TWO DIVISIONS.

DIVISION I.

EMBRACING THE HISTORY OF THE ROSE, THE FORMATION OF THE
ROSARIUM, AND A DETAILED ACCOUNT OF THE VARIOUS PRACTICES
ADOPTED IN THE SUCCESSFUL CULTIVATION OF THIS POPULAR FLOWER :
ILLUSTRATED WITH NUMEROUS ENGRAVINGS ON WOOD.

DIVISION II.

CONTAINING AN ARRANGEMENT, IN NATURAL GROUPS, OF THE MOST
ESTEEMED VARIETIES OF ROSES RECOGNISED AND CULTIVATED IN THE
VARIOUS ROSE GARDENS, ENGLISH AND FOREIGN ; WITH FULL DESCRIP-
TIONS AND REMARKS ON THEIR ORIGIN AND MODE OF CULTURE.

'Η Σαπφὼ τοῦ ῥόδον ἐρᾷ, καὶ στεφανοῖ αὐτὸ ἀεί τινι ἐγκωμίῳ· τὰς καλὰς
τῶν παρθένων ἐκείνῳ ὁμοιοῦσα.

Sappho was enamoured of the Rose, and bestows upon it always some distinguished praise :
she likens it to the most beautiful of maidens.—PHILOSTRATUS. Ep. 73.

BY WILLIAM PAUL, F.R.H.S.

SECOND EDITION.

LONDON :

KENT AND CO., 23 PATERNOSTER ROW,

AND TO BE HAD OF ALL BOOKSELLERS.

—

1863.

TO THE

ROSE AMATEURS

OF

GREAT BRITAIN AND IRELAND.

THIS WORK

IS MOST RESPECTFULLY INSCRIBED

BY

THEIR HUMBLE SERVANT,

THE AUTHOR.

PREFACE TO FIRST EDITION.

In submitting the present work to the public, it is thought desirable to state that it contains an exposition of the principles followed in these Nurseries, where the Rose has been extensively and successfully cultivated, under the author's superintendence, for many years. A chief inducement to its publication was, the writer's desire to improve the condition of a favourite flower. It had long appeared to him that a work entering into the detail of Rose-culture, elucidating the various practices by means of Wood-engravings, and furnishing Coloured Plates of some of the choicest kinds was a desideratum; and that the non-existence of such a work proved a formidable barrier to the agreeable and satisfactory prosecution of this branch of Floriculture.

Holding these views, it was his wish to publish, in a form and at a price, which would place the work within reach of the humblest cultivator; but the great expense attending the production of Coloured Plates in a highly-finished style, and the knowledge that the circulation of a class-work must necessarily be limited, pointed out the impracticability of pursuing such a course, and the idea was ultimately, though with reluctance, abandoned.

The publication did not, however, appear unadvisable because it could not be made more generally accessible. On the contrary, it was evident, from conversation with numerous Amateurs and professional Florists, who from time to time visited the Nurseries, that it was greatly required. It was argued that there were more lovers of flowers seeking amusement in the culture of the Rose at the present time than at any previous period; that the most difficult and important branches of cultivation were nowhere fully and clearly treated of; and that although other favourites had figured liberally in the Floricultural Periodicals of the day, this had remained almost unnoticed, no series of Coloured Drawings having appeared later than 1820, since which period the Rose had undergone a thorough change. Into the causes of this it is needless to inquire. Suffice it to say, that the neglect could not have originated in an indifference to the merits, or a supposed unpopularity of the flower. We can scarcely enter any garden, however humble, which does not contain a Rose-tree; and many of the noted establishments in England have, like in Rome of old, places set apart expressly for their cultivation. And it is not a slavish obedience to fashion that has led to this. Although cherished alike by peer and peasant, the popularity of the Rose rests on a surer foundation—its intrinsic merit. What other genus of plants embraces so great a variety of character, or gives forth such a number of delicious blossoms for so long a period? Moreover, it is easy of culture ; suited to a great variety of soils; lives and blooms even when neglected; yet yields an abundant return for whatever labour may be bestowed upon it.

The ROSE GARDEN is arranged in two Divisions. The First includes Chapters on The History of the Rose, the Formation of the Rosarium, and the various practices of Cultivation. The Chapters on Hybridizing and raising Seedlings are, it is believed, altogether new, and likely to prove interesting and useful at this particular era in Rose-culture. The Second Division embraces a natural arrangement of all the approved Roses known, with full descriptions of their colours, sizes, forms, degrees of fulness, habit, rates of growth, and purposes for which best suited. The descriptions are chiefly the result of close personal observation, having been taken from living specimens at a great cost of time and labour; which will be granted readily, when it is stated that above 2000 varieties are described. Nevertheless, it was judged desirable to pursue this course, in order to attain to that accuracy in the descriptive part of the work which should render it a safe and efficient guide in selecting varieties.

The execution of the Coloured Drawings has been entrusted to eminent artists, whose design has been, not to fabricate a pleasing flower, but to produce exact representations of nature. This feature of the work presents the cultivator with *Roses at all seasons;* —alike when the blasts of autumn scatter his favourites without doors to the winds of heaven, and the rigours of winter surround them with the garb of death.

Before concluding, the writer would acknowledge his obligations to numerous Correspondents for suggestions received from time to time during the period of publication. Such Letters as contained hints on cultivation he has inserted in the Appendix as advertised ; and regrets that want of space should have compelled him to curtail some interesting communications. The article on the " Botany of the Rose," contained in the Appendix will, he thinks, prove particularly interesting, and should be read by all who feel inclined to enter upon the pleasing task of raising seedlings.

PAUL'S NURSERIES, WALTHAM CROSS, N.

PREFACE TO THE SECOND EDITION.

A Second Edition of the "Rose Garden" being called for, the Author is enabled to realize his wish of publishing in a form and at a price which will place the work within reach of the humblest Cultivator.

To accomplish this aim, it was found necessary to omit the coloured plates; a point deemed of little importance, as a series of new plates, representations of more modern varieties, is in course of publication in the Author's "Rose Annual."*

The present Edition of the "Rose Garden" has been carefully revised, and in part re-written. There is, indeed, a great change in the descriptive part of the work. Many of the varieties described, and even recommended at the time the first Edition was published, are now withdrawn, because surpassed in excellence by more modern varieties.

It was at first the intention to insert in the present Edition only such kinds as could be recommended; and this principle will be adhered to in the issue of the Yearly Catalogue. But in a work like the present, it was thought likely to prove of some service to lovers of the Rose, to include the many questionable varieties, floating about, if only to fix their position.

The original edition of the Rose Garden has been translated into Danish,† and my consent was asked and granted to the publication of editions in German and French also; but as I have never met with the work in either of the latter languages, I do not know if the translators' intentions have been carried out.

Paul's Nurseries, Waltham Cross,
  March 1863.

* The Rose Annual, by William Paul, F.R.H.S., 8vo., 4 Coloured Plates. Kent & Co., Paternoster Row.

† Rosengartneren &c. En Oversaltelse af Pauls Rosegarden afpasset efter danske Forholde ved Bentzien og Skoldager, Kjöbenhavn, 1855

CONTENTS.

DIVISION I.

TABLE OF CHAPTERS.

DIVISION II.

TABLE OF GROUPS.

Class I.—SUMMER ROSES.

Class II.—AUTUMNAL ROSES.

DIVISION I.

EMBRACING THE HISTORY OF THE ROSE,

THE FORMATION OF THE ROSARIUM,

AND A DETAILED ACCOUNT OF THE VARIOUS PRACTICES ADOPTED IN THE

SUCCESSFUL CULTIVATION OF THIS POPULAR FLOWER :

THE SUBJECT ILLUSTRATED WITH NUMEROUS ENGRAVINGS ON WOOD.

1 0

CHAPTER I.

THE HISTORY OF THE ROSE.

THE Rose, which is the leading flower of the day, the acknowledged favourite of the two greatest nations in the world, is to be found, in a wild state, very generally spread over the earth's surface.

As if too beautiful to be excluded from the natural Flora of any one of the ancient divisions of the world, it graces alike various countries of Asia, Africa, and North America, and extends over the whole of Europe, where, blooming in its native wildness and simplicity, it is universally prized and admired.

But although the geographical distribution of the various species makes the Rose an inhabitant of nearly the whole of the Northern Hemisphere, some species are far less plentiful than others, or, if plentiful in certain localities, have a less extended range. Here is one, confined to some particular and favoured spots; here another, not content with ranging one quarter of the globe;—the ROSA CANINA for instance, the one most commonly seen adorning our wilds and hedge-rows, is found also in Africa and Asia.

It is a remarkable fact, that Australia has naturally no Roses; and none have yet been found wild very near to, or south of, the Equator. It is in the temperate regions of Asia, and throughout Europe generally, that those species abound, from which nearly the whole of the present garden varieties have sprung. But if we extend our view, we find some growing on the mountains of North America, whose tops are covered with eternal snow; and others in the dreary wilds of Greenland, Kamschatka, and Iceland; while in Siberia there are several interesting species. On the other hand, if we turn to warmer climates, we discover that Mexico, Abyssinia, China, Persia, India, and Egypt have their Roses; and even on the outskirts of the mighty Sahara one species is found, gladdening the approaches to the desert with its clusters of white flowers, though often

——Born to blush unseen,
And waste their sweetness on the desert air.

Who were the first people to bring this flower from its natural habitats, to be a dweller in cultivated grounds, must ever remain a matter of conjecture. Doubtless it attracted the notice of the virtuoso in plants at a very early date ; probably when they were merely valued as objects of natural history, or for their medicinal properties. We may follow in imagination the busy doings of the plant-collector in the earliest times; we may fancy him gathering, and fixing in one spot, the beautiful productions scattered around him ; and it is natural to suppose that the most beautiful, or most useful, would be first collected. This surely would give an early date to the civilization of the Queen of Flowers. And doubtless the Rose has a claim to our regard as well for its antiquity, as for its beauty, variety, and fragrance. The famous gardens of Babylon, which are supposed to have existed 2000 years before the Christian æra, would probably number it among its treasures. This, of course, can be but conjecture ; though the probability is increased when we consider that the neighbouring country, Persia, has ever been famous for the Roses it naturally produces. In the Sacred Scriptures we read of " him who was to make the wilderness be glad, and the desert to blossom as the Rose": we read also of "the Rose of Sharon," and " the Rose of Jericho."

It has been questioned whether the flowers met with in translations of the ancient writers are identical with those known under like names in the present day. Indeed, what is commonly known as the Rose of Jericho, is a little cruciferous plant, with white flowers, very different from our Roses. I do not feel disposed to enter into this question ; indeed it would be out of place to do so here : but I would remark, in passing, that the non-existence of the wild forms in those countries, at the present time, is not conclusive evidence to me that they never flourished there ; or even were it so, the productions of other countries might have been introduced, to administer to the comforts and enjoyments of this people.

In the Book of Wisdom (chap. ii. ver. 7, 8) the following passage occurs :—" Let us fill ourselves with costly wine and ointment, and let no flower of the spring pass by us. Let us crown ourselves with Rose-buds before they be withered." Hence it is apparent that the practices so common with the Greeks and Romans of crowning themselves with flowers at their Bacchanalian feasts, and on various other occasions, were resorted to in these early times, and most probably were borrowed from the Jews. Again, in the Book of Ecclesiasticus (chap. xxxix. ver. 13) we find the following passage :— " Hearken unto me, ye holy children, and bud forth as a Rose growing by the brook of the field." Homer, the most ancient of all the profane writers, uses the Rose figuratively, both in the Iliad and Odyssey; and above 2000 years have rolled away since Sappho christened it the "Queen of Flowers." Philostratus (Epistle 73), writing of this lyric Poet, says, "Sappho was enamoured of the Rose, and bestows upon it always some distinguished praise : she likens it to the most beautiful of maidens." Such was the Rose then, and it still maintains as distinguished a position.

It were scarcely necessary to search the Greek authors for quotations to shew in what esteem that people held our flower. Ancient history, by which their customs are handed down to us, bears sufficient evidence of its popularity. The Rose, with other flowers, was used by them in times of public rejoicings, in their religious ceremonies, and the youth of both sexes wore them in the fêtes. They consecrated it to Venus, Cupid, Aurora, and also to Harpocrates, the God of Silence. If it was dedicated to Venus as an emblem of beauty, and to Cupid as an emblem of love, we may conjecture wherefore it was also dedicated to the goddess of the morning: it was the symbol of youth. But, beyond this, the Greeks doubtless were alive to the fact, that the Rose is most beautiful at sunrise: then, newly expanded by the breath of morn, there is visible all that freshness, in which consists so much of its peculiar beauty, and which soon vanishes before the radiance of a summer's sun. From its being consecrated to Harpocrates, the God of Silence, probably arose that custom practised in the north of Europe, but now almost fallen into desuetude, of suspending a Rose from the ceiling at convivial or other meetings, to signify that what transpired was of a confidential nature. "The White Rose has long been considered as sacred to silence: over whatever company it was suspended, no secrets were ever revealed, for it hung only above the festal board of sworn friendship. No matter how deep they might drink, or how long the wine-cup might circulate round the table, so long as the White Rose hung over their heads every secret was considered inviolable ;—no matter how trivial, or how important the trust, beneath that flower it was never betrayed ; for around it was written the sentence—

He who doth secrets reveal
Beneath my roof shall never live.

What faith, and what confidence must there have been between man and man in the olden time, when only the presence of a flower was needed to prevent the maligning whisper—to freeze up slander's hateful slime—and destroy that venom, which, when once circulated, proves so fatal to human happiness!"—*The Poetical Language of Flowers*, by Thomas Miller. Bogue. London.

Sappho having named the Rose the "Queen of Flowers," other

of the Greek writers would naturally consider it a subject worthy of their attention. This was eminently the case. Theocritus, on account of its transitoriness, compares it to the course of human life. The gay Anacreon alludes to it in several of his Odes, calling it "the most beautiful of flowers," "the delight of the gods," "the favourite of the muses"; and says its leaves are full of charms. He speaks of it still more definitively as useful in diseases. The Rose is made the particular subject of his Fifty-third Ode, wherein the poet considers it sacred, and accounts for its origin in a mar vellous manner.

> While Spring with lavish flow'rets glows,
> From the gay wreath I'll pluck the Rose,
> The queen of fragrance will display.—
> Oh ! pour, my friend, th' accordant lay.
> Dear to earth, thy smiling bloom !
> Dear to heav'n thy rich perfume !
> Sacred to the sportive hour,
> When the loves, from flower to flower,
> Blithely trip ; the Graces fair
> Bind thy treasures to their hair ;
> By the Paphian queen caress'd,
> Seated on her snowy breast.

> Nymphs, who haunt th' embow'ring shades,
> Poesy's enchanting maids,
> Woo thee, Rose ; thy charms inspire
> All the raptures of the lyre.
> Cull we straight th' inviting Rose ;
> Shielded by the thorn it grows.
> Cull the Rose : what boots the smart !
> Boundless sweets regale the heart.

> Pluck it not : the flow'ry gem
> Unwilling quits its parent stem.
> Round the feast of fragrance rove ;
> But gently touch the Rose of love.
> Mid the sons of Comus spread
> Blooms the Rose's living red ;
> Chaplet for the thirsty soul,
> Well it crowns the purple bowl.

> Hark, the bard ! his numbers pour
> Incense to the sacred flower.
> The rosy-fingered beam of light
> Undraws the curtain of the night.
> Health's blushing Rose the virgin streaks,
> And paints the down of Venus' cheeks.

Lovely Rose! thy genial power
Sweetly soothes the sickly hour:
O'er the grave thy fragrance shed;
We sink in quiet to the dead.
When the envious hand of Time
Nips the harvest of thy prime,
Dead in youth thy odours bear
Sickness to the unloosed air.

Say from whence the Rose divine
This th' unrivalled lustre shine?
From the liquid caves of night,
When Aurora waked to light—
Waked from her Neptunian bath,
To fill with love the circling earth;
From the forehead of her sire,
When Pallas sprung with martial fire,
Nature gave the Queen of Flowers,
Coeval sister of the Powers.

When th' immortals frolic souls
Glow'd with Nectar's copious bowls,
Perchance, upon a blooming thorn,
Such as the heavenly seats adorn,
Prolific fell the ethereal dew:—
Consecrated Roses grew.
The topers hail'd the plant divine,
And gave it " To the god of wine."

(ANACREON, Ode 55. Translated by GREEN.)

It appears that the Greeks also cultivated this flower with the view of extracting the perfume from its petals. And Theophrastus, who lived about 300 years before the Christian æra, tells us it was common to set fire to the Rose-trees in Greece: and that unless this practice was resorted to, they would not produce any flowers. Is the writer in earnest? If so, this does not say much for the knowledge they possessed of the art of culture in those days. But although flowers were so much used on special occasions, it is generally admitted that gardening, considered as an art, was neglected by the Greeks.

If the Greeks considered the Rose worthy of adoration, the Romans were by no means less lavish in the praises they bestowed on it. They regarded it with that veneration and enthusiasm which the high encomiums passed on it by a people they so much admired might be supposed to give rise to. It has been said by some writers that the Romans acquired their taste for these flowers from the Egyptians, who, during the early ages of the Republic, sent quantities of them to Rome every year. But it appears to me more probable that the taste was acquired from the Greeks, although the Egyptians might have administered to, and further developed it. Virgil, the " prince of Latin poets," makes frequent mention of the Rose in his writings. In the opening of the Fifth Pastoral he contrasts the pale sallow to the blushing Rose :

> Puniceis humilis quantum saluinca rosetis ;
> Judicio nostro tantum tibi cedit Amyntas.
> [*Ecloga* 5. ver. 17, 18.

In the Georgics he speaks of " Pæstum Roses with their double spring" :

> Forsitan et, pingues hortos quæ cura colendi
> Ornaret, canerem, biferique rosaria Pæsti.
> [*Georg.* lib. iv. ver. 118, 119.

In reference to the latter quotation, Botanists who have visited Pæstum have not been able to meet with Roses flowering in autumn ; and some people have pronounced them creations of the poet's fancy. Be this as it may, it might be accounted for, I think, by presuming the adoption of a particular mode of culture. The culture of Roses was a trade at Pæstum ; and might not the cultivators have forced the plants, to induce them to flower early in the spring ? After this, they might rest them for a period ; and then, by pruning and watering, backed by the influences of their climate, induce a new growth, and consequently a second development of flowers. I can quite conceive of the practicability of this, although no one who cared for the ultimate weal of his plants might be disposed to practise it. Or, again, is it not probable that some of the Roses raised from seed were of this nature, though lost during the barbarous ages which succeeded the downfall of Rome ?

Cicero, Ovid, and Martial, speak of Roses ; and Pliny, who wrote on Gardening towards the close of the first century, devotes some considerable space to them. He mentions those of Carthage, and others of Miletus (supposed to be R. GALLICA). He tells us they used to obtain Roses before the natural season, by watering the plants with warm water so soon as the buds were visible. Whether such was the plan pursued by the Roman gardeners we are at perfect liberty to doubt, although it is certain they had, under the reign of Domitian, abundance of Roses in winter. Martial, the famous epigrammatic poet, ridicules the Egyptians for sending them Roses when they had already plenty, and asks them to send corn instead. Dr. Deslongchamps relates, on the authority of Seneca, that the Roman gardeners had at this time found out the means of constructing hot-houses, which they heated with tubes filled with hot water, and thus induced Roses and Lilies to flower in December. (*La Rose*, &c., par Dr. Deslongchamps.)

On the authority of Horace, it appears that Roses were grown in beds; and Columella mentions a place being reserved expressly for the production of late Roses.

With regard to the culture of this flower in those times, M. Boitard says, " The cultivation of flowers, and particularly of Roses, was carried on upon a grand scale, both at Pæstum and in the environs of Rome. The sale of the flowers was ordinarily in the hands of the prettiest girls of the place; and the Latin Poets have immortalized the names of several of these charming flower-girls, and have even deified some of them. The divinity of Flora, the goddess of flowers, has no other origin." (*Manuel Complet de l'Amateur des Roses*, &c., par M. Boitard. Paris, 1836.)

If there is any one period in the world's history, when flowers engrossed too much the attention of a nation, it was under the reigns of Augustus and subsequent Emperors of Rome. The love of flowers was then carried to excess; and the Rose seemed to bear away the palm from all. It was customary for the wealthy inhabitants to take their meals resting on Rose-leaves,—a practice which Cicero loudly condemns. Roses were scattered upon the beds and floors of the chambers of their guests. At their festivals they put the flowers in their cups of wine. In times of public rejoicing the streets were strewed with flowers, and the statues of their deities were adorned with crowns and garlands of Roses. Cleopatra, in a feast given to Marc Antony, is said to have expended a talent in their purchase; and the room of entertainment was strewed with them to a considerable depth. Suetonius, the Latin historian, relates of the Emperor Nero that he spent four millions of sesterces, amounting to more than 30,000*l*., in procuring Roses for one feast. Alas, that these gems of earth should have been so perverted from their just use! Here, instead of opening up a source of pure and intellectual enjoyment, we see them debased, and administering to the lust of a luxurious people.

It was customary with both Greeks and Romans to bring in flowers, Roses especially, at their Bacchanalian feasts, placing them on the tables, and ornamenting their persons with them, believing they preserved them from the intoxicating influences of wine.*

We have heard Anacreon's tale of the origin of this flower; and writers subsequent to him, struck probably by the beauty of his

---

* It is said that the Esquimaux and the Georgians, in the present day, decorate their hair with the flowers of the wild kinds which adorn their respective countries.

composition, or willing to keep up so agreeable a delusion, have also attributed to it a supernatural origin. They do not, however, agree as to the source from whence it sprung. Bion, in the Epitaph of Adonis, tells us it arose from the blood of this lovely youth, who was destroyed by a wild boar. Others of the ancient poets say it was changed from white to red by being stained with the blood of Venus, whose feet were lacerated by its thorns in her endeavours to save Adonis. Spencer makes a beautiful allusion to this latter fancy in the Daphnaida :

> White as the native Rose before the change
> Which Venus' blood did in her leaves impress.

But of the English Poets hereafter.

From the fall of the Roman empire there exists a chasm in the history of gardening which cannot be filled up. The world, sunk in a state of barbarism, had neither inclination for, nor opportunity of, enjoying pursuits of this kind ; and Roses share in the general oblivion. As, however, mankind emerged from this state—as wars became less frequent, and men felt the blessings of peace—they found time to attend to the comforts and enjoyments of life. Charlemagne, who flourished in the beginning of the ninth century, enumerates the Rose, among other flowers, and shews his fondness of it by desiring it to be grown in his garden.

The Rose was the favourite flower with the Moors of Spain, and they paid considerable attention to its cultivation. They sowed the seeds ; and it has been said they had blue Roses, which were obtained by watering the plants with indigo-water. That they had such cannot for a moment be supposed ; and the means by which it has been said they obtained them are still more questionable. Nevertheless, a French writer (Marquis D'Orbessan, *Esai sur les Roses*) states that he saw them. I have heard persons, unacquainted with Floriculture, maintain that they have seen pure yellow Moss Roses ! a deception probably practised on them by some charlatan, or witty friend. Is it impossible that the same thing might happen with the Marquis D'Orbessan ?

Pierre de Crescent, an Italian, who wrote early in the fourteenth century, mentions the Rose. It has also, for some ages, been a custom of the Roman-Catholic Church for the Pope to consecrate a golden Rose, and send it to the monarch of some State, as a token of his particular esteem. Two of our kings received this mark of distinction—Henry the VIth and Henry the VIIIth. "They made," says M. Boitard, "the delicate and ephemeral Rose emblematic of the frailty of the body, and the short duration of

human life; while the precious and unalterable metal in which it
was modelled alluded to the immortality of the soul."

It is now customary throughout Italy, as it was in ancient
Rome, to use flowers in times of feasting, and in the ceremonies of
religion; and the Rose is an especial favourite.

But let us glance hastily to the land of the East—Persia. The
Poets of that country idolize this flower, placing it, in song, in
company with the nightingales. That it holds a high rank there
may be gathered from the following fable:—"One day," says
Saadi, " I saw a tuft of grass which surrounded a Rose-tree. What!
cried I, is this vile plant, born to be trodden under foot, come to
dwell in company with Roses? I stooped to pluck it out, when
it modestly said to me, Spare me, I pray thee: I am not a Rose it
is true, yet by the perfume which I exhale you may perceive at
least that I have dwelt with Roses." (*Manuel Complet de l'Amateur
des Roses*, par M. Boitard. Paris, 1836.)

In Persia, and throughout the East generally, Roses are grown
in considerable quantities, for the manufacture of Rose-water, and
the famed Attar of Roses, which has been sold for six times its
weight in gold. The Musk Rose is, I believe, the variety cultivated.
The Attar, or Otto, of Roses is manufactured chiefly at Ghazeepore,
in Bengal; but it is also prepared in Persia, in all parts of India,
Upper Egypt, and in Tunis. In the Bengal Dispensatory there
(*The Bengal Dispensatory*, by W. B. O'Shaughnessy, M.D., Calcutta,
1842) is a paper, drawn up by Dr. Jackson, on the Cultivation of
Roses, and the Manufacture of Rose-water and Attar of Roses.

" Around the station of Ghazeepore," says this author, " there
are about 300 beegahs, or about 150 acres, of ground laid out in
small detached fields as Rose gardens, most carefully protected on
all sides by high mud-walls and prickly-pear fences, to keep out
the cattle. These lands, which belong to Zemindars, are planted
with Rose-trees, and are annually let out at so much per beegah*
for the ground, and so much additional for the Rose-plants;—generally five rupees per beegah, and twenty-five rupees for the Rose-
trees, of which there are 1000 in each beegah. The additional
expense for cultivation would be about rupees 8.8; so that for
rupees 38.8, you have, for the season, one beegah of 1000 Rose-
trees.

" If the season is good, this beegah of 1000 Rose-trees should
yield one lac of Roses. Purchases of Roses are always made at
so much per lac. The price of course varies according to the year,
and will average from 40 to 70 rupees.

* A beegah is half an acre.

" The Rose-trees come into flower at the beginning of March, and continue so through April.

" In the morning early the flowers are plucked by numbers of men, women, and children, and are conveyed in large bags to the several contracting parties for distillation. The cultivators themselves very rarely manufacture.

" There is such a variety of Rose-water manufactured, and so much that bears the name which is nothing more than a mixture of sandal-oil, that it is impossible to lay down the plan which is adopted. The best Rose-water, however, may be computed as bearing the proportion of 1000 Roses to a seer* of water: this, perhaps, may be considered as the best procurable. From 1000 Roses most generally a seer and a half of Rose-water is distilled; and perhaps from this even the Attar has been removed.

" To procure the Attar, the Roses are put into the still, and the water passes over gradually, as in the Rose-water process. After the whole has come over, the Rose-water is placed in a large metal basin, which is covered with wetted muslin, tied over to prevent insects or dust getting into it: this vessel is let into the ground about two feet, which has been previously wetted with water, and it is allowed to remain quiet during the whole night. The Attar is always made at the beginning of the season, when the nights are cool: in the morning, early, the little film of Attar, which is formed upon the surface of the Rose-water during the night, is removed by means of a feather, and it is then carefully placed in a small phial; and day after day, as the collection is made, it is placed for a short period in the sun; and after a sufficient quantity has been procured, it is poured off clear, and of the colour of amber, into small phials. Pure Attar, when it has been removed only three or four days, has a pale greenish hue: by keeping, it soon loses this, and in a few weeks' time becomes of a pale yellow.

" From one lac of Roses it is generally calculated that 180 grains, or one tolah,† of Attar can be procured: more than this can be obtained if the Roses are full sized, and the nights cold to allow of the congelation.

" The Attar purchased in the bazaar is generally adulterated, mixed with sandal-oil or sweet-oil. Not even the richest native will give the price at which the purest Attar alone can be obtained; and the purest Attar that is made is sold to Europeans. During the past year it has been selling from 80 to 90 rupees the tolah: the year before it might have been purchased for 50 rupees.

" At the commencement of the Rose season, people from all

---

* A seer is two pounds troy.   † A tolah is seven pennyweights.

parts come to make their purchases; and very large quantities are prepared and sold. There are about thirty-six places in Ghazeepore where Rose-water is distilled.

"The chief use the natives appear to make of the Rose-water'is at the period of their festivals and weddings. It is then distributed largely to the guests as they arrive, and sprinkled with profusion in the apartments.

"I should consider that the value of the Roses sold for the manufacture of Rose-water may be estimated at 15,000 rupees a year, and from this to 20,000; and from the usual price asked for the Rose-water, and for which it is sold, I should consider there is a profit of 40,000 rupees. The natives are very fond of using the Rose-water as medicine, or as a vehicle for other mixtures; and they consume a good deal of the petals for the Conserve of Roses."

But Roses are grown for the purpose of manufacturing Rose-water in other countries beside Persia. At Provins, a town forty-seven miles S. E. of Paris, which has long been celebrated for its conserve of Roses, the French Rose has been cultivated; and in the environs of Paris, the Damask, and other kinds. In some parts of Surrey and Kent, in our own country, they are grown in considerable quantities—the Provence, Damask, and French kinds, indiscriminately. In the process of distillation, six pounds of Rose-leaves are said to be enough to make a gallon of Rose-water; but much depends on the stage in which the flowers are gathered, the best stage being just before full-blown.

The Rose has been valued in Medicine from the remotest times: it was so in the time of Hippocrates; and the Romans believed the root to be efficacious in cases of hydrophobia: hence probably the term 'DOG-ROSE.' Many writers have attributed to it virtues which it does not possess; though it is still used in medicine, and valued for its tonic and astringent properties. The hips of the Dog-rose, when reduced to pulp, are also used in pharmacy, to give consistence to pills and electuaries.

But to return more immediately to the history of the Rose.— This flower, having been considered as the emblem of innocence and purity from remote times, seems so far to have influenced the early Christian writers, as to induce them to place it in Paradise. It is well known, also, that the seal of the celebrated Luther was a Rose.

In Hungary our flower is held in great esteem. I am informed by a friend who has resided in that country, that it is customary with ladies of rank and fashion to take bouquets of Roses and go into the woods to bud the wild kinds which they may encounter in their rambles. It must be an agreeable and exhilarating task to go in search of Roses during the flowering season; for I am assured it is no uncommon thing to meet with the finest varieties blooming in the most unfrequented places.

In Holland the Rose seems to have made but little way, although it was from that country the most beautiful of the tribe—the Moss Rose—was first introduced to England, from whence it found its way to France. The transactions which took place in Holland during the Florimania associate no unpleasant ideas with our flower. The Rose was without the pale. The Tulip, the Hyacinth, the Ranunculus, the Anemone—these, with a few of minor importance, were the pride of the seventeenth and eighteenth centuries: these were the flowers of Holland; and the enthusiasm with which they were cultivated there had rendered them popular in other European countries. Thus the Rose lay neglected. Its capabilities of improvement were not thought of, or unknown. The unlocking of its treasures was reserved for more recent times. The skilful and persevering individuals, to whose labours we are indebted for the choicest ornaments of the Rose Garden, still live to admire the productions of their genius, and to witness their favourite flower reigning without a rival in the Floral world.

Let us turn to France, a country naturally rich in Roses. According to Decandolle, she has no less than nineteen species growing spontaneously in her hedges, woods, and wilds. The chief among them is the ROSA GALLICA, or French Rose, which has produced some of the most brilliant and regularly-formed flowers of the genus.

The country abounding in Roses, we should expect its poets would not fail to notice them ; and perhaps in no other language have so many beautiful comparisons been instituted, or so many verses written in their praise. Delille exclaims, " Mais qui peut refuser un hommage à la Rose?" (Who can refuse homage to the Rose?) And Bernard, Malherbe, Saint Victor, Roger, Leonard, and others too numerous to mention, have made it the subject of the most delightful strains.

Rapin, a French writer of the seventeeth century, gives a pleasing and ingenious tale, which I shall venture to insert.

" Rhodanthe, Queen of Corinth, having enamoured several princes with her beauty, and having disdained their proffers of homage, three of them, furious to see themselves despised, besieged her in the temple of Diana, where she had taken refuge, followed by all the people, who, dazzled by her extraordinary beauty, made her assume the place of the statue of the goddess. Apollo, enraged by the indignity offered to his sister, changed Rhodanthe into a tree which bore the Rose. Under this new form Rhodanthe is always queen, for she became the most beautiful of flowers. Her subjects pressed around her, seem still to defend her, metamorphosed, as they are, into prickly thorns. The three princes were changed; the one into a butterfly, and the two others into winged insects, which constant in their love, flutter without ceasing around their cherished flower." (*La Rose, &c.,* par Dr. Deslongchamps.)

There exists at the present day, in the village of Salency in France, a custom which is of very ancient date. As early as the sixth century, the Bishop of Noyon offered a prize of a crown of Roses, to be given yearly to the maid of the village who should have earned the greatest reputation for modesty and virtue. The villagers have the power of appointing her who shall receive it ; and it is awarded with much ceremony and rejoicing.

It is the opinion of some of the French authors on this flower, that Roses were cultivated far more extensively in France in former times than at present; which they arrive at from the statements made, by early authors, of the great quantities which were used on particular occasions. I have sometimes thought it a matter of surprise that the Rose should have taken the precedence of all other flowers in France at an earlier period than in this country, especially when we consider it is our national emblem, and that to the enterprise of English collectors Europe stands indebted for many species which were sent from this country to France and elsewhere. It was so with the Tea-scented, the Chinese Rose, the Banksiæ, the Microphylla, the Macartney, the Multiflora, and others.

But it was fashion paved the way for its general reception in France. At the commencement of the present century, the Empress Josephine acknowledged it as her favourite, and caused varieties to be collected throughout Europe, and brought to her garden at Malmaison. The late Mr. Kennedy was provided with a passport to go and come as he pleased during the war, in order that he might superintend the formation of that garden. The patronage of the Empress gave an impetus to Rose-culture. Establishments were soon formed, solely for the purpose, among the earliest of which were those of M. Descemet and M. Vibert, and the taste spread throughout Europe. It has been said that the collection of the former at St. Denis was destroyed by the English troops in 1815, but I believe they were removed to a distant part on the approach of the allied troops.

Monsieur Vibert, of whom we have just spoken, was one of the most celebrated cultivators among the French. He founded his establishment in the vicinity of Paris in 1815, at which time the only Moss Rose known in France was the red, or common one. He removed, a few years since, to Angers, where the climate is more favourable for the pursuance of that science to which he was entirely devoted. To him we owe the existence of those old favourites, Aimée Vibert, Cynthie, d'Aguesseau, Julie d'Etangés, Blanchefleur, La Ville de Londres, Madeleine, Gloire des Mousseuses, Jacques Lafitte, General Brea, Ornement des Jardins, Pius the 9th, and a host of striped and spotted Roses. It is worthy of remark, that the latter, though much admired and cultivated in France, have never gained any great popularity here.

M. Laffay, another distinguished cultivator, owns a list of names no less worthy. Who, even among modern Rose cultivators, is not familiar with Archduc Charles, Fabvier, Brennus, William Jesse, Madame Laffay, Coup d'Hébé, La Reine, and Duchess of Sutherland ; these and others, of nearly equal merit, were raised in his garden. His residence at Bellevue, near Paris, where these Roses were raised, was a most enviable one : he lived surrounded with Roses and Chestnut-trees ; and his garden, although not extensive, commanded a wide and most agreeable prospect. The soil was a stiff—I had almost said rank—clay, and never appeared to have had much labour bestowed on its amelioration.

Both M. Vibert and M. Laffay were engaged in the cultivation of Roses for many years ; and their enterprise and industry brought them a full reward. Having realized a comfortable independency, and attained to the highest eminence in their profession, they seem content to recline beneath the laurels they have so peacefully won.* In the Preface to his Catalogue, published towards the close of 1846, M. Vibert writes to this effect :—" My establishment, which I founded in 1815, and where Roses only are cultivated for sale, is the first of the kind which had existence in France. Thirty-five years' practice in this branch of Horticulture, with numerous and reiterated experiments made on every mode of cultivation ; a long habit of seeing, studying, and of comparing the productions of this beautiful genus ;—such are, at the least, the claims I have to public confidence. But I know all the obligations under which I remain, from the long and sustained kindness with which amateurs and the members of the profession have honoured me ; and it is in reply to the honourable proofs of concern which have been so often addressed to me, that I am resolved not entirely to renounce my profession. To cover the expense of my garden, and to use my time sparingly, is the end which I propose to myself. Without seeking to extend my connections, I shall receive willingly orders from persons sufficiently reasonable to value what time and care it costs in the present day to obtain novelties really decided. I shall always continue the cultivation of my seedlings ; I shall

---

* Since the publication of the first edition of this work, both M. Vibert and M. Laffay have retired from the profession.

never renounce them; I shall rather increase them; and shall propagate but few others."

M. Laffay wrote to me in the autumn of 1847 : " C'est mon intention de cèsser le commerce. Mon projet était de quitter cet automne, et de m'installer dans le sud de la France, sous le climat des Orangers et Palmiers ; mais mon Père, qui est très âgé, ne veut pas que nous le quittions cet hiver, ce qui dérange un peu nos projets d'émigration, qui ne sont que retardés. Aussi il est bien possible que je vous offre encore quelques bonnes Roses, surtout des Mousseuses Hybrides, car je me dispose à faire un semis de plusieurs milles graines de ces variétés. Ainsi je présume que ma Pépinière sera encore bonne à visiter quelques anneés. Je suis persuadé qu'a l'avenir nous verrons de bien belles Roses, qui effaceront toutes celles que nous admirons maintenant. Les Mousseuses joueront bientôt un grand rôle dans l'Horticulture."

"It is my intention to cease cultivating the Rose, in a commercial sense. My project was to do so this autumn, and to instal myself in the south of France, in the land of orange and palm-trees ; but my father, who is very aged, wished that we should not quit Paris this winter, which deranges a little our plans of emigration, although they are only retarded. But it is very possible that I may yet offer you some good Roses, especially of the Hybrid Moss, for I intend to make a sowing of several thousands of seeds of these varieties. Thus I presume that my seed-plot will be worth visiting for some years to come. I am persuaded that in future we shall see many beautiful Roses, which will efface all those that we admire now. The Mosses will soon play a grand part in Horticulture."

It is somewhat remarkable, that while M. Vibert's operations have produced chiefly French and Provence, and, of late years, a few varieties of Moss and Hybrid Perpetual Roses, the results of M. Laffay's labour have been chiefly visible among the Hybrid Chinese and Hybrid Perpetuals. We can only account for this by supposing each cultivator to have had his favourite group, which he strove to improve. I should think one half of the Hybrid Perpetual Roses known up to the year 1850 originated with M. Laffay.

The trade of cultivating Roses in France is in the hands of many individuals ; and to visit that country with the view of forming a collection is (I speak from experience) a laborious undertaking. As far as my powers of observation serve me, I should think the establishments where they are grown for sale, in the neighbourhood of Paris, vary in extent from one to five acres ; and there are others, situate in various parts of France, nearly all of like extent. It is thus that English amateurs, who may chance to visit any of them, are usually disappointed, owing to the contrast of their Rose Gardens with those of England, which are much more extensive. The most splendid collection in France is that in the Jardin du Luxembourg at Paris, formerly under the superintendence of Monsieur Hardy. Most of the plants there are of some age, and flower profusely in the season. They are seen from the public promenades. It is true they look rather drawn; but when we consider their proximity to the heart of the city, it is surprising that they flourish so well.*

M. Hardy is no stranger in the Rose world : one of his varieties alone (Madame Hardy) would have sufficed to render his name popular ; but he has been fortunate enough to raise many others of first-rate properties, some bearing the after appellation of " Du Luxembourg." And how could it be otherwise, when he has devoted so many years to the cultivation of this flower, and raised so many thousands of seedlings ? He never practised selling his Roses, but exchanged with his friends for other plants. He retired from the superintendence of these gardens some three years ago, and was succeeded by Monsieur Riviere, under whose charge the Roses now are.

The Rose amateurs of France, who are exceedingly numerous, are enthusiastic in the cultivation of their favourite. So soon as they hear of any new variety, possessed of merit, they cease not to importune the raiser till he places it within their reach.

While admitting France to have been more prolific than England in the production of new Roses, it is yet worthy of remark, that *the English cultivators produce far handsomer plants* than the French. Although I may be ranked among the former, I state this boldly; not from prejudice, nor from interest, but from a thorough conviction of its truth. If proof be needed, it may be found in the large exports of the *French varieties, of English growth, to America*

---

* Every one who has visited Paris will not fail to have remarked the clean appearance of the buildings, compared with those of London, which is due to the burning of wood instead of coal. It is the extensive use of the latter which exerts so injurious an influence on vegetation in or near London. I recollect, upon one occasion, seeing a Honeysuckle and a Rose growing up a house in a street in Paris, the name of which I do not remember, but it was not far from the Hôtel de la Monnaie. Both looked flourishing ; and the Rose, which was of the Sempervirens kind, was in bloom. Independent of its appearing to thrive there, a second cause for surprise was, the fact of its remaining untouched, which it apparently had done for a length of time, and did, to my knowledge, for five or six days, although within reach of every passer by.

and elsewhere. It may not be generally known, that some of the finest and most esteemed Roses in France do not succeed well in this country. On the other hand, many kinds are developed in far greater perfection here than there. The flowers of Roses generally cannot bear the scorching of a summer's sun : it is during our cloudy days, or when refreshed with a soft shower or a fall of dew, that the buds expand in fullest beauty.

I cannot help mentioning the jealousies which exist among some of the "Cultivateurs de Rosiers" in France. I once visited the gardens of a noted grower, in company with a grower of less celebrity. I was surprised to see so little in these grounds, and to find the owner careless as to shewing what he possessed. Although exceedingly polite and talkative on other subjects, he was disinclined to speak on Roses. The mystery was cleared up by a letter received soon afterwards. In it were words to this effect : "If you visit my establishment again, which I beg of you to do, pray do not bring any French Rose growers with you, for I cannot shew them my rarities and beauties." This opened my eyes : I concluded I had not seen "the lions ;" and an after visit proved this to be the case.

It has been said that little dependence can be placed on the transactions of the French growers ; and I am sorry that my experience does not allow me to meet this assertion with a direct negative. *Old Roses have been sent to this establishment under new names, and charged at high prices.* This, however, might occur by mistake, and seldom happens with *the respectable growers.*

But let us trace the history of the Rose in our own land. It is again matter of surprise to me that the Rose should not have been more extensively cultivated in England at an earlier date, when it is considered that it must have been brought prominently before the eyes of our forefathers in the wars of the Houses of York and Lancaster ; or, as they are often termed, the wars of the Roses. But perhaps this was the very cause of its unpopularity. It might have been the remembrance of those sanguinary struggles, which, casting a halo around this emblem of innocence and purity, made our forefathers shrink instinctively from cherishing a flower that recalled to mind scenes or tales of carnage and of woe—whose leaves were once saturated with the blood of England's bravest sons.

It may not be considered out of place to give an account here of the origin of the Red Rose in the arms of the House of Lancaster. About 1277, Guillaume Pentecôte, Mayor of Provins, was assassinated in a tumult ; and the King of France sent Count Egmond, son of the King of England, and who had assumed the title of Comte De Champagne, to that city, to avenge his death. After staying some time there, he returned to England, and took for his

device the Red Rose, which Thibaut, Comte De Brie, and De Champagne had brought from Syria some years before, on his return
from the Crusades.   This Count Egmond was the head of the
House of Lancaster, and which preserved it in their arms. . (*L'An-
cien Provins*, par Opoix.
   The Damask Rose being the wild kind of Syria, it would hence
appear that it was *this* gave rise to the Red Rose of the Lancas-
trians, and not the French Rose, as asserted by some.   The White
Rose was probably assumed by the Yorkists in contradistinction to
the other.
   Chaucer, our first great English author, who wrote in the middle
and toward the close of the fourteenth century, alludes in his early
pieces to the poetical worship of the Rose and the Daisy.   And
others of our early poets were not unmindful of its charms.   Har-
rington speaks of "cheeks that shamed the Rose ;" Marlowe, of
"beds of Roses," &c.
   Spenser, whose genius sheds a brilliancy over the age in which
he lived, makes frequent mention of it.   Every one is familiar with
his fable of the Oak and the Brier, contained in the Shepherd's
Calendar.   Of the latter he says—

> It was embellished with blossoms fair,
> And thereto aye wonted to repair
> The shepherd's daughters, to gather flowers
> To paint their girlands with his colours.

   The poet makes the "bragging Brere" vaunt his own praises, to
the disparagement of his neighbour the "goodly Oak."

> See'st how fresh my flowers been spread,
> Dyed in lily white and crimson red ?
> .   .   .   .   .   .
> The mouldy moss which thee accloyeth
> My cinnamon smell too much annoyeth.
> [*Shepherd's Calendar*, Eclogue 2.

   Again, in the Shepherd's Calendar (Eclogue 4) we meet with
the following :

> See where she sits upon the grassy green,
>   (O seemly sight !)
> Yclad in scarlet, like a maiden queen,
>   And ermines white ;
> Upon her head a crimson coronet,
> With *damask Roses* and daffodillies set :
>   Bay-leaves between,
>   And primroses green,
> Embellish the sweet violet.

c 2

In the next verse he speaks of

> The red Rose meddled with the white yfere.

In the "Fairy Queen," especially in the Second Book, he makes several allusions to it, and also in the Epithalamion.

Shakspeare often introduces the Rose in his writings. In the following passage he compares the extinction of life to the plucking of a Rose:

> When I have plucked thy Rose,
> I cannot give it vital growth again:
> It needs must wither :
> I 'll smell it on the tree.   [*Othello*, Act 5.

In one of his Sonnets, the comparisons of the greatest English poet are obviously so much to the advantage of our favourite, that I cannot help inserting it.

> O how much more doth beauty beauteous seem
> By that sweet ornament which truth doth give !
> The Rose looks fair, but fairer we it deem
> For that sweet odour which doth in it live.
> The canker blooms have full as deep a dye
> As the perfumed tincture of the Roses ;
> Hang on such thorns, and play as wantonly,
> When summer's breath their masked buds discloses ;
> But, for their virtue only is their show,
> They live unwooed, and unrespected fade;—
> Die to themselves.   Sweet Roses do not so :
> Of their sweet deaths are sweetest odours made.
> And so of you, beauteous and lovely youth,
> When that shall fade, my verse distils your truth.

I have made the above quotations to shew that the Rose was not unregarded by the early English poets ; but were I to pursue this plan of quoting all the agreeable things which our poets have written of it, that matter would occupy the whole volume ; for who among them has not heaped upon it the riches of his fancy ?

> In every love-song Roses bloom.

From the allusion of Chaucer, it is evident the Rose was a favourite flower, at least among the poets in England, some centuries since; and this I should have thought a sufficient passport to public favour.   That they did not owe their love and respect for this flower to the existence of superior garden varieties, or to an interest displayed in their cultivation by their countrymen, will, I think, soon be sufficiently evident.   But the wild forms of Roses are beautiful; and they probably gave rise to these effusions. Or the poets might owe their veneration for them to the writings of the ancients, with which they were familiar. But we must quit the land of poetry.

Lobel, who had a garden at Hackney, and who was appointed Royal Botanist by James the First, published, towards the close of the sixteenth century, a work entitled " Plantarum seu stirpium Icones." In this work he describes ten species.

" In 1622, Sir Henry Wotton sent from Venice, to the Earl of Holderness, a double yellow Rose of no ordinary nature, which was expected to flower every month from May till almost Christmas, unless change of climate should change its properties."—Johnson's *History of Gardening.* This most probably was the old double yellow Rose, so notorious for refusing to unfold its blossoms in our less propitious climate. With regard to its *flowering from May till Christmas !*—this no doubt was an embellishment, to which an enthusiastic collector may be readily excused for giving ear.

Parkinson, an early English writer on Gardening and Botany, in his " Paradisus," published in 1629, speaks of the " white, the red, and the damask," as the most ancient in England He enumerates twenty-four varieties; and speaks of others, but does not specify their names. He treats, in a separate chapter, of the propagation of Roses by budding and by seed. The red Rose of which he here speaks was no doubt the Cabbage, or Damask; and the white one, an old variety of ROSA ALBA. In how many old English gardens do we find trees of the apple-bearing Rose still occupying a conspicuous position, and whose ancient appearance denotes them to have withstood the changes of many a by-gone year. Some-times, indeed, the scathing hand of time has severely marked them, and they are hastening to decay.*

There is now before me a work published on Gardening in 1654, entitled " The Countryman's Recreation, or the Art of Planting, Graffing, and Gardening, in three Books." In a work with such a title we might expect to find a variety of flowers treated of. But no : fruit-trees seem then to have been the chief ornament of country gardens : the *utile* was preferred to the *dulce :* in truth, the attention of our forefathers seems to have been *chiefly* directed towards the "making of good cyder," and the "keeping of plummes" ! In the above-mentioned work there is but one flower named, and that is the Rose ! Here is the article as it appears in the original :

* I recollect meeting with two or three of this description in the gardens of Bruce Castle, Tottenham, a short time since : they were of prodigious height and size, resembling apple-trees more than Roses. But alas they are no longer there.

" To Graffe a Rose on the Holly.

" For to graffe the Rose, that his leaves shall keep all the year green, some do take and cleave the holly, and do graffe in a red or white Rose-bud ; and then put clay or mosse to him, and let him grow. And some put the Rose-bud into a slit of the bark, and so put clay and mosse, and bind ʻhim featly therein, and let him grow, and he shall carry his leaf all the year."

This is a recipe for obtaining evergreen Roses ! *Satis superque.* Must we infer that practical men in those days held tenets such as these, or that they were merely the effusions of the brain of some would-be *savant* in horticultural matters ? As gardening was then a practical art, we cannot suppose the former to have been the case, since the very first experiment would throw a doubt on such a proposition, which the failure of every subsequent attempt would confirm ; and thus the most credulous would soon be undeceived. The latter would certainly seem the juster inference. Without wishing to be too severe against the early writers on Horticulture, we certainly were not aware that the sun of Horticultural science had reached the meridian so long since as 1654, and feel some concern, as well as humiliation, that nearly two centuries should elapse without our profiting by so wonderful a discovery ! We cannot forbear quoting certain lines of Virgil, met with in our school-days, and to which, perhaps, the above writer was indebted for his idea :

> Inseritur vero et fœtu nucis arbutus horrida ;
> Et steriles platani malos gessere valentes :
> Castaneæ fagus ornusque incanuit albo
> Flore piri, glandemque sues fregere sub ulmis.
> [*Georg.* lib. ii. ver. 69—72.*

Such are the workings of the imagination, that the black Roses produced by grafting on black-currant bushes, the blue Roses of the Moors, and the oft-talked-of yellow Moss, are already before our eyes ! Could we but retain them there ! But, alas ! this were impossible. Creatures of the imagination, a moment's sober reflection dissipates you in thin air !

But to be serious. As late as 1762, Linnæus appears to have acknowledged only fourteen species. In an edition of Miller's

* The thin-leaved arbute hazel-graffs receives,
  And planes huge apples bear, that bore but leaves.
  Thus mastful beech the bristly chestnut bears,
  And the wild ash is white with blooming pears.
  And greedy swine from grafted elms are fed
  With falling acorns that on oaks are bred.
  [*Dryden's Virgil.*

Gardeners' Dictionary, published in 1768, thirty-one species are described. It was only at the close of the last century, and the dawning of the present, that the garden varieties of Roses were really recognised and esteemed. In 1789 the Chinese Rose was introduced ; and in 1810 China furnished us with the Tea-scented also. At this period nearly all the varieties known bloomed in summer only : there were few autumnal Roses. In 1812 came forth that exquisite variety, the " Rose du Roi," or Crimson Perpetual, which was raised in the Royal Gardens of St. Cloud, then under the care of Le Comte Lelieur.

In 1799 Miss Lawrence published " A Collection of Roses from Nature," which contained ninety coloured plates, including many of the most beautiful species and varieties then known. In 1820 the " Rosarum Monographia," by J. Lindley appeared ; in which seventy-eight species, besides sub-species, are described, and thirteen of them figured. This work is of a scientific character, and the system there adopted has been followed, more or less, by many subsequent writers on the botany of the Rose. About this time the types of the Bourbon and Noisette Roses appeared, and in a very short period the varieties were increased and improved beyond what the most sanguine could have anticipated. Loudon, in the Encyclopædia of Gardening, published in 1822, says, " The lists of the London and Paris Nurserymen contain upwards of 350 names." . . . . . . " New varieties are raised in France and Italy annually. L. Villaresii, Royal Gardener at Monza, has raised upwards of fifty varieties of Rosa Indica, not one of which has, as far as we know, reached this country. Some of them are quite black ! others shaped like a Ranunculus ; and many of them are highly odoriferous." With regard to those *quite black*, as none of them have *yet* reached this country, it may be presumed the writer made this statement on the authority of the continental growers, whose vivid imaginations often lead them to portray in too glowing colours any new production.

It may be thought reasonable that I should allude to the Nurseries here, which have been so long famous for Roses. They gained considerable renown in the time of my late father, from the continual flowering of a plant of the old double yellow Rose (R. Sulphurea), which had become established on a west wall about the close of the last century. Flowers from which to draw were sought from various parts of the country. The plant produced them with such regularity, and in such gay profusion, that an amateur eventually purchased it to transplant to his seat in Yorkshire; and he did this with considerable success, for, although of great size, it flourished, and continued to flower well.

In Sweet's Hortus Britannicus, published in 1827, there are 107 species given, and 1059 varieties; the greater portion of the latter being French or Gallica Roses.

In 1829, M. Desportes and M. Prevost each published in France a Catalogue of Roses. In the Catalogue of the former cultivator above 2000 varieties are described. These Catalogues, with others which appeared in England and France, both before and after this time, were calculated to infuse fresh ardour into the minds of the improvers of this charming race of plants, and at the same time to spread a taste for its cultivation.

The Rose amateurs of England are so numerous in the present day, that it were almost impossible to enumerate even those who possess collections of great merit. A few, however, occur to me, which have especial claims to notice as being the earliest of any extent.

At Dane-end, near Munden in Hertfordshire, the seat of Charles S. Chauncey, Esq., was formed one of the earliest and best collections; and to which this county is no doubt indebted, in some degree, for the celebrity she enjoys for Roses.

Mr. Sabine formed a collection of the species, some years back, at North Mims, Herts; and a vast number of species were once growing in the Gardens of the Horticultural Society at Chiswick.

About thirty-five years ago, Mrs. Gaussen formed a Rosarium at Brookmans, in Hertfordshire, which contained many varieties. The form of the ground it occupied was an oblong square, walled in, the walls covered with climbing Roses and other plants. There was a variety of beds formed and planted with much taste: in the centre stood a temple covered with climbing Roses. The whole was blinded from distant view by a wide laurel bank; and the surprise created on suddenly entering was most agreeable, and the effect magical. " Here," says an eminent cultivator with whom I was in conversation the other day, " I first saw the Rose Ruga, which was then recently introduced; and I remarked to Mr. Murdoch, who was gardener there, that it was a hybrid of the Tea-scented. It was beautifully in bloom, and struck me at the time as a gem of the first water. I had not at this time met with any of the Sempervirens Roses; the first of which, the ALBA PLENA, I saw in flower soon afterwards, on a wall at Dropmore, the seat of Lady Grenville."

The next collection which demands our notice is that at Brox-bournebury, the seat of George J. Bosanquet, Esq., where there are at the present time a great number of very fine specimens.*

* The greater part of this, once the finest collection in England, was destroyed by the severe winter of 1860-61, and has not yet been thoroughly restored.

In addition to the above, there are superior collections of Roses at the following places:—Poles, near Ware, the seat of Robert Hanbury, Esq.; Youngsbury, near Ware, the seat of C. W. Giles Puller, Esq., M.P.; Bayfordbury, near Hertford, the seat of W. R. Baker, Esq.; and Danesbury, near Welwyn, the seat of W. J. Blake, Esq.

It might have been foretold, that the rare beauties the gardens above mentioned contained—whether viewed on the plants, arrayed in the simple loveliness of nature, or when dressed for the tables of the Floral fêtes—would captivate all lovers of flowers, and spread a taste for their cultivation. And such was really the case. They became known and their worth appreciated. Florists and amateurs vied with each other in the cultivation of their favourite, each desirous of producing it in the most perfect state. Its characters were thus fairly developed; improvement followed on improvement; and it soon became universally popular. And why? Shall Anacreon answer? 'Ρόδον ὦ φέριστον ἄνθων, " The Rose is the most beautiful of flowers."

CHAPTER II.

ON LOCALITY AND SOILS; AND THE IMPROVEMENT OR ADAPTATION OF SOILS FOR ROSE-CULTURE.

IF we were called upon to select a spot as best suited for the cultivation of Roses, we should seek one at a distance from large towns, that we might secure the advantages of a pure air. It should lie open to the south, and be so far removed from trees of every description, that their roots could not reach the soil of our Rose-beds, or their tops overpower us with shade, and prevent a free circulation of air. If, in addition to this, we could choose our soil, that preferred would be a strong loam ; if rich, so much the better ; if poor, we would enrich it by the addition of manures. It is generally known, that the Dog-Rose delights, in a stiff, holding soil ; and it is on the Dog-Rose the choice garden varieties are usually budded. We do not intend by this to recommend soils commonly termed clayey, for in such there is often too great a deficiency of vegetable substances ; lighter soils, too, are found better suited for such kinds as thrive best grown on their own roots ; but this may be managed by the addition of a little light turfy loam, peat, or leaf-mould, at the time of planting. An open, airy, situation, and a stiff loamy soil, are, we say, what we should prefer, were our choice of locality and soil unlimited. With these at our command, we should expect to carry Rose-culture to perfection. "But," says the amateur, "all gardens must have Roses, and how few are there thus favourably circumstanced. Many are close to large towns, where the air is rendered impure by the clouds of smoke constantly streaming into them. Others are of small size, and are often hemmed in by trees on all sides ; on this with a neighbour's favourite chestnuts ; on that with a group of sombre-looking firs ; and on another with a row of towering elms. And although we may think it not right that our less majestic denizens should suffer at their hands, we have no help for it. They have their pets as we have ours. They find as much pleasure in the blossoms of their chestnuts, in the agreeable shade of their elms during the sultry months of summer, or by the privacy afforded them by the impenetrable darkness of their fir-trees, as we do in the perfect form and varied tints of our Roses. We cannot rid ourselves of their shade. We have no right, indeed, to wish to do so. But we might not hesitate to dock their roots, should they, in their peregrinations, enter our domain, to gormandize on the provision made for our favourites. This, we think, would be justifiable. We are acting in self-defence. They are robbers, and deserve punishment, although it must not be such as to do them permanent injury. Then, again, as to soils : some are sandy ; others are clayey, wet, cold, and altogether uncongenial to vegetation. In a word, we cannot always suit our gardens to your Roses : your Roses must therefore be brought to suit our gardens."

Those who are free from all these annoyances may think themselves fortunate. The number of complaints of this kind received from amateurs possessing small gardens, which they make their chief source of relaxation and amusement, satisfy us they are great. It must be admitted, that localities are often unfavourable, and hardly capable of improvement. With this, then, we must endure, and seek the remedy in the choice of varieties ; selecting such as our own experience, or that of our friends, points out as succeeding best under such circumstances. It is well known that some kinds will grow and flourish where others will scarcely exist. Were this fact taken advantage of by those who plant in unfavourable situations, or unkindly soils, doubtless less failures in Rose-culture would ensue. But it may be said, Some of the most delicate in habit are the most beautiful of Roses, and how can we dispense with such ? That the varieties possessed of the most bewitching forms and tints are most difficult of culture, is, to a certain extent, true ; but we opine, that a Rose, which will flourish and blossom in a doubtful situation, or in an unfriendly soil, is greatly to be preferred for such, to one which would only exist there as an unhealthy plant, though the latter were naturally its superior in point of beauty. I have known instances in which varieties of the most delicate growth have been selected, time after time, to occupy the most unfavourable situations ; and this against all remonstrance, and the knowledge of the cultivator, *bought by experience,* that they will not succeed. Varieties are often chosen and planted, without paying sufficient attention to their aptitude for the purpose or position they are wanted for. They are chosen because admired most—because they are *the most beautiful.* Now what are the consequences ? That which should yield pleasure, produces, by constant failure, indifference or disgust, and their culture is abandoned. This is to be lamented ; for if circumstances are unfavourable for the cultivation of particular varieties, others, that are likely to succeed, should be chosen. And the amateur need not be altogether without his favourite kinds. If unsuited for out-of-door culture in some places, they may be grown to perfection in pots, under glass. In this manner, with due care, they always succeed well ; and, by the increased beauty of their foliage and flowers, fully compensate for the additional attention paid to them. I here allude only to such as are very susceptible of frost, or of weak and delicate growth, confining the suggestion to no one group in particular, nor excluding varieties of such character from any group. If an illustration be needed, we may instance Cardinal Patrizzi and Princesse Imperiale Clotilde, (Hybrid Perpetuals), Eliza Sauvage, and several others of the Tea-scented. These, and the like, will not thrive in unfavourable situations or unkindly soils. And whatever the situation may be, they assume a decidedly improved appearance when grown in a frame or greenhouse. An unfavourable locality or soil should never deter the lover of Roses from entering on their cultivation ; for such is the diversity of character of the varieties belonging to the genus, that some may be found suited to, or capable of flourishing in, the least desirable localities ; and the soil may be improved, or dug out, and the beds re-filled with prepared soil. For the encouragement of those whose situation may be decidedly unfavourable, it may be stated, that thousands of Roses grown at this establishment are sent annually into the neighbourhood of London and the large manufacturing towns in England and Scotland. And it is pleasing to see, in their perfect production there, how far the art of culture can be brought to triumph over circumstances. In such situations, the practice which seems to have been attended with the most marked success, is that of syringing the plants frequently with clean water, which frees the leaves of the impurities which settle upon them. Thus, it will be seen, none need despair of securing a moderate share of success in, and of realizing the pleasures afforded by, the cultivation of this richly-varied flower.

We have said that soils are capable of improvement, and may suppose that every one has his garden under his own control, so far as improvement goes. To this point let us now direct attention.

In the first place, if our soil be wet it should be drained. Roses will never flourish in a soil naturally wet. As few plants will, if a garden be of this nature, it would seem desirable, before attending to other improvements, to drain it wholly and thoroughly.

Let us suppose we have a piece of clayey undrained land, which is the best our limits contain, and on which we are about to form a Rosarium. We defer planting the Roses till spring, availing ourselves of the autumn and winter for the amelioration of the soil; unless, indeed, there has been an opportunity of working it during the previous winter and summer, when autumn planting is preferable. There is not, however, always an opportunity of doing this; and we will suppose it taken in hand in October, just after a crop has been removed from it. Our first object is to secure a perfect drainage. This may be done by digging drains three feet deep, at about ten yards apart, and laying draining-tiles in at the bottom. In digging the trenches, they may be cut sloping from eighteen inches at top to two inches at the bottom. We must find out the lowest ground, and secure a gentle fall from the higher ground, that the water may run away freely.

If we do not choose to lay drain-tiles in the trenches, bushes may be put there, or stones, brick-bats, clinkers from the furnaces, broken into moderate-sized pieces, or any description of rubble. These will accomplish the same end, if laid sufficiently deep, though not so perfectly, as the soil will find its way amongst them in course of time, and choke up the passages through which the water should find egress. Having laid the soil dry, the next object should be to expose it, as much as possible, to the fertilizing influences of the sun and air. To accomplish this, the ground should be dug one spit deep, or more; but instead of laying it level at the surface, let it be thrown up in ridges in the roughest manner possible. In this state it may lie till near the end of winter, fully exposed to the action of sun, air, rain, and frost. The surface of the ridges will gradually crumble down, and the soil become pulverized. Now for the next step. What description of soils or manures can be brought to bear upon it with the greatest prospect of improvement? Chalk, lime, peat, sand, and burnt earth will improve it; and stable manure, with any decayed vegetable substances, the refuse of the garden, may be added to advantage. And now is the time to apply these. First level the ground, and lay on the top a good dressing of any of the above soils that may be accessible, or thought most suitable. Having done this, in the next place trench the ground two spit deep, well mixing these foreign matters with the staple in the operation. The ground is laid level this time, and when finished, the places where the Roses are to be planted should be marked out, and the holes dug, the earth taken out being laid up in ridges round their sides. The holes should remain open till the time of planting, that the soil, placed in immediate contact with the roots, may become further mellowed. From the end of February till the end of March is a good time for spring planting, choosing an opportunity when the ground works well.

But some gardens are so situated that it is not easy to drain

them. A make-shift system may be adopted in such cases. The
soil may be thrown out of the walks in the immediate vicinity
of the plants, to a good depth; and loose stones, or rubble of
any description, be placed at the bottom, covering with bushes,
over which the soil may be restored. Among the substances
mentioned above as calculated to improve wet or clayey soils,
is burnt earth. Of its value in the improvement of such for
Rose-culture I have been an eye-witness; and in a Letter to the
Gardeners' Chronicle of 1844 (p. 67), I gave an account of the
results of its application to some Dwarf Roses.* Subsequent experiments have increased my faith in it: and as the burning
of earth is considered by many to be a difficult process, I shall
give a succinct account of the plan pursued here.

Earth may be burnt at any season of the year. It has been
the custom here, for some years, on the decline of spring, when
the operations of pruning, grafting, &c., are ended, instead of
suffering the rough branches to lie about, presenting an untidy
appearance, to collect them in a heap. A wall of turf, about
three feet high, of a semi-circular form, is then built round them.
The branches are set on fire, and when about half burnt down,
seed-weeds, and such rubbish as collects in every garden and will
not readily decompose, are thrown on the top, and earth is
gradually cast up as the fire breaks through.

During the first two or three days great care is requisite to
keep the pile on fire. Here is the point where many fail. They
allow the flame to break through and expend itself before the
heap is thoroughly kindled. Constant watching is necessary at
this juncture. As the fire breaks through, the heap should be
opened and a layer of bushes and weeds should be added, and
then a layer of earth. Follow up this plan, and the fire will
spread through the whole heap; and any amount of earth may
be burnt, by continually adding to those places where the fire
appears the strongest. The soil burnt here is the stiffest loam
that can be found within our limits, and which is of rather a
clayey nature ; also turf from the sides of ditches and roads, in
itself naturally sour and full of rank weeds.

Burnt earth has been found beneficial in every instance where
applied. In black garden mould, rather wet, in which peach-trees
were disposed to sucker and canker, despite of the use of various
manures, two or three annual dressings of it appear so to have
altered the nature of the soil, that they now grow clean, vigorous,
and healthy, are free from suckers, and produce roots completely

* Published also in Lindley's Theory of Horticulture, Second edition, p. 566.

matted with fibre. The like success has attended its application to various other trees.

But to our Roses. In the summer of 1842, six beds of Tea-scented Roses were manured with the following substances : 1. bone-dust ; 2. burnt earth ; 3. nitrate of soda ; 4. guano ; 5. pigeon-dung ; and, 6. stable manure, thoroughly decomposed. The soil in which they grew was an alluvial loam. The adjacent fields, which are of the same nature, grow large crops of wheat and potatoes. The particles of the soil run together after rain, presenting a smooth cemented surface ; the soil, in dry weather, becoming hard and harsh. But for the results. The guano produced the earliest visible effects, causing a vigorous growth, which continued till late in the season ; the foliage was large, and of the darkest green, but the flowers on this bed were not very abundant ; the shoots did not ripen well, and were consequently much injured by frost during the succeeding winter. The bed manured with burnt earth next forced itself into notice : the plants kept up a steadier rate of growth, producing an abundance of clean, well-formed blossoms ; the wood ripened well, and sustained little or no injury from the winter's frost. The results attendant on the use of the other manures were not remarkable : they had acted as gentle stimulants ; the nitrate of soda and bone-dust least visibly so, although they were applied in the quantities usually recommended by the vendors.

The beds of Roses were all planted at the same date, and in the same soil ; and there was no undue advantage given to any one kind of manure. The fertilizing influences of the burnt earth were no doubt due partly to its drying and opening the soil, thus rendering it more permeable to air ; and partly to the power it is said to possess of fixing the ammonia conveyed to the soil by rain. But further, earth is reduced, by burning, to its inorganic constituents, and thus becomes a concentrated inorganic manure, from which many soils benefit largely ; and the ashes of the wood, and other substances used in burning, although of small amount, would add to its value under this point of view. A portion of the earth comes from the heap red and hard, and a portion black or dark brown. The latter, which may be more correctly called charred earth, is highly beneficial to most soils. I think charred earth the best manure that can be applied to Roses in wet or adhesive soils, and would advise all who cultivate such to use it.

Peat soils, although not of the best kind for Roses, are found to grow them tolerably well. For the improvement of such, if wet, the first effort should be to drain them. After this, stiff loam, or pulverized clay and burnt earth, may be brought upon the surface, digging two spit deep, and well mixing the foreign substances with the natural soil, as advised in the improvement of clay soils.

The worst soils for Roses are those of a sandy or gravelly nature. In such they often suffer fearfully from the drought of summer, scorching up and dying. Soils of this kind are sometimes bad beyond remedy. The best plan to pursue under such circumstances, is, to remove the soil to the depth of about twenty inches, as the beds are marked out, and fill up again with prepared soil. Two-thirds loam—the turf from a pasture, if attainable—and one-third decomposed stable manure, will make a good mixture. If a strong loam is within reach, choose such in preference to others; and if thought too adhesive, a little burnt earth or sand may be mixed with it. A good kind of manure for mixing with the loam is the remains of a hot-bed, which have lain by for a year and become decomposed.

Opoix, a French apothecary, whom we have previously quoted, attributes the superiority of the Roses grown for medicinal purposes, in the neighbourhood of Provins, to peculiar properties of the soil, which contains iron in considerable quantity. We are told that the selection of inorganic manures for plants may be fixed upon by an examination of the composition of their ashes.* We know, by the research of chemists, that the petals of the ROSA GALLICA contain oxide of iron; and I have long thought that the iron which abounds in the soil of one of the nurseries here is an ingredient of importance in the culture of Roses. I would not say that it is indispensable, but beneficial; and am almost confident that it heightens the colour of the flowers. On turning up the soil, its ferruginous nature is in places distinctly seen. In an un-drained field adjoining the Nursery the water frequently collects on the surface in the form of a thick brown liquid, like so much rust, which is covered here and there with a film, on which the sky is distinctly mirrored. When the soil in this nursery is hoed or forked, the rapid increase of growth of vegetation is striking beyond measure. This practice is known to promote growth in all soils; but the extent to which it does so here, is, I think, due to the oxygen of the air changing the iron contained in the soil from a substance pernicious to vegetable life, into one favourable to its development.

We have hitherto been speaking of the improvement of soils preparatory to the formation of the Rosarium, or beds of Roses. But it is often desirable to improve the soil in beds already formed, and which probably have existed for a number of years. This is

* Liebig.

usually done by the addition of animal or vegetable manures, which are very good so far as they go, but are not in every case *all* that is required. Roses increase in bulk every year, and draw inorganic as well as organic matter from the soil. Although a portion of this may be returned by the fall of the leaf in autumn, and by the manures employed, yet a great deal is deposited in the branches and stem : and when we consider what a quantity of branches we cut from some Roses, and carry away every pruning-season, it will appear reasonable that we may, in the course of years, impoverish the soil as regards its inorganic constituents, and yet leave it rich in vegetable matter. Thus, we think, every two or three years a dressing of chalk, lime, soot, or like substances, would prove highly beneficial to the beds of the Rosarium.

But let it be remembered, that if the soil is wet manures are of little value : often, indeed, they sour in the soil, and are worse than useless. In all such cases, then, the first effort must be to lay the soil dry. After this, add such manures as the character of the soil may point out as likely to prove most beneficial. Animal and vegetable manures of all kinds may be used, but not in a fresh state ; they should be well decayed : for Roses, though delighting in a rich soil, dislike green manures more than most plants. In heavy soils a good dressing of chalk, peat, burnt earth, or sand may be used ; not to the preclusion of, but in addition to, the animal or vegetable manures. In light soils, especially such as are of a gravelly or sandy nature, stiff loam may be applied to advantage. These substances may be thrown on the surface of the beds with the usual manures, and forked in at the same time.

We would remark here that stable manure, which is excellent in most cases, and the kind in general use for Roses, is not of the best description *for light soils.* Its tendency is to render them still lighter ; and if it can be dispensed with on light soils we think it desirable to do so. Manures should be applied here in a more concentrated form. Cow-dung is excellent, especially for the Tea-scented Roses ; and pigeon-dung, rabbit-dung, and night-soil, are all great improvers of light soils. The unpleasantness attending the preparation and use of night-soil may in a great measure be done away with by pursuing the following plan. A basin, or reservoir, should be formed on the ground, to hold a given quantity. In the bottom of this, loam may be thrown, heavy or light, turfy or not, as may be at our command, or whichever is thought best suited to the character of the soil we intend to manure. Upon this the night-soil is lowered from the cart, and a sufficient quantity of loam thrown in to absorb the whole. The heap should then be covered over closely with a layer of earth, about a foot thick, and

D

remain closed for about six months. It may then be broken up, more or less, according to its state, mixing dry soil, or ashes, or *burnt earth* with it in the operation, and casting it up in ridges. About a month afterwards it may be turned over again, that the night-soil may be well mixed with the loam. In autumn it may be carried to the places where required, and forked in as other manures ; or it may be scattered over the beds immediately after they are forked in spring, when it will be washed down by the rains. We cannot conceive of any description of manure to surpass this, applied *to Roses on light soils.* By its use, we administer at the same time a cool and rich fertilizer, and a substance calculated to be of permanent benefit to the soil.

It may be thought that guano should be a good manure for Roses on cold and poor soils. It probably might prove so if used sparingly, and *in conjunction with vegetable manures.* I do not, however, think guano the best thing for Roses in the generality of soils. It certainly increases the vigour of a plant, but seems to act more favourably on the foliage than on the flowers. It may be said this is due to the use of it in excess. But this I am not disposed to grant. In the spring of 1846 I scattered guano, *in variable quantities,* over some newly-forked beds of Roses, just as the buds were pushing forth. The soil where this experiment was made is a dry loam, rather stiff, of excellent staple, but poor. The subsoil, to the depth of twelve feet, is a yellow loam or brick earth. Below this is gravel. In every instance where the guano was applied the growth was more vigorous, and the foliage developed of extraordinary richness and beauty ; *but, mark !* it was at the expense *of the flowers.* Such were the consequences attending its use to plants in full health on one soil : on soils otherwise constituted the results might be different.

Roses should have manure applied to them at least once a year. It should be in a decayed state, and may be dug in, when the borders are dug, in spring ; or laid on the surface afterwards, to be washed in by the rains. When manure is applied in such state as to be capable of yielding immediate nourishment to a plant, spring would seem the better season to apply it. The roots are then in full action, and every shower of rain places an abundant supply of food within their reach. If manure is applied in autumn, a great part of its nutritive properties may be carried beyond the reach of the roots by the frequent and heavy rains of winter.

CHAPTER III.

REMARKS ON THE FORMATION OF THE ROSARIUM, AND ON THE INTRODUCTION OF ROSES TO THE FLOWER GARDEN.

In the formation of a Rosarium, it appears to me that the simpler the forms of the beds the better. The plants of which it is composed are for the most part budded on stems, and decidedly artificial objects; and parallelograms, squares, circles, ovals, and other regular figures, are in perfect harmony with the character of the plants; admit of the most perfect arrangement; and display the Roses to greatest advantage.

When the Rosarium is intended to be of large or even moderate size, there should be two compartments; the one for the summer kinds exclusively, the other to contain the autumnals. The boundary of each may be defined by planting a single row of Pillar-Roses at intervals of a yard apart. When they reach the height of five feet, each alternate plant may be removed, and small chains be fixed from pillar to pillar, hanging in graceful curves the entire length of the line. Over these some of the branches may be trained to form elegant festoons, two or three shoots being allowed to ascend the pillar until they reach such height as circumstances or taste may point out as desirable.

If Pillar-Roses are not approved of to form the line of demarcation, the same end may be accomplished by a rustic fence, which should be covered with some particular kind of Rose suited for the purpose. It should be a good, free flowering, hardy variety, whether a summer or autumn bloomer: if the latter is preferred, the Bourbon or Noisette offer the best kinds. Or again, this would seem a fitting opportunity of introducing the Sweet-briar, which should abound in every Rosarium; for the delicious fragrance of its young leaves in the earliest of spring, the delicacy of its blossoms in summer, and the gay appearance of the scarlet hips it produces in the autumn, must recommend it to every observer.

The walks of the Rosarium should be invariably of grass, which sets off the plants, when in flower, to much greater advantage than gravel. Grass walks are objected to by some because unpleasant to walk upon early in the morning, or after a shower of rain;

but they give such a finish to the Rosarium, and lend such a freshness and brilliancy to the flowers, that it were a pity to forego
these advantages solely on this account. And if the grass is kept
closely mown, the force of this objection is greatly abated.

When the walks are of grass, it is perhaps not desirable to plant
edgings to the beds. When they are of gravel, it is decidedly
necessary to do so; and Box, or fancy tiles, may be used. In many
instances, too, the Pompon and Fairy Roses may be introduced as
edgings, with a very happy effect, to form a complete hedge, of less
than a foot in height, covered with their miniature blossoms; the
one variety blooming in summer only, the other throughout the
autumn. ·

It is desirable that the Rosarium should have a raised spot in its
vicinity, from which a bird's eye view of the whole may be obtained
during the season of flowering. A mound of earth thrown up is
the simplest plan; and some burs and stones may be placed upon
the surface. The sides of the mound may be planted with Ayrshire, Sempervirens, and other running Roses, or climbing plants
of various kinds: on the top may be formed a Rose Temple, or a
cluster of Pillar-Roses. From this spot we obtain, in the flowering
season, a view of the Roses *en masse*, as they lie beneath us, the
effect of which is agreeable and striking; and indeed every one can
appreciate the beauty of the picture thus submitted to him. It
needs neither the knowledge of the Florist nor the refined taste of
the connoisseur; the beauty and effect of the *coup d'œil* thus obtained
is acknowledged alike by the skilled and unskilled in these matters.
This we regard as one important point gained in the formation of
the Rosarium; but there are others deserving of attention.

When *the Amateur* forms a Rosarium, *he* does not usually plant
for effect: he views his plants individually, rather than collec-
tively. And we should suppose that, to meet his approbation, the
Rosarium should be so formed that he may attend to, and examine,
each plant, without risking an injury to the rest. He may be
delighted with viewing his collection as a whole; and, in addition
to this, the knowledge that his friends, who may be less skilled in
floriculture than himself, would derive the highest gratification
from such a sight, would induce him not to neglect this point. But
he finds greater pleasure in looking at his favourites separately.
What would be tedious and uninteresting to them, is to him highly
amusing. Each of his plants has a name by which he distinguishes
it. He regards them as so many friends or acquaintances, every
one of which has a claim upon his attention. He therefore wishes
them so disposed that he may attend to each in turn, without
annoying the rest. How often have I seen, *in large beds of Roses,*

the soil round a favourite tree trodden as hard as a gravel walk! I have also seen the adjoining trees, whose beauty was only dimmed by the presence of a brighter gem, seriously rubbed and broken, being altogether unheeded in the eager haste to inspect some more inviting specimen.* It would seem desirable, then, that the beds be so formed that each plant may be seen from the walks. No one who really loves Roses will be content with viewing a plant placed in the back of a bed some six or seven yards from a walk. To fully appreciate its beauties—to be satisfied—one must have it directly under the eye, or how can he mark the exact colour, form, and various characters, and last, but not least, inhale its perfume? If the plant is so placed that we cannot do this from the walks, the beds must be trampled on; the temptation is too great; we cannot resist it.

When forming a Rosarium, it is at the option of the cultivator to set apart a spot for growing plants from which to save seed. If he desire to raise seedlings, this should be done; for the plants become impoverished by the ripening of the seeds, and therefore those from which he wishes to obtain large and perfect flowers should never be suffered to seed. He should select the sunniest spot in the garden in which to plant the seed-bearers, in order to secure every possible advantage for accelerating the period of maturity. Autumn pruning should also be adopted, as a means to this end, by inducing an early development of flowers. Our climate is not the most favourable for this branch of Rose-culture: we therefore must not waive even the slightest advantage which may be obtained either naturally or artificially.

In preference to giving new plans only, we shall present our readers with some which already exist, and which have obtained the approval of those who have witnessed the effect they produce. For the reasons above stated, we believe the simpler the form of the Rosarium the better. It is therefore thought not necessary to give many plans; but besides those given, we shall offer a description of several places noted for Roses, or where the plants appear arranged with taste.

The most renowned Rosarium in Europe is that of the Jardin du

* I have a vivid recollection of committing this error. I once stepped on a seedling in the garden of a Rose-grower in France, which was planted in a very injudicious position. A glimpse of La Reine, for the first time, was the cause of my misfortune. I was made acquainted with the real state of things by a very un-Frenchmanlike roar. Fortunately the plant was not seriously injured, but the flower-bud was destroyed; and the amount of mischief done was the keeping of the owner in a state of suspense for a month or two longer. I afterwards learned that I was very near annihilating a very fine variety.

Luxembourg at Paris. The interest attached to these gardens arises principally from some of our finest varieties having been originated and nurtured there, and to its possessing some unusually large specimens. I remember seeing there, in the month of June, on my first visit to Paris, a Standard of the Tea Princesse Hélène du Luxembourg, of an immense size, with hundreds of its fine flowers in beautiful condition. The tree called to mind the large-headed Hybrid Roses occasionally met with in this country. We shall proceed at once to describe these Gardens.

The wood-cut No. 1, on the annexed page, is a ground plan of the Rosarium, in which the entire collection of the Luxembourg is planted. It is situated on the right of the public walk leading from the Palais du Luxembourg.

It is below the level of the public promenades, as shewn at e.

In summer, when the Roses are all in flower, they produce a splendid effect viewed from the public walks above, and over the parapet-wall c, e. If we descend to the walks f f we lose this effect, as the Roses are then brought on a level with the eye. The little round marks in our engraving shew a line of fruit-trees originally planted in the borders surrounding the Rose-beds, forming a sort of back-ground, but these are now removed.

There are two other Rosariums, similar in design, situated on the same side, between rows or groves of trees, *but they are on a level* with the public promenades. In consequence of this, and being surrounded by trees, the effect they produce is very inferior to that of the one just mentioned. No. 2 is an isometrical view of one of these : the other is so similar in design to No. 1, that we think it unnecessary to introduce it. The double lines here are intended to shew the edgings of the beds, which are of Box. The vases in the centre are planted with Geraniums, Verbenas, &c., during the summer months. It is wholly surrounded with trees ; but they are shewn here on two sides only, in order that the plan of the Rosarium might not be interfered with. The presence of these trees could be dispensed with to advantage. By excluding sunlight and a free circulation of air they produce most pernicious consequences, which the drawn and weakly state of some of the plants sufficiently prove.

The gardens of the Luxembourg are enclosed by a kind of fence, made of light sticks, which are much used in France for similar purposes. The manner of planting adopted is this :—The beds are about seven feet wide, and contain two rows. Two plants of each variety, a standard and a dwarf, are planted side by side, at distances of about three feet. They are so disposed that every standard has a dwarf behind it, and in consequence every dwarf is

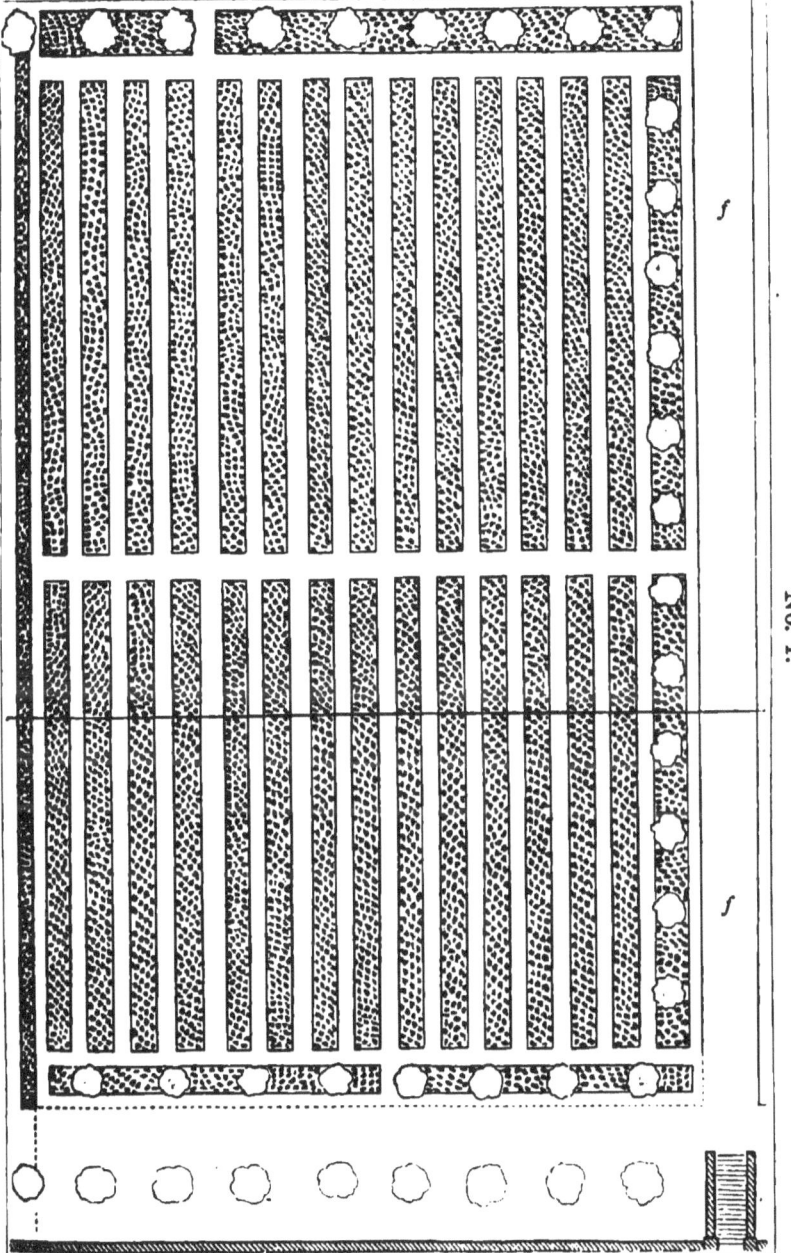

No. 1.

No. 2.

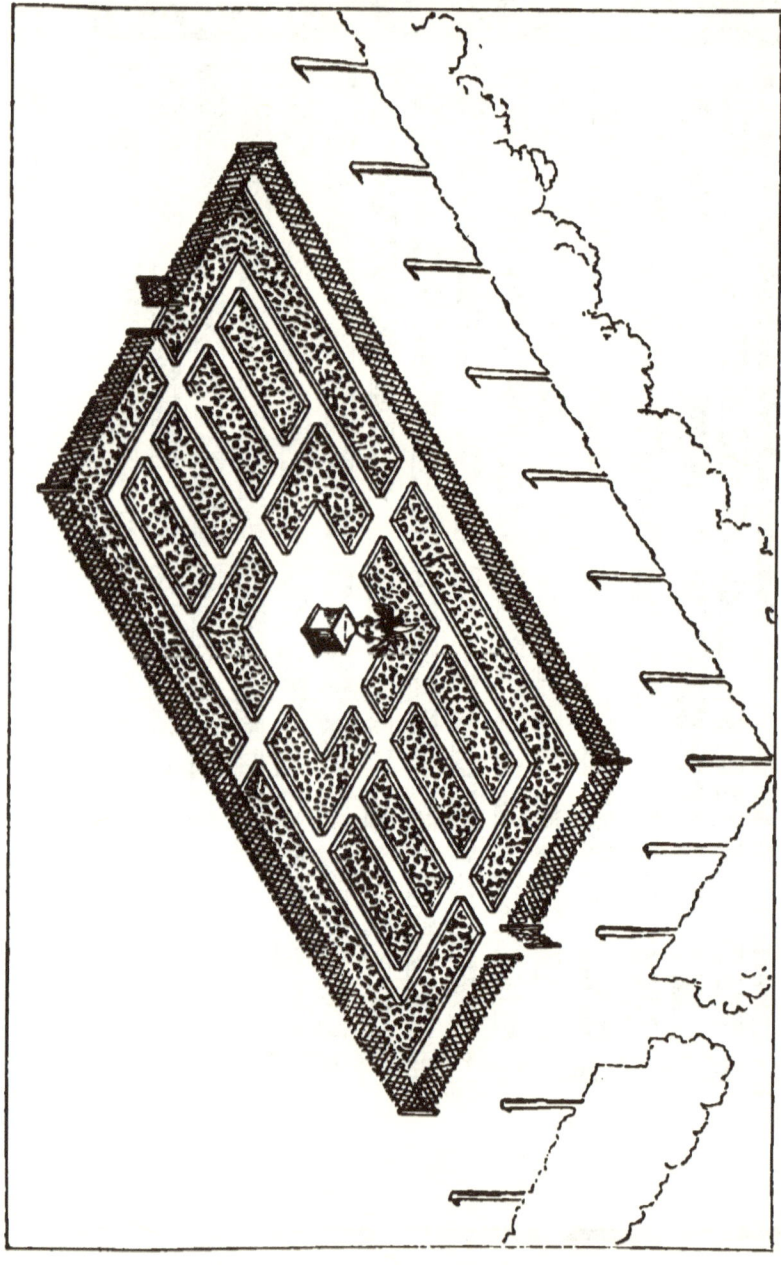

backed by a standard. The number of plants contained in the Rosarium of which No. 1 is a ground-plan is about 1800. The Roses in No. 1 are apparently planted without any design of keeping the respective groups together. In the other gardens, however, one is planted solely with Autumnals, and the other with the various groups of Summer Roses. The extreme simplicity in their formation renders them not very brilliant objects on paper; but although the design be simple, the effect is good. Now, without holding these gardens up to view as perfection, I do think two principal points in the formation of the Rosarium have been perfectly wrought out. Here is a terrace, from which we can look down upon the plants; view them as a whole (which is indeed a grand sight); and they are so arranged, that we can look closely at each by descending to the walks. The greatest objection appears to me to exist in the non-arrangement of the varieties in separate groups, according to their external characters; and which might have been done without lessening the effect produced as a whole.

We shall now present our readers with two original plans, designed expressly for this work by Messrs. Major and Son, the eminent landscape gardeners of Knosthorpe, near Leeds, and on which they make the following remarks :—

" In grounds sufficiently extensive for the introduction of various scenes, the Rosarium is one calculated to produce considerable interest; and being formal, and a separate scene, it is necessary that it should be masked out from the general pleasure-ground by shrubs and *low* ornamental trees, blending with the adjoining ground in the natural or English style. In situations where the ground is too limited for the introduction of a Rosarium, we prefer assembling the Dwarf Roses in groups or small masses in front of the shrubberies; and arranging the Standards irregularly here and there just behind some of the lower shrubs, so that the stems for the most part may be covered. The heads appearing above the shrubs has a highly interesting effect.

" In the designs for the Rosariums, we have arranged the whole of the beds and Standard Roses as near each other as they should be placed, even in the most limited grounds; but in situations where a little more space of lawn can be allowed, it will be better to keep them more apart, the same character being kept.

" If an extensive Rosarium is required, it is only necessary to increase the number of beds and Standards, and to preserve the same proportions in the beds and lawn as shewn in the plans No. 3 and No. 4 : it would only be required to throw the shrubbery farther back, and form another range of round beds between it and the Standards ; and, if necessary, the shrubberies enclosing the

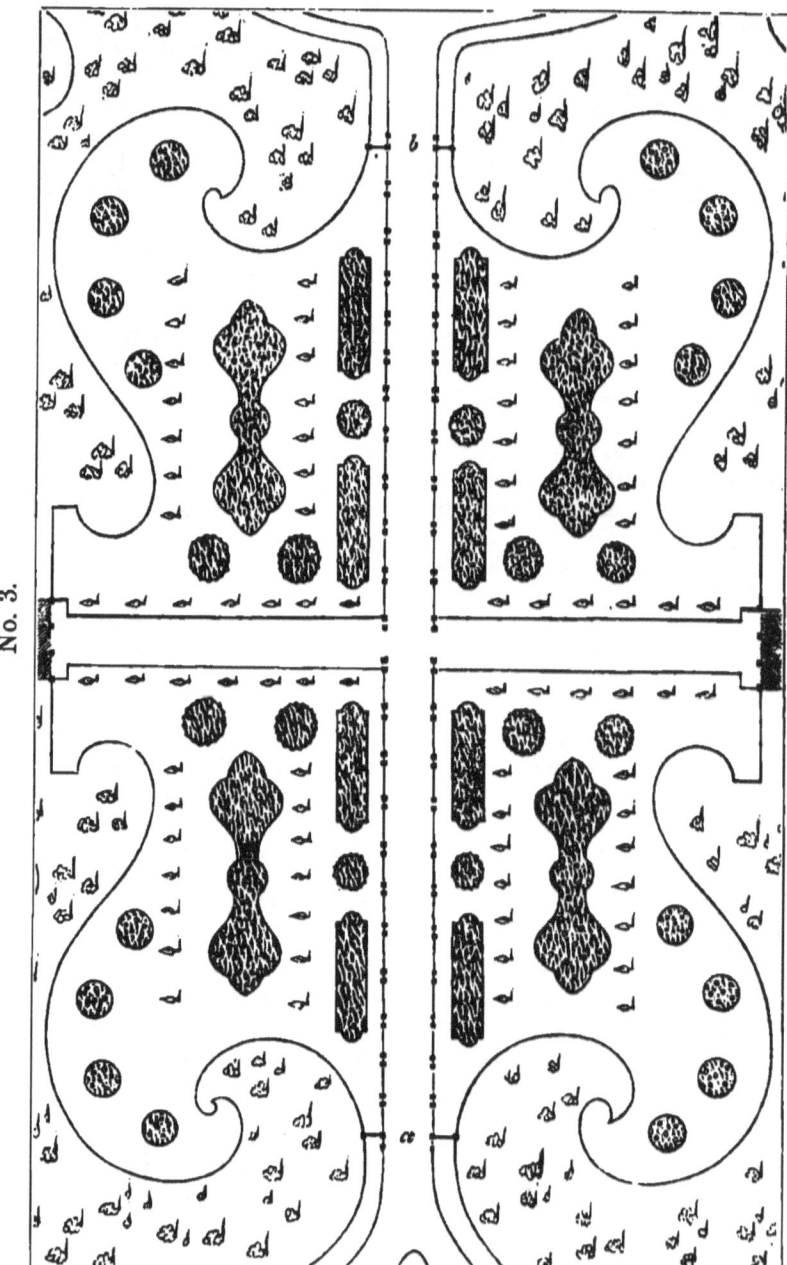

No. 3.

No. 4.

Rosariums may be fronted both with Standards and Dwarf Roses. We adopted this plan, a few years ago, in arranging a Rosarium, the area of which was nearly half an acre in extent; but the collection being very extensive, we found it necessary to front the whole of the shrubbery enclosing the compartment both with Standards and Dwarfs; and during the blooming season it presented a scene truly splendid, surpassing the assemblage of any other family of plants we ever saw, even a splendid collection of Rhododendrons which composed another scene in the same grounds.

"The arcades in both designs are for exhibiting Climbing Roses, which we need not say will produce a very imposing effect. They should be formed of latticed pilasters, twelve inches wide, and about six feet high to the spring of the arches, each pilaster having four uprights one and a quarter inch square, placed two and two, an inch apart, with balls between them at proper distances, and filled up in the middle with lattice-work, shewing five-eighths of an inch in front. The openings between the pilasters may be from four to five feet, according to the height. The arch over the walk must be of lattice-work. Some of the round beds may be of basket-work, twelve or fifteen inches deep, especially those shewn with a varied outline.

"In order to make the Rosarium as interesting as possible, the beds might be planted with patches of early flowering bulbs to precede the general bloom of Roses; which bulbs, after flowering, might be lifted, and their places supplied by different kinds of Annuals, to succeed the general Rose bloom. So that there would first be a show of early bulbous flowers; then the grand display of Roses; and, lastly, the show of Annuals."

But it may not suit every one's inclination or convenience to form a Rosarium, however desirous he may be of cultivating a few choice specimens of Roses. In small gardens it often happens that there is little room, or the proprietor's favourite may be another flower. He may wish not to exclude Roses altogether, although he has not space to cultivate many.

It is therefore necessary that we should consider how they may be introduced, to form an agreeable feature in the Flower Garden.

Various methods have been suggested, and many carried out with good effect. With regard to Standards, they have been grouped in beds on lawns; planted in continuous lines, running parallel with walks; in square beds, or parallelograms; and they are also not unfrequently planted singly on lawns. Dwarfs are planted in single beds, or groups of beds; sometimes a single variety to each bed, to obtain masses of well-contrasted colours;

sometimes the varieties are mixed, and the colours blended. Each of these plans is good under particular circumstances; for we have not always the exact plot of ground at our disposal necessary to carry out certain forms, and besides which our tastes vary.

Perhaps the best mode of introducing Roses to the Flower Garden is, by a group of beds thrown together on a lawn. In these, if the proprietor be a Rose Amateur, he would most likely be desirous of obtaining as great a variety as possible ; and a bed should be set apart for each group, or for a certain number of his favourite groups, if he be confined for space. There is a very elegant arrangement of clumps on the lawn at Southgate House, the seat of Sir John L. M. Lawrence, Bart. The ground they occupy is a strip taken in from the park, about one hundred and thirty yards long, and eight yards wide : it lies open to the east. There are fifteen clumps formed in a single row, some two, and some four yards apart, excepting the sixth and seventh clumps, between which there is a clear space of sixteen yards. Their forms are circles, segments of circles, ovals, parallelograms, octagons, and the like. In front of the lawn is a broad gravel walk, and at the back a wire fence, separating the lawn from the park. The clumps were originally planted with the following groups, in the order in which we place them, commencing with that nearest the dwelling-house : 1. Bourbon ; 2. French; 3. Provence ; 4. Damask Perpetual ; 5. French ; 6. Moss; 7. Noisette ; 8. Bourbon Perpetual ; 9. Hybrid Provence ; 10. Hybrid Perpetual ; 11. Hybrid Chinese ; 12. Damask and Alba mixed ; 13. Bourbon ; 14. Sweet Brier, and its hybrids ; 15. Hybrid Perpetual. This series of clumps still exists, but the varieties being mostly destroyed by the winter of 1860-61 the beds have been recently re-filled with miscellaneous Roses. It is situate on the right-hand side of the gravel-walk when proceeding from the house. To the left are walks leading to the Flower Garden, some fine Horse-chesnut trees, and a few clumps to contain Geraniums, Verbenas, and various other plants. Behind these is a wall, on which fruit-trees are planted. At the further end of the Rose-clumps is a group of ornamental trees, opposite to which is a Summer-house. With regard to the arrangement, the plants intended for the centre, or centre rows, were selected on stems about three feet and a half high : the others gradually decrease in height as they approach the edges of the beds. The greatest distance from plant to plant is three feet ; and the smaller growers, which have place towards the circumference of the beds, are planted nearer to each other.

The natural soil here is clay upon gravel. In preparing the ground to receive the Roses, the soil was removed from the beds to the depth of two feet, and replaced with good loam—the washings of the park and fields, which had been collected from the gutters there.

The earth from the walk was removed *to a greater depth* than that of the beds; and various substances were placed in the bottom to form a drain, in order that the latter might be laid quite dry. This was taking a great deal of pains with a soil not irremediably bad—with a soil *which might have been rendered suitable for Rose-culture* with less labour than that bestowed on it. But the additional painstaking was more than repaid by the complete success attendant on the transplantation of the trees. Of 319 specimens transferred from the Nurseries here, not one died! The greater part, too, flowered beautifully the first season after transplantation, which is not generally the case. They were planted with great care, and no doubt received the strictest attention during the spring and summer. But although the success here must be chiefly ascribed to the above-mentioned circumstances, this case must not be considered as one of common occurrence. We record it here because remarkable; for, with the most skilful management and utmost care, individual instances of failure will almost invariably ensue.

When Roses are planted in the manner of which we are now speaking, if the proprietor of the garden be a lover of flowers in general, without caring to enter into the detail of the matter, planting in masses of colour will probably suit his taste better than making up each clump with mixed varieties. In this case the beds should be of smaller dimensions than when filled with various kinds, or there is an appearance of too much sameness. *We here plant for effect;* and if the plants are Dwarfs, full scope may be allowed for the exercise of taste and ingenuity in the construction of the beds : the simple forms recommended to the Amateur for Roses on stems may be cast aside. The effect of planting masses of colour is truly splendid, and such as cannot be accomplished simply by a mixture of varieties.

Let us suppose a group of beds formed on a lawn within sight of the drawing-room, and filled with the freest flowering Roses. Let Chinese Fabvier (scarlet) fill one bed; Bourbon Queen (salmon) another; Géant des Batailles (crimson) a third; Narcisse (yellow) a fourth; and, in continuation, selecting kinds to introduce as agreeable a contrast of colour as possible, and of as nearly equal growth, as the form of the series of beds may require. If we prefer Summer Roses, there are kinds among them quite as suitable for the purpose. Can we doubt the effect of this mode of planting? Could we introduce a more agreeable feature to the Flower Garden? If formed of the Autumnals, we have flowers springing forth in the earliest of Summer, and continuing to blossom till November;

bidding defiance to the slight frosts of Autumn, which check or destroy the less hardy races, that contribute so much to the adornment of the garden.

In small gardens, where variety is desirable, a bed of moderate, or large size, produces probably a more agreeable effect than numerous small beds : the latter are, however, better, if well-contrasted *masses of colour* are desired.

Standard Roses, planted in lines running parallel with garden-walks, are shewn to great advantage, and this method is in many cases to be recommended; the borders beneath being planted with bulbs, herbaceous plants, annuals, or others of humble growth.

There is one practice which has been too frequently adopted in planting Roses singly on lawns, that of placing the turf close up to and around the stems immediately after planting : this cannot be too highly deprecated. The starved and unhealthy appearance the plants usually present tells unmistakeably their dislike of such treatment. Why, then, should they be submitted to it ? Were they allowed to become thoroughly established, the turf might then be laid on without producing such injurious consequences. But it is desirable to avoid even this. For of what avail, we ask, can the soft genial showers of spring, or even the heavier rains of summer, be to the roots of a tree, when they have first to pass through the thirsty turf, and give sustenance to the blades composing it. And again, the turfing of the ground prevents in some measure the air from permeating the soil, which practice proves so beneficial to the growth of plants. It may be said that an open space round a plant on a lawn is objectionable ; but this may be overcome by placing a few white flints or burs on the soil ; or sowing it with Annuals of small growth, which will diversify and add to the beauty of the garden.

Some varieties of Roses, which form large heads when grown as Standards, look well planted in avenues.

In small gardens, Standards of various kinds may be planted completely round the outside of the lawn, at equal or various distances.

Weeping Roses form beautiful objects when planted singly on lawns ; and it is surprising that they are not more generally cultivated. Are they so rare that few have yet witnessed them in complete beauty ? It may be so. There is a Letter now before me, from an Amateur in Devonshire, who purchased from here, some years since, a plant of the Ayrshire Ruga, with a stem eight feet high. It has been trained as a Weeper ; and the tips of its branches now rest upon the grass below : an arbour is formed by it, and there is a seat within. The branches are, in the flowering season, covered with blossoms from the head to the ground, and the sight is described as magnificent.

There are but few kinds *naturally suited* for this mode of growth; although many may, by a course of pruning and training, be brought to form handsome specimens. Of natural Weepers, the Ayrshire and Evergreen are the best. Of others, such of the Austrian, the Boursault, the Hybrid Chinese, the Hybrid Noisette, the Noisette, and Bourbon, as are of pendulous growth, should be chosen. The latter groups introduce a pleasing variety of character and colour, points well worth gaining, especially if many Weepers are wished for.

We cannot conceive a more beautiful object on a lawn than a Standard Rose trained as a Weeper,* covered, in summer, with its thousands of blossoms, relieved and admirably set off by the careless grace of its growth, and the agreeable colour of its foliage. By a careful choice of varieties, and a judicious system of pruning (see article " Pruning"), the long pendulous branches may be made to droop from any moderate height to the ground, producing flowers their whole length.

We should fancy that Roses of pendulous growth, worked on short stems, and planted in vases, would have a pretty effect. Again, if the same kinds were planted as Dwarfs, in raised baskets, on lawns or elsewhere, and their shoots allowed to hang down on all sides, the effect of the masses of flower they produce, if equalled, could not be surpassed.

We occasionally see varieties of vigorous and straggling growth formed as plain Standard or Bush Roses. We must confess we do not admire them as such; and think them better fitted to form Climbers, Pillars, or Weepers. And if the Rose is more beautiful under one form than another, it is perhaps when fashioned as a Pillar Rose. Every Rosarium, and indeed every Flower Garden, should possess some of them. We have previously stated that they may be introduced to the Rosarium, to form the boundary-line of the summer and autumn gardens. In the Flower Garden they may be planted to form temples, avenues, single specimens on lawns, or in groups of three, five, or more. If planted in a ring round a circular clump on a lawn, at some distance from its circumference, we should conceive the effect to be good. The best kinds are, the Ayrshire, Sempervirens, Boursault, Hybrid Chinese, Noisette, Hybrid Perpetual, and Bourbon, some of which shew

---

* Where any particular mode of growing Roses is recommended, a list of a select few suited for the purpose will be given at the end of Div. 1.

themselves better suited for the purpose than others, and which we shall point out when we come to speak of Pillar Roses.

Climbing Roses may be introduced to the Flower Garden to advantage, as a cover for fences, or to hide any object disagreeable to the eye. When it is wished to cover a high fence or building quickly, some of the strongest growers should be chosen, budded on tall stems: the space left beneath may then be covered with kinds of less rampant growth. Climbing Roses may be planted to cover arbours, rustic seats, or to form arcades or arches over walks. I have seen them trained on arches by the sides of walks, a line of arches on either side running their entire length, not stretching over them. Such may be admitted, in certain positions in the Flower Garden, with charming effect, although they are not always in harmony with surrounding objects, or in good taste. When this arrangement may seem suitable, the arches should not be placed at too great a distance from each other; and the effect may sometimes be heightened by running chains, in curved lines, from arch to arch, covering them with the spare branches of the Roses. For this purpose the Evergreen Roses are perhaps the best, as they are very hardy, and hold their leaves longer in winter than any other Climbers.

The Evergreen and Ayrshire may also be planted in rough places in parks, to trail over waste ground, hillocks, or the like: they may also be made to climb old trees; in which way they present a very rustic appearance, and produce a pleasing effect. It appears to us better taste to plant *them* in such situations than budded plants, as the latter are only in character in dressed grounds.

A bank of Roses produces a very agreeable effect, especially when seen from the windows of the house. The Evergreen and Hybrid Chinese, owing to their vigour and density of growth, and the immense trusses of flowers they produce, are of the best kind for this purpose. They may be planted two or three yards apart, according to the quality of the soil. They will need only just so much training as to induce them to cover regularly and thickly the whole surface of the ground. As to pruning, the less the better; but we must of course keep the form of the bank elegant, and the plants in health and vigour.

If these same kinds were planted at the base of trees in the most open spots, near the confines, or within sight of the walks in shrubberies, we think they would introduce a pleasing feature there. In such places, how often does the gloomy and desolate triumph over the cheerful and beautiful! The trees are often bare, or dead branches only seen, for some distance from the ground; and the

E

beauty of their tops is not appreciable as we walk beneath. Who has not sometimes rambled in such walks, where the wild Honeysuckles have presented the most pleasing feature, if not the only one, to tempt him to pursue his walk? And beautiful indeed *they* are, creeping over the rugged branches of the trees, their tortuous stems shewing here and there, and their beautiful flowers and leaves glistening among the boughs above. And why should not Roses be brought to fill like positions. Let the Ayrshire be planted in spots where they obtain *a little light*, and they will do. But it will be well to give them every encouragement at the outset. Remove the soil at the root of the tree to the depth of eighteen inches, and for two or three feet square, filling up the opening with two-thirds good turfy loam, well intermixed with one-third manure, rich, but not too fresh. In this they may be planted. Train them for the first year or two, until they get good hold of the trees; then manure them annually. Prune very little; and there is no doubt they will flower well, and lend additional interest and beauty to the shrubbery-walks by the relief and variety they give.

In some places, where the shrubbery walks are extensive, we have seen groups of Roses introduced with good effect.

It is probably the best plan here to have the arrangement as simple as possible, that it may be comprehended at a glance. It should be entirely concealed from distant view, to the end that some little surprise may be created, by finding ourselves unexpectedly greeted in our course with a mass of these lovely flowers. Planting simply in straight rows about four deep appears an excellent method; and the plants may be arranged to slope gradually from the back to the front. The entrance at each end might be arched over with wire-work; or even two or three rustic poles fixed upright on either side the walk, and arched over, would be in perfect harmony with the design. Round and over these poles and arches Climbing Roses may be induced to grow, mingling the colours, or not, as taste may suggest, but taking care that the varieties be abundant bloomers, and of similar growth. If the arches are too long, the light is excluded from the interior, and the flowers all draw to the top, in which position they are not seen. If it is wished to have an arched Rose-walk, the arches should not exceed two feet in length, and they should be placed about a yard apart. The effect produced in viewing the walk from either end is the same as if the arches covered the whole space of ground; and when passing under them, the flowers hang drooping from the sides and top, and are then seen to advantage.

But to return. From the situation (the Shrubbery), the rare and perfect kinds of Roses will not be looked for here: the beholder

.will very probably not stay long enough to examine them critically, and the aim should be to produce an impression at first sight. This may be done by choosing the showy free flowering kinds, such as are famed for the quantity of flowers they produce, for beauty *en masse*, and brilliancy of colour, in preference to those possessed of great symmetry of form, or exactitude of habit. Many of the Chinese, Hybrid Chinese, Hybrid Perpetual, and Noisette Roses, are of this kind.

Such a plantation as that just described exists at Ponsbourne Park, Herts, the seat of Wynn Ellis, Esq. The entrance on either side is arched over with rustic poles, for a distance of a few yards ; the arch is so curved that the plantation is entirely concealed from view till you are within it. The walk, which is simply a continuation of the shrubbery-walk, is of gravel; the beds edged with the pretty Lawrenciana Roses. We can imagine the effect of such an encounter upon the mind of a visitor, who may have chosen to spend his early hours in the shrubbery-walks.

There is a very pretty arrangement of Roses introduced in the walks of the shrubbery in the gardens of the Misses Warner, at

No. 5.

Feet.

Hoddesdon. No. 5. is a ground-plan of the beds in which they are planted. The earth in the four beds which compose the inner circle is raised about four feet above the level of that which surrounds it; and upon this is built a temple, the frame-work being formed with iron rods. It is covered with Climbing Roses of various kinds. There are eight plants planted in each bed. No. 6. is a sketch taken of this temple when the Roses were pruned.

No. 6.

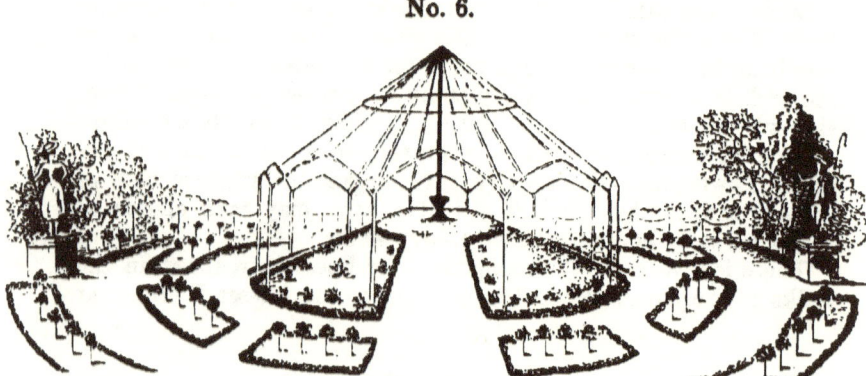

Although they cover it entirely, we have thought it desirable to omit them, in order that the construction of the frame-work might be clearly seen. The temple, to which there are four entrances, has at its circumference twelve gothic arches, the outer standards of which are seven feet three inches high, and six feet three inches apart. There are other iron supports between the outer standards and the centre one : the latter, which is placed on the top of the mound, stands ten feet clear of the ground. In the outer ranges of beds are planted a Standard and Dwarf Rose alternately. The diameter of the first circle is twenty-six feet, that of the whole, forty-eight feet.

When in the temple, looking down the walks, we see three rustic figures, modelled in lead, and mounted on pedestals, which vary and add to the beauty of the design. The fourth figure, which would seem required, to give grace and uniformity to the scene, is wanting, a brook running on one side of the circle occupying the ground where it should have place. A hedge of Scotch Roses is planted round the outside, over which we look upon an extensive lawn, with Pinuses and various plants shewing in the distance. Forming a part of the Shrubbery, we may suppose it is not entirely free from trees, but it lies open on one side ; and to this, united with skilful management, may be attributed the healthy and vigorous condition of the plants.

The space allotted to this branch of the work is already filled, which we regret, as there are many other Rose Gardens well worthy of notice.

One more we must just glance at, which is known as Rosenthal, and is the property of A. Rowland, Esq., situate at Lewisham, in Kent. The principal features in this garden are an arched Rose-walk, and a Temple of Roses. Water is introduced here from an artesian well 120 feet deep, which creates variety, and imparts fresh-ness and animation to the scene. There is a garden of about four acres, planted with the French, Provence, and Perpetual Roses, and Mr. Rowland has taken about fifty prize medals for roses exhibited at the various flower-shows.

CHAPTER IV.

ON THE CHOICE AND ARRANGEMENT OF VARIETIES, AND REMARKS ON PLANTING.

HAVING formed the Rosarium, it may be well, before proceeding further, to ask ourselves this question—Are the soil and locality sufficiently favourable to admit of the successful cultivation of all kinds indiscriminately ? If so, we are indeed fortunate ; for variation in character is certainly desirable, and each group possesses some particular feature to recommend it. There are the Damask Perpetual, and the Tea-scented, justly celebrated for their fragrance. The Hybrids of the Chinese have an equal claim, on account of their finely-shaped flowers and great variation in colour ; besides which, they are the hardiest of Roses, thriving in less favourable situations than most others. Then there are the Chinese, remarkable for great regularity of growth, and whose flowers are produced in gay profusion in Spring, Summer, and Autumn, and which only cease to blow when the chill breath of winter strikes them, heralding the approach of the season of repose. In addition to these, there are the Provence, the Moss, the Damask, the Alba, the Hybrid Perpetual, and the Bourbon—the two latter blooming almost as constantly and as long as the Chinese—and many other groups as interesting, if not so extensive, or so generally known. Can we, in planting the Rosarium, wholly dispense with any group ? We think not. To render the design complete, a few varieties from each should be chosen : the cultivator may have his favourite groups, and introduce *them* in greater quantity ; but if the soil and situation are good, he should not wholly exclude any.

We now intend to note the number of varieties we should draw from each group, were we about to plant a Rosarium for ourselves : this, we believe, will prove useful to some of our readers. And in order to do justice to so difficult a task, I have carefully considered the varieties separately, and in many instances weighed them the one against the other. Let us suppose a Rosarium to require from four to five hundred plants ; and as all have not precisely the same objects in view in planting, it may be well to offer two arrangements.

1. Where the design is to introduce as great a variety as possible, without sacrificing desirable qualities or beauty :

SUMMER ROSES : †The Boursault, 2. The Double Yellow, 1. The Scotch, 12. The Damask, 6. The Provence, 5. The Pompon, 4. †The Moss, 20. The French, 20. The Hybrid French, 6. †The Hybrid Chinese, 20. †The Hybrid Bourbon, 6. †The Hybrid Noisette, 2. The Alba, 10. The Austrian Brier, 4. *The Ayrshire, 6. *The Evergreen, 10. *The Banksiæ Rose, 4.

AUTUMNAL ROSES : *The Macartney, 2. The Microphylla, 2. †The Hybrid Perpetual, 120. The Bourbon Perpetual, 8. *The Rose de Rosoméne, 6. The Perpetual Scotch, 2. The Perpetual Moss, 8. The Crimson Chinese, 10. The Chinese, 10. The Fairy Rose, 4. The Tea-scented, 60. †The Bourbon, 60. *The Musk, 3. *The Noisette, 20.

From the groups marked thus †, the best Pillar or Pole Roses may be drawn : from those marked thus *, the best Climbing and Weeping Roses.

2. Where a principal view in the culture of Roses is to compete for prizes at the horticultural exhibitions :

SUMMER ROSES : Provence, 4. Moss, 10. Damask, 4. Alba, 4. French, 10. Hybrid French, 4. Hybrid Chinese, 6. Hybrid Bourbon, 6. Austrian, 1.

AUTUMNAL ROSES : Hybrid Perpetual, 100. Bourbon, 16. Noisette, 10. Tea-scented, 20.

When cultivating for exhibition, we think it advisable to reduce the number of varieties, and plant two or three specimens of each. It is not often that we can cut three fine trusses of flowers (which are required under the present mode of exhibiting round London) from a single plant at the same point of time ; and, from a glance at the rules of several Provincial Societies, I should say two or three plants of each, of a less number of varieties, offer advantages over double the number of which only single plants are grown. In addition to the reason given above, I would remark, that by reducing the number of varieties, we improve the quality of our Collection ; and although it may be difficult to cull the choicest where all are choice, yet he who has a thorough knowledge of the varieties, whose eye has been long practised among them, will discern slight differences, and know the true merit of each.

But sometimes circumstances are adverse to the cultivation of all kinds, and what must be done then ? This materially alters the aspect of affairs. The cultivator should then consider what

proportion may be planted to advantage, and make up his plans
with such. We have previously stated that it is unnecessary to
plant delicate Roses in unfavourable situations or unkindly soils,
as there are plenty of a nature and character adapted for all such
circumstances.

Let us, then, before we leave this part of the subject, offer a
classification of the groups, with the view of aiding the tyro in
selecting for himself.

1. The hardiest groups ; the varieties thriving in localities and
soils the least favourable to vegetation. *Summer Roses:* Boursault,
Damask, Hybrid Chinese, Hybrid Bourbon, Ayrshire, Evergreen.
Autumnal Roses: some of the Hybrid Perpetual, *some* of the
Bourbon, *some* of the Noisette. The plants here, whether dwarfs
or standards, should be budded, and not on their own roots.

2. Hardy groups ; the varieties thriving in ordinary soils and
situations, under common treatment. In addition to all the groups
mentioned in No. 1, the following may be classed here : *Summer
Roses :* the Scotch Rose, the Provence, the Pompon, the Moss
(budded), the French, the Hybrid French, the Hybrid Noisette, the
Alba, the Austrian Brier. *Autumnal Roses* : the Bourbon Perpetual,
the Perpetual Scotch, the Perpetual Moss, the Crimson Chinese,
the Chinese or Monthly, the Bourbon, the Musk.

3. Hardy groups, as regards soil, but requiring an airy locality and
slight protection against frost, if the weather be severe in winter.
Summer Roses: the Multiflora, the Banksiæ. *Autumnal Roses:*
the Macartney, the Microphylla, the Rose de Rosoméne, the
Crimson Chinese, the Chinese or Monthly, the Fairy Rose, the
Tea-scented, *some* varieties of the Noisette.

4. Groups not liable to injury from frost, but which require a pure
air. *Summer Roses :* the Double Yellow, the Austrian Brier.

5. Groups requiring a wall to develope their flowers in full
beauty. *Summer Roses :* the Banksiæ. *Autumnal Roses :* the
Macartney, the Microphylla ; also varieties from various groups,
whose flowers do not expand well under ordinary treatment.

6. Groups best adapted for the heaviest soils. *Summer Roses :*
the Boursault, the Damask, the Hybrids of the Provence, the
French, the Hybrid French, the Hybrid Chinese, the Hybrid
Bourbon, the Evergreen, the Multiflora. *Autumnal Roses :* the
Hybrid Perpetual, the Chinese or Monthly, *some* of the Bourbons,
the Musk, *some* of the Noisette.

For such soils as these the plants should be budded, and not on
their own roots.

7. Groups suited for the lightest soils. *Summer Roses :* the
Scotch Rose, the Provence, the Pompon, the Moss, the French, the

Hybrid Noisette, the Alba, the Ayrshire. *Autumnal Roses :* *some* of the Hybrid Perpetual, the Bourbon Perpetual, the Perpetual Scotch, the Crimson Chinese, the Fairy, the Tea-scented, *some* of the Bourbon, *some* of the Noisette. In soils of the above description the plants should, so far as attainable, be grown on their own roots : such as are not so cultivated in the Nurseries should be chosen budded on very short stems.

8. Groups best suited for Pot-culture, many kinds improving greatly in beauty when grown under glass. *Summer Roses :* *some* of the Hybrid Chinese, *some* of the Hybrid Bourbon. *Autumnal Roses :* the Hybrid Perpetual, the Bourbon Perpetual, the Crimson Chinese, the Chinese or Monthly, the Fairy Rose, the Tea-scented, *some* of the Bourbon, *some* of the Noisette. The plants may be budded, or on their own roots, at the option of the cultivator.

9. Groups best suited for forcing. The same as recommended for pot-culture in No. 8 ; and the plants should be budded on the Dog-Rose, the Manetti, or some free stock.

10. Groups which furnish the best Climbing Roses. *Summer Roses :* the Boursault, the Ayrshire, the Evergreen, the Multiflora, the Banksiæ Rose. *Autumnal Roses :* the Macartney, the Rose de Rosoméne, the Musk, *some* of the Noisette.

11. Groups which furnish the best Pillar or Pole Roses. *Summer Roses :* the Damask, the Moss, the Hybrid Chinese, the Hybrid Bourbon, the Hybrid Noisette, the Alba Rose. *Autumnal Roses :* the Hybrid Perpetual, the Bourbon, the Noisette. The *"vigorous"* growers from these groups must be selected, and the plants usually preferred are dwarfs on their own roots. These remarks are applicable to No. 10 also.

In selecting varieties to plant in the Rosarium, or to ornament the Flower Garden, if the individual have not a thorough knowledge of Roses, the better plan for him to pursue is, to make known his plans to a respectable Rose grower. Let him first name his soil and situation ; then the *particular object* he has in view in cultivating Roses ; whether he desires to compete for prizes at the horticultural exhibitions, or merely seeks, in Rose-culture, a quiet recreation ; or whether, again, his object be to create a display, to obtain a grand mass of flowers, or to produce effect from some particular spot. He should state whether he would wish Summer or Autumn Roses to preponderate ; and if he has some knowledge of the groups, let him name those which are most pleasing to his taste. In addition to this, he should state whether standards or dwarfs, &c. are most admired ; the colours preferred ; and give either the number of plants wanted, or the quality he requires, and the sum he wishes to expend.

This is undoubtedly the most advantageous plan for the purchaser. If the tyro select his own varieties from the Catalogues,
the chances are, that he will be taken with one or two points in a
Rose, and fix upon it without giving other points their due weight,
and thus disappointment not unfrequently ensues. For example:
the Rose Victor Trouillard (Hybrid Perpetual) is exquisite in
colour ; it is large, and very double. These qualities would recommend it; but it is a poor grower, and the arrangement of the
petals is indescribably bad.—The flowers of Toujours fleuri (Hybrid
Perpetual) are perfect in form ; the habit of the plant is also unique,
but the variety is a shy grower. The Rose amateur will usually
discover these points, but not so the tyro ; and no sale-catalogue
can afford space to describe, in full, all the good and bad points
of each variety. But if the purchaser give the information above
stated, and apply to a respectable firm, his objects may be fully
attained.. Let it be further remarked, that this plan of dealing is
also advantageous to the vendor ; and he compensates for the
accommodation afforded him, by sending a number of plants free
of charge, or prices the whole at a lower rate than he could have
done had the amateur selected them individually. The efforts of
the Rose-growers are, or should be, directed towards obtaining the
greatest possible quantity of the finest varieties ; and independent
of feeling it a duty to serve, in the best manner, those who confide
in them, it is their interest in two ways to supply only the choicest
varieties. In the first place, they have usually the largest stock of
such ; and then, it is these which will do them the most credit,
and recommend them to further transactions. It is no advantage
to them to send bad growers, or second-rate kinds : it is the reverse. The bad growers are *always* most difficult to propagate and
bring to a saleable condition, for which the trifling addition in
price does not compensate : and it is easier to grow four or five
thousand of a first-rate variety, than to grow a like number of
plants divided into fifty different kinds. We need not speak of
the disadvantage the vendor suffers from the sale of any but the
best kinds; and I believe he does this, even though the purchaser
select them himself. But beyond the advantages already mentioned
as derived on both sides from this method of dealing, the purchaser
obtains better plants. In a collection of six or seven hundred varieties,
there is a greater number of *first-rate* kinds than the most ardent
cultivator of Roses would be likely to purchase at one time ; and
if the plants of any particular variety are small or weakly that
season, they are excluded, and can be added to the collection at subsequent periods.
　Let us now proceed to make a few remarks on planting. We

will suppose the beds ready formed and prepared, and the order of planting arranged. There is a sufficient number of plants at hand of the required heights and kinds to fill them. If it be a Rosarium or a series of beds we are about to plant, we may suppose that each group will have a bed to itself; or if our plans are not sufficiently extensive to admit of this, each bed should be planted with varieties of one group only, or at furthest with a combination of such as resemble each other in external characters. We are speaking now of planting the Rosarium, or a series of beds : in a single bed or clump it is desirable to mix the groups.

The disposing of the plants will vary so much, according to the plan of the Rosarium or the taste of the individual, and is withal so simple, that it does not appear necessary to enlarge on this particular point. One thing in planting should be borne in mind— Never suffer the roots to lie exposed to the sun and wind, not even for an hour. I fancy I hear, as I have heard some say, "Nonsense! the Dog Rose is so hardy that you may expose it for a month to all weathers, wind, frost, or sunshine, without fear of injuring it." I have often heard this asserted, and have tried experiments, which it is not necessary to record here, to convince myself of a simple fact, which it may be said no one ought to have doubted. One experiment I will relate. In planting some French Roses, two plants of the same kind were left out of the ground for two days and two nights in December. They were budded on the Dog Rose. The days were sunny, the nights were frosty, the mercury falling to about 28° Fahrenheit. Numerous other plants, whose roots were kept covered, and which were planted at the same time, grew and flourished without one exception. And these two *did not die;* but for three years they maintained a miserable existence, neither growing as the others grew, nor producing any creditable flowers; and yet they were as robust and vigorous as any, if, indeed, not more so.

If there are two employed in planting, the one may dig the holes at proper distances, mixing the soil taken out with some well-pulverized manure, and laying it on the sides of the holes ready for use in planting. If the soil be light, he may, notwithstanding the dressing it may have previously received, add a few spadesful of loam for any very choice kind : if the soil be heavy, he may add a few spadesful of leaf-mould. This latter substance is an excellent addition to heavy soils, and almost indispensable when the Tea-scented Roses are planted there: it tempts them to root vigorously, and strong well-flowered plants are the result.

If Standards only are planted, three feet apart is a good distance; and if there is an objection to planting Dwarfs among Standards, and it is still thought desirable to cover the ground below during summer, this may be accomplished by planting Annuals, such as Mignonette, Viscaria oculata, Dianthus Heddewegii, and any others of slender growth. These cannot injure the Roses: in hot dry seasons we believe they prove beneficial, by the partial shade they afford; but they should be planted very thinly, and those kinds chosen which are of the most slender growth. When Dwarf Roses only are planted, from one to three feet, according to the vigour of the kinds, is the distance usually chosen.

A few words on arranging plants in single beds may not be misplaced here. We first take the centre of the bed, where we place the tallest plant, and which should be a robust grower, an abundant bloomer, and an attractive Rose. In reference to this plant, whatever may be the shape or size of the bed, the others are disposed. They should incline gently from it in any or every direction, till the plants at the edge be on very short stems or perfect dwarfs. An inclination of one foot and a half, from one row to another, admits of a very pretty arrangement. Supposing the centre plant to be five feet, the next row may be three feet and a half, the next two feet, and so on. Let it be borne in mind, that the strongest growers should be planted nearest to the centre; and in consequence of their more vigorous growth, greater space should be allowed from plant to plant there than at the circumference of the bed, where the smaller growers are planted. When the holes are opened for planting, throw a little manure in the bottom, and mix it with the soil there; then place the plant in the hole, filling in with the manure and soil laid ready above, treading them firmly about the roots. After planting, give each Standard a stake, to secure it from the action of the wind, and the operation is finished. Be it remarked, that planting deep causes Roses to throw suckers: if the roots are from three to six inches under the soil it is quite enough.   .

The Tea-scented, Chinese, tender varieties of Noisette, and Lawrenceana Roses, should never be planted in the autumn. Let the beds or places which they are intended to fill remain open till spring. The plants of these groups are sometimes small and delicate, and if put into the ground in autumn they often suffer fearfully from the winter's frost. But plant them in spring; if they are a year old, in April; if younger, in May or June; and they have the growing season before them: they get a firm hold of the ground by winter, and are more gradually hardened to, and better capable of supporting, the changes and severities of that season.

It is important that the ground be in good working order at the time of planting, for on this depends greatly the measure of success.

If it be wet, it hangs to the spade and to the heels of the operator, and prevents him from doing his work well. But worse than this: the moving of ground when wet causes the particles to combine more intimately: it becomes close and dead, and, if thrown about the roots of a tree in this state, acts most prejudicially. Choose, then, a dry time, when the earth bounds clean and free from the spade; and if subsequent dry weather points out the necessity of using the watering-pot, by all means do so: far better this, than to plant when the ground is in bad order.

CHAPTER V.

PRUNING.

I BELIEVE pruning to be the most important practice in Rose culture, and, at the same time, the most difficult to obtain the mastery over, and to apply with success.

The difficulty arises chiefly from the extensiveness of the genus, which is made up of varieties differing so much from each other in habit and character. What a striking contrast does the tiny Lawrenceana, seldom exceeding eighteen inches in height, present to the other extreme of the genus, the Ayrshire and Sempervirens, which will form shoots fifteen feet long in a single year! And there are kinds of every intermediate degree of vigour and character, and hence the difficulty—the great variation required in the application of pruning.

But, beyond this, the manner of pruning is partly determined by the object the operator has in view, or by the condition and health of the plant. A Rose intended to form a standard would require different pruning to one wanted to form a Pillar Rose, although the variety were the same. When flowers are desired of the largest size, as for exhibition, the plan should differ from that pursued to obtain masses of flowers. Again, a Rose in vigorous condition, when healthy and full of sap, requires *less* pruning than when, owing to soil, situation, or other causes, it is of moderate or weakly growth. *The same degree of pruning applied to each condition would produce opposite results.* Close pruning would be the means of improving the health and flowering of a weak tree : it would induce a vigorous one to form wood-shoots only, no flowers.

From the above remarks it will be seen, that after the fullest and most careful examination of the subject, pruning depending so much on circumstances, a great deal must be left to the judgment of the operator : *a certain degree of practice is necessary* before any great attainment in this art *can be arrived at*, and I would not advise the uninitiated to trust himself too far, before he has well marked the manœuvres of some skilful friend or practitioner.

I know many instances in which amateurs, who take delight in attending to their own Roses, mar the beauty of their trees for want of considering the principles of Rose pruning. Many trees, from too much pruning, grow most luxuriantly, but shew little disposition to flower; others, from too little pruning, produce abundance of flowers, but they are poor in quality. These are known facts of every day occurrence; and what are the consequences? Probably the varieties are condemned as worthless, though of first-rate merit, and only requiring a skilful application of the knife to cause them to flower perfect, and in gorgeous abundance.

But it is not a question of flowers only. On pruning depends the formation of the trees; whether they be handsome, or irregular and misshapen. Regarding this branch of cultivation, then, as one of primary importance, I shall give myself full scope in discussing and illustrating it.

There are two seasons of the year at which pruning is usually performed; November, which is termed Autumn-pruning; and March, or Spring-pruning. Winter-pruning cannot be recommended, as there is a risk of the trees being injured by the action of wet and frost upon the fresh wounds. Thinning in Summer is advocated by some; and of this we shall have occasion to speak by and bye.

Which is the better season for pruning, Spring or Autumn, is a point concerning which Rose-cultivators are not altogether agreed. To enable our readers to judge for themselves, it may be well to state the condition of the trees at each season.

In November, Roses may be said to be at rest; for although there is always a circulation of the sap, at this particular time it is less active than in Spring or Summer.

As a proof of this, if we remove a Rose in Autumn, the roots are then, to all appearance, inactive; but if we remove the same in March, or often, indeed, earlier, we shall find numerous white rootlets, which have been newly formed, and which, sponge-like, are continually sucking moisture from the earth, thereby favouring the circulation of the sap, and promoting growth. Hence the different state of a tree in Autumn and Spring is, that at the former period it is sinking into or at rest, and in the latter rising into life and action. Now, it is evident, that the greater quantity of nutritious matter that can be collected in the immediate vicinity of the buds intended to remain for bloom, the more vigorous will the growth be, and the finer the flowers. Autumn-pruning favours this storing of the juices of the plants; for by cutting away the superfluous shoots in Autumn, the buds on those left behind are placed in contact with a greater supply of food, by the lessening of the number of the channels through which the sap has to pass: the buds increase in size, become plump, and, when Spring arrives, vegetate with great vigour. An earlier bloom is also produced than when pruning is deferred till Spring; and the shoots and flowers are formed with more regularity, and in greater abundance.

It may be said that many of the Summer kinds, being more disposed to produce growing than flowering-shoots, Autumn-pruning is calculated to favour this tendency. True, and to counteract this, the operation should be performed with less rigour at that season than when deferred till Spring.

But Autumn-pruning has its disadvantages, the greatest of which is this:—A few mild days in Winter often excite the buds of Autumn-pruned Roses, and they push forth; severe weather follows; the young shoots are frosted; and the bloom injured. This is more particularly the case with the Chinese, Noisette, Bourbon, Tea-scented, and the Hybrids of these kinds, which we shall term *excitable*, because they are quickly excited to growth. The Provence, Moss, French, Alba, and others, rarely suffer from this cause, as they are not so readily affected by the state of the weather. Be it remarked, however, that the quickness with which buds are roused into action depends much upon how far the shoots were matured the previous Autumn: the less mature the more excitable. It will be perceived, then, that there is a difficulty in the way of Autumn-pruning, when applied to the excitable kinds, which can only be remedied by affording them protection from frost, should a mild December or January be succeeded by severe weather. But this would entail great additional trouble, and cannot always be done. Let us now turn to the other season.

The chief advantage gained by deferring pruning till Spring is, that the flower-shoots are placed beyond the reach of injury by frost. If, during Winter, any buds push forth in unpruned Roses, it is those at the ends of the branches, and they will be removed by pruning. But there is an evil attendant on this apparent advantage. When pruning is put off till Spring, the buds placed at the extremities of the shoots are often found in leaf, and in the operation we cut off some inches from a shoot in this state. The tree is denuded of its leaves, and thereby receives a check. The sap, being in active motion, exudes from the fresh wounds. The lower buds find themselves suddenly in contact with a great supply of food, by the cutting away of the buds beyond them. There is a pause. Soon one or two buds at the extremity of the pruned shoots take up the work: they swell, are developed apace, but all below remain dormant! Thus Spring-pruning is unfavourable to an abundant and regular development of branches and flowers, and, consequently, to the well forming of a tree. The flowers are also usually produced later in the season, and of less size.

Thus it may be said that each season has its advantages and disadvantages ; but is it impossible to draw from both ? We think not ; and would strongly recommend that *all but the excitable kinds be pruned in Autumn : thin out these at the same time, but leave the shortening of their shoots till Spring.*

For pruning Roses two instruments are necessary, a knife and a saw. The knife I use is one with a straight blade : the saw is a double-toothed one, small, with a handle about a foot long and a blade of rather less length : the point is narrow, to admit of its being easily worked among the close branches. Armed with these we are ready for action ; and it is necessary to bear in mind that they should be kept very sharp, in order that the work may be well done.

In France it was formerly the practice to clip the heads of the Standard Roses with shears; but I believe this practice is now abandoned there, and scissors used in their stead. I have tried the latter, but find, in my hands, the knife executes the work better, and more expeditiously; although, as to the latter point, something may depend on use. The scissors are, however, very convenient for gathering flowers, and for cutting off the flower-stalks when they grow shabby, or begin to decay.

There are three principal ends sought in Rose pruning, each of which carries with it a degree of weight, and should be kept distinctly in view ; and let it be borne in mind, that on the judicious use of the pruning knife their perfect accomplishment more or less depends : they are—

1. To maintain a plant or tree in full health and vigour.

2. To induce it to assume a form at once agreeable to the eye, and advantageous for the development of its blossoms.

3. To secure an abundance of good flowers.

1. *To maintain a tree in full health and vigour.*

We are told that the extraordinary vigour. and beauty of some plants on which goats had been browzing first gave the ancients the idea of pruning. Certainly no one in the present day would dispute the advantages of it. Cultivators can only be at variance as to the mode of action, and the season at which the operation should be performed. If we leave a Rose-tree unpruned for one year, a great number of buds will burst forth, producing a vast quantity of blossoms, but both shoots and flowers will be comparatively thin and puny. If such tree be left unpruned for two or three successive years, it will become greatly enfeebled ; the ends of the yearling shoots will die back for want of nourishment, and thus are reduced the number of buds capable of development during the subsequent year. Here we see one end of pruning naturally accomplished. But it is not sufficiently so. The flowers continue to degenerate, till at length they can be scarcely recognised : the tree dwindles, presents an unhealthy appearance, and pruning must be the first means applied for its restoration.

2. *To induce a plant or tree to assume a form at once agreeable to the eye, and advantageous for the development of its flowers.*

The formation of a tree is a point deserving of the closest attention ; for if the form is inelegant it cannot but displease, however healthy and vigorous the tree may be, or whatever the degree of beauty the flowers it produces. Should the latter be forming small, their size may be increased by lessening their number, or by a timely application of manure-water ; but for the improvement of the form of a tree there is no such ready remedy. The flowers, too, are but transitory : the shape of the tree is lasting ; it remains to view after they are gone. To form a handsome tree, it is necessary to take it in hand when young : it is then easy to fashion, as taste, or a view to its permanent weal, may require. But if it has become straggling, from unskilful management or other causes, it is often difficult to re-model, sometimes requiring the patience and skill of two, or even three seasons. Before we commence the pruning of a Rose, whether it be a bush or a tree, it is therefore well to determine the shape it shall assume, and then frame all our operations with a view to its accomplishment. Perhaps a form at the same time pleasing and advantageous is that of a half oval ; for in such all the shoots and branches get a due portion of air and sunlight, and the under ones are not excluded from view, which they often are in round-headed trees. The varieties of spreading growth are most easily brought into this form, but the principle is applicable to all.

The next aim in Rose pruning is

3. *To secure an abundance of fine flowers.*

If the health and vigour of a tree are affected by pruning, the flowers, depending so much on these conditions, must also be affected by the same operation.

When about to prune a Rose, I first look to the name, that I may know the habit and character of the variety I have to deal with. I must know whether it is a summer or perpetual bloomer ; a strong or weakly grower ; and whether the flowers are produced fine from low, middle, and top eyes indiscriminately, or not. It is only by knowing and considering these points that we can prune with accuracy, and ensure full success.

It is an axiom in Rose pruning, that the more vigorous in habit a plant is, the more shoots should be thinned out, and the less should those which are left be shortened in. This has in view, in particular, the production of flowers in the most perfect condition. The eyes near the base of those kinds which form short shoots (especially the Autumnals), usually produce the best flowers; and in the vigorous growers we prefer, for the same reason, the eyes about the middle of the shoot, or nearer its summit if the wood be well ripened. But there is a question arising here which it may be well to glance at before proceeding further. All Roses make two growths in the year; first in Spring, and again in Summer shortly after they have flowered. Some of the Autumnals start afresh at short intervals throughout Summer and Autumn; but we wish at the present time to speak of the Spring and Summer's growth only, and to ask which we should look to as calculated to produce the best flowers.

When the shoots formed in Summer are well ripened we should prefer them, and for these reasons. The growth at that season is generally more rapid, and the shoots, although usually of less strength, are freer in the bark; the eyes are more plump and prominent, and well stored with the juices required to supply nourishment and promote growth.* Nevertheless, it is only a question of neat perfect flowers that would induce us to prefer the Summer wood; for when we desire large flowers, or to keep elegant the form of the tree, we shall find it necessary, in most cases, to prune back to the growth of Spring. Still it is well to bear in mind that the wood grown during Summer usually produces the most refined flowers, that we may make the best of the materials beneath our hand; for it does sometimes happen that we may prune to the Summer's growth with advantage to the tree, and it is often a matter of indifference whether we do so or not.

With these remarks on pruning in general, we proceed to consider it in its special application, under the following heads, as applied to Standards and Dwarfs indiscriminately: 1. Long Pruning, suited to varieties of vigorous growth. 2. Close Pruning, suited to kinds of small growth. 3. Pillar Roses. 4. Weeping Roses.

1. Long pruning.—This must be applied to the strongest growers : such are, the greater part of the Hybrid Chinese, the *vigorous* in the groups Moss, Damask, Noisette, and Bourbon, &c., which form large heads, of rather loose, but not always inelegant growth.

If we remove many shoots from a strong growing Rose, or shorten the shoots in very closely, the result, as previously stated, will be a vigorous growth, ·but few or no flowers; and the shoots *may be* developed so gross, as to destroy the balance of the tree,

---

* Hence the flowers, if not so large, are less coarse and more perfect.

F 2

and render the flowering for the subsequent year partial or void. This is more to be feared when dealing with Summer Roses and established plants, than with the Autumnals or newly-planted ones. To what endless disappointment have those fine old Roses, Brennus, Fulgens, and the like, given rise from not blooming freely. I have heard them branded as shy, bad bloomers, not worthy of place in any garden. "Grow they do," says the cultivator, "and that most vigorously, but refuse to shadow forth a single blossom." Now we would ask, Should the blame, if blame there be, be attached to the varieties? *Is it natural for them not to flower?* Or does this state of things arise from the system of cultivation? We sometimes see them produce abundance of flowers, and pronounce them perfect; then surely the former is not the case. They, and numerous others of like habit—*vigorous growers*—require *long pruning;* that is, a sufficient portion of the shoots should be cut away at their base, which is called thinning out, to allow a free admission of air and light into the heart of the tree; then the shoots which remain after thinning should be left long. If they are cut close, the eyes are developed as wood shoots, and not as flower-shoots; and this is the cause of their not blooming.

The treatment of plants from the bud will be alluded to elsewhere (see Budding); and as few comparatively have to deal with them in this rude state, I shall commence here with one-year budded plants, such as are usually purchased at the grounds of the Rose-growers. Of such No. 7 is a representation. Let us look closely at it, and, while doing so, bear in mind that it is *a young plant.* Now what is the object of paramount importance *this year?* Let us assume the first effort to be to establish the plant, and to put it in a right course of formation. With this end in view, we prune more closely the first year after transplanting than at any subsequent period. Let us suppose the specimen before us required to take the shape of a half oval. What is the first step? It has been budded in two places, and has seven shoots. This is too many: we must therefore remove some. In this stage of a tree, pruning is not complicated: the number of shoots is few, and we see our way pretty clearly. Three shoots are thought sufficient to remain here, and let us select any three which may seem most advantageously situated, and imagine the others absent. We may try this experiment on different shoots, if we are not satisfied with our first choice. To us the shoots shewn by the dark shadowing seem best placed, and our first step is to thin out the others shewn by the single lines. This renders the object clear, and, if it be one of the exciteable kinds, finishes Autumn pruning. In Spring we shorten the shoots that remain, at the termination of the dark

No. 7.

Long Pruning, Stage 1.

shadowing (a). The plant is pruned, and it may be said with
truth, its appearance is not improved. But the question is not,
How does it look when newly pruned? for when properly pruned it
often presents a sorry appearance. The question is, *How will it
look* when each of the shoots left triples or quadruples itself? Many
cultivators spoil their trees by pruning in fear. It is well to be
cautious, but it is seldom that the novice errs by pruning too much.
But what considerations have guided us in our operations here? Seven
shoots is the *greatest* number that should be suffered to remain on
a young plant, and, in general, a less number is preferable. One
or two should rise perpendicularly about the centre of the tree,
and round this or these all others should be regularly disposed;
and the more equal and greater distances that can be contrived
from shoot to shoot the better. The shoots, wherever they arise,
should have a tendency to grow *from* the centre; for if they grow
towards it they will eventually cross each other, forming a confused and crowded head. In the above illustration it will be seen
that every shoot has this tendency.

The aim in thinning should be to leave those shoots which are firmest and healthiest, provided they are placed at nearly equal distances. Care should be taken to cut the shoots close to their base : the wounds then heal over in Spring and Summer, and the trees are grown clean and perfect. If the cut is not made quite close, an eye at the base may burst forth and grow with extraordinary vigour at a point where not wanted, and rob the other branches of their food, and produce an uneven plant. Or should it not be so, the wood will die back, sometimes introducing decay into the heart of the tree. Sear snags and stumps, which are sometimes met with in old specimens, are due to the slovenly practice of leaving an inch or so on the bottom of shoots which should have been cut clean out.

When shortening in, the lowest shoots should, where practicable, be left the longest; and the others may be shortened in closer and closer as we rise towards the summit of the tree. The centre branch will, from its position, command a free supply of sap, and it is likely that it will maintain the ascendancy. Now the shoots

No. 8.

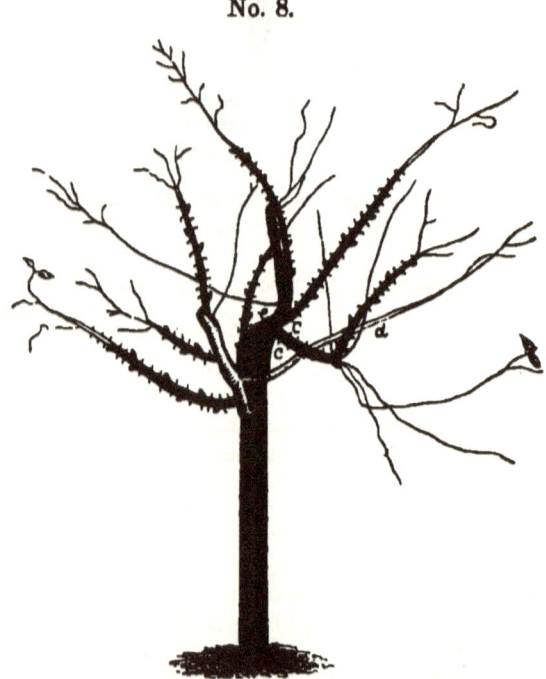

Long-Pruning, Stage 2.

No. 9.

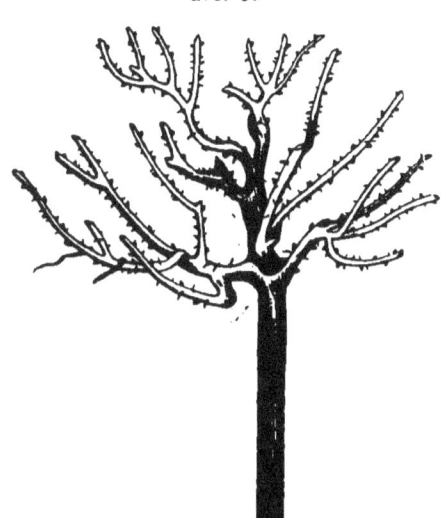

Long-Pruning complete.

shortened closest, will *cæteris paribus*, produce the strongest growth,
with the greatest tendency to rise perpendicularly, and thus the
head is formed as desired.   In shortening the branches, we should
insert the knife at *b*, on .the opposite side of the shoot to that on
which the bud next below is placed; and we should cut in a direction slanting upward, about the eighth of an inch above the bud.

But let us turn to the next stage of the above plant, No. 8.   We
left it pruned for growth, and the additional shoots now seen are
the product of the past Summer.   Pruning is now more complicated: there are more shoots to dispose of.   The operator should
examine the tree thoroughly before he commences.   He should
look not only at it, *but through it,* and this from two or three points
of view.   He should picture to himself this and that shoot removed, and what will be the comparative advantages to the tree.
He thus studies the position and relative bearing of the shoots,
and will soon discover which should be thinned out.

In No. 8 it is thought best to remove those shewn by the single
lines, and the others are shortened in at the termination of the

dark shadowing. It will be observed, the shoots are left of greater length than in the previous year's pruning, for which we give two reasons : First, The plant being established, will have a greater command of food from the soil ; its growth is therefore likely to be more vigorous : Secondly, Having been put in the right course of formation last year, in this pruning we have an eye to the production of flowers.

It may appear to the looker-on that it would have been better to have removed the shoot between cc, and shortened in that shewn by the double line at d. This would have made the art appear more simple, and simplicity in Gardening operations (and indeed where not ?) is a desideratum. But there was a cause for not doing this which the tree before us serves well to explain. The shoot marked d had been produced late in the year, and, to use the technical phrase, was not well ripened—was little more than pith and bark. Such was not fitted to produce either shoots or flowers in good condition, and therefore it was removed. We also think it advisable to shorten in close at e the centre shoot left last year, to keep the head compact. The best shoots having in this instance arisen from the base of the head, we do this to decided advantage. We follow on this system through subsequent seasons, continuing to thin and shorten the shoots ; the tree, if properly managed, increasing in size for several years.

No. 9 is a fair illustration of a full-grown tree to which long pruning has been applied.

2. Close Pruning.—We have been speaking of pruning hitherto in its application to the most vigorous growing Roses : let us now turn to another class, and consider pruning as applied to the small kinds. Such are, some of the Hybrid Perpetual, the Chinese, the Tea-scented, the moderate-growing French and Bourbon, &c., which make compact and neat, but rather formal heads.

No. 10 represents a young plant of this description. Here we have a crowded head the first year : the shoots are of less length than in our former specimen, but more numerous. We proceed to thin as before, but often less severely. The shoots may stand closer to each other here, because those they give birth to will be less robust, and produce smaller foliage. The shoots shewn by the single lines *are not in this instance all removed because disadvantageously situated ;* many are thin and weakly, wholly unfitted to remain. If such exist in a favourable position, it must be an extreme case to justify us in leaving them. Rather would we go a little out of the way to secure a good strong shoot, as such offers a better chance of perfecting our plan. Be it observed, the shoots left after

No. 10

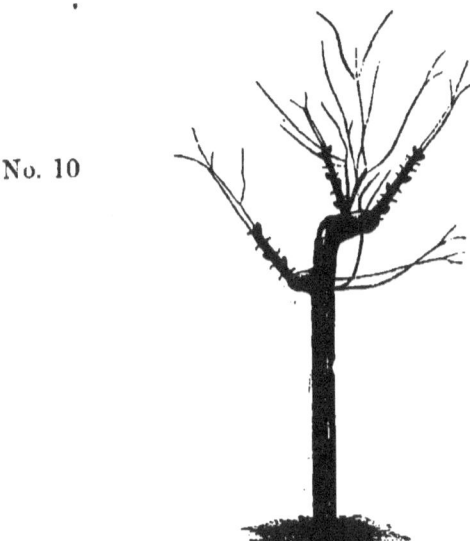

Close Pruning, Stage 1.

No. 11

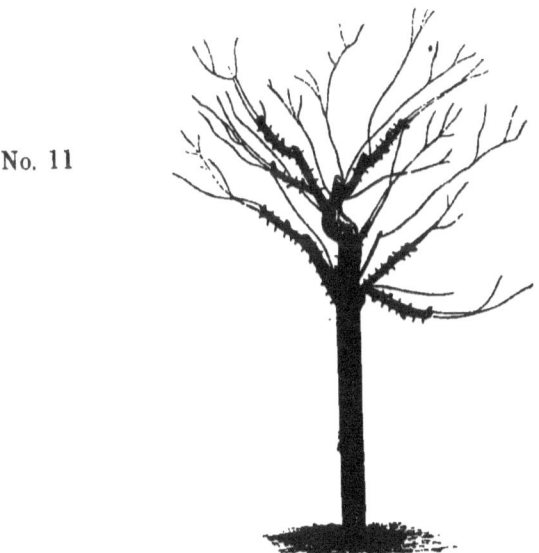

thinning are shortened in closer here than in No. 7. This tree
looks a complete stump, and, as a Summer Rose, will probably not
bloom the first year. But supposing it to be an Autumnal, *it will
then assuredly bloom the first Autumn*, and most probably during
Summer.

No. 11 represents this tree taken from another point of view, as
it appears the next year. Here, as in long pruning, we see the
addition of branches has been great, and we thin out in Autumn
the shoots shewn by the single lines, and shorten the others where
shaded, in Spring, as before. This we do on the supposition that
it is an excitable kind: if not so, we complete the operation at once,
by shortening in Autumn.

No. 12 shews a full-grown plant to which close pruning has been
applied.

Most persons prefer plants budded in two places : we have therefore given examples of such. For my own part, I like a plant with
a single bud best. It is enough for every purpose, and the head is
more easily fashioned. It is thought not necessary to give an
example of such ; for to know how to prune a plant properly with
two buds renders the dealing with a single bud extremely simple.

No. 12

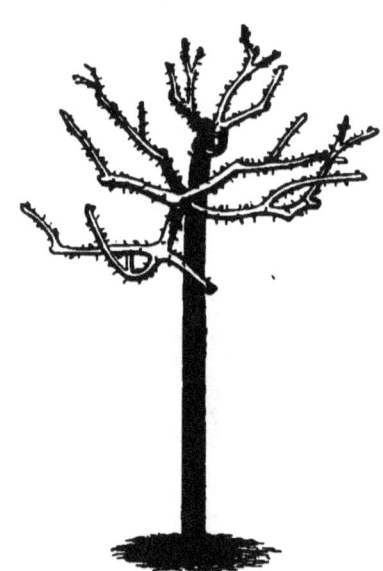

Close Pruning complete.

It would seem well to mention here, that a modification of long and close pruning, which we call moderate pruning, is necessary for certain varieties. Practice alone can inform us correctly which they are ; and we give the result of our practice with some varieties in the Second Division of this work.* But it should be remembered that the plan of pruning must be regulated in some measure by the object sought. We have been treating of it with the view of forming handsome plants, and producing flowers in the greatest degree of beauty. But where the object is merely to enrich and ornament the garden by a great display; where the aim is to have a mass of bloom, and the individual size and form of the flowers are not of first importance ; a less rigorous system should be adopted. Prune, then, only just so much as seems necessary to keep the trees in health and shape.

But there are particular forms which Roses are capable of taking, and these are in a great measure brought about by pruning and training. Such are Pillar Roses and Weeping Roses.

3. Pillar or Pole Roses.—Most kinds may be formed into pillars, short or tall ; but the kinds usually understood by this term are such as will reach at least to six feet. There are many beautiful Roses which will do this ; and some kinds, when established, grow as if there would be no end to them.

It is in this instance thought unnecessary to show the plant in its first year's growth.

No. 13 is a representation of a young plant possessed of five shoots. It had three only last year, and these were cut off nearly level with the ground soon after it was planted, to induce a vigorous growth. We now cut out the three shoots shewn by single lines, and shorten the others as shewn by the shadowing (*f*). After pruning, the branches should lie at full length on the ground, and be fastened down with some little pegs to keep the wind from blowing them about. Owing to their recumbent position, the buds will break regularly their whole length, and by the end of April they may be tied up to the pole, either in an erect position, or made to entwine around it, as shewn in our drawing. We have introduced the poles here from the first stage, but this is a matter of indifference : a good stake will answer every purpose for the first two years.

In No. 14 we see the same plant as it appears the following year,

---

* The terms "robust," "vigorous," "moderate," and "dwarf," attached to the varieties in the descriptive part of this work, will be found almost invariably a correct guide in pruning.

No. 13   No. 14

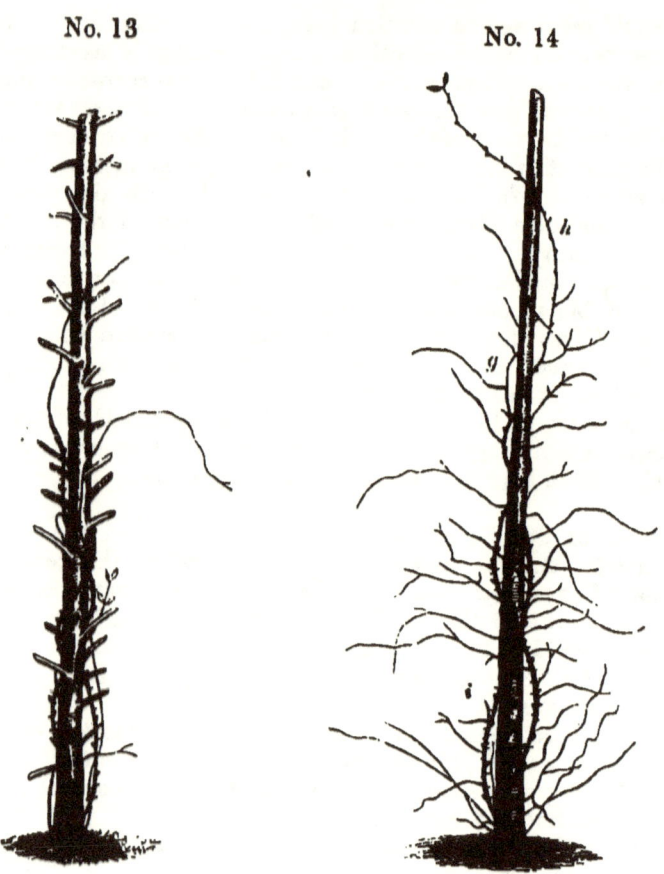

Pillar or Pole Rose, Stage 1.   *Pillar or Pole Rose, Stage* 2.

before it is pruned.   It has grown well, and there is a prospect of a
complete Rose pillar being speedily formed.

We commence pruning at the bottom of the pillar by thinning
out the vigorous shoots formed there.   Two are cut off within a
foot of the ground, and left to fill the base.   This must be our first
aim ; for it is easy at any time *to extend the growth*, and thus increase its height.   We ascend the pillar, thinning as we proceed,
till we reach the top.   Here we select one or two of the strongest
and best-placed shoots *g h* to continue the ascent, and tie them up.
From their position an abundant flow of the sap furnishes them
with means of free growth, and favours the rise of the plant.   The

small lateral or side shoots are now cut back to three or four eyes. If in any spot, as at *i*, the pillar is thin, we cut a shoot back to one or two eyes, and thus get a strong shoot or two, by which we fill the vacuity the next season. We do not reckon much on flowers the second year, if desirous of perfecting the pillars quickly; but the third Spring after planting we find them of considerable height, and in every condition to produce an abundant bloom. Another year, and they blaze forth in all their magnificence.

We continue to follow this method of procedure from time to time, tying up the leading shoots till the pillar is covered the desired height, which perhaps should *not exceed* twelve feet. The lateral shoots of short growth with well-ripened wood are those which produce flowers with the greatest certainty : they may be shortened in, to four or six eyes.

Pillar Roses send up almost invariably strong shoots from the base of the plant during Summer and Autumn. These, if not wanted, may be cut out as soon as discovered ; but it is well to leave one or two, as they may often be made use of to keep the pillar in a vigorous state when perfected, or to renovate it when decaying: by keeping up a constant supply of young shoots the old hide-bound stems may be removed as they exhibit symptoms of debility, without marring the beauty or deteriorating from the effect of the pillar. The branches of Pillar Roses in general do not maintain their vigour for many years, which is probably owing to the little pruning they undergo ; and these strong shoots, arising from their base, offer alone the means of their perfect restoration.

It is more difficult to prune a Pillar Rose than any other form : it requires closer attention, and thoroughly tests the skill and judgment of the operator. When properly managed, and of full size, it should be well and regularly clothed with branches, and in the flowering season with flowers, from the summit to the base. When the tree is once formed, masses of flower being the object sought, and not individual size, it is necessary to guard the unpractised hand against over-pruning : it is on this side that he is most likely to err.

Every year, immediately after pruning, it is well to look to the poles to see that they are in sound condition; and at the same time tie the Roses afresh with small willows, tar-twine, or twisted bast.

The annexed (No. 15) represents a Pillar Rose of full size just pruned. Its main branches have not been twined round the pole as in the previous illustrations, but that practice is a good one, for it favours a moderate and regular growth.

We would just say a few words here in reference to Climbing Roses, which are considered by many as identical with Pillar

No. 15.

Pillar or Pole Rose complete.

Roses. I wish we could make a distinction that would be generally acknowledged. By Pillar Roses we would understand the erect-growing vigorous kinds : by Climbing Roses, those of twining and pendulous growth which are usually still more vigorous than the former. These do not make the best Pillar Roses, nor do the former make the best Climbers, though each is often planted to fill the purpose of the other.

Climbing Roses are usually required for covering walls, fences, arbours, rustic arches, and the like. The first object sought is to cover well and quickly a given space. To effect this, pruning and training are directed. The system of pruning is but a slight modification of that just described : they require, perhaps, rather less of it. The first season that they are placed in the situation they are intended to occupy, each shoot should be shortened in two or three eyes. The result will be a few vigorous shoots, sometimes extending to an extraordinary length, which will depend much on the season, the situation, soil, and attention paid to them ; also on the habit of the variety. Thus the plant becomes established. With regard to covering the space, remember, close pruning will produce a few vigorous shoots ; long pruning a greater number of less vigour. Which are wanted? However the case may be, prune accordingly. Be it remarked, that when a plant is full grown close pruning is not advisable, for the object here, as in Pillar Roses, is masses of bloom.

No. 16.

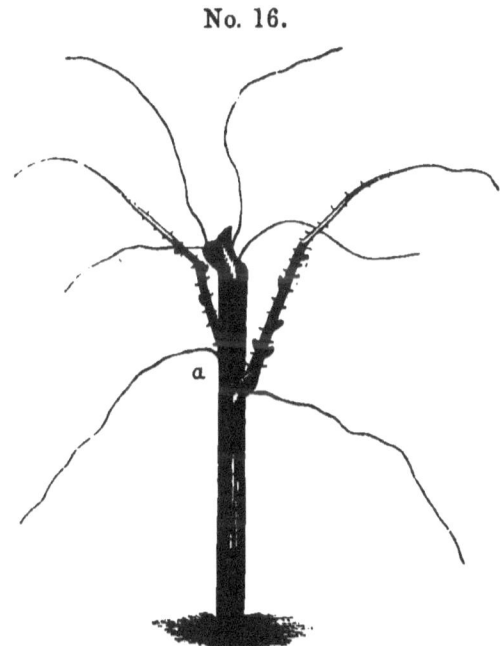

Weeping Rose, Stage 1.

4. Weeping Roses.—Weeping Roses are the kinds of vigorous and pendulous growth worked on stems of five feet or upwards.

No. 16 gives a fair specimen of one of these the first year after budding. This plant has two buds, which are certainly prejudicial, not only from the obstacles they present to the perfecting of our design, but because they have been placed too far apart. As with Pillar and Climbing, so with Weeping Roses, the shoots should be cut in closely the first time of pruning, to induce a vigorous growth. In this case, the lower bud has given birth to the strongest and best shoots : we therefore remove the upper one, cutting the stem away just above the lower junction *a*. Having removed the upper bud, we thin out the two shoots shewn by the single lines, and shorten the others to the dark shadowing. Hence, shoots push vigorously; and the habit of the varieties being pendulous, they soon reach the ground.

No. 17 shews the growth of the tree the first year after it has been pruned with the view of forming a Weeper. We continue the operation. We here find it advisable to shorten closer *a a*, the

No. 17.

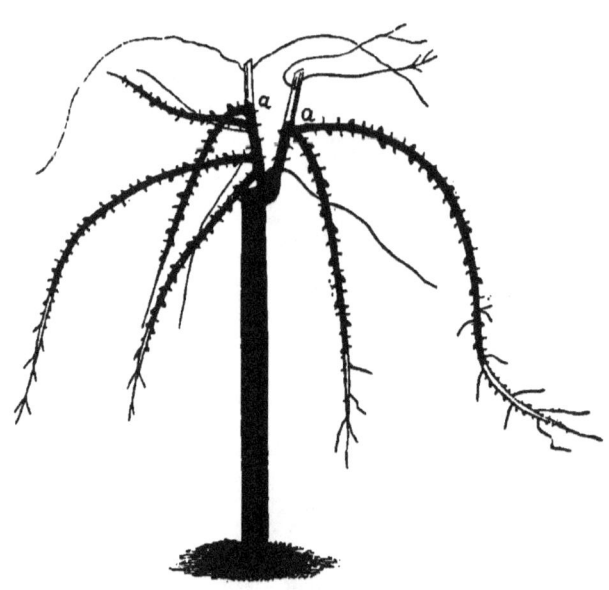

Weeping Rose, Stage 2.

shoots left by the last year's pruning. In the next place, we cut out the shoots shewn by the single lines, and shorten the others a few inches only. From their drooping position the flow of the sap is equalized, and the eyes will break regularly nearly their whole length. Single blooms will occasionally be produced from them, and the following year these short bloom-bearing branches may be spurred ; that is, pruned to about two eyes. Henceforth there is but little difficulty in bringing the tree to perfection. The main shoots should not be shortened till they reach the ground : prune the laterals only ; when flowers are produced all along the branches from the head of the tree to the ground, forming a beautiful half-globe one mass of flower.

About the second or third year it is well to attach a hoop to the head of Weeping Roses, as shewn in No. 18, to keep the branches free from injury by the action of the wind, and to assist in arranging them properly.

I have sometimes seen wire-work, in the form of an umbrella, placed under the head of a tree intended to be trained as a Weeper. The shoots are drawn through this and tied down, and thus a

No. 18.

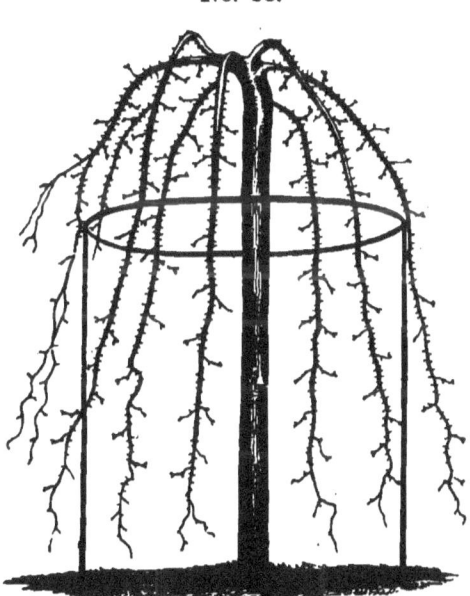

Weeping Rose complete.

drooping form is given to the tree. Sometimes, also, the shoots are tied into the stem with bast or tar-twine, or fastened down to pegs driven into the ground.

No. 18 shews a Weeping Rose of full size, pruned and trained.

After a Rose tree, of whatever form or kind, is put into the desired shape, supposing it to be healthy and vigorous, we prune so as to increase its size every successive year. This *must be done* with the vigorous growing kinds, or they are over-pruned. It should be done with the moderate growers ; for as the roots extend their growth, and the stem increases in size, the plant is capable of supporting a larger head, and perfecting a greater quantity of flowers. This increase of size must be accomplished by thinning. Thin out well then ; *leaving shoots at the farthest limit of the plant that you can, to allow of its being well furnished from base to summit.*

In pruning Roses that have attained to some age, it may be necessary to remove an old branch or two occasionally, to keep the head from becoming straggling or ill-shapen. As soon as any branch shews symptoms of decline, it should also be cut out. The saw will be found useful here, as well as in removing small shoots, which, from their position, it may be difficult to reach with the pruning-knife; also for cutting away dead branches, which should never be done with the knife, because it takes away the edge. In all cases where the saw is used, the cut should be made nearly close, and afterward pared down with the pruning-knife.

A few remarks on old plants which have been neglected in the early stages of growth may not be misplaced here. Such are often met with. Usually the fault has been the fear of pruning too much : the branches have consequently become straggling, and the tree unsightly. To deal with these, the best plan is, to cut back some of the branches almost close to the base of the head, either main branches or yearling shoots, one here and there in different places. These will produce shoots near home, and, by pruning such close the following year, the head is brought into a more compact form.

We have here a plant (No. 19), the form of which, we think, none will be bold enough to advocate. The flowers are produced just at the top of the branches, and numerous naked, weak, unsightly branches appear near the base of the head. But, we must remodel this tree, and, in attempting this, we first cut the main branches off at *a a.* But, says the tyro, there are no buds left visible on the stumps. True; but the practised hand knows well that they exist there, although not visible. It is our business to develope them. If we shorten in the surrounding branches tolerably close, leaving only that part of the tree which is shown by the dark shading, we shall succeed in doing this: the eyes, too, will most likely shoot forth with uncommon vigour. We view this as we should a young tree : our first aim is to form it aright. This we may often do in one year, by the help of disbudding ; without it, two years will be required.

No. 19.

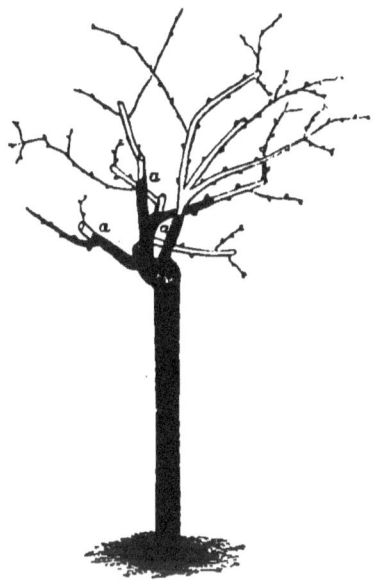

Attempt to recover an old plant that has suffered from neglect, or too little pruning.

Trees that have become weakly are generally much improved by close pruning; so are those small growing kinds which flower so constantly that it is rare to see a shoot not terminated with flowers, at whatever season it may be developed. Of these, we may give Comte d'Eu and Madame Angelina (Bourbons), as examples; and be it remarked that a rich soil is found as indispensable a condition for their well-doing as close pruning.

Close pruning, when applied to trees in a weakly condition, has great renovating power. I recollect well, when pruning some Roses in pots, noticing a plant of Archduke Charles (Chinese) in a very bad state. It had produced such puny flowers, that, during the flowering season, I more than once doubted whether the variety was Archduke Charles. The stock was hide-bound—*i.e.* had ceased to swell—and the shoots were stunted and scrubby. The latter were all thinned out but three, two of which were shortened in to three eyes. The remaining one, which was the strongest, was shortened in to one eye. The plant was afterwards treated as the others. The single eye on the strong shoot was developed with

G 2

surprising vigour, and in the ensuing autumn I found the hide-bound bark was burst asunder by the swelling of the stock, and beneath a new bark was forming. The plant gradually improved, and became as healthy as any in the collection.

To do justice to the Autumnal Roses, they should be pruned a second time in summer, just after flowering, removing as few leaves as possible in the operation; or, if the summer flowers are not much regarded, prune just before flowering, by which the vigour and beauty of the later flowers will be increased.

The tender kinds, such as the Chinese and Tea-scented, are not unfrequently severely injured by frost. When this is the case, all the dead wood must be cut away : I have, under such circumstances, pruned level with the ground, and obtained an abundant flowering. Necessity, however, urged this, rather than prudence. A too vigo-rous growth not unfrequently arises from it, followed by its evil consequences, of late flowering only, unripened wood, and great susceptibility of frost.

There are some Roses which, although at times very beautiful, do not in general expand their flowers. From some cause, which has been said to be too great a degree of fulness, the buds remain sealed at the top till they drop from decay. Examples of such are Melanie Cornu, (Hybrid Perpetual), and Reine des Belges and Princesse Hélène du Luxembourg, (Tea-scented). In France many of this nature take rank among the finest of Roses : they are also excellent with us when grown in the forcing-house. Too much moisture, combined with great heat or cold, favours this tendency, and thus the seasons have a great influence over these kinds. But another favouring circumstance is, too great a degree of vigour in the plant. The first cause is evident. Let us illustrate the second. In the spring of 1844 a few plants of the Duchesse de Nemours (Hybrid Perpetual) were neglected : the soil in which they grew was neither manured nor forked; the plants were not pruned, the variety being counted worthless. They grew, but their vigour was greatly diminished; and what were the consequences? The flowers were produced in surprising beauty, the novelty and richness of the colour attracting every one's attention, and all who beheld admired them. But, mark! a plant that had been treated well, in common with other Roses, dropped every bud before expanding.

Pruning, in the light in which we have hitherto considered it, may be said to consist of thinning and shortening; but it has long appeared to me that thinning might be in part done away with, by practising disbudding; i. e. rubbing or cutting out some of the buds when swelling in spring. The Rose, when in robust health, throws forth a great number of shoots during the season of growth, and the merciless havoc, that is made with them in the pruning season must, by the waste it creates, and by the wounding of the plant, prove highly injurious. True; it is necessary some should be removed when such numbers are present; but why are more than will be required suffered to grow? It is questionable whether the theory of branches and leaves elaborating the crude sap, and thereby fitting for assimilation a greater quantity of food, is in favour of their development. A few vigorous branches, with healthy well developed leaves must, I think, better accomplish this end, than a great number crowded together, the leaves becoming puny and sickly through the exclusion of air and light. Now, by rubbing out a portion of the buds when swelling, and others at any season when they may sprout forth in a position where shoots are not wanted, the remaining buds form stronger shoots; and thus, perhaps, a larger—certainly, a healthier—surface of foliage is the result. It is bad practice, then, to suffer more buds to be developed as shoots than are required for forming the tree, or for flowering; for by cutting away these when pruning, there must be a waste of the elaborated juices of the tree. But this is not the only evil : beyond this, the tree is sorely maimed in the operation. Now, if the nutritive matter, which has been supplied in the development and sustenance of numerous branches, was confined to a lesser number, they would have been more powerfully developed, and the loss by removal, and the injury the tree suffers by thinning, would have been avoided. *I believe disbudding to be the system best calculated to produce flowers in the finest possible condition, to keep a plant in full health and vigour, and to bring it to the highest pitch of beauty.* It has been successfully applied in the cultivation of other trees, and why should it not answer when applied to Roses? But it does answer, and, as one fact is said to be of more weight than a load of argument, I will relate an experiment commenced in the spring of 1844. I marked, at that season, from 50 to 100 Dwarf plants, which were budded in the previous summer; consequently, they were what is termed in bud. My object was, to test the efficiency of disbudding. They were intended to be grown in pots for exhibition, and each plant possessed two sound healthy buds, formed closely together. Two buds were, in this instance, preferred, because the aim was to get large plants in a little space of time. So soon as these buds had shot forth about six inches, they were stopped, and, in due course of time, two, three, or four laterals were produced from each. These were drawn out to sticks stuck in the ground a good distance apart, that the shoots might receive the full advantage of the sun and air. The surface of the soil was once or twice loosened with a Vernon hoe. The Summer

No. 21.

Disbudding. Persian Yellow.

sometimes three buds together, as shewn by the open buds in
No. 21, and leave one, as shewn by the shaded buds. On the
Coupe d'Hébé (No. 20) every other bud is removed. By the
accompanying illustrations it will be seen that we remove seven
or eight buds from a branch of the Persian Yellow, of equal length
with one of the Coupe d'Hébé, from which we remove two or three
buds only. But disbudding is not the work of spring alone ; it
must be attended to all through the growing season. The plants
should be looked through at least twice before the time of flowering,
and again soon after the flowering is over. The remains of the
flowers should be cut off, unless seed is sought, and only so many
eyes be allowed to develope themselves in the second or summer's
growth as the state of the tree and the considerations before
mentioned may render advisable.

In rubbing out the buds, it is sometimes difficult to decide which
to remove. The tendency of a bud should be almost invariably
outwards ; and in buds, as in shoots, the greater distance, in
moderation, they are from each other the better. Should two buds

threaten, when developed, to cross or crowd each other, the one taking the least favourable course of growth should be removed.

I have often heard amateurs, when admiring some of the large specimens in the Nurseries here, express astonishment at their prodigious size, which they attribute to great age and good soil. But it must be told, that the system of pruning has as much to do in this matter as the age of the trees, or the soil in which they grow. The oldest *of the large trees* here cannot number more than twelve years, though there are others much older not half the size. Often have I seen Rose trees full of shoots, nearly all proceeding from the base of the head, owing principally to injudicious pruning. When the knife is applied, whether in autumn or in spring, the greater part must be removed, for there is not room enough for the whole to be developed. There are, perhaps, not more branches than the tree can advantageously carry, but they are badly placed. Why should they not be obtained in such positions that they may be of permanent benefit to the plant—be made to extend its size, and render less thinning necessary? This may be done.

A few years ago, after having pruned a number *of large specimens*, in which I had observed this error, I watched for the bursting of the buds, with the view of practising disbudding. When they had shot forth about half an inch, I took a knife, with a sharp point, and commenced my search at the heart of the tree. From here I rubbed off, close to the bark, a great number of buds, leaving only such as, from their position, promised to increase the size or im- prove the *contour* of the head. If a bud was pushing where there was a gap, such was left ; the others were thinned, leaving those which took a lateral and outward course of growth. Proceeding upwards, I cleared the centre of the tree pretty freely, leaving only just so many buds as seemed necessary to preserve it from becoming straggling. Towards the top and circumference, also, the buds, where crowded, or likely to cross each other, were re- moved. A month after the first looking over, fresh buds had broken, and thus was opened a prospect of more gaps being filled, the outlines of the heads being still improved, and their size extended. They were looked over again and again, and the same plan followed out. The growth was, in consequence, more vigorous than that of the previous year, and the flowers fine. On the fall of the leaf in autumn the succeeding course of action was apparent. The trees were pruned as usual, and there was little mind exercised in the operation—little thinning required—no necessity to look at the tree for some minutes before one could determine where to begin, which, in my early attempts, I must confess I have often done, owing to the interminable interlacings of the shoots. The

second and third year the same plan was followed, and the trees
are now of handsome form, large and healthy, producing an abundance of good flowers. It should be stated that the first year
they were taken in hand they were watered once a-week for two
months with liquid manure. The sole reason for this was that the
soil in which they grew had become impoverished.

We apply the plan of disbudding to Pillar and Weeping Roses
as to others, by rubbing out any buds that may appear disadvantageously situated. In the youngest stage of the tree, the buds left
to produce flowers and flowering shoots for the subsequent year
should stand about six inches apart on the main branches: intermediate buds should be rubbed out. The laterals produced in
after stages may also be disbudded; but, masses of flower being
the object sought here, the practice should not be too freely resorted to.

A few words on Summer Pruning, or Thinning, seem called for
before closing this chapter. If disbudding can be carried out,
there is no need of summer thinning; but if it cannot, then the
latter practice may be followed to advantage. So soon as the plants
have done flowering, look them carefully over, thinning out the
weak, unhealthy shoots, and even some of the stout and healthy
ones, where they approach each other too nearly: each shoot left
should stand free and exposed on every side. It is surprising to
see how stout and firm the shoots become, and how the leaves increase in size after summer thinning.

The Summer kinds submitted to this treatment *usually* continue their growth by the elongation of the main shoots, the buds
in the axils of the leaves remaining dormant; but with the
Autumnals, the buds push forth the entire length of the shoots,
and the second flowering is complete. The trees are improved in
both cases, for the shoots of Autumnals grown at this period of the
year will produce the most perfect flowers in the subsequent
season.

CHAPTER VI.

ON HYBRIDIZING.

GARDENING, especially that branch of it termed Floriculture, is acknowledged to be replete with interesting detail; and if one department is more fascinating than another, it is perhaps that of Hybridizing and Cross-breeding, with the view of raising Seedlings. By Hybridizing is understood the bringing together of individuals of different species; by Cross-breeding, individuals of the same species; with the view of raising up new beings, differing from, and superior to, those already existing.

How different, how far less interesting to us, would be the forms which compose the Vegetable Kingdom, had the Creator made them incapable of variation ! Not that we despise the wild flowers scattered over the earth's surface, decking mountain and meadow, met with in every hedge-row and valley wild : their beauty is cheerfully acknowledged. But Nature's plants are prone to improvement : by cultivation they increase in size ; the flowers assume new forms, new tints ; the fruits new flavours.

> " The earth was made so various, that the mind
> Of desultory man, studious of change,
> And pleased with novelty, might be indulged."

And what a kind dispensation of Providence is this ! how it strengthens the inducements to labour ! What a charm it throws around the toilsome duties of a rural life, cheering on the labourer with higher prospects than those of mere pecuniary reward ! Compare the present breeds of corn with the wild forms of the cereal plants from which they are descended; or the Pinks, Pansies, Dahlias, and Roses of our gardens, with their types growing naturally in various countries ; and, while struck with the contrast, we wonder at the inexhaustible treasures of Nature, and admire the improved races, we need not withhold from man his humble due, remembering that these alterations are not the work of Nature unaided and alone, but are in greater part owing to the untiring perseverance and assiduous care of the plant-cultivator.

The raising of seedling plants is indeed a delightful occupation. The work is varied ; there is such a wide field for speculation and experiment; and the pleasing state of expectancy in which the operator is kept as to the results of the turn he gives to the workings of Nature surrounds it with more than ordinary interest.

The improver of plants is, so to speak, moving continually amid ideal scenes ; he works in an enchanted sphere ; he is striving to raise up new forms, knowing what he wishes, what he works for, but not what he will obtain. The seeds ripen beneath his care, and he sows them ; but as to the issue of events, he remains in ignorance profound, until, by the flowering of his pets, the magic wand of Nature dissolves the spell, and realizes or dissipates his hopes. And, may we be permitted to ask, is it unworthy of the chief actor in these terrestrial scenes to employ his hours of relaxation in striving to diversify and increase the beauty of the natural objects scattered around him, thereby holding up to view the wonders of the Infinite, and administering to the necessities and enjoyments of his fellow-man ? As a recreation, who can object to it ? Its tendency is useful. It is harmless, healthful, and exhilarating, and calculated to soften down the asperities and ills of life. There is philosophy in striving to improve the simple Pansy, counted as a weed in our corn-fields, as well as in turning the attention towards the amelioration of those more valuable plants which constitute the food and raiment of man.

But it is with the Rose we have to deal at present, and let us turn immediately to the subject.

The improvement of this flower by cultivation has been wrought out chiefly by foreign cultivators. But why seedling Roses should not be raised in England, is a question I could never yet determine. I know it has been said by some, "We do not understand the business;" by others, "Our soil is not suitable;" and, again, "The climate of England will not admit of the seed ripening perfectly." But these are seeming objections—mere obstacles of the imagination, the semblance of which is greater than the reality. For, if our soil is not naturally suitable, we can render it artificially so : if we do not understand the business, surely we can learn. We are not isolated from our fellow-labourers; we cannot be so satisfied with our own doings as to refuse to learn a lesson from them : or, even were it so, the great book of Nature is open to us all, in which "we may read, and read,

> " And read again, and still find something new :
> Something to please, and something to instruct."

To me the difference between the climates of England and France seems the only point worthy of consideration ; and that difference, although great, is not of such magnitude as to raise an insuperable barrier against the successful prosecution of the art. If we compare the climate of London with that of Paris, where the greater part of our modern Roses have been originated, it will be found that rain is less frequent in Paris during Summer and Autumn; there is also a greater intensity and duration of sunlight there, which increases the temperature of the atmosphere and soil, and thus accelerates the period of maturity.

The above is also true as regards the climate of Angers and the south of France, only in a still greater degree ; and who would doubt those districts being eminently more favourable than Paris for the pursuit ? No one. But suppose the Parisian growers had rested contented with these reflections, what position would the Rose now hold in the floral world ? And if English cultivators had joined ardently in the pursuit, who can say to what pitch of beauty the Queen of Flowers might have attained ?

What country ranks equal with England in the art of Gardening ? yet how many are there more favourably circumstanced. This, it may be said, is partly due to the great liberality of its patrons, and to the admirable contrivance of its plant structures. But still the English cultivator has great disadvantages to contend with, especially in raising plants under glass. His skill and perseverance, however, overcomes them all, and obstacles surmounted encourage him to go on : he continues to battle with the elements, and his intellectual powers seem to brighten in the contest. He produces Grapes superior to those brought from the Land of the Vine, and Pine Apples infinitely so to those of West-Indian production. These are facts known to every one ; and will it yet be maintained that he cannot raise seedling Roses ?*

But, it may be said, Hybridizing and Cross-breeding are not the work of the gardener. It requires an uninterrupted course of study to enable any one to carry them out with success : and his multifarious duties render it next to impossible that he should pursue this. There is much truth in this assertion, and the nurseryman

* So was it said, not many years ago, that Standard Roses could not be grown in England—that the climate of France was essential for their development. Thus prejudice, for a time, triumphed over reason, and they were imported from that country for years. And the reason why so few seedling Roses have been originated in England is doubtless this—nurserymen have found sufficient occupation in multiplying the kinds put into their hands; amateurs in admiring and attending to the varied wants of their favourites.

may certainly put forward a similar plea. The weight of the burden, then, would seem to rest with the amateur. And it has always appeared to me that his is the proper sphere for the raising of seedlings, and that greater objects are accomplished in this line when pursued as a relaxation rather than as a profession. If the amateur has had less experience in gardening matters, this seems compensated for by a less divided attention and greater assiduity.

If the Tea-scented and Chinese be the kinds the operator prefers seeding from, it will be necessary to grow them under glass, as they are longer in bringing their seeds to maturity than most other kinds. The majority of seed-bearers, however, need no such protection: they thrive and complete their work perfectly out of doors.*

It is now many years since I first took up this branch of culture: I have reaped some reward, and am still sanguine of greater success. I started a tyro, with little knowledge in store, and had to pay for learning by the way. The first and second years of my practice I gathered the seeds promiscuously during winter, seizing every pod that appeared large and plump, whether ripe or green. The production of these sowings was a motley group; among them some good double Roses, and many very brilliant-coloured semi-double ones; but nothing worth bringing before the public— no star of the first magnitude.

The subsequent year I took one step farther, and kept the seeds of each group separate, to ascertain to what extent the offspring departed from the parent in external characters. This was done for two years, and enough of the plants raised from these flowered to afford a little insight into the probable results.

According to the statements of M. Boitard, there is scarcely any limit to the variation of Roses produced from seed. He affirms that M. Noisette, a French cultivator, has never sown seeds of the Chinese Roses (R. INDICA) without raising some Scotch Roses (R. SPINOSISSIMA) from them. He states, This fact is not supported by a solitary occurrence, but has been frequently observed by that cultivator, and is further attested by the evidence of M. Laffay, who has raised seedlings on an extensive scale, often as many as 200,000 in a single year.

It were easy to conceive a mistake occurring in the gathering,

---

* Since penning these remarks, I have raised from one sowing Moss Princess Alice, and Hybrid Bourbon Vivid, both superior varieties in their day. From a more recent sowing I have raised Beauty of Waltham, in every respect a first class Rose: Red Rover, Lord Clyde, and many other sorts useful for garden decoration.

storing, or sowing of the seeds; but when the facts have been noticed repeatedly, and by different individuals of known probity and great horticultural attainments, the evidence, we think, must be deemed conclusive.

Thousands of seedlings have been raised here, and I have been searching them through to see if any thing corroborative of the above statement can be brought forward; but I have met with no success. I find the variation of character greater than I had expected; and many of the seedling plants approach nearer to the wild forms than to those from which the seeds were gathered. The offspring of all kinds does not vary in the same degree. The plants raised from seeds of the Chinese are all Chinese or Tea-scented; those from the Bourbons seem Bourbons, Hybrid Bourbons, and Hybrid Chinese; and while the French Roses (R. GALLICA) appear true to their kind, the Perpetuals have given birth to Hybrid Chinese and Hybrids of other Summer Roses, very few having proved Autumnal bloomers.

Since observing and penning the above I have met with a remark of M. Desprez, the celebrated Rose amateur at Yebles, that he has sown thousands of seeds of Du Roi (Crimson Perpetual), and never obtained a Perpetual Rose. In all, the characters of Rosa Gallica were visible. But we must remember this variety partakes largely of the nature of the Gallica or French Rose.

In examining my seedlings I found a seed of the Moss du Luxembourg had produced a French Rose; a seed of William Jesse (Hybrid Perpetual), a blush Hybrid Chinese; a seed of Mrs. Bosanquet (Chinese), a pink Chinese, resembling its parent in every respect save colour; Chénédolé (Hybrid Chinese) had produced a brilliant-coloured Hybrid Perpetual, and a numerous progeny of Great Western retain exactly the foliage and habit of that variety. Tea Goubault crossed with Bourbon Souchet has produced two Summer Roses, the one having the characters of the Hybrid Chinese, the other those of the Hybrid Bourbon.

My friend M. Laffay once told me that he raised many of his splendid Hybrid Perpetual Roses from Athelin and Celine (Hybrid Bourbons), crossing them with the free-flowering varieties of Damask Perpetual and Bourbon. A few years since he took up a new idea—that of obtaining Hybrid Moss and Perpetual Moss Roses by crossing the Moss with the Hybrid Bourbon and Damask Perpetual. He has since raised several seedlings, some Perpetual Moss and some Hybrid Moss, the latter possessing the foliage and vigour of the Hybrid Bourbon Roses. The Princess Adelaide (Moss) was obtained in this manner. On the success of these and the like unions some of the French raisers are very sanguine, and say, much as they have done with Roses, they anticipate doing far more, and raising up such hybridizations and novelties as shall astonish the floral world. As they have already done so much, their intentions and prophecies deserve our respect. But why should France labour alone in this field? why should she have all the fame, reap all the profit? Cannot we assist her! Time is short. Some of the French growers are already past the meridian of life, and the raising of seedling Roses is a tedious operation.

If the Hybrid Bourbon crossed with the Moss produce perfect seeds, we may presume that the intermixing of the pollen grains of other species will be productive of like results. This, it will be seen, demolishes the idea of the necessity of restricting ourselves to the crossing of individuals of the same group. Not only may we choose the parents from different groups, but from different species. Where, indeed, is the line of demarcation? There appears no limit to the field of labour. We have to prove by actual experiment what can and what cannot be done.

It should be known, in choosing varieties for this purpose, that the least double kinds do not always perfect their seeds best. Such, upon less mature consideration, might appear to be the case, and has been asserted to be so, which error must have arisen from the want of close observation. It does not depend so much on the degree of fulness in a Rose, as upon some other cause to me altogether inexplicable, and not to be interpreted even by the acknowledged laws of the effects of hybridization; for some Hybrids seed freely, whereas others are sterile, although of the same origin and apparently similarly constituted. That the power of producing perfect seeds does not depend on the degree of fulness, may be established by the fact, that Pourpre fafait, a mongrel-bred Bourbon Rose, and others, too full to open their flowers at all times, ripen their seeds, although very many semi-double varieties rarely form a seed-pod. That it does not depend on their being Hybrids, may be inferred from the fact, that many of the Hybrid Chinese Roses, which are decided Hybrids, seed freely.

I have, by the aid of the microscope, examined numerous flowers, with the view of solving this difficulty. I have arrived at conclusions which may be considered sufficient for practical purposes; or what will prove still better, may induce others interested in the matter to push on the inquiry.

The flowers were divided into three classes. The first class examined was that which shewed no disposition to seed, where the seed-vessels did not increase in size after the falling of the petals. In this case I found the pistils huddled together, if I may so express myself, and apparently sterile; or, if not so, petals usurped the place of the pistils and stamens, extending into the ovaria or seed-vessels. It was evident, then, that such *could not* seed.

In examining the next class, where there was a disposition to seed, where the seed-vessels increased in size after the falling of the flowers, but withered before arriving at maturity, I found the pistils placed separately, and they appeared perfect and healthy ; but the stamens were either so few or so encased within the petals, that the pollen could not escape, and thus the flowers remained unfertilized. In some cases the flowers were pendant ; owing to which position, and the relative length of the pistils and stamens, the latter rising above the former, the pollen fell away from, rather than upon, the pistils. In other cases, where the flowers stood erect, the pistils often rose above the stamens, when the same consequences were likely to ensue. Flowers of this kind will occasionally produce a pod of perfect seeds, which may be attributed to accidental fertilization, the conveying of the pollen by the insect tribe, or other causes.

The next class taken in hand was that which ripened its seeds freely.

The flowers here were found to have both stamens and pistils perfectly developed, the former abounding in pollen, which, in a more advanced stage of the flower, was seen plentifully scattered over the stigmas, whose cup-shaped summits were distinctly visible.

From these facts I draw the following conclusions :—1st, That certain varieties are sterile ; incapable of forming perfect seeds under any circumstances. Of these I find such kinds predominate as roll the petals inward, the centre of the flower being quartered in the manner of a crown. In others the pistils are weak or imperfect.

2dly, That many kinds, where the pistils are perfect, which in their natural state form seed-pods that wither before arriving at maturity, may be induced to perfect their seeds by artificial impregnation. This class of Roses is the best for him who intends raising seedlings to choose his female parents from, because there is little here to interfere with, mar, or counteract his plans. Be it remarked, however, that there are certain kinds which must not be confounded with the above—kinds which, owing to the length of time the seed-vessels are in arriving at maturity, never perfect their seeds in this country.

3dly, That those kinds which we find seeding abundantly in their natural state are self-fertilized, and that their abundant production of seeds is due to this point mainly, the more perfect development of the sexual organs, especially the polleniferous parts of fructification.

Waiving for a moment the distinctions above shewn, I shall col-

H

lect here a list of a few kinds, which ripen their seeds perfectly
in this country in ordinary seasons :—Chénédolé, Général Allard
(*Hybrid Chinese*); Coupe d'Hébé Vivid, Charles Duval (*Hybrid
Bourbons*); Du Luxembourg, Celina (*Moss*); Madame Laffay,
William Jesse, General Jacqueminot, Géant des Batailles, Jules
Margottin (*Hybrid Perpetuals*); Harrisonii (*Austrian Brier*); Bou-
quet de Flore, Sir J. Paxton (*Bourbons*); Gloire de Rosomène (*Rose
de Rosomène*); Russelliana (*Multiflora*); Splendens (*Aryshire*).

These varieties are chosen because easy to deal with, and with
them, or any portion of them, the operator may commence. He
will see quickly the effects of his labour: there will be no disappointment, and he is thus encouraged to go on. He may then add
the less certain and more desirable seed-bearers at subsequent
periods, when he has acquired, by practice, more knowledge of the art.

Having chosen the varieties, they should be planted in the
sunniest spot in the garden, in a soil not too rich; for however
favourable this condition may be to the production of fine flowers,
it promotes a too vigorous vegetation for the perfect development
of seeds. In pruning, the branches should not be shortened in very
closely. Long pruning is most suitable here.

But the planting season has passed away, and a glance at our
seed-bearers satisfies us they will soon be in flower. It will be but
fair to suppose that they have had more, rather than less attention
paid to them than plants in common, for they are more than
usually interesting. The soil ought to have been hoed occasionally
during spring, and watered during dry weather. The caterpillar
should have been closely sought for by hand, and the aphis got rid
of by syringing repeatedly with soot-water or tobacco-water.

It is seldom that all the flower-buds can be developed to advantage, and as they increase in size it will be seen which had
better be removed. Secure a good portion of the earliest and
boldest buds, but not all of such: leave some in different stages
of forwardness, that the work may be spread over a greater
extent of time. Wherever buds are seen forming imperfectly, or
in an unfavourable position—where they do not obtain the full
sun—remove them at once.

Before we commence hybridizing, it is necessary that we should
have fixed ideas of what we are going to do: we should have certain objects distinctly before us, and for the realization of those
objects we must work. Without this, we cannot expect to obtain
a full measure of success.

As a first step towards the attainment of these ends, let us consider what constitutes a good Rose, and fix the results of this
inquiry firmly on the memory.

Those properties of the Rose to which we attach the greatest importance are — 1. Habit and constitution; 2. Form of the flowers; 3. Colour; 4. Scent; 5. Freedom, constancy, and duration of flowering.

1. Habit, &c.—The growth of a tree should be free, not dwindling or delicate. It may be considered immaterial whether it be pendulous, branching, or erect, as each growth is desirable for certain purposes. Handsome foliage is important, and should be kept in view under this head. The offspring of the tender Roses may also be rendered less susceptible of frost by intermixing the latter with the hardiest varieties of the same or kindred groups.

2. Form.—A Rose may be good, whether globular, cupped, compact, or expanded. But of whichever form it may be, the petals should be thick and smooth, and the outline circular.

Annexed are representations of four Roses which may be considered models of their respective forms, which are explained in Division II. Nearly all Roses may be brought under one or other of these forms : there are some few whose petals reflex in the full-blown and decaying stage of the flower, but we think the reflexed form untenable for a young bloom.

3. Colour.—This, of whatever shade or tint should be clear and full. The thick-petalled Roses usually present us with the richest tints, owing, I presume, to the greater body of colour : such are, therefore, desirable for this reason, as well as on account of holding

No. 22.

Globular. Général Allard.

No. 23.

Cupped.   Comtesse Duchâtel.

No. 24.

Compact.

No. 25.

Expanded.

their flowers perfect a longer time than others. Need we add the
desirableness of varying the colours of the groups ?

4. Scent.—All Roses should be sweet. We cannot dissociate
fragrance and the Rose.

> " The Rose of brilliant hue, and perfumed breath,
> Buds, blossoms, dies, and still is sweet in death."

There are, indeed, few kinds altogether scentless, although the
degree of fragrance varies remarkably.

5. Freedom, constancy, and duration of flowering.—Some Roses
are most profuse bloomers, presenting a splendid effect on the tree,
but when viewed separately they are poor and flimsy. Others
produce a less quantity of flowers at one time, but a regular succession, from which a good Rose may be gathered at almost any time
in the season of flowering. Then the flowers of some are very transient, lasting but a day, although others will retain their form and
colour for a week. These properties are inherent, for all kinds are
not influenced alike by the state of the weather. We should seek
to combine those kinds which possess the above-named properties
in the most eminent degree.

The above, then, are a few broad principles, which, duly considered and acted upon, seem likely to lead to the further improvement of our flower.

The question next arising is, Do certain properties proceed more from the one parent than from the other? and, if so, which and what are they? If we could ascertain this, we might then work by rule. It is the opinion of some Vegetable Physiologists that the offspring assumes the foliage and habit of the male, while the flowers are influenced more by the female parent. These may be the rules, but there are exceptions to them; and it would appear that there is nothing yet made known that can be taken as a correct guide in the matter. But if, in hybridizing, the operator follow the dictates of his own reason, and closely watch the results of his labour, he will, in all probability, not absolutely fail, and be at length enabled to build up a theory of his own. Until he has done this, he must be content to work by the light of others, or grope his way in darkness.

That certain cultivators have acquired by practice sufficient knowledge to enable them to attain *almost* to a given object, is my firm belief; and this is founded on the frequent appearance of the kind of plant, or an approach to it, that has been pronounced a *desideratum*. A case occurs to me which will serve to illustrate this remark. Within my memory we had no dark or very light Bourbon Roses; nearly all were of a rose or lilac hue; but there was a cry raised for dark ones. Proserpine first arose, and by her beauty captivated every beholder. Next came Paul Joseph, darker still, and still more beautiful. Then it was reported, and proved true, that one raiser was in possession of several very dark varieties, and some pale-coloured ones also appeared about the same time. Now what inference can we draw from these facts, when we consider that similar varieties proceeded from different quarters, unless it be that the skill of the cultivator was directed, and that successfully, towards originating them.

The dark Bourbon Roses, of which we have just spoken, are those introduced to England in 1843, under the names of Souchet, Charles Souchet, Dumont du Courset, Gloire de Paris, Princesse Clémentine, Souvenir du Dumont d'Urville, and Comte de Rambuteau. These were all raised from seed by one individual. I remember visiting the establishment of M. Souchet at Paris, where, alone, these Roses were to be seen, in the summer of 1842; and although a violent thunderstorm had just passed over the city, producing the usual consequences to the denizens of the garden, I could see from the wreck they were a splendid lot of Roses. There were at that time twelve varieties, the one a light-coloured one (Madame Souchet), but nine only were introduced to England. What became of the other three I could never learn. Probably they proved of little merit, and were therefore not offered to the public.

Now, with such an example as this before us, need we sigh over the improbabilities of improving or extending the range of colour in any other class of Roses? Surely not. Will not the same skill which produced dark and light Bourbon Roses prove adequate to any future reasonable demand?

But the plants are in flower, and there is no further time for talking : we are now called upon to act. Keeping in mind the points recently advanced, let us next inquire, What is there desirable among Roses that we do not already possess? The answer to this question, will be the things we should endeavour to obtain. But shall we be satisfied with merely crossing the varieties, and gathering and sowing the seeds indiscriminately ; or do we wish to know the results of the turn we are seeking to give to the workings of nature? I think this knowledge is desirable, and it certainly heightens the interest of the work. To carry it out with little trouble, it is a good plan to obtain some thin sheet lead, and cut it into strips an inch long and a quarter of an inch wide. On these may be stamped figures, from 1 to an indefinite number, and, as each flower is crossed, one of these numbered leads is wound round the flower stalk. The number is then set down in a book, and the name o-each parent, with the object in view, are entered opposite the number.

Here is an extract from my note-book.

Number.	Female Parent or Seed-bearer	Male Parent, or Fertilizer.	Object in view.
17	Harrisonii. (Austrian.)	Copper Austrian.	A double Copper Austrian Rose.
21	Général Allard. (Hybrid Chinese.)	Madame Laffay. (Hybrid Perpetual.)	To invigorate the habit, and perfect the tendency of Général Allard to flower in the Autumn.
42	La Reine. (Hybrid Perpetual.)	Du Luxembourg. (Moss.)	To obtain a large and globular - shaped Moss Rose.

In No. 17 fulness and colour are the points to engage our attention. The colour of the Copper Austrian Rose is distinct and beautiful, but the flower is single. I want a double one. The Harrisonii is double, and nearly allied to the other. I choose it for the female parent, because it is the best seed-bearer. This seems to me the most reasonable means to pursue in order to accomplish this end.

In No. 21 the female parent, Général Allard, is a model in form. I am satisfied with the colour, but it is a delicate grower, except when young, and not a free autumnal bloomer. I am seeking to remedy these defects, and cross with Madame Laffay, which is nearly of the same tint, and has the desired properties, deficient in the other, abundantly developed.

The subject of No. 42, La Reine, is an extraordinary Rose. I hybridize it with Du Luxembourg, with the view of obtaining a large, red, globular-shaped Moss Rose. As one parent here is an autumnal bloomer, there is also a chance of some of the offspring becoming such.

But we may proceed from individuals to classes. Two very desirable classes of Roses in prospect are Hybrid Moss and Perpetual Moss; and I look more to the hybridizing of the species for future improvements of the Rose, than to mere cross-breeding. The latter has already been pushed so far that fresh sources must be opened before any thing great can be accomplished. Thus it is, that while we view as doubtful certain things talked of, we hail with delight the prototypes of the Hybrid Moss and Perpetual Moss, which already appear in the horizon. We have some ; and what appears the most reasonable means to pursue to increase their number ? The Hybrid Moss, it would seem, may be obtained by hybridizing the Hybrid Chinese and Hybrid Bourbon with the Moss kinds, or *vice versâ ;* the more double and mossy the parent Moss is the better, that the offspring may produce full flowers, and not lose the mossy characteristics.

The Perpetual Moss would appear easiest obtainable by hybridizing the Hybrid Perpetual with the varieties of Moss, or *vice vers â,* using the Perpetual Moss kinds already obtained, on either side, according to whether they produce seeds or pollen.

Of other Roses wanted may be instanced striped Hybrid Perpetuals, which may probably be obtained by bringing the most constant flowering varieties of that group in union with the Rosa Mundi, or any of the striped French Roses.* Then there

---

* Since the first edition of this work was published, we have obtained several striped " Hybrid Perpetual" Roses, and some valuable " Perpetual Moss." The greatest improvement, however, has taken place among the " Hybrid Perpetuals," although even here there are many wants still unsupplied which the lover of Roses may reasonably look for. Unless, however, new ground is broken, he must not expect, in the present state of the family, to meet with the broadly-marked improvements of former years, but rest satisfied with the more gradual development usual among plants which have been long cultivated.

are no striped Hybrid Chinese or Hybrid Bourbon Roses, which we should expect to obtain from the union of the striped French with the varieties of Bourbon or Chinese. There is no striped Moss Rose worthy of the name. Might not such be obtained by working various of the Moss kinds with the Rosa Mundi? There are few autumnals of growth sufficiently rapid to form high pillars. Here is a field for experiment! Is there not a fair chance of obtaining these from between the most vigorous growers of summer and autumn Roses? We hear talked of Yellow Moss and Yellow Bourbon. As an *attempt* to obtain the former, cross the palest Moss Roses with Emerance (Provence); for the latter unite the yellowest tints of the Tea-scented with the Buff and most colourless Bourbons. But we have not space to pursue these remarks further. We need not confine ourselves to the instances above quoted: they are merely given as examples. The work may be varied *ad infinitum :* any thing that reason may suggest the head and hands may work for.

It is desirable, before crossing or hybridizing, to see if the flowers about to be crossed have any stamens. If so, they should be cut away with a pair of round-pointed scissors, just as the flowers expand. It is not known for certain whether superfœtation can occur in plants, but it is well to provide against it, especially where it can be done with little trouble. The plan I adopt when crossing is, to bring a flower of the male parent to the seed-bearing tree. If the weather be calm, I cut away the petals of the former, holding a finger over a flower of the latter, upon which I strike the flower deprived of its petals. The sudden shock drives the pollen into the other flower, and the work is done. But if the wind be high, this plan will not do. It is better then to collect the pollen on the end of a camel-hair pencil, and convey it thus to the styles of the other flower.

When the flowers have passed away we shall soon have the satisfaction of seeing the seed-pods swell ; and as they ripen it will be well to devise some means to protect them from birds. I have no direct proof to adduce that birds eat the seed-pods of cultivated roses ; but I have often seen the greenfinch feasting on the Sweet-Brier hips, and should these, by any chance, become scarce, or fail, he probably might not object to this slight change of diet. It is important to leave the seed-vessels on the trees as long as possible, and they never should be gathered until quite ripe. It is not enough that they are red : they should, if possible, hang till they grow black. So soon as gathered, let them be sown : they will then break through the ground in the following March, and probably some of the Autumnals will flower the first year.

CHAPTER VII.

ON CLEANING AND SOWING THE SEED, AND THE SUB-SEQUENT TREATMENT OF THE SEEDLINGS.

In the last Chapter we left the seeds sown prior to winter, that drear season at which the Flower Garden presents but few attractions. Its denizens, stripped of their gay attire, are sunk in repose; often bound fast in icy chains; all vegetation sharing in one general imprisonment, waiting for the balmy breath of spring to release them from their slumbers, to burst forth endued with fresh life and vigour. Let us momentarily retrace our steps to speak of the cleaning and sowing of the seed.

When removing the seed-pods from the plants on which they have grown, the seeds should be rubbed out between the hands previous to sowing. Some pods that are hard, or were not fully ripened when gathered, will require stronger measures to separate them. These may be rubbed through a coarse wire sieve, the hard coating of the seeds protecting them from injury in the process; and if any are found proof against this, they may be crushed beneath a rolling-pin, or slight taps of the hammer.

So soon as the seeds are broken up they should be laid out in the sun and air to dry; and when sufficiently dried it is easy to rid them of their pulp and external covering by sifting and winnowing in pans. The seeds then are sufficiently clean for sowing; and in what manner shall this be performed?

The French growers sow principally in the open ground, either in beds or in drills by the sides of walks; but M. Hardy, late of the Jardin du Luxembourg, preferred frames. I remember seeing there, some years since, a vast number growing in a wooden frame, the most of them apparently varieties of ROSA INDICA, and their healthful appearance and vigorous growth sufficiently attested the aptitude of the treatment.

If a frame cannot be spared for the purpose, *the tender kinds, at least*, should be sown in pans, thoroughly drained, and filled with equal parts of leaf mould and loam well mixed together. After the seeds are sown they may be watered, and covered over with about half an inch of the same soil, sifted, and mixed with a little sand. The pans must now be set in the best spot we can find for them ; in a cold frame or green-house, if accessible, where they should be kept in a state of equable moisture. Here they will vegetate as out of doors, and in autumn or spring may be transplanted as the others.

If it be the intention to sow in the open borders, a sunny but sheltered situation should be chosen : the aspect should be east, that the young plants may not be fatigued with the afternoon's sun. When preparing the ground for sowing, the soil should be well loosened with a fork or spade to the depth of eighteen inches or two feet, and made light and rich, the top being broken up fine, and laid level with a rake. If drills are preferred, draw them about six inches apart : if broadcast sowing, the ground is already prepared.

It is advisable to sow rather thick, for, in general, not one-fourth of Rose-seeds vegetate, and of these only a portion the first year. After the seed is sown, the earth should be trodden down or beaten with a spade, and watered, if dry, and covered afterwards with from half an inch to an inch of light free soil. Care must be taken to keep the earth moderately moist. About March some of the seeds will germinate, and others will continue to do so throughout the summer and autumn. So soon as they are seen rising through the soil means must be taken to protect them from slugs, birds, and worms.

Slugs have a great liking for seedling Roses, and will, unless prevented, eat them off close to the ground when rising, which usually involves their destruction. To guard against these pests, scatter soot or lime over the bed, which acts as a safeguard, and at the same time promotes the growth of the plants. Birds will occasionally pull them up when just sprouting forth ; and whether this is done to satisfy the palate, or merely from the love of mischief, I cannot determine ; but however it may be, we are equally the sufferers. The best scare-crow I can find is glass. Let a stick be stuck in the ground in a bending position, from the end of which two pieces of glass should be suspended with bast or twine, so that they dangle in the air : striking together with every breeze, they keep up a musical chaunt around the seedlings which the feathered plunderers seem unable to account for, and the most daring depredators are content to sit and chirrup at a distance.

Worms are often a great nuisance among seedlings, throwing up heaps of soil, which smother the young plants ; and sometimes they drag them into the earth, which destroys them. The best remedy here is lime-water, applied two or three evenings consecutively in dry weather. If the seeds vegetate very early, the young plants must be protected from the spring frosts ; and hooping the beds over with osiers and covering with a mat offers perhaps the simplest and most efficient means of doing this.

So soon as the seeds vegetate, the young plants require constant attention as to shading, watering, and weeding, as well as protection from their enemies. This will be cheerfully given, when the cultivator reflects that, by this care, many of the autumnals will be induced to flower the first year. This, however, holds good only with the autumnals, for the summer kinds will not flower for two, three, or even four years. Seedling Roses should be watered only when the soil is *really* dry, and then always in the evening, before sun-set. The same frame-work used to protect the plants from frost in spring will answer for summer shading; but shade only when the sun is powerful, and then only for a few hours in the middle of the day ; for shading as well as watering may be carried too far, and if so, favours the development of mildew. Watch your seedlings closely, to see what amount of sun they will bear without injury, and determine your movements accordingly.

At the time of weeding it is well to have a sharp-pointed stick in the hand, with which to stir the soil round the seedlings. This must be done with great care, or the plants just protruding will be injured; indeed, if they are germinating thickly, it is a dangerous operation, and perhaps better left alone.

So soon as the seedlings have formed their second leaves, if they should have sprung up so thick as to impede each other's growth, a part may be safely drawn out after a good shower of rain (raising the soil in the first instance with a hand-fork), and transplanted to a shady border in the evening of the day, watering and covering with a hand-glass until they take hold of the soil. Let it be understood, however, that transplanting at this season is not recommended : it is here chosen because less injurious than suffering the plants to remain crowded together. It may not involve any positive loss, but it ordinarily retards the period of flowering.

When the plants have formed a few leaves the pleasure attendant on the raising of seedlings increases ten-fold. In looking over the bed, how anxious are we to discover to what groups certain curious-looking individuals belong. We look, and look again, and often depart without coming to any satisfactory conclusion. The plants, however, increase in size, the scrutiny goes on, fresh features are noticed at each new gaze, until at length we have something tangible to work on. We pronounce this to be a Provence, and that a Bourbon : here is evidently a Hybrid, and there a Chinese or Tea-scented. Or if we feel inclined for a closer analysis by descending from groups to individuals, we may in some instances trace the seedling from a particular variety. Here is one evidently born of General Jacqueminot, there another from Gloire de Rosomène. Thus far we may amuse ourselves, and settle the matter in our own minds, although the flowering of these individuals may not always substantiate our pre-conceived notions.

I have seen seedlings of the Bourbon and Chinese Roses flower when little more than a month old. This, however, should be prevented rather than encouraged. It weakens the plants, and does not impart any real knowledge to their proprietor. The flowers may be white, they may be red, and this is the absolute amount of knowledge to be gleaned from them. As to size, form, fulness, and the other valued properties of Roses, no true idea can be formed. It is well, then, to pinch off the flower-buds immediately that they are seen, whereby the plants gain strength and produce better flowers later in the season : but it is advisable not to destroy any of the seedlings the first year. Let the whole remain till late in October, then take them up, pruning both roots and tops, and replant them in a soil moderately rich. It is of importance that they be transplanted from the seed-bed in autumn ; for if the operation be deferred beyond winter, there is danger of destroying the seeds which have hitherto lain dormant, and which often vegetate very early in the second spring.

When transplanting, sort out the strongest plants, and place them about a foot apart : the weaker ones may then be set together at less distances. After planting, it will be well to water and shade for a few days, should there be much sun, and even to cover against frost, if such occur before the plants are firmly settled in the ground. This may be done by sticking single boughs, or fern branches, among them ; or, better still, by the use of mats.

In the following summer and autumn the flowers of many will appear. All that are single, or not clear in colour, may be destroyed ; also any where the outline is irregular. But if the outline be good, the colour clear, and the flower possessed only of an ordinary degree of fulness, it should be preserved, even though apparently inferior to varieties already known ; for the seedling has not yet passed through the high routine of culture the named varieties have, and its properties are not fully developed. It is often capable of great improvement.

As the seedlings blow, whenever one strikes the fancy it should be tied up to a stick, a number attached to it, and its properties entered against the number in a note-book ; then watch for the

buds being in a good state, and bud one or two stocks to prove
the variety. As it would occupy much time to bud all the seedlings, the seedling plant of any that is of doubtful merit may be
grown for two or three years, when its real worth will become
apparent. But it should be told, that budding on the Dog-rose, or
any free stock, enables us to form a correct opinion of a variety
a year or two sooner than we can do by trusting to the seedling
plant. Therefore, if stocks are not scarce, and the cultivator has
leisure, it may be interesting to bud a plant or two of any variety,
the flowers or foliage of which may appear to him likely to make
it interesting.

Mildew is the most discouraging visitant among seedling Roses.
It is bad enough anywhere, but it seems to attack them here with
redoubled virulence, and it is astonishing how suddenly it appears,
spreading death and desolation in its track. It must be watched for,
and, when first discovered, dust the plants with sulphur, on a calm
evening if possible, having first sprinkled or syringed them, that the
sulphur may stick on. This sometimes requires repeating at short
intervals, for it is not always a preventive, but a temporary cure.

As winter approaches, it is necessary to provide some protection
against frost. The plants of the tender kinds, being young, are
extremely delicate, and liable to suffer from frost. If such have
been sown in the borders, an advantageous point is gained by
sorting them out at the time of transplanting, and placing them in
a sheltered spot, where they may be shielded from the cutting
winds, and then hoop them over, covering, in severe weather, with
a mat, or some frost-excluding material. I have, in this edition of
the Rose Garden, advocated sowing in autumn, because calculated
to induce an earlier growth, whereby are obtained plants stronger
and better fitted to endure the cold of their first winter.

If autumn sowing be chosen, it will be necessary to guard the
seeds effectually against mice, as the length of time they lie in
the ground increases their chance of being eaten by these intruders.
It is a good plan to cover the bed with fine wire-work, or, if we
choose to act on the offensive rather than the defensive, the mice
may be trapped and destroyed. It will be well to have an eye to
this point, whether sowing in spring or autumn.

It is no uncommon occurrence, with seedlings growing out of
doors during winter, for the roots to be thrown to the surface,
the plants sometimes lying almost out of the ground. If left in
this condition, they wither and die. They should be replanted ;
and if the beds are hoed on a fine day in winter it will prove
advantageous, casting a little fine mould upon the surface in the
succeeding spring.

With regard to the pruning of seedlings, we have only one point to consider in the first instance—to obtain fine flowers. We sacrifice the shape of the tree to this point, if necessary, cutting back to any eyes that are plump and prominent, and situated on wood likely to produce fine flowers. We remove the gross shoots, if there be any, and thin out well, especially if the variety be an Autumnal, and, therefore, a certain bloomer.

CHAPTER VIII.

ON THE CULTIVATION OF ROSES IN POTS.

It is no longer said that the Rose is intractable as a Pot-plant; indeed, it is now sufficiently established that it is perfectly suited for such, and is consequently gaining a still wider circle of patrons and admirers. This furnishes no matter for wonderment, if we consider, that, in its present improved state, it possesses, in a greater or less degree, every quality that could be wished for in a plant designed for particular cultivation. The length of time the varieties continue in bloom; the delicious fragrance of the flowers; their richness and beauty; their elegant mode of growth and handsome foliage;—such a combination of desirable properties must necessarily secure for it a large share of favour.

The question has been, and still is occasionally, put to us, What advantage is gained by growing Roses in pots? The same question might be asked with equal propriety respecting any class of hardy or half-hardy plants. But we reply to it, by appealing to the unprejudiced judgment of horticulturists, by asking them whether the withdrawal of Pot-Roses from our green houses, parterres, forcing-houses, and horticultural fêtes, would not cause a very obvious blank. We think it would; and if so, it cannot be altogether folly to grow them in this manner. But there are more cogent reasons for the practice. Some of the delicate and more beautiful kinds have their flowers bruised and spoiled, even in summer, by the winds and rains of our unsettled climate, and many are incapable of enduring the cold of winter. Then, again, in some soils, as in low wet places, and in some localities, as in the neighbourhood of large towns, these same sorts will scarcely grow when planted out in the open air, but flourish and flower well when grown in pots under glass. It is such kinds we recommend *principally* for Pot-culture, introducing others merely to increase the variety. And surely the objects are worthy of this especial care. What other plants will conduce more to the enlivenment of the green-house? What others fill it with such a grateful perfume? I regard the Autumnals especially as of rare worth for greenhouse culture; for, by keeping three distinct sets of plants, we may ensure Roses all the year round. Five months may be allowed as their natural period of blooming out of doors, from June to October inclusive; then the shelter of a frame or greenhouse will prolong the blooming season till February; and during this and the three following months forced Roses may be obtained in beauty and abundance.

These are the principal advantages gained by growing Roses in pots. But we would not press our favourite immodestly on the attention of our readers. Suffice it to record our opinion : if the Rose is a suitable plant for Pot-culture, it will undoubtedly continue to gain friends; if not, no advocacy of ours can essentially serve it.

In entering on this branch of culture, the first point that should engage our attention is to provide a good heap of soil for the plants to grow in. The groups and varieties differing greatly in their nature and habits, it will appear reasonable that more than one sort of soil will be required, if all kinds are to receive that most suitable. All like a rich soil, which should be made light for the delicate-rooting varieties, and more tenacious for the robust hardy kinds.

To form a light soil, procure one barrow of seasoned turfy loam, half a barrow of well decomposed stable manure, half a barrow of leaf mould, and silver sand in proportion to the texture of the loam, which will in no case require more than one-fourth of its own bulk.

The heavy soil may be composed of one barrow of stiff turfy loam, one barrow of night-soil that has been mixed with loam, as previously advised, and laid by for a year, half a barrow of leaf-mould or well-pulverized manure, and sand as before recommended.

Night-soil may be thought too powerful a manure, but it may be used with safety, provided it has been mixed with loam, and well-seasoned previously by frequent turnings. The addition of about one-sixth of a barrow of burnt earth will be found to improve both composts. The materials should be thrown together at least three months before required for use, and turned frequently, that the integrant parts may become well incorporated, and ripened by exposure to the sun and air. The sieve is in neither case necessary, for as large pots will be principally used, the coarser, in moderation, the soil is, the better will the plants thrive.

It is our intention, at the end of this Division, to give a list of the kinds thought most suitable for Pot culture; but as many may prefer searching our descriptive lists for themselves, let us here consider what features are most worthy of notice when selecting for this

I

purpose. In my Pamphlet on the Cultivation of Roses in Pots,*
published some years since, the following points were given, and I
do not know that I can offer any further suggestions.—

1. Elegance of habit; regarding both growth and manner of
flowering.
2. Contrast of colour.
3. Abundance of bloom.
4. Form or individual outline of the flowers.
5. Duration and constant succession of bloom.
6. Sweetness.

What, says the tyro, can we find so many good properties combined in one variety? Can we obtain a Rose of an elegant habit,
an abundant bloomer, the outline of whose flowers is at the same
time perfect, remaining a long time in full beauty, and that is
very sweet? Truly such cases are rare. Few have a claim on all
these points, but some combine them more intimately than others;
and it is these we should choose.

Roses intended for growing in pots may be either on their own
roots or on short stems : the Tea-scented and Chinese kinds are
undoubtedly better in the former way. Let us suppose any number of young plants are obtained on their own roots in 60-sized
pots in the spring of the year. In the first place, they should be
shifted into 48 or 32-sized pots, according to the rate of growth
of the plant, and the quantity of roots it has made; then plunge
them, seeing that they are watered as often as the soil becomes
dry. I believe that Roses cultivated to bloom at their natural
period cannot be placed in too airy a situation; therefore I would
keep them constantly plunged in an open spot in the garden, removing the tender kinds only, on the approach of winter, for shelter
against frost.

Some object to plunging, and prefer placing the pots on the level
ground, packing moss, cinder ashes, or sawdust between them.
Practically speaking, it seems to matter but little; and whichever plan is adopted, there are two things to guard against—the
ingress of worms from the ground, and the egress of the roots from
the hole in the bottom of the pot. If the roots find their way into
the ground, there will be few formed in the pot; and the result
will be, a more vigorous, but less perfect, growth : and if the plants
are required to be removed at the time of flowering, they will receive a severe check. Both of these occurrences must therefore be

* Observations on the Cultivation of Roses in Pots, &c., by W. Paul.
Second Edition. Kent and Co., London.

prevented, by placing the pots on inverted seed-pans, or adopting some other plan which the ingenuity of the cultivator may devise. It must not be expected that the plants will all maintain the same rate of growth: some will grow vigorously, others not so. Now, although we would not wish to deprive the cultivator altogether of the reward of his care and labour—the flowers, yet we would say, a few only should be suffered to develope themselves the first year, and the seed-vessels should be cut off when the flowers drop. *The aim throughout the growing season should be to get a few stout, well-ripened shoots by autumn*—shoots that will bear strong pressure between the finger and thumb without giving any indication of softness, for it is these which will produce strong and perfect blooms.

The way to accomplish this is to place the plants a good distance from each other, and, as the young shoots form, they should be set wide apart, that they may enjoy the full sunlight. From the earliest period of growth, it is necessary to look them over occasionally, with the design of encouraging such shoots as maintain the best position, and checking those whose tendency is to exclude others from a fair rate of growth, and destroy the symmetry of the plants. Weak shoots should be cut out, and disbudding practised freely. If two or three eyes burst from the same point, threatening to crowd or cross each other, the least promising should be at once removed.

Most of the plants shifted into 48 or 32-sized pots in spring will, if they flourish well, require a second shift in July, when 24 and 16-sized pots may be made use of, and the same soil as before. When re-potting, the crock may be removed from the bottom of the ball, and the surface soil, which is apt to become sour, rubbed carefully away, so far as can be done without disturbing the roots.

A nice judgment is required in shifting the Chinese and Tea-scented Roses, as they are very liable to suffer from over-potting. As a guide on this point, turn them carefully out of the pots once or twice a year to examine the roots: if found protruding from the ball of earth in great abundance, place the plants in larger pots; if it be otherwise, put them back in the same. The hardy and robust growers may, however, be cultivated on the one-shift system, that is, changed at once from small to large pots; but this treatment will not suit the small and delicate growers.

Annexed (No. 26) is shewn a plant two years old, having been grown the first year in a smaller pot. It is now autumn, and it is losing its leaves. It needs no thinning, as it has been disbudded during spring and summer, on the principles advanced in our Chapter on Pruning. We now shorten the branches at the points

No. 26.

where the lines intersect; and, by continuing to practice disbudding, we obtain a handsome and well-flowered plant the following summer.

After it is pruned, the shoots should be staked out at as great distances as possible : those that are left long ought to be made to lie almost horizontal, by bending them down, that the buds may be induced to break regularly from their summit to the base. Great care is required in this operation, as the wood of some kinds is extremely brittle. If, however, the long shoots be allowed to maintain an upright position, the probability is, that two or three buds only at their top will break, which, by their exuberant growth, keep the lower eyes dormant, which are required to form a compact and well-regulated plant. But it is not necessary to keep them long bent; for so soon as the eyes have burst, the shoots may be tied up again. With regard to training, each cultivator will likely acquire a plan of his own. But of this hereafter.

Watering should be carefully attended to throughout the growing season. The quantity to be given must depend mainly on the state of the plants, the weather, and the porosity of the soil. As a general rule, Roses require but little water during autumn and winter. In spring, when the buds first break, occasional syringings are of infinite service. As the plants advance in growth, thereby acquiring a greater surface of foliage, and as the sun gains greater power, the quantity of water may be increased; and when in full leaf, and throughout the growing season, an abundance should be given. In making these remarks, we are supposing the water to have free egress through the rubble at the bottom of the pots, a condition essential for the health and perfect growth of the plants.

Manure water is beneficial. The use of it imparts a freshness and dark green hue to the foliage, and increases the vigour of the plants. It should not, however, be given too frequently, nor in too concentrated a form. If guano is used, an ounce to a gallon of water is sufficient. It is well to watch the effects of the dose given, to guard against an overgrowth, and regulate the supply accordingly. Perhaps the plants cannot grow too vigorously, provided the wood can be well ripened before winter. There is the point. But, as we cannot ensure a sunny autumn, which is necessary for the perfecting of strong shoots, a moderate growth is safer. Camphor-water an eminent Rose Amateur once advised me, from his own experience, to try ; but I am unable to report any satisfactory results. It is said to add new brilliancy to the flowers. Certainly, it is a safe application, and no *injurious* influences are likely to arise from its use.

In addition to our pains-taking to promote the growth of our plants, we have to guard against enemies and diseases. The Rose grub, which is most prevalent early in the season, requires close watching, and should be destroyed by hand-picking. I have picked a score off a single Pot-plant. Wherever a curled leaf, or shoot without a growing point, meets the eye, this destructive insect will be found. The mischief has perhaps been done in part, for it is seldom that he can be discovered, except by the effects he produces ; but let us catch him as soon as we can, and much mischief is prevented. He eats and destroys when young, but when he arrives at maturity he is a perfect gourmand, travelling from shoot to shoot, spreading devastation in his track ; and if he reach the moth state we may calculate on a numerous progeny the next year. I had a lot of plants remarkably free from these pests one season, which I could only account for by the fact that they were closely sought and destroyed the year before.

The Aphis, or Green-fly, may be destroyed by removing the plants to a pit or house, and smoking them : it may be kept away by dipping the ends of the shoots in, or syringing with, tobacco water, or by laying the shoot in the palm of the hand, and brushing the fly off.

There is a very small canary-coloured fly, which did great mischief among Roses one season. They are generally found on the back of the leaf, close to the midrib, eating the leaf, working from the under side, and not only disfiguring, but injuring the plants. They are remarkably active. By giving the plant a tap, they will rise instantly in the air, fly round, and settle again on the leaves. As they were too nimble to be dealt with as their more sluggish compeers in mischief, I applied sulphur and snuff in equal portions, dusting the mixture on the back of the leaves when wet, and found it prove an excellent remedy.

A long thin caterpillar, the larva of a saw-fly, sometimes commits great havoc among Roses. They came in such myriads upon a Rose Garden in this county a few years ago, that the plants were almost stripped of their leaves before their course could be arrested. Hand-picking was resorted to, by which means they were ultimately got rid of.

The red fungus, which often attacks Roses out of doors late in autumn, may visit the Pot-plants ; and should it do so, the leaves where it appears should be carefully rubbed between the finger and thumb, using a little sulphur in the operation.

Mildew is sometimes a source of great annoyance. Dusting the leaves with sulphur is the best remedy. Watering with a solution of nitre is also said to destroy it. If the situation is airy and sunny, there is little to fear on this account. Forced Roses are more subject to it, and, when speaking of these, it will require a brief notice.

We have followed our plants through the first training season. They have been shifted twice, once in spring, and again in July. In autumn they will be well established, when a portion may be selected for forcing, and part left for blooming at other periods.

If to produce large and handsome specimens *quickly* is the point aimed at, we would advise sacrificing the bloom in part, even the second training season, by pinching out some of the flower-buds so soon as they are formed. The same routine of culture will require to be gone through now as in the first season, availing ourselves of whatever knowledge we may have gained by experience and observation. But a new source of amusement now opens upon us, and one which will discover and exercise our taste. The first year little training is necessary ; but it has now become an important part of the business.   If skilfully and tastefully done, it greatly enhances the beauty of our favourites : if otherwise, it has a contrary tendency.   Often we see well-grown plants, which reflect great credit on the cultivator, spoiled in the training.   To manage this properly, the shoots should be tied out to sticks immediately that the plants are pruned ; and when the newly-formed shoots are three or four inches long, they should be tied out also, training according to some preconceived plan.

We agree that the fewer sticks used the better ; but we fear Roses cannot be managed nicely without the help of some.   We do not like to see a plant with as many sticks as it has flowers, and almost a hedge-stake used to support a branch which a privet-twig would hold in place.   This is bungling and unsightly, equalled only by the want of design often apparent in the training.   The sticks should be chosen as slight as will support the flowers, and the shape of the plant should be determined before we commence to fashion it.   Not that we are obliged to follow such form, if, by any occurrence, we discover one more suitable in an after stage of

No. 27.

growth.   The sticks used in tying out and training, if painted, should be painted green, as near the colour of the foliage as possible, duller, not brighter, or they will create a glare, and detract from the beauty of the plant. To us the system of a tall shoot in the centre of the plant, with all the others disposed around it gradually decreasing in height as they recede from the centre—in a word, a pyramid, presents the most pleasing object. No. 27 is a newly-pruned plant grown and trained on this system.

Immediately after pruning, we draw the lower shoots downwards over the rim of the pot, just beneath which a wire should pass, to which the bast may be fastened. When the plants are of three or four years' growth, and have been previously trained upon this plan, tier above tier of branches may be arranged, each decreasing in circumference in the ascent, till we terminate in a point. Trained on this plan, the plants require constant care and attention during the season of growth to keep them well balanced. Strong shoots must be stopped as occasion may require, and weak ones encouraged.

A round bush is quite in character in some instances, especially for such kinds as are of lowly growth.

The plants may be trained to a face, the tallest shoots ranged at the back, the others gradually decreasing in height as they approach the front. This method has been successfully carried out at the various horticultural exhibitions, where only one side of the plant, or at most three-quarters of it, is presented to view.

Pruning may be applied here as elsewhere, excepting that, the growth of Pot-Roses being usually less vigorous than that of kinds under common treatment out of doors, they require rather closer pruning. Disbudding should be practised in Pot-culture especially: it is of great assistance in obtaining well-formed plants, which we expect to see when grown in pots.

But the second season has passed away, and we have entered upon the third. Our plants are not equal to what they are capable of becoming; but the accompanying engraving (No. 28) may be considered a fair illustration of a three-years' old plant that has been carefully and skilfully cultivated for two seasons. Its growth is too vigorous to be called perfect, for the flowers, are, in consequence, nearly all on the top of long shoots. This, however, is desirable at this stage of growth, and easily remedied the next year, by long pruning, and afterwards bending the branches down.

Roses are often lifted from the ground to be grown in pots, and it is necessary to say a few words about them. Early in autumn (September) is a good time to take them up; and if done immediately after rain, the roots are less liable to be injured in the removal. When potting, whether the plants are on their own roots or on stems, the straggling roots should be cut in so far as to

No. 28.

admit of their being placed comfortably in the pots. If any of the roots have been bruised in taking up, the bruised part should be cut away : let the cut be made clean with a knife, and fibrous roots will soon be emitted from its surface. When potting worked plants, we should have an eye to suckers from the wild stock, which should be cut off close to the stem, to prevent their springing into life at any future period. The sized pots most suitable for dwarf plants from the ground vary from Nos. 32 to 12 ; if a plant is of robust growth, strong and well rooted, it may be placed in the latter size : if the reverse, use the former. In reference to this, the judgment at the time of potting is the best guide. Placing the plants too low in the soil is a great evil: always keep the roots near to the surface, as they are sure to strike downwards.

It is essential here that the pots be thoroughly drained, and the soil should be well pressed or shaken down among the roots. The heads may be thinned out at the time of potting, leaving as many shoots as can be found properly situated to form the plant handsomely. The shortening of the shoots may be deferred till the plants are supposed to have made fresh roots ; remembering, however, that the time of pruning regulates the time of blooming : the earlier they are pruned the earlier they will flower.

After potting, the plants should be placed in a cold pit, where they may remain closed from the air for a few days. They should be syringed twice daily, or three times, and shaded also, if sunny weather. If taken up in September or October, when the leaf is green, and kept in a close pit, well syringed and shaded, they will retain their leaves almost as fresh as if left in the ground, and soon renew their hold of the soil.

I have removed the Autumnals from the ground in June and July, just when they had completed their first flowering, and, by treating them in the manner above described, have obtained complete success.

It is not necessary that they should remain in a pit for any great length of time. After the first ten days or fortnight air may be admitted gradually to harden them, when the hardy kinds may be plunged out of doors, in an airy situation, and the tender ones kept in the pit, or placed by themselves where they may be sheltered from severe frosts. The north side of a wall or fence will serve for this purpose, erecting a temporary building, open on three sides, the top covered with felt or fern, or any thing else that will exclude the rain and frost : the sides may then be closed in with mats in severe weather.

A few remarks on Roses grown in pots as climbers may not be altogether useless. If it be the wish of the cultivator to train a few upon this system, they should be invariably chosen on their own roots. But perhaps it may seem strange that we should suggest such a thing. What! cultivate Climbing Roses in pots! The idea is absurd! So it would be did we recommend the groups which are ordinarily spoken of as climbers ; namely, the Aryshire, Boursault, Banksiæ, Musk, Sempervirens, &c. But such is not our intention. Magnificent as these are when growing in the open ground, to the height of twelve feet, covered with their immense trusses of bloom, we are aware that their semi-double and transient flowers render them unsuitable for Pot-culture. But where else are varieties found that will climb? This question will be replied to in the list given at the end of this Division.

We have now to point out the end in view, and the means by which it is to be accomplished. Some kinds, which are indispensable even in a small collection, cannot be grown to advantage

except as climbers; such are, Lamarque, Solfaterre, Jaune Desprez, and others. As to the shape they are brought to assume,
the taste of the cultivator will perhaps be the best guide. Circular trellises may be formed, varying in height and diameter,
that they may be fitted to any particular variety, according to its
rate of growth. None should exceed four feet in height. Round
these the shoots may be trained, according to the accompanying
illustration (No. 29), so as eventually to hide the trellis, and to

No. 29.

produce a dense, but not shapeless, mass of foliage and flowers. It
is necessary, in the first instance, to practise close pruning, to
induce the shoots to grow vigorously : they should then be trained
in their proper course during the season of growth. Now, the great
point to be kept in view here is, so to prune and train that the
plant may produce flowers from its summit to the ground ; for it is

evident that if only a few flowers are to be produced at the top, then
the dwarfer it is grown the better.   Here, as in all gardening
operations, Nature requires time to perfect her work.   The plants
will not be complete the first year : they may not the second.
Much, of course, will depend on the treatment they undergo, their
strength when put to the trellis, and the size of the latter.   But
little pruning is necessary : each year the weak and unripened wood
only should be removed, tying the rest to the trellis, till it is

No. 30.

covered.   With respect to the shortening of the shoots, they should
be cut back to eyes that are well ripened, and no farther.   Cover
the trellis as thoroughly and quickly as possible, and then prune as
directed for Climbing Roses.

No. 30 is a sketch of the beautiful yellow Rose Solfaterre, taken from a plant in bloom which had been treated as above described. We said, at the opening of this Chapter, that Roses may be had in flower all the year round. Let us revert to that point. We must divide our plants into three lots, varying the colours in each as much as possible; securing the fullest kinds for forcing, and the least double for winter flowering. From June to October, inclusive, may be considered the natural season of flowering. By forcing, of which we shall speak in the next Chapter, we may obtain flowers from February to May. It is now our intention to relate how we secure flowers from November to February. This is the most difficult point to attain. Nevertheless, it is done, *by inducing the Autumnals to grow and form flower-buds late in the autumn, and by preserving these flower-buds from wet and frost.* I do not say this plan is new, or has not been adopted by others; but I certainly am one who read the lesson from the book of Nature, and afterwards practised it with complete success. Walking one October evening among some Chinese and Tea-scented Roses which had been transplanted in spring, and had grown and flowered but little during a dry summer, I could not but remark how thickly the trees were then covered with small flower-buds. The first inquiry was, as to the cause of this, which was soon discovered. A dry spring had been succeeded by rain late in summer, and the plants were now growing vigorously. Pleased at first by the prospect of so late a bloom, it did not strike me that it would be the middle of November before the flowers could be perfected. However, frost and rain set in, and the consequences were soon apparent—the flower-buds were blighted and decayed. One kind alone, Chinese Fabvier, a semi-double scarlet one, braved the storm, and his rich warm tints were unusually beautiful, or perhaps apparently so, in contrast with the desolation that reigned around. The petals of the most double kinds had become glued together at their tops, which prevented their expansion, and the buds rotted. From these observations I inferred two things; 1st, That had these flower-buds been protected from frost and rain, they would have been gradually unfolded; for they continued advancing in size so long as the weather remained favourable. 2dly, That the least double varieties are more likely to expand their flowers perfectly late in the year than others, because less affected by damp; and, that the damp was as destructive as the cold, was evident, from the most double varieties, which retain moisture the longest, being in the worst state, and from the semi-double ones flowering, in spite of the adverse weather.

Building upon these inferences, late in the following summer (I think in August) I cut down *the main shoots* of several Autumnals that were then flowering in pots, leaving two or three eyes on each shoot to break from. They broke; and in October, the flower-buds being formed, the plants were removed to a cold pit, giving all possible air in fine weather. It was a mild winter, but a damp one. The flower-buds advanced steadily, although some became mouldy and damp, and, as it is termed, "*fogged off.*" Nevertheless, during November and December, many kinds flowered beautifully; and at Christmas I cut as fine a bunch of Roses as could be desired. In wet or damp weather the lights were kept on: in frosty weather there was the further addition of a straw-mat. Lovers of roses! what think you of this? Is a cold pit unworthily occupied with Pot-roses, which shall furnish you with flowers in full beauty in the depth of winter? It has been seen that the above succeeded well there; though it is questionable whether they would do so *every* season. Severe frost, should it occur, must injure, if not destroy, the flowers. Let them, then, have a place in a greenhouse, giving fire-heat only to dry up dampness and exclude the frost. So soon as they have done flowering they may be removed to a cold pit, giving air plentifully. In March they may be re-potted and pruned, and plunged out of doors, where they will flower again in July.

Once every year, late in September, or early in October, all, except the plants intended for winter flowering, should be turned out of their pots, shaking away a good portion of the soil, and re-potting them in new or clean pots, larger if thought necessary. Immediately after this operation they should be transferred to some situation where they have the morning sun only—a north border is a good place—and watering must be carefully attended to. When they have remained here for a week or ten days, the pots may be plunged in the ground up to the rims, having manure laid on the surface of the soil. At the time of re-potting, it is advisable, if disbudding has not been followed, to thin out such shoots as will not be required for the succeeding year.

Whenever plants are grown in cold pots, abundance of air should be given at all seasons. Indeed, the lights need only be used as a shelter against frost or wind, or heavy rain; dews and slight rains are beneficial in spring and summer. In the flowering season it will be necessary to shade during the middle of the day, when canvas lights should be used instead of glass ones.

CHAPTER IX.

ON FORCING.

OF all flowers induced to blossom, amid the chills of winter, there is perhaps none which excites so much interest as the Rose. And as this branch of culture is now so generally practised, it seems to demand more than a passing notice.

The art of forcing consists in accelerating the period of growth and flowering of plants, by means of artificial heat. In practising it, we change their seasons, inducing them to perform certain functions at other seasons than those at which they naturally perform them. With Roses, spring and summer is the natural period of growth, autumn the period of maturation, and winter that of repose. But supposing we commence forcing at Christmas, our winter becomes their spring, our spring their summer, our summer their autumn, and our autumn their season of rest. Thus, in forcing, although *we change all the seasons*, we take care *not to annul any one of them*, or we sacrifice the health of the plants. And these changes should be brought about gradually. The first year the plants are forced they should be advanced steadily, and should, in no case, be brought to flower earlier than the middle of March.

In the construction of the forcing-house, every chance of increasing the quantity of light should be accepted, remembering that, in their artificial spring, the plants will not have the advantage of so long or so powerful a sunlight as in the natural one. A house has been built here recently, for the express purpose of growing Roses in pots to bloom in the spring of the year. Measured from the inside, it is fifty feet long, and eighteen feet wide. It has a span-roof, facing east and west, with glass ends and upright sashes at both fronts. The top lights are moveable, that air may be given as required ; and it is intended to substitute canvas for glass in the summer season. This house was built *for Pot-roses only ;* but if flowers are not wanted before March or April, we think a desirable point would be gained by omitting the stages on which the pots are placed, and forming, in their place, a

bed of good soil, in which standards and half-standards might be
planted ; say three or five rows—a row of tall plants along the
centre, and shorter ones on either side.

In forcing Roses on a small scale, a pit with a span-roof may be
constructed at a very trifling cost ; and an Arnott's stove, pro-
portioned to the size of the pit, proves an effectual and wholesome
heating apparatus. A pit 20 feet long, and 15 feet wide, of
sufficient height to enable one to walk conveniently down the
middle, will hold 100 *large* plants; and to heat this structure a
moderate-sized Arnott's stove is sufficient. A pan of water should
be placed on the top, to preserve a proper degree of moisture in
the atmosphere. Plants removed from the ground will, if on their
own roots, require to be grown one year in pots before forcing.
Their early treatment is the same as that of other Roses in pots,
which is fully described in the last chapter. To this, then, we
need not revert, but will suppose the amateur in possession of
strong plants of at least two years' growth, whether of his own
raising, or purchased at the Nurseries. When about to force
Roses on their own roots, we should ascertain whether the pots
are full of sound healthy roots; for if they are not, only partial
success can be obtained. If fine flowers are wanted, the last week
in December, or the first week in January, is early enough to
commence forcing, and but little fire-heat should be given in the
first instance. This is their artificial spring, and a low night
temperature must necessarily be secured. The Rose is not a lover
of a powerful heat : it must be forced steadily, increasing the
temperature by degrees, if flowers are required very early. Where
bottom-heat can be readily obtained, we think it advantageous,
although by no means necessary. A good point to start from
in forcing is 50 to 55 degrees by day, and 40 degrees by night.
The temperature of the house requires close attention ; and the
state of the atmosphere, as regards its humidity, although often
overlooked, is equally important. Too dry an atmosphere causes a
drain upon the nutritive organs, and will cause the young leaves to
wither and fall off; it also encourages red spider. A too damp
atmosphere is favourable to the production of mildew, especially if
the temperature should fall suddenly, from the effect of atmo-
spheric changes from without, or other causes. A dry air may be
remedied by syringing the plants copiously, and, if found necessary,
by pouring water on the floor of the house. A damp atmosphere
is best remedied by giving air. Unless the weather be very frosty,
air should be admitted freely for the first fortnight, to strengthen
the growing buds ; but so soon as leaves are formed, it will be
necessary to keep the house constantly closed, except the air be

very mild, which it seldom is at this season of the year. By the admission of cold air, the young leaves may, from their extreme tenderness, be blighted in an hour. The plants being once fairly aroused, and their roots in action, the temperature may be gradually raised till we reach 50 degrees by night, and 75 degrees by day. A higher temperature than this should not, I think, be produced *artificially*. Towards the spring, sudden bursts of sun- shine will occasionally raise the house 10 degrees, without pro- ducing any injurious effects : still, if the weather be mild, we would counteract this by giving air; if keen and windy, by shading. A temperature of 90 degrees, or even 100 degrees, caused by sunshine, is, however, productive of less injury than a keen frosty air.

In case of severe weather, as was experienced in February 1845, on the 12th of which month the thermometer sunk as low as 6 degrees, there will probably be some difficulty experienced in main- taining the temperature previously recommended. Under such circumstances the plants will receive no injury from a slight decrease of heat, which is indeed much to be preferred to a high forced temperature, produced by great effort. If the house or pit is so constructed that it can be conveniently covered up with mats or cloths, radiation is prevented, and the advantages are very great : and this is desirable on the score of economy, for a great expenditure of fuel is saved ; but it is still more desirable for the health of the plants, because the less artificial heat employed the better.

In the early stage of growth, little water need be given : the plants may be syringed occasionally with manure-water of moderate strength. I have sometimes used soot-water in lieu of the above, and the vigour of growth, the dark-green hue of the foliage, and the prominence of the buds, sufficiently attest the value of it. It may, however, be dispensed with so soon as the branches begin to harden and the flower-buds are formed. It is advisable to syringe the plants twice daily in the early stage of growth ; in the morning, just as the sun falls upon them, and again in the afternoon. But should several cloudy or rainy days follow consecutively, once syringing, and that in the morning, is sufficient. Disbudding should be practised here, as before recommended. We would not, in forced Roses, destroy dormant buds, for they·are of no injury to the growing shoots, and in them we have embryo shoots, ready to be awakened, and capable of producing flowers at our will.

The Rose, when forced, has as much to contend with from the insect tribe as when growing naturally in the garden. Here, as elsewhere, the Rose-grub will require close seeking, for the treat-

K

ment which causes the production of Roses before their natural time produces him also.

The red spider is sometimes productive of sad results, for which moisture is the best remedy. Syringe the plants abundantly and daily with tepid soot water, perfectly clear, driving the water with some force against the young leaves *through a fine rose-syringe*, so as not to bruise or injure them. The pipes may also be washed with sulphur and soot formed into a liquid, laying it on when they are in a warm, not hot state.

For the destruction of the aphides the usual plan of fumigating with tobacco must be had recourse to, and this upon their first appearance. The atmosphere of the forcing-house seems particularly congenial to them. To-day you will see a few fat comfortable-looking ones stalking up and down the shoots : disregard them for a week, and you will see thousands. To avoid the unpleasant situation of being enveloped in a dense cloud of tobacco-smoke, the following plan is now adopted in many places : a portion of tobacco, judged sufficient for the size of the house, is mixed with an equal portion of damp moss. and placed in a fine wire sieve over charcoal embers. This gradually smoulders away, and the house is filled to perfection. In a large house a sieve at either end is advisable. Fumigation will require to be repeated frequently : for if only one or two aphides escape, the house is soon swarming again, and no plant can thrive while covered with these numerous sap-suckers.

The mildew will sometimes appear, and is a pest of no ordinary kind. I have seen the beauty of a house destroyed by it for the season. Sulphur, dusted on the leaves when wet, is the remedy usually applied. Experience and observation tell us that the best preventive, as well as cure, is to keep the atmosphere in a wholesome state. Sudden and violent changes should be avoided. Every effort should be used to keep the plants vigorous and healthy. If they suffer from being crowded, or for want of light and a free circulation of air, they become drawn and weakly, and are very liable to its attacks. On the first appearance of mildew, such as are suffering from it should be removed, to prevent infection.

During their growth, the plants should be looked through frequently, and the surface of the soil stirred, using due care not to injure the fibrous roots, which often lie near the top in great abundance. At the same time suckers should be removed ; those from the stem cut off close, and the under-ground ones drawn out.

So soon as the leaves are of fair size, and the flower-buds are forming, a free supply of water is required. Manure water should be given occasionally, not cold, but of the temperature of the house. If worms are troublesome, lime water may be administered. But the reward of our care is at hand. The buds are strongly formed, and shew colour, and syringing must cease. Now which do we prefer, a great display at one time, or a regular succession of flowers? If the former, lower the temperature of the house *gradually*, and run a thin canvas* over the glass to create a slight shade. This will give the buds longer time to expand, and the flowers will be increased in size, improved in colour, and last longer. A continual succession of flowers may be obtained by removing the plants, at different stages of forwardness, to a house with a lower temperature, where they get the sun and air. It is plain that the time of flowering will be regulated by the temperature of the house; and plain, also, that the finest flowers will be produced if a moderate degree of heat be maintained. Has our treatment, then, guided, as in some measure it must be, by the state of the weather without doors, caused them to flower by the end of February, or is it March? Whichever it may be, here they are, delighting us with their gay and varied colours, and shedding around a delicious perfume. The Rose in bloom in winter, too! Truly, this is a charmed flower.

Here is a pause in the process of cultivation; the Amateur has breathing time. He has only to see that his favourites do not suffer from drought, and all will go on well. But an active mind, which the cultivation of flowers usually engenders, will find plenty of amusement in attending to his plants out of doors. Besides, is it likely that a house of forced Roses should be known to exist without drawing the proprietor's friends, or some anxious connoisseurs, around him? And here is one charm hanging over the pursuit: not only does the votary of floriculture derive, from the purest sources, a calm and intellectual enjoyment, but he is at the same time enabled to exhibit the science, in its most pleasing dress, to those around him.

When the flowering is over, it is advisable to remove the summer bloomers. Do not take them at once from the forcing-house and place them out of doors, for the sudden change would prove injurious. Gradually harden them, by help of a cold house, if standards, or a pit, if dwarfs. When the summer kinds are removed, fresh plants, kept in reserve for the purpose, may, if the Amateur wish, be brought to fill their places. The autumnal bloomers may, however, be treated somewhat differently: their shoots should be

---

* The Tiffany, recently brought out by Mr. Shaw, of Manchester, is an admirable material for the purpose.

cut back to three or four eyes with good leaves, and they will give forth a second crop of flowers in grand perfection during April and May. At the time they are cut back, it is well to remove a little of the surface soil, replacing it with well-pulverized manure.

After April, very little fire heat is required for the forcing-house : indeed, if the weather be warm and sunny, none is needed. After the second flowering, the admission of air should be gradually increased for a few days, when the plants may be re-potted and removed from the house. In the operation of potting it will be found necessary to shake away a portion of the soil, sometimes using larger pots, and sometimes others of the same size : the old pots should not be used again till they have been washed or well rubbed out. After potting, plunge the plants in an airy and sunny situation, where they may remain till required for forcing the following year. Having been early excited, they will be disposed to rest early ; and thus are obtained specimens in the best condition for forcing. I have observed plants, which have been forced for several years in succession, cease growing about Midsummer, and shed a portion of their leaves shortly afterwards. If, from much rain, the bark and soil become thoroughly moistened, they are aroused, a second growth occurs, and the best wood is lost. To prevent this, the plants should be pruned so soon as the wood is matured, and the pots laid on their sides under a north wall or fence. The Autumnals removed from the forcing-house in May will, if suffered, produce flowers again in September and October. But this is working them rather hard ; and if we are anxious to secure good plants for the next forcing season, the flower-buds should be nipped out so soon as formed, and all gross shoots stopped back or destroyed. It is the shoots formed after the first flowering that we are looking forward to for fine flowers the next year, and the eyes on them must be kept dormant. Roses thus treated will flower well forced several years in succession.

It is not intended to be expressed that Roses newly-removed from the ground will not bear forcing. If worked on the Dog-rose, or any free stock, they do not absolutely require to go through the preparatory course recommended for plants on their own roots. If taken up early in September, they may be forced the first year with success, as far as regards the flowers, although they do not form regular and handsome plants. For several years past it has been customary here to place the new varieties in the forcing-house, to their merit before offering them to the public, and some le flowers are thus produced ; certainly not in full and perbeauty, though sufficiently good to form an opinion of their ue. But this is treading on the very confines of the laws of nature, and is one of those things which *may be done*, and not what should be recommended. Small plants, *established*, are preferable to large ones newly-potted. In fact, the former, if in a good state, will produce flowers equal to those of larger plants : the difference will chiefly consist, not in quality, but in quantity. Plants of this description, after having been in the house for a short time, should be shifted into 32 or 24-sized pots, using a rich light soil, and taking care not to bruise the tender roots, or loosen the ball of earth in the operation. With regard to the description of Roses best suited for forcing, some varieties, which do not expand their flowers freely out of doors, are beautiful when forced ; and some kinds, of rare beauty in the garden, are of little worth for forcing. A list of the best will be furnished hereafter.

Many who might not have convenience or inclination for forcing Roses, would yet willingly appropriate a pit to secure a good bloom in April and May ; and this may be attained without much trouble. Let the plants be pruned and placed in the pit early in November. Keep them as close to the glass as possible. Give air abundantly in mild weather, covering the glass with mats or fern on cold nights, or even during the day in the event of severe frost.

CHAPTER X.

REMARKS ON SUNDRY OPERATIONS IN THE ROSE GARDEN.

CERTAIN branches of cultivation have been made the subject of separate chapters; but there are others, important in themselves, yet not of sufficient magnitude to require this : such it is our intention to include in the present chapter.

Let us run hastily through the year, commencing with the spring. The last operation performed in the Rose Garden has been pruning, and now, forking the beds over requires to be done.

When Roses are newly planted, they need a little extra attention. They should be mulched and watered occasionally, if the spring or summer prove dry. As care in childhood and early life determines the constitution of the man, so attention at this epoch of a plant's existence establishes a vigorous and healthy subject. Unless it is the intention to supply the plants with manure-water during that part of the growing season which precedes their flowering, now is the time to enrich the soil. If the ground has been prepared the previous autumn, this will be unnecessary, but under all other circumstances it should be done. The manure should be well decayed, and a thick coating laid on the beds previous to forking, that it may be turned in in this operation. *An annual forking is indispensable;* and if the beds are also hoed with a Vernon hoe three or four times in the course of the summer, as the nature of the soil or the season may require, the plants will be largely benefited. The latter practice is especially recommended for stiff and adhesive soils.

Rose-trees require a careful looking over during April and May, to remove the Rose-grub, which, if allowed to pursue its ravages, proves most destructive to the early bloom. Tobacco-smoke, and tobacco-water, seem alike inefficient; soot-water is evidently disagreeable to them, but they survive it; and the only effectual remedy I know of, is to search diligently, in the early stages of the young shoots' growth, and draw the vagrants from their flimsy hiding-place. I believe the *tom-tit* frequently makes a meal off them, but his operations are too irregular to be relied on. The green-fly abounds everywhere; syringing with tobacco-water, or dusting with snuff and soot when the leaves are damp, that the mixture may adhere thereto, destroys or disperses it. It is also a good practice to smoke the trees with tobacco, using the fumigating bellows, first enclosing the head with some material that will prevent the escape of the smoke.

In Standard Roses, suckers from the stock often shoot forth, and will impoverish the tree if allowed to remain. They should be watched for, and invariably removed so soon as seen: if proceeding from beneath the ground, it is necessary to remove the soil, for which purpose a spade is best, and they should be cut off close to the stock whence they spring. If this is strictly attended to for two or three years, Roses will cease to throw suckers. On the specimen plants here, which are of some age, it is rare that a sucker is seen.

At the same time that we are on the look out for suckers, it may be well to have an eye on the heads of the trees, to establish a regular growth. Besides the shoots produced at stated periods,—in spring, and in summer immediately after flowering,—it is not unusual, when a plant is in full vigour, for buds that have lain dormant even for a year or two, to burst into life, producing very gross shoots. If such proceed from the Summer kinds, they rarely flower, and, not ripening well, are of little use: if they arise from the Autumnals, a large truss of flowers is often produced, but their quality is quite mediocre. In both cases, by drawing to themselves the nutritive juices of the plant, these gross shoots weaken the more moderate and valuable branches. But what shall be done with them? They are fine shoots, and it seems a pity to destroy them. But if the plant is already well furnished with shoots, it is certainly best to destroy them, by cutting them off close to their base, so soon as discovered. If, however, there are but few shoots, or a tree is ill-shapen, they may be turned to advantage. Under the latter state of things, pinch out their tops when they have reached an advantageous height, which the looker-on must determine, and thus they may be brought to fill up a scanty tree, or balance a mis-shapen one. But supposing, when such shoots arise, a Summer Rose has an abundance of vigorous shoots, or an Autumnal is scant of bloom, though at the same time in such a state of health and vigour as to warrant us in concluding there is a sufficient command of food to support and develope existing branches and anticipated flowers; this may render it advisable to allow such shoots their natural course of growth, when the Autumnals—and here we refer to the varieties of ROSA INDICA especially—often terminate with a large cluster of flowers. But remember, *the most vigorous shoots in Summer Roses are least likely to flower; in Autumnals they do not produce the best flowers*

We would treat these gross shoots in the same way when they arise on Dwarf or Pillar Roses.

As a general rule, so soon as the flower-buds are formed, if we are seeking large flowers in preference to numbers, it will be well to nip out first those that seem imperfect, and afterwards such as are smallest and most backward. It has even been recommended to cut off the early flowers of the Autumnals, *on the ground that there is an abundance of other Roses in June,* and the practice causes a finer and more certain production in autumn. Yet we see no need for destroying the first flowers of the former. Let them bloom; and when the flowers drop, remove the soil an inch or two deep for a good space around each plant, placing a spadeful of manure there. Cover this over again with the soil, and water the plants twice or thrice if the weather continue dry. This treatment will induce a fresh and vigorous growth, ensuring, as a consequence, fine flowers. *The secret of securing a good bloom of Roses in autumn exists in keeping the Autumnals growing during summer and autumn.* Do this, and there is no fear of failure.

The Autumnals perhaps give a better succession of flowers when grown on their own roots, than when budded, because their growth is less regular : shoots spring into life at shorter intervals.

These are some of the operations necessary to be attended to *previous to the flowering season,* in order to secure the well-being of our favourites. Some of them may appear tedious, but to those who love flowers there is an interest felt in the simplest operations of culture ; for he who plants a tree adopts it as his own, appoints himself its protector, and delights in administering to its wants. Every act of labour bestowed increases his attachment to it, and every stage of progress offers beauties to his sight. As he wanders in the Rosarium, and sees the plants covered with flower-buds, what agreeable anticipations does he indulge in, heightened, perhaps, by the occasional recognition of a flower blossoming before its time. Every succeeding walk shews him an increase in the number ; till at last he beholds them flushed with blossoms, yielding a rich harvest for the labour he has bestowed.

> Well they reward the toil. The sight is pleased,
> The scent regaled. . . . .
> Each opening blossom freely breathes abroad
> Its gratitude, and thanks him with its sweets.

What a delightful month is June for the lover of Roses! and what time is equal to the morning for inspecting the flowers? What floricultural enjoyment can surpass that afforded by a walk in the Rosarium at grey dawn, when

The lamps of heaven grow dim, and jocund day
Stands tiptoe on the misty mountain's top ?

Then the White Roses first shew, and how inexpressibly pure
they seem in the twilight ! The deeper tints,—the blush, the pink,
the rose,—follow in rapid succession ; and as darkness flies away
the crimson and the blacker hues rise in rich effulgence to complete
the picture. How beautiful the foliage appears glistening with
dew ! The flowers, too, are rife with freshness and beauty. Is
there not life in every fold ? And what a delicious odour is borne
on the surrounding air ! As we gaze and admire there is little to
disturb our meditations ; the warblings of the feathered choristers
alone break in upon the slumbering scene. Here is the consum-
mation of our hopes in Rose-culture. And what a recompence for
the toil we have sustained ! Do we not feel as we admire, that

" Nature never did betray
The heart that lov'd her : 'tis her privilege,
Through all the years of this our life, to lead
From joy to joy."

Next to the morning's walk in the Rosarium a ramble at even-
tide is, perhaps, the most delightful. The colours of many kinds
have the same fervid glow ; the same perfumes scent the air, but
(alas that the life of our favourites should be so fleeting !) instead
of the young and promising beauties of the morning, we gaze on
Roses of mature age.

But these are not all the sweets attendant on the cultivation of
flowers. As the Amateur scans the beauties which surround him,
when satiated—if indeed satiety can be experienced here—with the
sight, the reflections awakened by association in floricultural nomen-
clature afford him new sources of enjoyment. What an amount
of virtue, learning, wit, valour, often congregate on a small plot in
the flower-garden ! How proud is the florist of his Catos, his
Socrates, his Butlers, his *peaceful* Alexanders and Cæsars ! There,
kings and emperors are placed beside the subverters of dynasties
and empires ; there, warriors who have indulged in deadly strife
exist together in the strictest amity—a Charles beside a Cromwell,
a Scipio in company with an Hannibal. In " rigid Cincinnatus,
nobly poor," he reads a lesson on self-disinterestedness and magna-
nimity ; in Napoleon, however much he may be dazzled by the
splendid genius of the man, he cannot but recoil from one who
drenched the earth with blood as he ponders over the futility of
human ambition. Then let him contrast the consequences of the
tyranny and licentiousness of an Antony with those arising from

the virtues and philanthropy of a Howard: the one, through his
vices, lost a kingdom; the other, though an humble individual,
conferred lasting benefits on thousands of his race, and earned in
the work an honoured and imperishable name. And in admiring
the objects bearing names like these, and indulging in the reflections awakened by association, does he not feel the mind expand,
refine, aspire to imitate the good and shun the evil?

But we have digressed very far, and must return to the practical part of our subject. With regard to the manner in which
Roses should be grown, the habit of the variety may be taken as a
guide. The vigorous growers would seem best adapted for Standard
or Pillar Roses, unless of slovenly growth, when they are suited
only for covering banks or for climbers. Annexed are engravings

No. 31

Standard Rose.

of two Standard Roses in flower: they are both vigorous growers,
and have been submitted to long pruning (see Chap. V.)

No. 32.

Pyramidal-headed Standard.

The habit of No. 31 is branching, that of No. 32 is erect: the latter has, by a little variation in pruning, been made to form a pyramidal head. The kinds of moderate growth look well on Half-Standards, of which the annexed engraving (No. 33) is a representation. The kinds of delicate or dwarf growth are best on dwarf stocks or on their own roots; they rarely succeed well as Standards: besides which, a small head on a long stem is unsightly. No. 34 was taken from a dwarf variety of the French Rose.

But let us note a few thoughts respecting Climbing Roses. The groups best suited for this purpose are named in Chap. 15. For covering walls and fences with north, north-east, or north-west

No. 33.

Half Standard Rose.

No. 34.

Dwarf Rose.

aspects, the Ayrshire and Sempervirens are the best, because they
are free bloomers and very hardy.

When Climbing Roses are planted to cover unsightly trees,
standing in positions where it is thought desirable they should
remain, the same annual pruning and manuring is all the culture
they require.

Pillar Roses are comparatively of recent introduction. They
present a new feature in the Rose Garden, and deserve to be more
extensively cultivated.   No. 33 was sketched from a plant of the

No. 35.

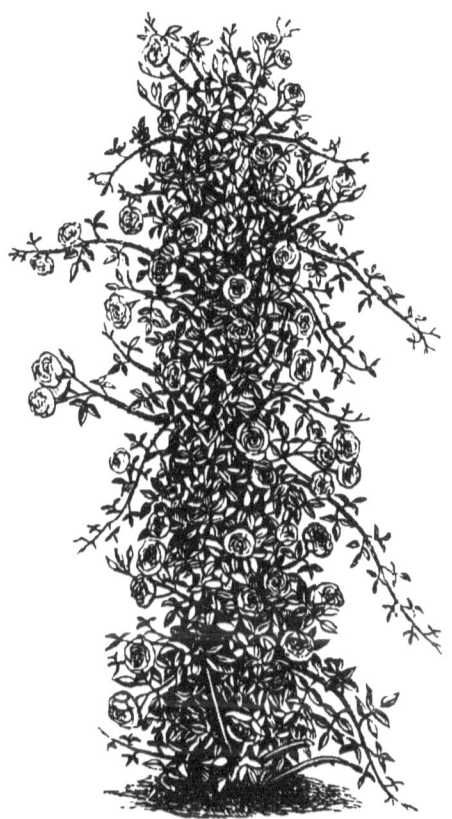

Pillar or Pole Rose.

Ayrshire Splendens, the best of the group for a Pillar Rose. The groups thought most suitable for this style of growth are named in Chapter 15 ; but it must not be inferred that *all* the varieties of these groups are suitable : they require selecting, and those denominated *vigorous*, or *robust*, in the descriptive part of this work, are best for the purpose. But what are the proper supports for Pillar Roses? Iron is doubtless the most durable, but also the most expensive : nevertheless, where expense is not a primary consideration, it is thought preferable. The supports more generally used are larch poles, which have a very rustic appearance when cut from the woods with the snags left projecting a few inches :

these hold the shoots in place, and prevent them from being torn about by the wind. But the want of durability is a great drawback on the value of these poles. In the course of three or four years, just as the Rose has covered the pole, the latter often decays at the surface of the ground, a strong gale of wind lays it prostrate, and the result is sometimes disastrous to the plant. To counteract this as far as possible, it is well to char about two feet of the lower end of the pole, inserting eighteen inches only in the ground. The advantage of larch poles for Pillar Roses is, the rustic appearance they present, relieving the often-tiring niceties of the Rose Garden : the advantage of iron supports is their durability.

Two or more plants of different colours are sometimes placed together, and their branches so interwoven that a pied pillar is formed. This, to my taste, is as objectionable as two sorts on one stem, and the effect is not equal to that produced by plants of opposing colours placed side by side. Pillar Roses require more manure than others. In addition to the supply granted in spring when the soil is forked over, it is necessary to give a second supply in June, just after the plants have flowered, as recommended for the Autumnals. Pillar Roses are often found bare of branches and flowers at their base, due, usually, to their having been carried up too quickly, or to poverty of soil. To remedy this defect, reduce their height when pruning, and enrich the soil, when eyes will be developed at the base, and the upward growth may be again encouraged.

The Weeping Rose (No. 36) is the last form of which we have to speak. Can any thing be more beautiful? In windy situations an iron trellis is indispensable : in sheltered places a hoop, as shewn in No. 19, is sufficient. It accelerates the perfecting of the Weeping Rose to thin out the supernumerary shoots in July, after the tree has flowered. We advise cutting off the flower-stalks in all cases so soon as the flowers have decayed ; for in addition to the neat appearance it gives to the Rose Garden, it prevents the formation of seeds, which, when suffered to ripen, draw to themselves that matter which should be stored in the branches.

After worked Roses have been planted some years—say from six to ten—the health of the plants often becomes impaired ; the wood annually produced grows weaker and weaker, and does not attain that maturity and size necessary for the production of fine flowers. The stems, unless washed occasionally, become covered with moss and lichens, and, if the soil be at all inferior, they probably cease to swell. Too little pruning will produce this state of things ; but there are other causes. If we carefully remove a tree in this condition, we shall find it abounds in large sucker-like roots, about

No. 36.

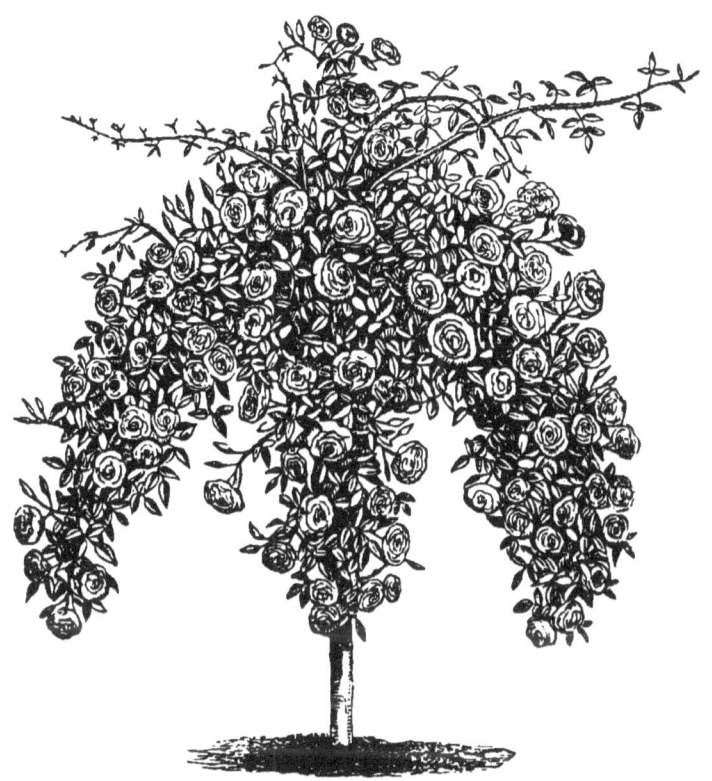

Weeping Rose.

the thickness of one's little finger, almost destitute of fibre, and which have been burying themselves deeper and deeper in the earth every succeeding year. Thus they become placed farther and farther from the reach of nourishment, while the tree, increasing in size, requires a greater supply. The consequence is, the tree dwindles and becomes debilitated. This is especially the case when deep planting has been practised. When this state of things is visible, the plants should either be root pruned, or, which is better, taken up altogether and replanted. Let this be done *early in the autumn;* and when the plants are out of the ground *cut off all the suckers,* and shorten the roots moderately close, which will induce an abundant emission of fibres. Prune the heads closely *in spring:* never mind sacrificing the flowers: the removal of trees of this age, and the shortening of the roots, would alone prevent a perfect flowering the first season : look only to the formation of the tree. It is, perhaps, not advisable to remove the whole at once : let ·a few be thus treated every year; for the second year after replanting, having regained their vigour, they may be expected to flower as beautifully as ever. Every Rose-tree should be named. Wooden labels answer very well. They should be three-quarters of an inch wide, three inches long, and about the eighth of an inch in thickness. In one end of these a hole may be pierced with an awl, and copper wire passed through, by which they are fastened on the branches. Wooden labels are preferred for naming plants in the ground. If well painted, and *the names written with a dark pencil when the paint is wet*, the writing will remain plain for four or five years, and often much longer. When stuck in the ground, the lower end of the stick should be covered with pitch for an inch or so above the line of the level of the ground.

To have Roses in bloom during the chilly months of autumn is the greatest triumph of modern cultivators ; and perhaps this property of the Rose has recommended it to popular notice more than any other. Now, although we do not, in a general way, recommend summer-pruning, yet it is desirable to practise it to obtain late Roses. At the end of August 1846 I cut back the main shoots of about thirty sorts of Autumnals, when the flower-buds were about as large as a French bean ; and on the 17th of November I gathered flowers as fine as I had ever seen in summer. Some *buds*, which were gathered at the same time and placed in a vase in a warm room, continued to unfold for several days. It is especially necessary to remove decaying flowers during autumn, as, from the moisture they retain at that time, they cause the rapid decay of those which surround them : a pair of scissors is very useful for this purpose.

It is an excellent plan to wash the stems of Rose-trees in the winter, which is a time of leisure in the garden. A mixture of cow-dung, soot, and lime, two parts of the latter to one of each of the former, serves for this purpose. This will destroy insects which may have sought shelter in the crevices of the bark, and also the moss and lichens which often grow there. It will further soften the bark and favour the swelling of the stem.

It is not an infrequent occurrence that the pith of a shoot decays from an old wound in pruning, leaving the living wood hollow like a flute. It is well to place on the end of such shoots a little of the composition used in grafting (see " Grafting"), which will exclude the wet, shut up one hiding-place of insects, and preserve the branch from decay.

As winter approaches, it is necessary to devise some means of protection against frost for those kinds which are susceptible of its influences : such are, the Tea-scented and some of the Chinese and Noisette. It is surprising what a little shelter suffices : branches of the common fern, which grows plentifully on most wilds, answer for the purpose, as do laurel or fir-boughs : the latter, having a more lively appearance, are preferable. They should be stuck *loosely* among the plants, if dwarfs, that the air may circulate freely ; if standards, a branch or two may be placed in and round the heads, securing them in the most favourable position by a tie with bast. All the Tea Roses form beautiful objects as Standards : the only objection to the culture of many, as such, is their extreme tenderness. I have often thought this difficulty might be overcome by the use of bee-hives. Drive three stakes into the ground triangularly ; on these nail a board with a hole cut in one side extending to the centre, that the stem of the tree may be drawn in so that the head rests immediately upon the board ; fasten it there, and then place a hive over the head. This will undoubtedly form sufficient protection for the tenderest : it is not very troublesome or expensive ; and if the hives are painted they are not unsightly, and their durability is increased. The framework may remain during winter ; the hives are required in frosty weather only. In March this protection may be withdrawn, at which time the tender Roses may be pruned. Intense cold doubtless kills many tender kinds *when left wholly unprotected ;* and the alternations of frost and thaw are often severely destructive to plants on their own roots, raising them out of the ground, and exposing their roots to the drying winds of spring. In the winter of 1846-47 I witnessed many die from the latter cause, which had been uninjured by the severe frost. To prevent these consequences, a little fresh soil should be thrown over the roots immediately after a thaw, and, when the ground is tolerably dry, press it firmly around the stems.

CHAPTER XI.

ON PROPAGATION.

THE Rose is capable of being propagated, 1. by seed; 2. by cuttings; 3. by budding; 4. by grafting; 5. by layers; and 6. by suckers.

The first method, which is adopted only as a means of obtaining new varieties, has been already fully entered into, and needs no further notice here.

2. *By Cuttings.*—Cuttings may be made, with varied success, at any time. The seasons which offer the greatest advantages are summer and autumn; but where there is a house of forced Roses cuttings may also be taken from March to May. Let us first offer a few remarks on summer propagation. Immediately after the plants have flowered, select well-ripened shoots, of moderate strength, taking care not to remove any whose loss would destroy the symmetry of the plants. In taking off the cuttings they should be cut close to the old wood, with a heel, as it is technically termed, which increases their chance of rooting. The cutting, of which No. 37 is a representation, should be made from two to three inches long, consisting of from three to five joints. An inch at least of the lower end should be inserted in the soil, and the part left above should have two good leaves. From four to six of these cuttings may be placed round the inside of a large 60 pot, in a compost consisting of equal parts of leaf mould, turfy loam chopped fine, and silver sand. After insertion, they should be well watered through a fine-rose pot, to settle the mould closely around them. When the soil is drained and the leaves dry, the pots may be removed to a cold frame, or placed under hand-glasses, keeping them closed from the air and shaded from the sun, sprinkling them twice daily for the first fortnight. The sprinkling usually keeps the soil sufficiently moist, though it is sometimes necessary to give water in addition. We need scarcely say that the leaves should be retained on the cuttings as long as possible; but if they decay they should be removed immediately, or the contagion spreads, and numbers may be sacrificed. Where damping or fogging-off occurs, the admission of air or more sunlight proves the best remedy.

No. 37.

A Cutting.

In about a fortnight after the cuttings are made they will have formed callus, when they should be removed to a pit with bottom-heat. Here they root quickly, and may be potted off singly into small or large 60 pots, according to their strength. Place them in bottom heat again for a few days, and they become established, when they may be removed to a cold frame, and air gradually admitted to harden them. " But," says the Amateur, "is bottom heat indispensable? I have no bottom heat; or, at least, I have but little, and to that a variety of plants lays claim. There are my Azaleas, my Geraniums, my Fuchsias, my Cinerarias; they require all the room of this kind that I have. Surely Roses, hardy plants as they are, will strike without bottom heat." We answer, "They will." We do not say this condition is indispensable, but advantageous: they may be kept in the cold till rooted, or indeed throughout the year.

But there is another season at which propagation may be carried on with success, namely, autumn, just before the fall of the leaf. In June the Autumnals only need be cared for; now, both the Summer and Autumn kinds demand attention. Among the latter, the Bourbon, Tea Noisette, Chinese, and Tea-scented should be placed in rows under a hand-glass, or round pots in a closed frame, for few of these do well planted as cuttings in the open ground. The hand-glass should be lifted off occasionally on a bright day

L 2

during winter, to dry the dampness of the soil, when any decayed leaves or cuttings may be removed. Water, under these circumstances, is rarely required till spring, though if worms be troublesome in raising the earth, a little lime-water may be given, supposing the soil to be well drained, which is a point of primary importance. These cuttings will not be rooted till April, when they may be taken up and potted, and placed in a frame for a few days, kept close, shaded, and syringed. Now for what purpose are the plants required? Are they wanted for pot-culture? or is planting out the end in view? If the former, treat them as recommended in the chapter On the Cultivation of Roses in Pots: if the latter, plant them out in May. Cuttings of the hardy kinds, such as the Hybrids of the Chinese and Bourbon, the Boursault, the Ayrshire, the Evergreen, the Multiflora, and the Hybrid Perpetual, may be planted in beds in the open grounds. By October there will be plenty of well-matured wood on the old plants, and judicious thinning will benefit rather than injure them. The cuttings in this instance should all be made with heels, by which rule only one cutting can be made from a shoot. The tops may be used, but they are not so likely to take root. The cuttings here must be longer than those placed in pots, to allow of their being firmly fixed in the ground. Nine inches to a foot is a fair length, and two or three eyes should remain above ground. When prepared, the best method of planting them is to dig the soil, cutting down a trench every nine inches, in which a row is inserted at about an inch apart from cutting to cutting. A few boughs should afterwards be stuck rather thickly between every two rows, to accomplish the double purpose of shielding them from the sun and to prevent the ground from becoming frozen very hard. Branches of some evergreens should be used, and as the leaves fall they should be cleared away, or a dampness will be engendered, resulting in loss. The branches may remain till spring, and after their removal it will be well to hoe the soil to loosen the surface. After this, it will be seen which are on a fair way to make plants: the others should be removed, to give the prosperous ones a full chance of success, and plenty of room to grow. Here they must remain till autumn, when they may be conveyed to any position they are destined to fill.

But we have alluded to another season at which propagating by cuttings may take place, and which requires a few passing remarks: this is from March to May, when the cuttings are taken from plants that have been forced. They are treated in the same manner as related of June cuttings, excepting that the latter are first placed in a cold frame, and the former are placed in bottom heat at once. Cuttings so made strike very readily; yet we apprehend this plan is least of all suited for the Amateur. First, it involves the necessity of keeping the cuttings and plants in bottom heat for six weeks or two months in the spring; a time when, to the generality of cultivators, heat can ill be spared. And then it is questionable whether, by such culture, we obtain the robust, hardy-constitutioned plants that we do by raising in the open air, or with merely bottom heat at rooting time.

3. *By Budding.*—Before we enter upon the detail of this practice, let us note a few thoughts respecting stocks.

The kinds most commonly used are, the Dog-rose, the Boursault, and the Manetti. The former abounds in the hedges throughout Europe, where it delights us with its delicately-tinted blossoms in June and July. It is, however, a bad subject there, and all who value a good fence will rejoice over its removal. There cannot be a good hedge where the Dog-rose abounds. The autumn is the best time to remove them, and a mattock is the fittest instrument for the purpose. Before replanting in the garden the roots should be trimmed close with a bill, bruising them as little as possible in the operation, and the tops shortened of various lengths, according to their size or straightness. The Boursault and Manetti Rose may be either struck from cuttings made in autumn, or purchased at the nurseries. The crimson Boursault is allowable as a stock for Tea-scented and Chinese Roses intended for pot-culture. The Manetti is desirable for Roses in pots, and admissible for hardy kinds when an extremely vigorous growth is desired. The latter has been recommended for kinds of delicate growth, which do not thrive well on the Dog-rose, but *my* experience does not uphold the recommendation. If a change of stock is necessary for such, it would seem that one *of a finer, not coarser nature* than the Dog-rose should be employed. That the plants grow more vigorously on the Manetti *the first year* we do not deny, *but their subsequent decline is also more rapid.*

As the stocks shoot forth in spring they will sometimes produce buds from the base to the top: all should be removed but two or three nearest the summit. Three placed triangularly are best, when the two lower ones—which should range on opposite sides—may be budded, and the upper one cut away so soon as the stranger buds are developed.

The operation of budding consists in transferring from one tree a small piece of bark containing an embryo bud, and inserting it beneath the bark of another tree. This piece of bark is called the bud, *d*: the tree in which it is inserted is called the stock. The only implement necessary in the operation is the budding-knife, of

No. 38.

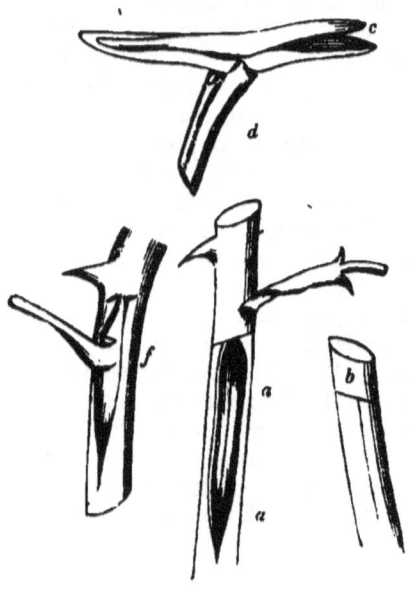

Budding.

which there are various forms, but that called Curtis's is perhaps
the best.   Let us suppose we have a stock which we are wishing to
convert into some favourite variety.   In the first place, obtain a
shoot from the tree whose identity we wish it to bear; from this the
leaves are cut off, leaving, however, about half an inch of the leaf-
stalk to every bud.   Before proceeding farther, the prickles should
· be rubbed off both stock and scion, that they may not interfere
with the operation, or annoy the fingers of the operator.   Now
take the budding-knife in the right hand and make a longitudinal
cut, *a a*, about an inch in length, terminated at the top end, *b*,
with a cross-cut.   In using the knife, take care not to cut too deep :
through the bark is all that is necessary; deeper is, indeed, injurious.   Now turn the handle of the knife to the incision, running
it up and down the cut *a a*, twisting it slightly on either side
to raise the bark.   All is now ready for the reception of the
stranger bud.   Take the shoot which is to furnish it in the left
hand, with the thicker part towards the finger-ends.   With the
knife in the right hand commence cutting about half an inch behind the bud, passing the knife upwards under the bud, and to

about the same distance beyond it. The knife should have a keen edge, that the bark may not be ruffled in the operation. In cutting out the bud, the knife should pass through almost level: it may, however, in some cases, dip a trifle when passing directly under the bud, as the wood before and behind it are not always on the same level. If the bud be cut ever so skilfully there will be a little of the wood adhere thereto. This some advise the removal of; others say, let it remain. Much depends on circumstances. If the shoot is not fully ripe, or if, from the nature of the variety, the wood is soft when taken, cut the bud as shallow as possible, and place it, with the wood, in the stock. But the shoot is usually firm and ripe, and then the wood should be withdrawn. To do this easily, place the bud between the forefinger and thumb of the left hand, with the cut uppermost, and with the upper end pointing from the hand. Insert the point of the knife just beneath the wood, c— that is, between the wood and the bark—and by a skilful twist of the knife, which can only be acquired by practice, the wood may be jerked out. Now, with the same hand place the bud on the bark of the stock parallel with the longitudinal incision, and with the upper end towards the top of the shoot; then with the handle of the knife raise the bark on the side opposite to that on which the bud is placed, pushing two-thirds of the bud beneath the bark with the thumb. Now raise the bark on the opposite side, and the bud may be gently pushed under with the handle of the knife, or will probably drop in. When properly placed, the eye of the bud should be directly under the opening caused by the raising of the edges of the bark of the longitudinal incision f: if it be not so, the handle of the budding-knife should be inserted beneath the bark, to push it to a right position. But if the bud be not deprived of the leaf-stalk, if that is allowed to protrude from the opening, the eye will be secured in the best site. After being inserted, the bud should be drawn upwards to the cross-cut, and the upper end cut at the same angle, that its bark may abut against the bark of the stock laid open by the cross-cut b. The bud then is inserted, and it now remains to bind it in. For this purpose take cotton or bast; the former is generally preferred. Commence tying at the bottom of the cut, passing upwards till the whole length of the incision is bound over. Where the buds are feeble, or where success is deemed important, it is customary to tie a little damp moss or a leaf over the bud after the operation is completed, which is in no case objectionable, except on account of the additional time it occupies.

About three weeks after the operation has been performed the cotton may be removed. If the bud is not well united, let it be tied up *loosely* again: if it is, leave it untied, and there is an end of care till the following spring. In February the wild shoot may be cut away two inches beyond the bud, when the latter will break, and soon form a tree. It is often said that it is unnecessary for the bud to remain so long dormant, and that it may be made to break; and, if an Autumnal Rose, even to flower the same year. We admit the truth of this statement, but condemn the practice. It is accomplished by cutting off the wild shoot a few inches above the bud, or by tying a ligature tightly round it at the same distance. The object sought is, to cut off certain channels through which the sap naturally flows, that it may become concentrated in the vicinity of the bud. The results are, usually, premature development, and an unsound plant. Let a certain number of plants be treated thus, and allow the buds inserted in others to lie dormant till spring: defer judgment for one year, and see, at the expiration of that term, which form the healthier and sounder plants. Unquestionably the latter. If the buds break soon after inserted the shoots are puny and weakly, evidently suffering from want of nourishment; if allowed to lie dormant till spring, they have a rich store of food at their command, and grow with surprising vigour. When a bud has shot a few inches, and formed three or four good leaves, the heart of the shoot may be pinched out, when, from the axil of each leaf, an eye will in time push forth. In May the stock may be headed down close to where the bud has been inserted, and if the growth be vigorous the wound made in so doing will quickly cicatrize, and a perfect plant is the result.

If the best time for budding be demanded, we should give July. It does not, however, require great penetration to see that this point depends in some measure on the season. The practised hand will cut and raise the bark to ascertain when it parts freely from the wood; the tyro will find a criterion in the prickles. If slight pressure cause them to separate from the bark, the stocks are in good order, and the fitness of the shoots or scions may be ascertained by the same test. If the weather be hot and sunny, morning and evening are the best periods for budding. A July sun pouring down his rays upon the operator is not altogether pleasant, and, in regard to the operation, does not increase the chances of success. The shoot from which the buds are to be taken should not be cut from the tree till we are ready for action; and the less time that elapses between the different branches of the work the better: the bud should be cut out, inserted, and tied immediately.

The Wild-roses are sometimes budded in the hedges where they grow, which is called " Hedge-budding." If it be intended to remove them afterwards to the Flower-garden the practice is not worthy of attention : it is far better *to transfer them* as stocks*, and bud those which grow after removal. But if done with the view of ornamenting parks, &c., by leaving the plants in the hedges, the idea is a good one. Bud them as heretofore described, taking care to eradicate suckers, which usually arise in great abundance, and soon starve the plants if left unchecked.

4. *Grafting.*—It is sometimes asked whether grafted Roses are equal to budded ones? When the junction becomes perfect they are quite as good, but the scion and stock do not always thoroughly coalesce ; owing to which, more imperfect plants are raised by this mode than by any other.

In selecting stocks for grafting, whether they be Manetti, Boursault, or Dog-roses, they should be secured of various sizes ; the majority, however, about the thickness of an ordinary cedar-pencil. It is well to pot them in 60-sized pots one year before required for use. The best time for grafting Roses in pots is January, and the stocks should be placed in bottom heat a week or ten days beforehand. *All kinds will succeed* grafted, but the hard-wooded ones do the best. The forms most generally practised are, 1. Cleft-grafting, 2. Wedge-grafting, and 3. Whip-grafting.

No. 39.

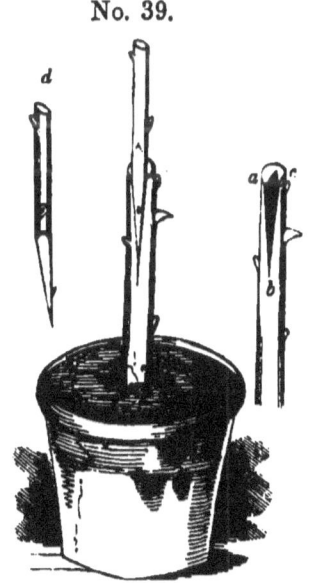

Cleft-grafting.

1. Cleft-grafting.—We shall first describe and illustrate this mode, and afterwards refer briefly to the others. Here the stocks should be larger than the scions. The latter, which may be taken from the plants as required for use, should be well-ripened shoots, cut into lengths of about an inch and a half. The tops of shoots are seldom fitted for scions; two-thirds of their length is, generally speaking, as much as can be used with advantage. Each scion should have two, three, or four buds : two are sufficient to produce a fine plant. In performing the operation, first cut the stock quite level at the top ; then insert the point of the knife at a, drawing it down towards the root in an oblique direction. Now make a corresponding cut, commencing at c, so that the two cuts terminate in a point b. Thus a piece of the stock is cut out, and the opening made is in the form of the letter V. With regard to the width and length of the cut, this must be regulated by the size of the grafts in hand : as to depth, the wound should not extend quite so far as the centre or pith of the stock. The piece being removed, the scion d must be cut to fill up the vacuity ; and the better it does this the greater is the chance of success. The most essential point is, *to bring the inner bark of the scion in exact contact with the inner bark of the stock.* When the scion is fitted in, it should be bound securely there with soft bast. It is then necessary to cover the place of junction with some composition that will effectually exclude air and water. For this purpose, take the following ingredients: five-eighths black pitch, one-eighth each of bees'-wax, tallow, and resin. Put them together in a glue-pot and melt them down over a slow fire. The best way of laying on the composition is by the use of a flat stick. It is not necessary to cover the whole of the bandage. Take care, however, that the lines where the barks join—indeed whatever part the wound extends to—be rendered impervious to air and moisture. The wound at the top of the stock should be covered, and also the summit of the scion. Care must be taken not to apply the composition too hot, or the bark will be scalded, and success rendered doubtful. A good way to test its fitness for use is, to place a little on the finger of the operator, when, if it does not cause any unpleasant sensation, it may be used without fear. This composition, though soft and pliable in a warm state, becomes hard and impenetrable when cold.

2. Wedge-grafting.—This is more simple than the foregoing. In many points the modes of procedure are the same : we have only to notice the differences. Instead of inserting the scion in one side of the stock, we here split the stock down the centre to the extent of an inch or so, and insert the graft in the slit. In preparing the graft, pare off equal parts from two opposite sides, that the lower

end may be in the form of a wedge. Push the wedge in the slit of the stock, binding it firmly in, and covering with the composition as before.

3. Whip-grafting.—It is not important here that the stock and scion be of the same size. The former should be cut level at the top, as before, to within a few inches of the base : both should be cut in an oblique direction, taking care to make the cuts smooth and even, and of the same length and slope, that the bark of the scion may lie exactly upon the bark of the stock. In laying the scion on, it is a good plan to hold the pot containing the stock in the left-hand, and the knife must occupy the right. Insert the knife an inch or an inch and a half below, drawing it up obliquely to, the summit. In making this cut, do not remove more than one-fourth of the diameter of the stock. Care must be taken to prevent the knife twisting, or the consequence will be an unlevel cut. The stock being prepared, take the scion in the left hand, giving an eye to the size of the piece of wood removed from the stock : while in this position, pass the knife downwards, repeating the movement till a clean level cut is made, and the size of the lower end such that it may, when united to the stock, exactly replace the part removed. Thus, if one-third of the stock is removed, supposing that and the scion to be of equal dimensions, two-thirds of the latter must be cut away. The unpractised eye and hand will not always be able to fit the stock by the first cut; and as it is important that the two barks should join, he may have to take a second or a third slice from one or the other. Well, he had better do so than leave the stock and scion badly placed. But the less of this hacking work the better. It is far easier to make a clean and level cut *by a single draw of the knife*, than by the most delicate after touches. When the scion is placed in a right position, it should be securely held there by the thumb and fingers of the left hand until it is bound firmly on the stock with the right. With regard to the treatment of the newly-grafted plants, if the stocks have been in bottom-heat before grafting, they must remain there ; if taken from the open air, bottom-heat is not absolutely necessary, although it will increase the amount of success. Suckers are sure to spring from the stocks, and they often do so in an annoying abundance. They must be kept in check by pinching out their tops till the stock and scion are firmly united, and the latter pushed into growth, when they may be entirely eradicated.

When the scions first shoot the young leaves are very tender, especially when developed in heat. In most cases, too, they are but ill supplied with food in this early stage of growth, and shading is especially necessary. A strong current of air, or a hot sun, will injure them greatly. When the shoots are two or three inches long, the plants that have been grown in heat may be removed to a cold frame, where air should be admitted gradually, to harden them. Some will bloom the same year; but they should not be left to flower in heat, or they become drawn and weakly, producing thin and badly-coloured flowers.

It is advisable to remove the ligature in grafted Roses, and this should be done so soon as we suppose, by the growth of the scion, that the union is complete. If, when untied, the junction is not perfected, a single tie at top and bottom is sufficient to render all secure.

In plants grafted out of doors the composition should not be removed for two or three months; and that which covers the summits of the stock and scion may remain till it naturally disappears.

In reference to grafting Standard Roses, as they are invariably done in the open air, March is the best season. As fine and mild a day as March is likely to afford should be chosen. Grafting requires at all times an ordinary share of patience and perseverance; and if the practitioner be not possessed of more than an ordinary share, he had better not attempt it out of doors on a true March day; for to be kept in one position five minutes at a time, with a cold wind whistling round one's ears, is a trial of no common order. What a contrast between this and budding in a sultry July day! In grafting Standard Roses, the stock is of course considerably larger than the scion, and Cleft-grafting is the mode I have pursued with the greatest success.

In grafted plants, as in budded ones, if the buds or eyes be allowed their natural course they break and form long single shoots. If these are stopped so soon as they have three or four good healthy leaves, a bud from the axil of each leaf will be developed, and a round bushy plant is formed.

5. *Layers.*—This mode of propagating is not so commonly resorted to as the others. Dwarf or bush Roses only are commonly layered. It is first necessary to dig with a fork for some space around the bush, breaking the soil quite fine, mixing in a little pulverized manure in the operation. The instruments wanted are, a knife, a flat trowel, and some pegs. All things being ready, select some of the best shoots, stripping off a few of the leaves at a distance varying from six inches to two feet from the point of the shoot *a a*. Now take the shoot in the left hand, and the knife in the right: insert the latter just beyond an eye *b*, on the upper side of the shoot, and pass it upwards steadily and evenly, cutting about half through the shoot, and for an inch and a half or two inches in length. This done, drop the knife and take the trowel. With the left hand bend the shoot close to the ground, that you may see the

No. 40.

Layering.

best spot in which to bury it, drive the trowel into the ground, working it backwards and forwards till a good opening is made, throw a little sand in the bottom of the opening, and press the shoot into it, pegging it down two or three inches under the soil. It is well to twist the shoot a little after the cut is made, so that the end of the *tongue*—as it is technically termed (*b*)—from which the roots will be emitted, may take a downward direction. Having made all secure, close in the soil, pressing it firmly round about the layer. It is a good plan to give each layer a small stick (*c*), to keep it from being agitated by the motion of the wind. As to the length of the shoot that should remain above ground, much will depend on the state of the wood. We should make the cut or tongue in wood that is young, yet firm. The larger the layer, of course the larger will be the plant, though not always the better rooted: the contrary is often the case. June, July, and August, are the months for layering; and should the weather continue dry, the layers should be occasionally watered. If layered in June and July, the free rooters will be ready to take off in November. It is well, however, to examine one or two of each kind, to ascertain this point, as some root in an amazingly short space, others advance very slowly. When rooted they may be cut off within an inch or two of the tongue, taken up, and transplanted into beds, or to various spots in the garden. In the spring they may be cut down to within three or four eyes, and some of them will bloom in the first summer or autumn. Their after treatment is the same as that of other Roses.

6. *Suckers.*—This is the least artificial of the artificial modes, though the Rose is not so much *inclined* to multiply itself by suckers as are many plants. The Scotch Rose (R. SPINOSISSIMA) is perhaps, next to the Dog-rose, most given to this peculiarity. It pushes its shoots along under the ground, and they break through the surface at various distances. It is not very often they can be separated from the parent with roots ; yet the underground stems will put forth roots, if carefully severed and transplanted. The autumn is the best time for doing this, and a spade with a sharp edge is the fittest instrument for the purpose.

CHAPTER XII.

ON TEA-SCENTED ROSES.

Some one has called these flowers the *élite* of the Rose-world. And if elegance of form, with tints and odours rare as they are delicate, entitle them to this distinction, it was a happy thought, for they possess these in a remarkable degree. There is a sprightliness of bearing, a careless grace in plant and flower that is without parallel among the most distinguished of other groups. Look at that long primrose-coloured bud of the Jaune just unfolding, how exquisitely the petals are arranged. Can any thing surpass in fragrance those half-expanded flowers of Madame de St. Joseph? What a treasury of beauty is presented to the eye and mind by the myriads of apricot-coloured blossoms clustering upon that pyramid of Safrano! The large snowy blossoms of Niphetos, too, are nowhere equalled, and Adam, Comte de Paris, Devoniensis, President, Souvenir d'un Ami, and many others, can hardly be too highly commended.

But beautiful as these Roses sometimes are in favourable soils and situations out of doors, they must be grown under glass to ensure a constant development of flowers in that state of perfection to which they are capable of attaining.

Some years ago, in Paxton's Magazine of Botany, I called attention to the culture of Tea-scented Roses under glass. Convinced, by experiments already tried, that a house of Tea-roses would prove an interesting feature in these Nurseries, and tempted by the reasonable rate at which such a structure might be built, I erected here, two years since, a house expressly for the purpose. It has a span roof, sloping to the east and west. It is 50 feet long, 20 feet wide, 10 feet from the ridge to the ground, with lights opening at the top and sides. There is a bed all round the inside next the walls, and a bed in the centre, and a walk between the centre and side beds. The beds are raised a few inches above the level of the walk, the edgings of which are of four-inch brickwork : the house is not heated, and the entire cost was under £50.

Conceiving that it may be interesting to the uninitiated to follow the details of this system of culture, I shall here endeavour to describe my practice as clearly and briefly as possible.

The house was finished the first week in June. Before planting, the natural soil was loosened one spit deep, and the beds afterwards filled to the top of the brickwork with a prepared compost of turfy loam, decayed manure, and washed road-sand. Early in July, when the newly-placed earth had become solid, I planted all the really valuable varieties of Tea-scented Roses, and among them a few high-coloured Hybrid Perpetuals and Bourbons to increase the variety. The kinds of climbing habit were placed against the walls, with the view of training them up the rafters in the way of vines : in the centre bed, under the ridge, were planted the robust growers, that they might rise to the top and spread along the ridge ; the dwarf and moderate-growing kinds were, lastly, planted next the walks, with the view of fashioning them into pyramids. When all were planted, the earth, which had become rather dry, was thoroughly soaked with water.

It was with me a leading idea to preserve the temperature of the house similar to that out of doors. But as the sun had more power and the wind less, and as dew was altogether excluded here, I endeavoured to neutralise the excess of sun-power, and to realise the advantages of the other natural aids to growth, by admitting abundance of air, by frequent syringings and occasional waterings on the floor of the house. As the plants were in a growing state when planted out, the growth continued unchecked, and flowers were sufficiently plentiful till the end of November, when the plants were brought to a state of rest by withholding moisture from the air and soil. Early in February the plants were cut in rather close, and the surface of the soil was stirred with a hand-fork, the lights being left open night and day, except in frosty weather till the beginning of March. By this time the buds had begun to break, when less air was admitted, and frequent syringings resorted to. The green-fly was kept in check by the combustion of tobacco-paper. On the first appearance of mildew the plants were dusted all over with sulphur immediately after syringing, and this dusting was repeated at brief intervals throughout the year. With May the blooming season arrived. So vigorous had been the growth, that some shoots reached the top of the house the first year, and now completely overarched the walks. To look up at them from beneath was a delight as new as it was pleasurable. Large handsome flowers, supported by a profusion of beautiful green leaves, hung drooping as if to meet the eye, which might range at pleasure from their circumference to their very centre, while the air was laden with their delicious perfume. Never before had I really *seen* Tea-roses. I had often *looked at* them as they hung drooping from the bushes out of doors, and raised the flowers individually to trace their outline and varied colours, but this conveys no idea of the effect produced by masses of these lovely flowers so disposed that all their beauty is seen and comprehended at a glance. I do not remember that any thing in the whole range of my horticultural experience ever afforded me more gratification and delight than this house of Tea-scented Roses.

It should be remarked, that the plants and house were kept scrupulously clean throughout the year. Falling blossoms, decaying leaves, weeds, and every other source of impurity were cleared away at least once a week. The soil, too, was often stirred, and, whenever it became dry, thoroughly watered with rain-water.

The reader will have already seen that my object in this attempt was not to obtain *forced*, but *early* Roses. No heating apparatus was employed, because I did not want Roses here till May. But with the aid of hot-water, and a slightly modified system of culture as regards the time of resting the plants and after pruning, flowers may be had in March, as easily as in May.

Tea-scented Roses may also be grown to advantage in pots. The light soil recommended in our chapter on Roses in Pots is most favourable to their growth, and in this state care must be taken that they are neither over-potted nor over watered. They also require less pruning when in a young state than the Hybrid Perpetual and other hard-wooded Roses.

Those who have light dry soils, and sheltered situations, may grow the Tea-scented Roses out of doors ; but under such treatment they should be invariably protected from the winter's frost. One of the hardiest of this race is also one of the freest and most beautiful,—Gloire de Dijon,—and there are different degrees of hardihood amongst the various kinds. Some recommend taking these plants up every autumn, and placing them in a sheltered spot to be replanted in spring. Others have said, protect them where they stand by encircling them with fir or furze-branches. We regard these as mere make-shift appliances, uncertain in their results, and not likely to prove entirely satisfactory to the skilled cultivator. If Tea-roses must be grown out of doors, bud them plentifully every year, and a goodly number will, in this dormant state, pass securely through nineteen out of twenty of our winters. It is here the lover of Tea-roses should look for the chief supply of flowers out of doors.

M

CHAPTER XIII.

ON NEW ROSES.

In the winter of 1856-57 I found myself unexpectedly involved in a controversy in the pages of " The Gardeners' Chronicle," on the respective merits of new and old Roses. My opponents fought valiantly and well, all honour to the brave ! Some were sharp, others witty, and, as is usually the case in such controversies, a great deal was said which had nothing to do with the question at issue.

I then asserted, that every year brings forth some novelties well worth adding to our collections, though it may be difficult to pick out the few real gems from amongst the shoals of mere paste imitations with which they are so skilfully commingled.

It was the opinion of those who were best versed in Rose-culture, that my position was not only tenable, but strong, although it was difficult—nay, impossible—to demonstrate this otherwise than by the test of time. That time has now passed, and established the general truth of my argument. General Jacqueminot, and Gloire de Dijon were then unproved ; and since then we have added Anna de Diesbach, Beauty of Waltham, Comtesse de Chabrillant, Duc de Cazes, Empereur de Maroc, François Premier, General Washington, Gloire de Santenay, Lord Raglan, Louis XIV., Madame Boll, Madame C. Crapelet, Madame Furtado, Mdlle. Bonnaire, Senateur Vaisse, Triomphe d'Alençon, Victor Verdier, and—shall I go on, or content myself with saying, a host of others scarcely less noteworthy. Without entering further on this subject, I would refer those of my readers who may take an interest in it to the Gardeners' Chronicle of 1856-57.

Let me first bring under notice the novelties of 1861-62, of which we have some actual knowledge ; and I state fearlessly, at the outset, that this was the richest freight of new Roses that ever reached our shores in a single year. I find, on reference to my note-book, that I bought sixty-two new kinds that year, fifty-six of which bloomed with me, and twenty-four of these I have marked as decided acquisitions.

Charles Lefebre is a glorious Rose, with flowers of a rich glowing crimson, shaded with maroon, of good petal and perfect outline, cupped, of large size, full, and particularly solid-looking.

Duc de Rohan is a large and very bright vermilion-coloured Rose, full, and of globular form, of vigorous growth and handsome foliage.

Emile Dulac is a rose-coloured variety, with large, full, and deeply-cupped flowers, the best of this strain that I have yet met with.

François Lacharme is a large full flower, of rosy-crimson hue and good form, the colour peculiarly rich and fulgent.

Gloire de Chatillon is an expanded Rose, of immense size, and truly magnificent : the colours are the same as in Madame Masson —crimson and purple shaded. It has been said by some to be too near the latter to be desirable, but if it maintain the character it has acquired here it will certainly surpass that old favourite.

La Brillante is a cupped, large, and *almost* double Rose. The colour is of the most bewitching rosy scarlet when the flowers first unfold, but is withal so fleeting that it scarcely waits the breath of the fire-king to tarnish its beauty. It should be looked for early in the morning of a cloudy day.

Louise Darzins is a very distinct Rose, of first-rate properties : the flowers are pure white, large enough, nicely cupped, and quite full ; the shoots are thorny, the growth vigorous, and the flowers, which are produced in great abundance, resemble those of Madame Hardy.

Mrs. Charles Wood is a large showy Rose, of free habit; the flowers are vinous crimson, cupped and full; the petals large, of good form and substance.

Madame Ernest Dreol has rosy pink flowers, of more than average size, and has probably sprung from between Baronne Prevost and Alexandrine Bachemeteff, but is a brighter, thicker, and more solid-looking flower than either.

Madame Julie Daran figured conspicuously at the Exhibitions of the past year, and appears a good hardy Rose. The flowers are sometimes dull in colour, but, when in their usual dress of glossy vermilion, their large size, fulness, and globular form, render them very attractive.

Marechal Vaillant is a large, full, well-formed Rose, with fine purplish-red flowers, the reverse of the outer petals glaucous red : it is an abundant bloomer, with handsome foliage.

Maurice Bernardin is, in my judgment, one of the best, ; the flowers are of the most beautiful vermilion, large, full, and well imbricated. I have seen hundreds of flowers of this Rose which fully support the above description.

Monte Christo was, with me, the most striking Rose of the season : the flowers are blackish purple, often dashed with scarlet, but not in such manner as to mar or destroy the evenness of colour, which resembles that of Alexandre Dumas, but the flower is larger, fuller, and of a superior build. We must add, the constitution of the plant seems any thing but hardy.

Olivier Delhomme is a large, full, crimson-coloured Rose, of perfect shape, well set off with handsome foliage.

Prince Camille de Rohan, although not a full Rose, possesses the quality of distinctness in an eminent degree ; the flowers are dark velvety maroon, shaded towards the circumference with blood-red : it is not of more than average size, but the colour is exceedingly rich and beautiful.

Professor Koch was quite first-class here ; the flowers are scarlet crimson, beautifully cupped, in the style of Coupe d'Hébé, the outline perfect, colour splendid. This will probably make a good Pot-Rose.

Robert Fortune produces large rosy-crimson cupped flowers, of a fine full colour, and appears likely to prove a good useful Rose : it is also very sweet.

Souvenir de Lady Eardley is of the most vigorous growth, yielding an abundance of large, almost full, reddish-scarlet flowers.

Souvenir de M. Rousseau was one of the most beautiful in the forcing-house here last year ; the flowers are almost scarlet when first opening, gradually changing to crimson, shaded with maroon, very rich and velvety : the plant is of a nice compact habit, blooms freely, and the flowers remain on the plant a long time.

Souvenir de Comte Cavour, (Margottin), is a very effective Rose : the flowers are crimson shaded with black, large and full, of good form.

Triomphe de Guillot fils belongs to another group, being a Tea-scented Rose ; the flowers are white shaded with rose and salmon, very large, full, and sweet ; growth vigorous.

Turenne is unfortunately not very double, and the petals are often incurved during the summer flowering : it was, however, one of the most beautiful of the autumnal Roses, with large cherry-coloured flowers, composed of petals of great size and substance.

Wilhelm Pfitzer is less certain than some of the foregoing : the flowers are crimson maroon, shaded, large, almost full, and occasionally of splendid colour when newly expanded.

Beauty of Waltham, a seedling of my own raising, has more than equalled the description originally given of it ; the flowers are brilliant cerise, large and full, the petals beautifully imbricated in the way of Madame C. Crapelet. It is of vigorous growth, with splendid foliage ; sweet as the Provence, and hardy as the Dog-rose.

In addition to these, the following may be considered good useful Roses :—Alphonse Damaizin, Adolphe Noblet, Alexandre Dumas, Belle Chartronnaise, Bicolor incomparable, Charles Robin, Comtesse de Seguieur, Comtesse Ouvaroff, Christian Puttner, Eugene Bourcier, Gloire de Bordeaux, François Louvat, Madame Caillat, Mdlle. Claudine d'Offay, Madame Henriette Dubus, Marguerite Appert, Paul Feval, Reynolds Hole, Vicomte Vigier, Vulcain, &c. &c.

But of the Roses of the present year—the forthcoming brood—what expectations and interest cluster around them. Although I have seen the greater number of these varieties blooming in the hands of the raisers, and have made copious notes for temporary use, I should like to confirm these by growing the plants in the climate of England, before hazarding an opinion of their respective merits. Accordingly, I shall at present merely enumerate them, appending the raisers' descriptions, reserving for next year the task of re-describing and criticizing them.

1. *Alba Rosa* (Tea-scented), flowers white, centre rose, large, full, opening freely, and very sweet. A seedling from Devoniensis, of vigorous growth, flowering abundantly.

2. *Alfred de Rougemont* (H. P.), flowers crimson purple shaded with fine red, very bright, large, full, and well formed, growth vigorous.

3. *Amelia Mountclare* (Moss), flowers pale flesh, almost white, large, full, and produced abundantly, form fine, growth vigorous.

4. *Arthur Young* (Moss), flowers very dark purple, cupped, large, full, and well formed, growth vigorous.

5. *Baron Adolphe Rothschild*, (H. P.) flowers fiery red, often tipped with white, large, full, and well formed, growth vigorous, very effective.

6. *Baron Rothschild* (H. P.), flowers dark reddish carmine, some-times shaded with violet, very large, full, well formed, habit good, growth vigorous. A seedling from General Jacqueminot.

7. *Baronne Athalin* (H. P.), flowers slate colour, sometimes striped with white, large, full, and produced abundantly, habit good, growth vigorous.

8. *Baronne de Lassus de Saint Genies* (H. P.), flowers reddish cerise shaded with purple, large, of globular and perfect form.

9. *Beauté Française* (H. P.), flowers velvety violet red, the reverse of the petals fiery red, large, full, and well formed. A seedling from Lion des Combats.

10. *Belle des Massifs* (H. P.), flowers bright rose, the reverse of the petals paler rose, anemone-shaped, large, produced in clusters from June till November. Good for masses.

11. *Bellotte* (H. P.), flowers rosy flesh, of medium size, full, form perfect, growth vigorous.

12. *Blanche Simon* (Moss), flowers pure white, large and full, growth vigorous.

13. *Caravane de Nismes* (H. P.), flowers reddish scarlet, very large, and produced abundantly, habit good, growth vigorous.

14. *Colonel Soufflot* (H. P.), flowers bright fiery red, large, full, and produced abundantly.

15. *Comtesse de Brossard* (Tea-scented), flowers bright yellow, large, full, almost flat, produced abundantly, growth vigorous.

16. *Comtesse de Courcy* (H. P.), flowers rose shaded with red, of medium size, full, produced abundantly, growth vigorous.

17. *Comtesse de Polignac* (H. P.), flowers brilliant velvety red shaded with fiery red, colours superb, large and full, growth vigorous.

18. *Deuil de Prince Albert* (H. P.), flowers blackish crimson, shaded in the centre with fiery red, large, full, and well imbricated.

19. *Duc d'Anjou* (H. P.), flowers crimson shaded with dark red, imbricated, very large and full, growth vigorous.

20. *Duc de Bassano* (H. P.), flowers dark velvety crimson, cupped, large and full, growth vigorous.

21. *Emotion* (Bourbon), flowers white tinted with rose, of medium size, full, form perfect, colours exquisite, flowers abundant and prolonged, growth vigorous.

22. *Grandiflora* (H. P.), flowers clear brilliant red, exterior and reverse of petals bright rose, form and fragrance of the Cabbage Rose, very large and full, flowers freely, opens well, growth vigorous, habit good, with beautiful light green foliage.

23. *Gustave Rousseau* (H. P.), flowers Bishop's purple shaded with violet red, large, well imbricated, produced in clusters, form good, growth vigorous.

24. *Henri IV.* (H. P.), flowers bright purplish red, of medium size, full, produced abundantly.

25. *Henri Martin* (Moss), flowers brilliant red, large, full, and globular, growth vigorous.

26. *Hortense Blachette* (H. P.), flowers white with rosy centres, of medium size, full, growth vigorous.

27. *Imperatrice Maria Alexandrina* (H. P.), flowers white, medium size, full, form good, growth moderate.

28. *Jean Goujon* (H. P.), flowers beautiful clear red, large and

full, growth vigorous. A seedling from Triomphe de l'Exposition.

29. *John Hopper* (H. P.), flowers rose, crimson centres, reverse of petals purplish lilac, large and full, growth vigorous, foliage fine.

30. *La Esmeralda* (H. P.), flowers bright cherry colour, large, full, and of good form. A seedling from Jules Margottin, which it resembles in growth and habit.

31. *La Globuleuse* (H. P.), flowers pale glossy rose, globular, very large and full.

32. *La Tour de Crouy* (H. P.), flowers rose shaded with white, very large and full, growth vigorous.

33. *Lady Emily Peel* (H. P.), flowers white, bordered with carmine, of medium size, full, well shaped. Probably a good perpetual climbing Rose.

34. *Laurent Descours* (H. P.), flowers velvety purple, large, almost full, form globular, excellent for masses.

35. *L'Eclatante* (H. P.), flowers bright red changing to violet red, large, full, and of good form, colours and habit fine, growth vigorous.

36. *Le Juif errant* (H. P.), flowers blackish violet purple, large and full.

37. *Le Rhone* (H. P.), flowers vermilion, large, full, and well shaped, colour rich and brilliant, growth vigorous, excellent for masses.

38. *Lord Clyde* (H. P.), flowers scarlet crimson, deeply shaded, large and full, fine foliage and vigorous growth.*

39. *Lord Herbert* (H. P.), flowers rosy carmine, the petals reflexing at the summit in the way of Beauty of Waltham, large, full, finely formed, and altogether of first-rate excellence.†

40. *Lord Macaulay* (H. P.), flowers velvety crimson, in the way of General Jacqueminot, but brighter in colour, thicker in petal, and more double, habit good, foliage handsome.†

41. *Louise Margottin* (H. P.), flowers delicate satin-like rose, of medium size and excellent form. A seedling from Louise Odier.

42. *Madame Alfred de Rougemont* (H. P.), flowers pure white shaded with rose and carmine, large and full, shape of the Cabbage Rose.

43. *Madame Brianson* (H. P.), flowers reddish carmine shaded

---

* This Rose was raised from seed by me, when partner and manager of the Roses in the late firm of "Adam Paul and Son," and not by the present firm of "Paul and Son," as represented in the Floricultural Magazine.

† These three varieties are at present solely in my possession.

with light red, very large, full, and produced abundantly, form perfect, growth vigorous, foliage fine.

44.· *Madame Charles Roy* (H. P.), flowers violet rose, very large and full, of globular and fine form, growth vigorous.

45. *Madame Crespin* (H. P.), flowers rose shaded with dark violet, of medium size, full, good form.

46. *Madame Emain* (H. P.), flowers fine purplish red, globular, large and almost full, growth vigorous.

47. *Madame Freeman* (H. P.), flowers lemon white, of medium size, globular and full, thoroughly perpetual, growth vigorous.

48. *Madame Helye*, (H. P.) flowers reddish crimson, shaded with lilac, large, full, and globular, growth vigorous.

49. *Madame Valembourg* (H. P.), flowers bright purplish red, sometimes shaded with indigo at the summer flowering, large, full, and well-shaped, growth vigorous.

50. *Mdlle. Adele Jougant*, (Tea-scented), flowers clear yellow, of medium size, almost full, growth vigorous, forces well.

51. *Monsieur de Linières* (Bourbon), flowers bright fiery red, of medium size, full, growth very vigorous. Probably a good Pillar-rose.

52. *Monsieur Eugene Petit* (H. P.), flowers bright carmine, large, full, well shaped, produced abundantly, shoots almost thornless, leaves beautiful dark green.

53. *Mrs. William Paul* (H. P.), flowers bright violet red, shaded with fiery red, produced constantly and in clusters, large and full. Raised by M. Verdier of Paris, the raiser of Madame Knorr, Madame Furtado, and many of our finest varieties.

54. *Murillo* (H. P.), flowers rich purplish red shaded with crimson and violet, large, full, well formed and produced abundantly, growth vigorous.

55. *Paul Desgrand* (H. P.), flowers clear red tinted with violet, full and globular, growth vigorous, foliage fine, excellent for masses.

56. *Peter Lawson* (H. P.), flowers brilliant red shaded with carmine, very large and full, growth vigorous.

57. *President Lincoln* (H. P.), flowers cherry-red shaded with brownish red, very large, full, and well-imbricated. A seedling from Lord Raglan.

58. *Prince Henri de Pays Bas* (H. P.), flowers bright crimson shaded with velvety purple, reverse of the petals lilac, of medium size, full, fine globular form, produced abundantly, growth vigorous.

59. *Princess Alice* (H. P.), flowers bright rose, the reverse whitish, very large, full, sweet, produced singly, growth vigorous and erect, shoots almost thornless.

60. *Red Rover* (H. P.), flowers brilliant red, very large, petals thick and durable, growth extraordinarily robust. Not double

enough for a Show Rose, but forms a splendid and most effective Pillar Rose, flowering up to Christmas, if not prevented by frost.†

61. *Rochambeau* (Bourbon), flowers beautiful bright rose, of medium size, full, produced in clusters, growth vigorous.

62. *Rouge marbrée* (H. P.), flowers velvety red, carmine edges, centre marbled and shaded with violet, large, full, form and colour fine, growth vigorous, foliage splendid.

63. *Sœur des Anges* (H. P.), flowers delicate rosy blush, changing to white, very large and full, growth vigorous. A sport from Duchesse d'Orleans.

64. *Souvenir de Charles Montault* (H. P.), flowers brilliant red, cupped, large and full, produced abundantly, habit good, growth vigorous.

65. *Triomphe d'Angers* (H. P.), flowers brilliant velvety red shaded with blackish violet, large, full, of good form, and produced abundantly, growth vigorous.

66. *Triomphe de Nancy* (H. P.), flowers blackish velvety crimson, petals large and round, cupped, very large and full, one of the darkest.

67. *Vainqueur de Goliath* (H. P.), flowers brilliant red, globular, very large and full, produced abundantly, growth vigorous.

68. *Veloutée d'Orleans* (H. P.), flowers brilliant velvety red, almost scarlet, large and full, growth vigorous.

69. *William Paul* (H. P.), flowers brilliant reddish crimson, large and full. Raised by M. Guillot of Lyons, the raiser of Géant des Batailles, Lord Raglan, Senateur Vaisse, and many of our finest Roses ; said to be a seedling from Senateur Vaisse, but more brilliant in colour.

CHAPTER XIV.

ON EXHIBITING.

EVERY one who cultivates Roses may not do so with the design of becoming a candidate for floricultural honours ; many are satisfied with the calm enjoyment which this, in common with other branches of Gardening, affords : the quiet mind, the heathful glow, yields them a sufficient recompence, and ample satisfaction. From such we must ask a little forbearance while we offer a few remarks on preparing for exhibition, for we should be doing an injustice to some of our readers were we to neglect this point altogether. Let us first consider the arrangement and exhibition of cut Roses. The old plan of shewing large crowded bunches is superseded by the more natural one of shewing three loose trusses of each variety. By the old method, a gorgeous display was created, but the principles of good taste were violated, and the connoisseur could find little to delight and interest him : each bunch was a confused mass of colour, with a ragged outline. By the method now in vogue, the flowers stand out separately, the variety is shewn in a graceful style, displaying flowers in different stages, from the tiny bud to the full-blown Rose. So far, great improvement has been made ; and we submit whether a classification of the varieties exhibited would not be another step in the right direction. A more heterogeneous mass could not be produced by any other genus than that commonly displayed by bringing together Roses of different groups, and arranging them indiscriminately. It is cheerfully admitted that certain groups may be mixed together without any grave offence against taste ; but I have seen the beautiful but tiny Moss de Meaux completely smothered between two large French Roses, and the richness and beauty of the full deep-colours of the latter marred by the soft and bewitching tints of an adjoining Tea-rose. And are similar cases unfrequent ? By no means. Why not, then, arrange the kinds according to the classification of some popular grower ? The beauty and extent of each group would thus become apparent, and the abrupt transitions complained of be avoided.

We think it a pity that Horticultural Societies *should limit the number of varieties* to be shewn. Would it not work bétter to reduce the number of trusses from three to two, or even one, *and append a notice to the schedule that a bad truss or variety will be counted against the exhibitor ?* This would guarantee the exclusion of all inferior kinds, and secure a great number of varieties in a small space, and in a state approaching more nearly to that of nature. But to limit the exhibition to a small number of varieties, when hundreds are grown, does not admit of classification, and renders it impossible to give a full and true account of the genus.

With this statement of our views on exhibiting cut Roses, we respectfully submit two arrangements for the consideration of those who prepare the prize-schedules for our flower-shows.

1st, Roses in a collection, the number of varieties unlimited, classed in groups according to the arrangement of (name who), one, two, or three trusses only of one variety.

Or, 2dly,

A. Climbing Roses in a collection, the number of varieties un-limited (one, two, or three), trusses of one variety.

B. Summer Roses (exclusive of the kinds shewn under letter *A*) in a collection, the number of varieties unlimited ; classed in groups according to   ; — trusses only of one variety.

C. Autumnal Roses in a collection, number of varieties unlimited, to be classed and shewn as in letter *B*.

By the arrangements above proposed we afford the tyro efficient aid in selecting varieties. The classification enables him to see at a glance the extent, variety, and beauty of each group, and he can select from each and every one a gradation of colour from the light-est to the darkest hues it may embrace. Or if he prefer one colour more than another, such can be noted down, and its free interspersion secured. Further still, while he admires the variety and rich-ness of colour existing in one group, the regular outline of another, and is charmed by the delicious odour of a third, he is enabled to form a correct judgment of the *comparative value* of each, from the whole, or the most worthy, being brought at once under the eye. But these remarks are sufficiently extended, and we have to speak of dressing the boxes, and gathering and arranging the flowers.

The boxes may be made of inch deal of the simplest construction, and painted green. By the laws of some Societies, framed for general convenience, the lids must shift off at pleasure : no boxes are allowed to be placed on the exhibition-tables whose dimensions exceed three feet in length, six inches in height when the lid is removed, and eighteen inches in width from front to back. A handle at either end is desirable, which should drop into the wood that the ends may approach closely. The box may be filled with moss, into which zinc tubes may be sunk, filled with water, to contain the flowers.   The tubes may be about three and a half inches deep, an inch wide, with a rim half an inch broad.   Nothing, perhaps, forms so agreeable a ground on which to place the flowers as green moss, which may be gathered in most hollows of woods, and from shady banks.   It is not, indeed, a bad plan to place the moss on the boxes a few days before they are wanted, keeping them in a light but shady place, sprinkling the moss with water once or twice daily.

With regard to the choice of flowers, we may presume that he only who had formed a tolerable collection, and must consequently have acquired some taste in Roses, would enter the lists as a competitor.   We would therefore say, cut such flowers as appear best at the time wanted: a good variety may be in bad condition at a fixed period, and a second-rate one unusually fine.   But the exhibitor must, in a certain degree, conform to the tastes of others; and there are points of beauty almost universally agreed on.   The *outline* of Show Roses should be circular, free from all raggedness; the flowers should be full, and the petals arranged as regularly as possible; the larger the flowers the better, provided they are not coarse; and the colours should be varied with due care.   In gathering the flowers, we would say, choose the morning for the purpose, ere the sun has risen upon them, or before he has had time to dim their beauty.   When the place of exhibition is at a distance, it is often necessary to cut them the morning before.   There is full occupation for two persons, besides the advantage of having a second opinion in cases where the merit of two or more flowers is doubtful. It is not always easy to determine this point satisfactorily, for we have not only to consider *what a flower is*, but *what it is likely to become*.   The business of one should be to cull the flowers; that of the other to name and arrange them in the boxes.   It is desirable that every stage of the flower should be presented to view; but if cut the morning before the day of show, the forwardest should not be more than three-quarters blown.   Some of the stiff-petalled Roses, which remain a long time in perfection, may be made exceptions to this rule; but their number is few.   When the flowers are gathered. on the morning of the show, some may be full-blown, when less judgment and foresight are necessary.

Some little success perhaps depends on the taste with which the flowers are arranged.   This requires a little study, and we would take nature for our model.   Let the exhibitor walk among his plants occasionally with an eye to this point, and he will not fail to single out certain flowers remarkable for elegance of position: this is the true source from which to copy.   A few leaves should be gathered with each kind, for the grace and beauty of the flowers are materially heightened by the judicious arrangement of foliage;

and this is a point by which one may judge of the habits of a variety. As to the arrangement of colours, little need be said on that point. Much will depend on the materials in hand. Contrast should, I think, be aimed at; but with regard to the exact tints fitted for each position, the eye of him who arranges is usually best qualified to determine.

A neat and commodious method of naming is, to procure some deal sticks, about four inches long and half an inch wide, gradually tapering to a point. Let them be painted white, the names written in a round legible hand with a good dark pencil. Or small strips of card-board, the names written in ink, placed in the front of each sort, are both neat and convenient.

But the flowers are arranged, and what is to be done with them during the interval that must elapse ere they depart for the scene of competition? Shall the lids be placed on the boxes, and the flowers be kept closed from the air? By no means. Seek as cool a place as possible, where there is no draft, and where the light is not too strong. There place them till the time of departure. So necessary do many exhibitors consider it that the flowers should not be wholly closed from the air, that they have several holes made in the ends of their box-lids with a small augur. This I have found, by experience, a capital contrivance to admit the dust; and if these holes are made use of, they should be stopped with corks when travelling on a dusty road.

But besides the flowers of Roses, the plants are exhibited grown in pots; and it remains for us to say something of them. The advantages gained by their introduction are, that the characters and habit of the variety are shewn. Cut-roses create a great display, but Pot-roses afford us more extensive information. We may propose to ourselves, while viewing them, these questions :— What is the habit of the variety? Is it a free bloomer, or otherwise? Is it a good trusser? a summer or autumn bloomer? These questions cannot be answered by presenting a mere flower, or bunches of flowers; but the introduction of Pot-roses offers the means of a ready solution. In cultivating these for exhibition, it is necessary to grow *at least* double the number required to be shewn. This is no overdrawn calculation, as all who have had any experience in the matter will testify. There is no difficulty in flowering *every* plant, but *there is a difficulty in bringing all to perfection by a given time*. Remember, the Rose is one of the most ephemeral of flowers, and the day of exhibition is a fixed one. These facts, however, should deter no one from growing for exhibition, for they affect all exhibitors alike: all fight on equal ground; and the greater the difficulties to contend with, the greater is the triumph when achieved. For exhibition-plants we should recommend most kinds to be grown on their own roots. Although with such the cultivator will not be able to appear in the field at so early a date, yet he may ultimately attain to a more distinguished position. Certain kinds will not last long in health when budded: superior skill and great attention may bring them to a high pitch of beauty; but despite of every after care, they canker and fall into a state of retrogression.

The principal shows near the Metropolis are in May, June, and July; and to be enabled to shew in each month the plants must be divided into three lots. Those intended for the May exhibition must be grown in a green-house or frame with bottom-heat. It is my practice to select a good portion of the Tea-scented and other *tender* Roses for the first show, because they cannot remain out of doors during winter, and they improve under this particular culture. They should be pruned early in January, and taken into the house or frame immediately, *giving plenty of air*, but keeping the frost out. By the end of February a gentle heat may be started, and increased as is found necessary to bring them in flower in proper time.

The plants intended for exhibition in June may be plunged out of doors in an airy yet *sheltered* situation, that the foliage may not be damaged by the wind. So soon as the buds shew colour, remove the plants to a frame or green-house, giving air abundantly night and day, and shading from the sun, so soon as the first flowers expand.

The plants intended to bloom in July may also be grown out of doors: they should be autumnals exclusively; and by stopping the young shoots in April a perfect flowering is secured at that season. It is the practice with some to cut off the flowers of the autumnals shewn in May, removing the plants to a warm frame, by which treatment they flower again in July: this, however, we hesitate to recommend.

The detail of cultivation has been given in the chapter on Roses in Pots; it is our province here merely to speak of the management for exhibition. As the plants approach the flowering season, some will be found forwarder than others, owing to their position, or the habit of the variety. It is necessary, then, to calculate which are likely to be in perfection on the coming day, when means of accelerating or retarding must be had recourse to with regard to the others. If the former, a house or frame with heat is the best contrivance: if the latter, place them in a cold north frame, *admitting air gradually*. Care and forethought are especially necessary here. These changes of temperature must be brought about gradually;

and a calm and sunny hour should be chosen to remove the plants from place to place. As well might an inhabitant of India be sent to dwell in the frozen seas, as a plant suddenly transmuted from a high to a low temperature. When the buds shew colour, any that are in advance of the mass may be plucked out, when the side-buds will rise and produce good flowers. Have we, then, reached this stage of growth? A canvas awning must now be raised to shade the flowers. It should not be so thick as to exclude the light : its purpose is merely to break the sun's rays. As our flowers advance, our pleasures and anxieties increase. It is difficult to judge correctly of the time a bud requires to expand : some remain as buds for weeks after they shew colour; others expand very rapidly. The hard buds, of which we may instance Hybrid Perpetual La Reine, are slowest in expanding, and remain longest in a shewable state. The less double flowers, as Hybrid Perpetual Jules Margottin, and Tea Safrano, advance more rapidly, and are in general proportionally ephemeral. This is the best guide we can offer to the unpractised eye, though by no means an unerring one. If, after all our care, our specimens are *far* too early or too late, it is better to allow them their natural course than to resort to violent measures : it is better to shew fine specimens not arrived at, or beyond their glory, than to produce what might be construed as bad cultivation. Roses will not submit to the treatment in this respect which Azaleas and some other plants will endure.

We have already stated our views on tying up and training; but there is some doubt whether that system tells best on the exhibition tables. There, one side is to the wall, so that at best not more than three-quarters of a round plant can be seen. Now it is evident, that by leaving the back of a plant bare, a greater display can be made with the same material; as of course the flowers which would have been needed there are brought into full sight. Yet a skilful judge will surely detect *the false show ;* and if the round plants are in other respects nearly equal, we opine he would give his decision in their favour. Be this as it may, *a perfect plant* must yield its possessor a greater pleasure and more solid satisfaction than an imperfect one.

These remarks bring us to the period of exhibition. If the distance be great, the plants should be packed for travelling the day before. All is bustle and anxiety. A light spring van is the best vehicle for their conveyance, the space in which, from six to eight large plants will fully occupy. The surface of the soil of the pots should be covered with nice green moss, which, if the plants have stems, may rise in the centre in the form of a cone. Each flower-bed must have a stick to support it during the journey,—unless the variety produce its flowers in trusses, when a stick to a truss is sufficient,—but should not be tied so tight as to prevent an easy motion. If the flowers are heavy, soft tissue paper should be drawn closely round them without compression : if produced in trusses, wadding may be placed among them, to support and prevent them from bruising each other. In packing, each plant should stand clear of the other, and all free from contact with the sides of the van. Between the pots, moss or sawdust should be *tightly* pressed, at least half their depth, to keep them from shifting. A light tilt must go over the van, to exclude sun, rain, or dust, the last of which, by the bye, it is not always easy to do. But all is ready, and there is nothing like being at the place of exhibition in time. A careful person ought to accompany them, as the pace at which they travel should be a steady walking one. Attention, John ! From home to the place of exhibition, *all* depends on you. You must neither trot, gallop, nor canter. If you do, the consequences will be disastrous. Put your horse to his easiest walking pace, having reckoned up beforehand the time he will require for the journey. Having arrived early, you will find the tents only partially occupied; but the place for Roses, as for other objects, is already assigned. The north side of the tent is the best ; indeed, for Roses as cool and shady a place as possible should be apportioned, as perfect flowers will wither in a few hours in a sunny or hot position. In proceeding to set up the plants, it is well to calculate the elevation at which they shew best ; to which raise them by means of blocks of wood, of different thicknesses, about the diameter of the bottom of the pots. The sticks used as supports in travelling should be withdrawn. When the plants are all nicely adjusted, each should have the name placed to it in a position where easily seen, written in a bold legible hand, or done in the Egyptian style with Indian ink. At the grand Metropolitan exhibitions visitors are often so numerous that many cannot approach the objects exhibited : for their information, then, this is particularly desirable. All is now finished, and we await the decision of the judges, viewing the productions of our contemporaries, and anticipating the result. Perhaps, on returning to the tents after judgment has been pronounced, our plants are not so high in the scale as we expected to find them. A feeling of disappointment may arise. Shall we take umbrage at it ? Certainly not. This would be unjust, ungenerous. Let us ask ourselves this question : Which is the more likely, that the Censors—men selected on account of their professional knowledge and known probity—which, we say, is the more likely, that they should have shewn an indifference to, or prejudice against, our plants, or that we, the owners thereof, have been indulging in an overweening fondness? The answer is apparent. And let us ask ourselves again, if there is any disgrace in being beaten? Certainly none. *Every place here is honourable.* If *A* produces good plants, it is no discredit to him that *B* produces better. Nor would it always be correct reasoning to say that the latter is the more skilful cultivator. The air, or the soil, or the means at the disposal of *B*, may enable him to accomplish with ease that which is impracticable with *A*. *If our plants are good*, never mind those of our contemporary being better. Are not both engaged in the same work, both interested in the advancement of a favourite flower? Let us persevere, and we may probably reach the summit of our ambition at some future time.

In packing for returning the same care is requisite as before, if the plants are intended to be shewn elsewhere, or indeed if any store is set by the flowers yet unfolded. Under other circumstances, the flowers may be cut off, which saves much time in packing and travelling. But if the flowers are preserved, the plants may serve for other shows, although they must be considered in greater perfection when possessed of expanded flowers and others yet to come, than when shewing expanded flowers only.

When the flowering is over, the flower-stalks should be cut off, and a second growth will shortly ensue. The Autumnals, which bloomed in May, will flower again in August; those of June, in September; and if those of July are placed in a warm green-house they may be kept in flower till Christmas.

CHAPTER XV.

SELECT LISTS OF KINDS SUITED FOR VARIOUS PURPOSES.

A. LARGE, full, well-shaped flowers, suited for Exhibition.
SUMMER ROSES. *Group* 4. *Damask :* Madame Hardy, Madame
Soëtmans. *Group* 5. *Provence :* Adrienne de Cardoville, Cristata,
New Cabbage. *Group* 7. *Moss :* Common, Comtesse Murinais,
Gloire des Mousseuses, White Bath. *Group* 8. *French :* Boula de
Nanteuil, Kean. *Group* 10. *Hybrid Chinese :* Chénédolé, General
Jacqueminot. *Group* 12. *Hybrid Bourbon :* Charles Duval, Charles
Lawson, Coupe d'Hebe, Juno, Paul Perras, Paul Ricaut.

AUTUMNAL ROSES. *Group* 23. *Hybrid Perpetual :* Adolphe Bossange,
Alexandre Fontaine, Alexandrine Bachmeteff, Anna Alexieff, Anna
de Diesbach, Auguste Mie, Baronne Prevost, Baronne Hallez,
Beauty of Waltham, Belle de Bourg-la-Reine, Caroline de Sansal,
Charles Lefebre, Christian Puttner, Clement Marot, Colonel de
Rougemont, Comte de Nanteuil, Comtesse de Chabrilliant, Duc de
Cazes, Duc de Rohan, Duchesse d' Orleans, Duchess of Norfolk,
Emile Dulac, Empereur de Maroc, Eugene Bourcier, François Arago,
François Lacharme, François Louvat, François 1er. General Jac-
queminot, General Washington, Gloire de Chatillon, Gloire de
Vitry, Gloire de Santenay, Joan of Arc, Jules Margottin, La Reine,
La Ville de St. Denis, Lælia, Lafontaine, Lord Raglan, Louise
Darzins, Louis XIV., Louise Peyronny, Madame Boll, Madame Bruni,
Madame Caillat, Madame C. Crapelet, Madame Charles Wood,
Madame de Cambaceres, Madame Domage, Madame Ernest Dreol,
Madame Furtado, Madame Hector Jacquin, Madame Julie Daran,
Madame Knorr, Madame Masson, Madame Pauline Villot, Madame
Rivers, Madame Vigneron, Madame Vidot, Mademoiselle Bonnaire,
Marechal Vaillant, Maurice Bernardin, Monte Christo, Olivier Del-
homme, Paul Feval, Praire de Terrenoire, Prince Camille de
Rohan, Prince Leon, Professor Koch, Robert Fortune, Senateur
Vaisse, Souvenir de Lady Eardley, Souvenir de M. Rousseau, Sou-
venir de Comte Cavour, Souvenir de Leveson Gower, Souvenir de
la Reine d' Angleterre, Triomphe d' Alençon, Triomphe de Lyon,

Turenne, Triomphe de Paris, Victor Verdier, William Griffith.
Group 24. *Bourbon Perpetual :* Baron Gonella, Baronne Noirmont,
Catherine Guillot, Louise Odier. *Group* 26. *Bourbon :* Acidalie,
Comtesse de Barbantanne, Dr. Berthet, Dr. Leprestre, Empress
Eugenie, L'Avenir, Marquis Balbiano, Souvenir de Malmaison,
Vorace. *Group* 30. *Tea-scented :* Adam, Archimede, Auguste Oger,
Belle de Bordeaux, Bougère, Comte de Paris, Comtesse Ouvaroff,
Devoniensis, Duc de Magenta, Eugene Desgaches, Gloire de Dijon,
Madame de Vatry, Madame Pauline Labonte, Madame Villermoz,
Moiret, Narcisse, Niphetos, President, Souvenir d' Elise Vardon,
Souvenir d' un Ami, Triomphe de Guillot fils. *Group* 32. *Noisette :*
Celine Forestier or Liesis, Cloth of Gold, Lamarque, Solfaterre,
Triomphe de Rennes.

B. Free-blooming and showy varieties, most valuable for the
effect they produce in the garden.

SUMMER ROSES. *Group* 10. *Hybrid Chinese :* Brennus, Chénédolé,
General Jacqueminot, Vivid. *Group* 11. *Hybrid Noisette :* Madame
Plantier, Madeline. *Group* 12. *Hybrid Bourbon :* Charles Duval,
Charles Lawson, Coupe d' Hebe, Paul Perras, Paul Ricaut. *Group*
13. *Alba :* Felicité, Madame Legras, Queen of Denmark. *Group* 14.
Austrian Brier : Harrisonii. *Group* 23. *Hybrid Perpetual :* Anna
Alexieff, Admiral Nelson, Beauty of Waltham, François 1$^{er.}$ Gene-
ral Jacqueminot, Henderson, Jean Bart, Jules Margottin, La
Brillante, Lion des Combats, Louise Darzins, Madame C. Crapelet,
Madame Charles Wood, Madame Knorr, Oriflame de St. Louis,
Pauline Lansezeur, Princesse Mathilde, Red Rover, Souvenir de
Lady Eardley, Souvenir de Comte Cavour, Souvenir de la Reine
d' Angleterre, Triomphe de l' Exposition, Triomphe des Beaux Arts,
Victor Verdier, Victor Trouillard. *Group* 25. *Rose de Rosomène :*
Comte d'Eu, Géant des Batailles, Gloire de Rosomène, Leonce
Moise, Souvenir de M. Rousseau. *Group* 26. *Bourbon :* Armosa,
Bouquet de Flore, Queen, Duchesse de Thuringe, Mrs. Bosanquet,
Sir J. Paxton, Souvenir de Malmaison. *Group* 27. *Crimson Chinese :*
Cramoisie Superieure, Fabvier, President d'Olbecque. *Group* 30.
Tea-scented : Abricoté, Canari, Caroline, Comte de Paris, Gloire de
Dijon, Madame Damaizin, Madame de St. Joseph, Marquise de
Foucault, Mirabile, Narcisse, Nina, Niphetos, Nisida, Safrano, Som-
breuil, Vicomtesse de Cazes. *Group* 32. *Noisette :* Aimée Vibert,
Celine Forestier, Fellenberg, La Biche, Jeanne d' Arc, Ophirie.

C. PILLAR OR POLE ROSES. SUMMER ROSES. *Group* 4. *Damask :*
La Ville de Bruxelles, Madame Hardy, Madame Soëtmans. *Group*
7. *Moss :* Alice Leroy, Baronne de Wassenaer, Comtesse Murinais,
Laneii, Luxembourg, Reine blanche. · *Group* 10. *Hybrid Chinese :*
Blairii No. 2, Brennus, Chénédolé, Frederic II., Fulgens, General

N 2

Jacqueminot, Velours Episcopal, Vivid. *Group* 11. *Hybrid Noisette* : Madame Plantier, Madeline. *Group* 12. *Hybrid Bourbon* : Charles Lawson, Charles Duval, Coupe d'Hébé, Paul Perras. AUTUMNAL ROSES. *Group* 23. *Hybrid Perpetual* : Admiral Nelson, Alexandrine Bachmeteff, Duchess of Sutherland, Enfant du Mont Carmel, General Jacqueminot, Henderson, Jacques Lafitte, Jules Margottin, La Reine, Lion des Combats, Madame Bruni, Madame Pierson, Madame Schmidt, Mdlle. Haiman, Mdlle. Louise Carique, Mère de St. Louis, Mrs. Elliot, Mrs. Standish, Oriflame de St. Louis, Pius IX., Princesse Mathilde, Queen Victoria, Red Rover, Reine des Violettes, Rosine Parron, Souvenir de Lady Eardley, Souvenir de Montceau, Souvenir de la Reine d'Angleterre, Sydonie, Triomphe de l'Exposition. *Group* 26. *Bourbon* : Acidalie, Empress Eugenie, Pierre de St. Cyr, Sir J. Paxton. *Group* 30. *Tea-scented* : Belle Chartronnaise, Belle de Bordeaux, Gloire de Bordeaux, Gloire de Dijon, Sombreuil. *Group* 32. *Noisette* : Celine Forestier, Claudia Augustin, Desprez, Du Luxembourg, La Biche, Jeanne d'Arc, Mdlle, Aristide, Ophirie, Triomphe de la Duchere, Triomphe de Rennes.

D. CLIMBING ROSES OF VIGOROUS GROWTH, for covering arches, trellis-work, &c., quickly ; suitable also for a north wall. SUMMER ROSES. *Group* 1. *Boursault* : Amadis, Gracilis. *Group* 15. *Ayrshire* : Dundee Rambler, Queen of the Belgians, Ruga, Splendens, Thoresbyana. *Group* 16. *Evergreen* : Felicité Perpetuè, Leopoldine d'Orleans, Myrianthes renoncule, Rampante. *Group* 17. *Multiflora* : Laure Davoust. AUTUMNAL ROSES. *Group* 25. *Rose de Rosomène* : Gloire de Rosomène. *Group* 30. *Tea-scented* : Amabilis, Gloire de Dijon, Homer. *Group* 31. *Musk* : Princesse de Nassau. *Group* 32. *Noisette* : Celine Forestier, Desprez, Ophirie.

E. CLIMBING ROSES, for a sunny wall or fence, aspect South or East ; and also for the conservatory. *Group* 18. *TheBanksiæ* : White, Yellow. AUTUMNAL ROSES. *Group* 21. *Macartney* : Single, Maria Leonida. *Group* 22. *Microphylla* : Rubra plena, Rugosa. *Group* 30. *Tea-scented* : Archimede, Auguste Oger, Bougere, Canari, Devoniensis, Eugene Desgaches, Gloire de Dijon, Madame de St. Joseph, Madame de Vatry, Madame Pauline Labonte, Madame Villermoz, Marechal Bugeaud, Marie de Medicis, Moiret, Niphetos, Safrano, Sombreuil, Souvenir d'un Ami, Triomphe de Guillot fils. *Group* 32. *Noisette* : Cloth of Gold, Isabella Gray, Lamarque, Ophirie, Solfaterre, Triomphe de Rennes.

F. TRAILING ROSES for covering banks, rock-work and Rooteries. Any of *Groups* 15 & 16, *Ayrshire* and Sempervirens, which also form the best WEEPING ROSES.

G. ROSES FOR POT CULTURE : those marked thus *preferable for forcing or greenhouse culture. SUMMER ROSES. *Group* 7. *Moss*. Captain Ingram, Clemence Beaugrand, *Common, *Crested, Felicité Bohain, *Frederic Soulie, Madame de la Rochelambert, Mdlle. Rosa Bonheur, Marie de Blois, Nuits d'Young, *Purpurea rubra, Reine blanche. *Group* 12. *Hybrid Bourbon* : *Charles Lawson, Coupe d'Hébé, *Juno, Paul Perras, *Paul Ricaut. AUTUMNAL ROSES. *Group* 23. *Hybrid Perpetual* : *Adolphe Bossange, Anna Alexieff, Anna de Diesbach, *Auguste Mie, Baronne Prevost, *Beauty of Waltham, *Cardinal Patrizzi, *Caroline de Sansal, Charles Lefebre, Christian Puttner, Clement Marot, *Comte de Nanteuil, *Comtesse de Chabrillant, Comtesse de Seguieur, Dominique Daran, Duc de Cazes, *Duc de Rohan, *Duchesse d'Orleans, Duchess of Norfolk, Duchess of Sutherland, Emile Dulac, Empereur de Maroc, *Enfant du Mont Carmel, Eugene Bourcier, *François Lacharme, François Louvat, François Premier, General Jacqueminot, *General Washington, *Gloire de Chatillon, *Gloire de Santenay, Jules Margottin, *La Reine, Lælia, Lord Raglan, Louise Darzins, *Louis XIV., Louise Peyronny, Madame Boll, Madame Caillat, Madame C. Crapelet, Madame Charles Wood, Madame Domage, Madame Ernest Dreol, *Madame Furtado, Madame Hector Jacquin, Madame Julie Daran, *Madame Pauline Villot, Mdlle Claudine d'Offay, Marechal Vaillant, Maurice Bernardin, Olivier Delhomme, Paul Feval, Professor Koch, Senateur Vaisse, Souvenir de Lady Eardley, Souvenir de Comte Cavour, Souvenir de Leveson Gower, *Souvenir de la Reine d'Angleterre, *Triomphe d'Alençon, *Triomphe de Lyon, Triomphe de l'Exposition, Triomphe de Paris, Triomphe des Beaux Arts, Victor Verdier. *Group* 24. *Bourbon Perpetual* : Baron Gonella, *Baronne Noirmont *Catherine Guillot, Louise Odier, Modèle de Perfection. *Group* 25. *Rose de Rosomène* : Géant des Batailles, Leonce Moise, *Souvenir de M. Rousseau. *Group* 26. *Bourbon* : *Comtesse de Barbantanne, *Souvenir de Malmaison, Mrs. Bosanquet. *Group* 30. *Tea-scented* : Abricoté, *Bougère, Devoniensis, Gloire de Dijon, Madame Damaizin, Madame de St. Joseph, Madame Villermoz, Narcisse, *Niphetos, *President, *Sombreuil, *Souvenir d'un Ami, Vicomtesse de Cazes.

H. WINTER ROSES, to bloom from November to February. *Group* 23. *Hybrid Perpetual* : General Jacqueminot, Henderson, Beauty of Waltham, Jules Margottin, La Brillante, Louis Gulino, Louise Darzins, Madame Laffay, Oriflame de St. Louis. *Group* 24. *Bourbon Perpetual* : Catherine Guillot, Louise Odier, Madame Comtesse. *Group* 25. *Rose de Rosomène* : Comte d' Eu, Comte Bobrinsky, Géant des Batailles, Gloire de Rosomène. *Group* 26. *Bourbon* : Comte de Montijo, Empress Eugenie, Justine, Madame Cousin, Prince de Chimay, Queen, Mrs. Bosanquet. *Group* 27.

Crimson Chinese : Cramoisie superieure, Duchess of Kent, Fabvier, President d' Olbecque. *Group* 30. *Tea-scented* : Abricoté, Bride of Abydos, Canari, Marquise de Foucault, Nina, Nisida, Safrano.

I. SEED BEARERS. SUMMER ROSES. *Group* 7. *Moss* : Celina, Luxembourg. *Group* 10. *Hybrid Chinese* : Chénédolé, Vivid. *Group* 12. *Hybrid Bourbon* : Coupe d' Hebé, Paul Perras. *Group* 14. *Austrian Brier* : Harrisonii. AUTUMNAL ROSES. *Group* 23. *Hybrid Perpetual* : Duchess of Sutherland, General Jacqueminot, Jules Margottin, Triomphe de l' Exposition, William Jesse. *Group* 24. *Bourbon Perpetual* : Louise Odier. *Group* 25. *Rose de Rosomène* : Géant des Batailles. *Group* 26. *Bourbon* : Bouquet de Flore, Sir J. Paxton. *Group* 30. *Tea-scented* : Canari, Nina, Nisida.

K. BEST YELLOW ROSES. *Group* 14. *Austrian Brier* : Harrisonii, Persian Yellow. *Group* 18. *Banksiæ* : Yellow. *Group* 30. *Tea-scented* : Abricoté, Auguste Vacher, Devoniensis, Eliza Sauvage, Enfant de Lyon, Gloire de Dijon, La Boule d' Or (under glass only), Louise de Savoie, Madame Falcot, Madame William, Narcisse, Safrano, Vicomtesse de Cazes. *Group* 32. *Noisette* : Celine Forestier, Cloth of Gold, Isabella Gray (under glass only), Lamarque, Solfaterre, Triomphe de Rennes.

L. VERY SWEET ROSES. *Group* 5. *Provence* : Cabbage, Crested. *Group* 7. *Moss* : Common. *Group* 23. *Hybrid Perpetual* : Baronne Prevost, Beauty of Waltham, Belle de Bourg-la-Reine, Colonel de Rougemont, Comtesse de Chabrillant, Du Roi, Duchess of Sutherland, Madame Boll, Madame de Cambaceres, Madame Furtado, Madame Knorr, Madame Vigneron, Monte Christo, Souvenir de Leveson Gower. *Group* 30. *Tea-scented* : President, Devoniensis, Goubault, Gloire de Dijon, Madame de St. Joseph, Madame Villermoz, Marquise de Foucault, Narcisse. *Group* 32. *Noisette* : Desprez.

M. MINIATURE ROSES FOR EDGINGS OR ROSE-BEDS.
The varieties of Pompon and Fairy Roses, Groups 6 and 29.

N. ROSES FOR HEDGES.
    Scotch, various, Group 3.
    Madame Laffay, Group 23.
    Cramoisie supérieure, Group 27.
    Common Chinese, Group 28.
    Armosa, Group 26.
    Mrs. Bosanquet, Group 26.

O. ROSES FOR THE SHRUBBERY.
    Scotch, Group 3.

Damask, Group 4.
Provence, Group 5.
French, Group 8.
Hybrid, Chinese, &c., Groups 10, 11, and 12.
Hybrid Perpetual, Group 23, and any other hardy kinds that may be bought at a low price.

END OF DIVISION I.

DIVISION II.

AN ARRANGEMENT, IN NATURAL GROUPS, OF THE MOST ESTEEMED
VARIETIES OF ROSES RECOGNISED AND CULTIVATED IN THE VARIOUS
ROSE GARDENS, ENGLISH AND FOREIGN; WITH FULL DESCRIPTIONS,
AND REMARKS ON THEIR ORIGIN, AND MODE OF CULTURE.

In Two Primary Classes.

CLASS I.
SUMMER ROSES; BLOOMING IN MAY, JUNE, AND JULY.

CLASS II.
AUTUMNAL ROSES; BLOOMING FROM MAY TILL NOVEMBER,
OR LATER, IF NOT PREVENTED BY FROST.

INTRODUCTORY REMARKS.

ON THE ORIGIN OF THE FLORICULTURAL GROUPS.

THE word " Rose" is generally allowed to have been derived from the Celtic *rhodd*, or *rhudd*, signifying " red," in allusion to the colour of the flowers of most of the species. We may trace a great resemblance in the names by which various nations distinguish this plant. In the Greek it is called *Rodon;* in Latin, *Rosa;* in French, *Rosier;* in Italian, *Rosajo;* in Spanish, *Rosal;* in Portuguese, *Roseira;* and in German, *Rosenstock.*

According to the authority of most Botanists, the genus ROSA stands divided into sections, which are subdivided into numerous species, the distinguishing characters of which consist in the colour, shape, size, &c., of various organs, such as the leaves, prickles, flowers, and fruit. On the value of these characters, as constituting distinct species, botanical writers are, however, by no means agreed. While in the "Rosarium Monographia" seventy-eight species are described (besides others recorded as doubtful species); and the Messrs. Loddiges had in their Catalogue a far greater number; M. Boitard, a modern French author, stoutly maintains there are but three.*

It is not my intention here to enter into the botany of the Rose†; but I would state it to be my impression, that the differences of opinion arise in some measure from the unsettled definition of the word " species" When in conversation with tyros, I have often been asked what constitutes a species. And this question seems so necessary to be answered, in order that the arrangement of the varieties may be rightly understood, that I shall here offer a reply.

* *Manuel Complet de l'Amateur des Roses,* par M. Boitard. Paris, 1836. His species are, 1. R. simplicifolia; 2. R. lutea; 3. R. mutabilis. He divides these into races and varieties; and, according to this arrangement, nearly all the varieties cultivated in European gardens belong to the third species, (R. mutabilis).

† I purposely avoid entering into the botany of the Rose, having the promise of a popular article on the subject, which will appear in the Appendix to this work.

Mirbel says, " A species is composed of a succession of individuals, which have descended one from the other, in a direct line,
whether by seed, or a simple separation of parts.
" We find commonly in the individual all the characters which
distinguish the species to which it belongs from all other species in
the vegetable kingdom."

M. Boitard accepts the first sentence, but repudiates the other,
and places in its stead, " Each individual of which is capable of
reproducing, by seed, fertile individuals, possessing one or more
characters in common with the parent, and invariable in all."

In the Introduction to Lindley's " Rosarum Monographia" we
find the following definition given :—" By species, I wish to be
understood here to mean, an assemblage of individuals, differing in
particular respects from the rest of the genus, but having more
points of affinity among themselves than with others ; their union
being therefore natural."—Ros. Mon. Intro. p. 18.

" We assemble under the name of species," says Decandolle, " all
the individuals will bear sufficient resemblance to each other to
lead us to believe that they have originally descended from a single
being, or a couple of beings.—Physiologie Végétale, tome ii. p. 688.

Although not agreeing altogether in the views of M. Boitard, I
would state my conviction, that most Botanists have been too ready
in admitting, as species, individuals of. a genus so remarkable for
its disposition to vary : and if we adopt Decandolle's definition, I
think that many of the so-called species are nothing more than
hybrids, which, to use his words, " have originally descended from
a single being, or a couple of beings." I have been led to this
conclusion more particularly from observations in raising seedlings,
among which it is not uncommon to find plants differing exceedingly
from their parents. I think we may accept the second definition,
because with an eye to that the genus was divided in the " Rosarum
Monographia;" and that the division there made has met the views
of many subsequent writers, may be gathered from the extent of
their extracts from that work.

But it is necessary to consider other questions, which the discussion of this invariably gives rise to. The tyro having satisfied
himself as, to what constitutes a species, we may suppose the next
questions to be, What was the origin of the Floricultural Groups?
what the real difference between these groups? and how may one
be enabled to refer any variety brought before him to its proper
position ?

We need scarcely say that the Botanist's sphere of labour is
widely different from the Florist's. The former collects and
examines the productions of nature, arranging them in classes and

orders; which he again divides into genera and species, pointing
out their properties and uses. The Florist here takes up the work.
Once in possession of species, he applies the art of culture, with the
view of fashioning them to his own taste. Let us confine our remarks to the department of the Florist; and as varieties usually
originate with him, we may presume that he is competent to answer
the above questions.

Having the species, or varieties produced from species, at his
command, he saves seed from them, which he sows; and from the
proneness of Nature's offspring to assume new forms and tints,
hence arise individuals differing from their parents. These are
commonly termed varieties; and he bestows names on such of them
as he deems improvements on former kinds, and therefore worthy
of public notice.

But the Florist does more than this. He does not rest satisfied
with the simple workings of nature. Her march is too slow for
him. He strives to anticipate her. He brings together varieties of
different species, and, hybridizing them, he effects new combina-
tions—produces new races*; the individuals of which differ widely
in appearance, and which may eventually become so numerous, as
to induce him to group them, that they may be the more readily
comprehended. To accomplish this end, he seizes hold of external
characters,—whether it be the colours of the flowers, as in Carna-
tions, &c., or the general appearance of the plant, as in Roses,—
and forms a system of arrangement of his own;—not strictly botanical, perhaps, but popular and useful. Such is the origin of the
Floricultural Groups. As to the differences between these groups,
we shall point out, as we approach each one, the characters which
distinguish it from all others.

Now, it will be tolerably evident, that, to be able to group

---

* M. Deslongchamps, in his work on the Rose, devotes considerable space
to a discussion on the subject of raising Roses from seed, and especially in
proving they vary from seed, without being hybridized. What practical
man has any doubt on the subject? But with the same stroke he endeavours
to establish that the so-called hybrids are not really such;—have not been
produced by the union of two distinct species, but by freaks of nature. In
this, if he admits as distinct species those plants which most Botanists do, he
appears to me to fail absolutely: and he admits that the authority of the
French Rose growers, most of whom devote a great part of their time to the
raising of seedlings, is against him. M. Vibert, one of the oldest and most
distinguished cultivators in France, goes so far as to say that he obtained
spotted Moss Roses by crossing the spotted varieties of the Rosa Gallica with
the Moss kinds. The plants produced from this experiment partook unmistakeably of the characters of each parent, and differed from all pre-
existing kinds.

varieties correctly, some practice among Roses, combined with previous study, is necessary. If an individual wish to become sufficiently acquainted with Roses to enable him to do this, I would say, let him first study the features of the species from which the Florist's groups have descended. Let the groups be considered next ; then the varieties ; which, though ever so variously hybridized, will for the most part be readily understood. A hybrid may sometimes be met with, whose place it may at first sight be difficult to determine ; but in such case a second or third inspection, and a little reflection, usually solve the difficulty. To illustrate this remark, let us suppose the existence of a variety due to the hybridizing of a Damask with a Hybrid Provence Rose. The Hybrid Provence being a hybrid between the French and the Provence, such variety might partake of the nature of both these species, and also of the Damask parent. These are, on the authority of .most Botanists, three distinct species. Well, supposing the features of each to be visible in the new variety, where is the place for such a hybrid ? We would say, Is it sufficiently original in character to demand the formation of a new group ? If so, this is the proper course to pursue ; and it is thus that several new groups have of late years been added. The Hybrid Perpetuals, for instance, are of modern date, and it must be admitted by all, that for these hybrids a new group was necessary. But supposing this new individual to possess no very distinct features : then will not the characters of any one species or group predominate ? Undoubtedly they will ; and the variety should be referred to that group, to which the preponderance of similar external characters denote it most intimately to belong.

If we glance at the species from which the beautiful varieties which decorate our gardens have sprung, we find nearly all are natives of civilized countries, and have been for some years known and cultivated in Europe. This will account for the number of varieties we possess from them. It is probable that many other species, which are at present only known as species, will eventually give birth to esteemed garden kinds ; that fresh groups will arise, possessed of distinct characters from those we already possess. If these anticipations be realized, what a genus will that of the Rose become ! And are we not strengthened in this supposition by the appearance at the present time of numerous varieties raised from the Rosa rubifolia, which till lately was only known to us as embellishing with its pale red blossoms the prairies and forests of North America ? There is no doubt some of the species are more disposed to improvement than others, but all are capable of it. I believe

that when our cultivators shall become tired of working upon the
garden kinds they already possess, they will direct their attention
to others of the species, and bring forth the treasures they are
capable of producing.

When we look at the species with single or semi-double flowers,
which are the types of the present garden varieties, and compare
them with those varieties, the contrast may well make us inquire,
Have the latter really descended from these species? So greatly
are they improved in form and texture of petal; increased also in
size; changed from single to double; and varied in colour to a remarkable degree; that I do not wonder at persons unacquainted
with the effects of cultivation on the wild species, wishing to know
the process of development, before they accredit statements such as
these. We may fairly presume, however, that such is their origin.
But if so, how has such a change been wrought? We reply, simply
by a long course of careful and systematic culture. What was the
Rose, comparatively speaking, fifty, or even thirty years since?
There are doubtless some admirers of the genus who can glance
retrospectively to the former period, and trace the gradual altera-
tion from flimsy semi-double varieties, few blooming in the autumn,
to the full, bold flowers of the present day, so exquisite in colour,
so symmetrical in form. In order to trace their descent, it is
necessary to revert to the species which we must suppose existing
in a wild state. We know little of cultivation as pursued in remote
ages, but may be justified in presuming that seeds of the Rose
were sown, as well as those of other trees and plants. It is recorded
that the Romans did this, but we now allude to times anterior to
these. Now supposing the seeds of the wild species to have been
gathered and sown, Nature's stores thus opened, she would yield
forth her treasures, here as elsewhere, in rich abundance; the
plants raised would produce flowers varying in colour, size, and
degree of fulness.* We may suppose the handsomest of these
would be cherished most, and the probability is, seeds would be
saved from such; hence we might expect to obtain a variety
as before, and a further advance in beauty. So on from
time to time, the improvement taking place so gradually, as to fix
the attention only of the curious in these matters; or if, at any
period, a great advance had been made, it would not have been considered worthy of record in less civilized times, when the constant

---

* In presuming thus far, we are supported by natural occurrences. The
flowers of the Dog-rose in the hedges and woods vary in size and colour, and
in the south of Europe some of the wild kinds have double flowers.

occurrence of important changes and stirring events, kept men in a state of excitement, disquietude, and doubt. Ages might thus roll away, and the species be not marvellously changed from their primitive form. But following the stream of time, we reach the period when the raising of plants became a settled occupation : soon men turned their attention to the improvement of races ; then the sexes of plants was generally acknowledged; and, finally, the effects of artificial fertilization were made known, and the art practised. The latter was indeed a grand stride in the path of improvement ; by its pursuance, man stepped in to the aid of Nature, and the results are strikingly visible.

Although departing from our subject, yet to render this hypothesis more plausible, let us glance for a moment at analogous cases.

Let us turn to the *Heartsease*, or the Dahlia, whose progress from the species to the present state has been more rapid, and has fallen within the pale of more general observation. It is well known that the beautiful garden varieties of *Heartsease* are descended from the Viola tricolor, and V. lutea of botanists, both species indigenous to Britain. They had long been grown in the borders of flower-gardens, and the flowers had no doubt become varied in colour and size ; but I believe it is not more than forty years since Mr. Thompson, of Iver, first commenced their cultivation with the expectation of improving them. They were then, perhaps, not very far removed from the species. He collected several kinds, and saved seed from them promiscuously. From the plants thus raised, some were larger and handsomer than their parents ; these he reserved, saving seed from such, and, by continuing to reserve and save seed from the finest varieties, and by planting them in the most favourable soil, he materially improved them. He did not long work single-handed : other florists joined him ; and the results are now before us—the flowers are changed from an irregular and indescribable form, and become quite circular. I do not know whether he adopted artificial fertilization in his course of practice, but others have done so.

Take another instance. The Dahlia, when first introduced to England, was single, the flowers had but one row of petals, the centre being occupied with a yellow disk ; they resembled a single Aster. The first double Dahlias had long, narrow, flat, pointed petals, and were very different in character from the present favourites. The florist and amateur disliked the pointed, flat-petalled flowers, and they raised an ideal standard of perfection. All their endeavours were directed towards the attainment of this.

Dahlias, said they, should not be flat flowers, but circular, forming half a ball; the petals should not be long and pointed, but short, rounded at the edge, and cupped. Now mark the change that has followed. The Dahlia has, so to speak, been re-modelled.

So doubtless it has been with the Rose, though its development has been more gradual, has been spread over a greater extent of time, and has, consequently, been less marked than in the above cases. We must remember that the Rose is not a flower recently risen into favour, deriving its popularity from cultivators of the present day alone: it is of the highest antiquity; and the ancients having cherished it so much, we may presume they would bestow some pains on its cultivation. It is not then, I think, surprising when we consider the length of time the Rose has been under cultivation, and how freely the numerous species of which it is composed intermix—it is not, I say, surprising, that the varieties are removed to a greater distance from the species than in either of the above-mentioned flowers.

The Dahlias are the offspring of a single species; the Heartsease arose from two; but the Roses of our day claim no less than twenty species as their progenitors. Should we not expect, then, from a larger surface on which to build, and a greater quantity and choice of materials, added to which, time almost unlimited, a super-structure to arise more grand, more varied, more perfect?

In grouping the varieties, I have endeavoured not to increase more than necessary the number of groups into which, on the authority of Rose cultivators, the Rose at present stands divided. It were easy to effect a different arrangement, and perhaps a better one; but it is questionable whether the improvement would be sufficient to compensate for the confusion that must necessarily arise from such a step. In one or two instances only have I therefore formed fresh groups; and where I have thought varieties to belong to other groups than those in which some cultivators place them, they will be removed to what appears to me a more correct position. To prevent confusion arising from this change, the names will be retained in their accustomed places, the reader being referred to the other groups for their proper descriptions.

It was conceived that the Hybrid Perpetual Roses differed too widely to remain grouped as heretofore. Witness, Baronne Prevost, Gloire de Rosomène, and Louise Odier being placed together.

The original group of Hybrid Perpetuals will be now divided into three, of which the varieties just mentioned may be considered the types. [There are one or two other like cases which will appear hereafter.

It is thought desirable, before proceeding further, to explain certain terms which it is found necessary to use in describing the varieties; and the first which present themselves are those relating to *the size of the flowers.* They are *five*, namely :

Very small, applied when the flowers are
                                          about 1 inch in diameter.
Small   .   .   .   .   .   from 1½ to 2   „
Of medium size   .   .   .   .   2 „ 3   „
Large   .   .   .   .   .   .   3 „ 4   „
Very large   .   .   .   .   .   4 „ 5   „

There are also *five* terms used expressive of *the degree of fulness; Single, Semi-double, Double, very Double, and Full.*

The Single are such as possess but one row of petals; example, the Single Austrian Rose.

The Semi-Double have from two to five rows of petals; example, Amadis (Boursault), Fabvier (Chinese).

The Double have more than five rows of petals, yet usually shew the stamens in the centre of the flower; example, General Jacqueminot, William Jesse (Hybrid Perpetuals).

The very Double have a sufficient number of petals to hide the central stamens; examples, Souvenir de Lady Eardley, Triomphe des Beaux Arts (Hybrid Perpetuals).

The Full have the petals placed closely together; examples, Comtesse de Chabrillant, Jules Margottin (Hybrid Perpetuals).

The flowers of some varieties vary a little as to fulness.

In reference to the *form of the flowers*, we have the terms *globular, cupped, compact, and expanded.*

The term *globular* is applied to such varieties as assume that form, in which the outer petals encircle the flower, the latter remaining closed, or almost closed, till nearly full blown: thus the flower, in its early stage, is a perfect globe. Examples of this term : the Cabbage Rose (Provence), La Reine (Hybrid Perpetual), Gloire de Dijon (Tea-scented).

It is worthy of remark, that Roses of this form usually remain perfect for a longer period than others. I have kept globular-shaped Roses in good preservation for a week or ten days after being cut off the plant.

The term *cupped* is applied in cases where the outer petals of the flower stand erect, or are slightly incurved, the petals within being in general of smaller size than the outer ones, the flower thus being a little hollow in the centre like a cup. Examples of this term : Madame Hardy (Damask), Coupe d' Hebe (Hybrid Bourbon),

Auguste Mie, Beauty of Waltham, Louise Peyronny (Hybrid Perpetuals).

The term *compact* is applied to those varieties whose petals are stiff and upright, the centre of the flower being almost level with the circumference, usually rising above it, rather than being depressed. Examples of this term: De Meaux (Moss), Boula de Nanteuil (French), Madame Boll (Hybrid Perpetual).

The *expanded* differ from the *compact* in this respect; the outer petals, instead of standing erect, lie almost horizontal, usually turning back upon the flower-stalks in the last stage of the flower. Examples: most of the French Roses, Colonel de Rougemont, Mathurin Regnier (Hybrid Perpetuals).

The words *good, fine, perfect*, which follow some of the above-named terms, are used only where the form is particularly elegant.

These are the terms which I have thought it expedient to make use of, to convey a correct idea of the size, form, and fulness of the different varieties of the Rose.

With regard to the form of a flower, it may be remarked, that it often varies as the flower passes through the different stages of its existence. Thus, a Rose which is cupped when half-blown, may become compact when full-blown; and a Rose that is compact in the former stage, may become expanded in the latter. And the same with regard to colour. A Rose may be pink or rose-colour when first opening to the sun, and fade to blush ere it decay. Now with regard to form, as it would be difficult in all cases to record such peculiarities, *I have contented myself with seeking out the most perfect stage of the flower*, and noting the form of such. As to colour, where this changes, it will be found noticed in the description.

The *habit of the plant* is the next character which presents itself. The terms used here are, *branching, erect, dwarf,* and *pendulous*.

By *branching*, I intend to point out the varieties whose shoots have a somewhat lateral tendency of growth, branching away from the centre of the plant. Examples: most of the Hybrids of the Chinese.

Erect is applied to those whose shoots rise perpendicular, or nearly so. Examples: most of the French.

Dwarf is applied to varieties of humble growth. Examples: the Miniature Provence or Pompon, and the Fairy Rose.

Pendulous is used to point out such as are of a pendulous or drooping habit. Examples: the Ayrshire and Sempervirens.

There are *four terms* used illustrative of *the rate of growth; vigorous, robust, moderate,* and *small.*

Vigorous is used to point out such varieties as form long shoots. Examples: Madame Hardy (Damask), Duchess of Sutherland (Hybrid Perpetual).

Robust alludes to those which form very stout shoots of less length than 'Vigorous.' Examples: Juno (Hybrid Bourbon), Lion des Combats (Hybrid Perpetual).

Moderate alludes to those which are of moderate growth : such usually form neat and compact bushes, or heads when on stems. Such are most of the French and Bourbon Roses.

Small is applied where any variety is of small or dwarf growth.

To know the rate of growth of a plant is of the highest importance in the selection of varieties. How otherwise can they be properly adapted for particular purposes? how else arranged correctly in Rose clumps, or in the formation of a Rosarium? One cannot always judge correctly of the actual rate of growth by a young plant : its vigour may be extraordinary, when the variety is in reality only a moderate grower. Hence it frequently happens that we find Roses in clumps, and elsewhere, badly placed, the guiding-line when planting having been the rate of growth of the young plants ; and thus a moderate grower fills a position suited only for a robust or vigorous one, and *vice versâ*.

It is the frequent meeting with cases such as these that has induced me to attach the rate of growth to the varieties, as far as it was practicable to do so. As this feature in description will be new to those who have not seen the Descriptive Catalogues of the Collection here, it may be well to give a table of the average height of the varieties of the different groups intended to be expressed by each term. The terms *vigorous, robust, moderate,* and *dwarf,* are applied to certain kinds, *viewed in comparison with others of the same group :* thus, *a growth of two to three feet* would entitle *a Provence Rose* to the appellation of *vigorous,* whereas *a growth of eight to ten feet* would be required to justify the application of the same term to *the Hybrid Chinese ;* because the latter are, as a whole, more vigorous than the Provence Roses.

The following Table is drawn up in reference to their growth in these nurseries, the soil of which is an alluvial loam. However they may differ *in extent of growth,* in other soils, I imagine *most groups* will remain *comparatively* the same.

TABLE OF THE AVERAGE HEIGHT OF VARIETIES OF EACH GROUP, TO WHICH THE TERMS, VIGOROUS, ROBUST, MODERATE, AND DWARF, ARE APPLIED.

CLASS I.—SUMMER ROSES.

GROUPS.	VIGOROUS.	ROBUST.	MODERATE.	DWARF.
1. The Boursault Rose . .	10 ft.			
2. The Double Yellow . .	. . .	. . .	3 ft.	
3. The Scotch Rose . . .	. . .	. . .	. . .	1½ to 2 ft.
4. The Damask Rose . .	4 to 5 ft.	3 to 4 ft.	2 to 3 ft.	
5. The Provence Rose . .	2 to 3 ft.	2 ft.	2 ft.	
6. The Pompon Rose . .	. . .	. . .	. . .	1 to 1½ ft.
7. The Moss Rose . . .	6 ft.	4 ft.	2 ft.	1 ft.
8. The French Rose . .	3 to 4 ft.	2 to 3 ft.	2 ft.	1 to 1½ ft.
9. The Hybrid French . .	3 ft.	2 to 3 ft.	1½ to 2 ft.	1 to 1½ ft.
10. The Hybrid Chinese . .	8 to 10 ft.	6 to 8 ft.	2 to 3 ft.	1 to 2 ft.
11. The Hybrid Noisette .	6 ft.	. . .	2 ft.	1 to 2 ft.
12. The Hybrid Bourbon .	6 to 8 ft.	4 to 6 ft.	2 ft.	
13. The Alba Rose . . .	4 to 5 ft.	2 to 3 ft.	1½ to 2 ft.	1 ft.
14. The Austrian Briar . .	. . .	3 ft.		
15. The Ayrshire Rose . .	15 ft.			
16. The Evergreen Rose . .	15 ft.	. . .	6 to 8 ft.	
17. The Multiflora Rose . .	10 to 15 ft.			
18. The Banksian Rose . .	15 ft.			

CLASS II.—AUTUMNAL ROSES.

GROUPS.	VIGOROUS.	ROBUST.	MODERATE.	DWARF.
19. The Perpetual Scotch .	. . .	. . .	2 to 3 ft.	
20. The Perpetual Moss . .	. . .	2 to 3 ft.	1½ to 2ft.	
21. The Macartney Rose . .	6 to 8 ft.			
22. The Microphylla Rose .	. . .	. . .	3 ft.	
23. The Hybrid Perpetual .	5 to 6 ft.	4 to 5 ft.	1½ to 2 ft.	1 ft.
24. The Bourbon Perpetual .	. . .	. . .	2 ft.	1 ft.
25. The Rose de Rosomène .	6 to 8 ft.	. . .	2 to 3 ft.	1 ft.
26. The Bourbon Rose . .	6 ft.	4 to 6 ft.	2 to 3 ft.	
27. The Crimson Chinese .	3 ft.	. . .	2 ft.	1 ft.
28. The Chinese, or Monthly .	3 to 5 ft.	. . .	2 ft.	1 ft.
29. The Fairy Rose . . .	. . .	. . .	. . .	1 to 1½ ft.
30. The Tea scented . . .	8 ft.	3 to 4 ft.	2 ft.	1 ft.
31. The Musk Rose . . .	8 to 10 ft.			
32. The Noisette Rose . .	8 to 10 ft.	4 to 6 ft.	2 to 3 ft.	1 to 2 ft.

In the above Table I have avoided the maximum and minimum of height, and endeavoured to secure the mean. In poor soils I doubt not they will sink below this, and in rich ones they may rise above it. Certainly the most vigorous kinds, which are usually grown as Pillar or Climbing Roses, may, by skilful pruning and training, be brought to exceed the heights given.

Much confusion has arisen from there being no acknowledged standard of reference for the names of particular forms of Rose-trees. Thus the terms *low standard*, *half standard*, and *dwarf standard*, are used synonymously by some. Before proceeding further, it may be well to intimate what is here intended by the use of certain names :

Weeping Roses are kinds of vigorous and pendulous growth, worked on stems of 4 feet or upwards.

Standard Roses are any kinds on stems of about 3 feet.

Tall Standards . . . . 4 to 5 feet.

Half Standards . . . . 1½ to 2½ feet.

Dwarf Standards . . . varying from 6 to 18 inches.

Dwarfs are budded or grafted close to the ground, and termed *worked dwarfs;* or are grown from cuttings or layers, and spoken of as *on their own roots.*

Climbing Roses are the most vigorous kinds selected from various groups.

Pillar Roses are analogous to the last; but the best forms of these are kinds of more erect habit, and less vigorous growth, than are usually chosen for Climbing Roses.

Pot Roses are any of the above grown in pots.

CLASS I.—SUMMER ROSES.

BLOOMING IN MAY, JUNE, AND JULY.

ROSA ALPINA.

GROUP I.—THE ALPINE OR BOURSAULT ROSE.

THE Boursault Roses are very distinct from all others. The shoots are long, flexible, very smooth, in some instances entirely free from thorns; the one side often of a pale green, the other of a reddish tinge: the eyes are formed further apart than in common. The flowers are produced in large clusters. By these features are the varieties of this group readily distinguished. The Boursault Roses, though of vigorous growth, are not of a sufficiently pendulous habit to make perfect "Weeping Roses" without assistance from the cultivator. When desired to be formed into such, the branches should be drawn to the ground with tar-twine, or twisted bast; when the immense trusses of flowers they bring forth give to the tree an appearance truly gorgeous. One inducement to grow them in this manner is, that most Roses of a pendulous growth producing pale-coloured flowers, they introduce a charming variety among Weeping Roses; for the Boursault are mostly purple or crimson. Besides forming good Weeping Roses, they are fine grown either on pillars or on fences with a northerly aspect, a situation where few other kinds succeed well. It might be supposed that they are very hardy, growing naturally, as they do, on the Alps of Austria and Switzerland. And such is indeed the case: they will bloom well in situations where they scarcely obtain a gleam of sunshine. The popular name of the group "Boursault" is due to the first double Alpine Rose being so named in compliment to M. Boursault, a French cultivator.

Boursault Roses should be well thinned out in pruning; but the shoots that are left for flowering should be shortened-in very little.

1. AMADIS; flowers deep crimson purple, shaded more or less (*Crimson*) with vivid crimson, large and semi-double; form, cupped. Habit, erect; growth, vigorous; the young wood of a whitish green. A showy rose; excellent as a pillar for distant effect.

2. GRACILIS; flowers lively cherry, shaded with lilac blush, of

medium size, full; form, cupped. Habit, branching; growth, vigorous. Prickles singularly large and long; foliage of a rich dark green, the variety evidently being a hybrid.

———

ROSA SULPHUREA.

GROUP II.—THE DOUBLE YELLOW ROSE.

THIS Rose may be distinguished by its flat glaucous leaves, usually of a pale or yellowish green. The vigorous shoots grow erect, the weaker ones rather twisted, and both are covered with long thin prickles.

It is generally allowed to be a native of Persia, first introduced to England from Constantinople. It is notorious for refusing to expand its blossoms, and has been the subject of much discussion. It was apparently unfavourably known in this respect two hundred years ago. John Parkinson, who wrote on Gardening early in the seventeenth century, says of it: " The flower is so thick and double, that very often it breaketh out on one side or another, but few of them abiding whole and fair in our country." As he does not give us any means of remedying the defect, we may presume that that was a puzzle to him which still remains so to us. At least, if we can advance a reasonable supposition as to the cause, we have not yet been able to provide a remedy. The methods of treatment and aspects which different writers have recommended, to induce this capricious plant to flower, are very various; but all seems of little use. Different aspects have been chosen, and different modes of culture followed; but what has succeeded in the hands of one individual, has, in like situations and circumstances, failed in the hands of another.

. In the first volume of the Gardeners' Chronicle (1841), the Editor invites his correspondents to a discussion on this plant; and, at p. 811, winds up the subject with a leading article. It is there remarked:—

" In what aspect it most flourishes may perhaps be gathered from this, that in ten cases success is connected with an east aspect, in eight with a north, in seven with a west, in six with full exposure all round, and in only one case is the south spoken of: this, however, is by W. Leveson Gower, Esq., whose Roses at Titsey, near Godstone, are well known for their beauty; and this gentleman finds them do better there than on a north or west wall.

" Nothing can be more conflicting than the evidence about soil.

The majority of cases of success occur in light land, gravelly, sandy, loamy, and even marly.

" But, on the other hand, we have some instances of success in the stiffest land. Mr. Bowers, of Laleham, grew it in Northamptonshire, in cold clay, 20 inches deep; an anonymous correspondent asserts that he has had it in the greatest perfection in the blue clay of Essex, and that he has never known it to fail when it was put into clay in a north aspect; and another writer testifies to success in strong, wet, undrained clay, in the same county."

The Double Yellow Rose certainly is very beautiful when perfect; and could any system of cultivation be divulged, which, followed, would ensure a successful issue, I should consider pages well occupied in doing so. But although my anticipations are not thus sanguine, the subject yet deserves a little consideration.

Some have said, Grow it on its own roots; others, Bud it on the Dog-rose; and others, again, Bud it on the Chinese. At East Lodge, on Enfield Chase, the seat of the late Hon. Mrs. Elphinstone, there was a plant on its own roots, growing at a distance of about ten yards from a wall with a north-eastern aspect. It here produced its beautiful yellow blossoms abundantly, covering the bush on all sides, during the flowering season, for several successive years. This situation is high and exposed: the soil is *naturally a heavy loam*, but was somewhat lightened and enriched by the frequent addition of stable manure.

In certain districts of Suffolk, in Sussex, and in the Isle of Wight, it is said to bloom well generally.

I am informed by a friend, a great Rose amateur, that at Ballater, in Scotland, both this and the Austrian Rose flower beautifully. He has seen them there growing most luxuriantly, in a very exposed situation, covering a wall of great height and extent, laden with perfect flowers.

The late Mr. Cunningham of Edinburgh once informed me that there was a plant *on a south wall* in that neighbourhood which flowered to perfection every year. The main stem and branches were as large as those of a Pear-tree, and bushels of flowers might be gathered from them in the season.

In the Nurseries of my late father the plant to which allusion is made in the First Division of this work was grown on its own roots, trained to a *west wall*, where it flowered constantly and well. The soil in which it grew *was originally* a heavy loam; but having been occupied as garden ground for a century or two, it presents more the appearance of black garden mould. The sub-soil is gravel.

In some parts of Italy perfect flowers are produced with so much certainty, that it is cultivated as a market-plant; and it is often met with in the markets in various parts of France.

I think one thing is tolerably clear : our climate generally is not suited for its cultivation; and this presents a difficulty not easily overcome. Locality is evidently of vast importance ; and a locality with a pure dry atmosphere is preferable to any other. In dry, mild seasons it has flowered in its favourite haunts in England better than at other times; and then in places where, in less favourable seasons, it would not flower. I have never heard of its flowering near London, or in the immediate neighbourhood of any large manufacturing town. There we may plant it ; but no one can say whether it will ever produce perfect blossoms or not. The fact of its doing so, is an anomaly—rather the exception than the rule. Notwithstanding this, its beauty, when perfect, tempts many to cultivate it : and let us consider the most reasonable means of obtaining success.

I believe one point has been too much overlooked, both by cultivators and writers on this subject—the general health of the plant. Let the cultivator procure, in the first instance, a healthy and vigorous plant, and, if possible, keep it in a healthy condition. It must be borne in mind, however, that it is *possible* to produce an over-growth : a moderate course is best. Do not tempt it to grow too exuberantly, nor suffer it to dwindle, producing shoots resembling weak straws. Half the plants which I have seen have been in this latter condition, unhealthy, debilitated, literally starved, and often swarming with insects. Can such be expected to develop perfect flowers ? This state of things may answer (barring the insects), applied to some varieties, whose flowers are too full to expand under ordinary circumstances : indeed it does answer; but it will not do so in this instance. I would advise all who desire to cultivate the Double Yellow Rose to plant it on a border with an eastern or western aspect; not training it to a wall, but growing it as a round bush. Let the locality be airy, the soil rather heavy, and tolerably rich. So soon as the buds break, set a watch over the plant to keep it free from the insects which almost invariably infest it, and which may be done by brushing them off into the hand, or syringing with tobacco-water. When the flower-buds are forming, have an eye to their growth : if weakly, or seeming likely to become so, water the plant twice or thrice a week with a solution of guano, using about two ounces to a gallon of pond or rain-water. As soon as the flowering season is past, remove some of the shoots, if they have been produced in such number as to crowd each other, when those suffered to remain will become thoroughly matured by fuller exposure to sun and air. By this procedure one grand

point is gained—the formation of wood in the most favourable con--
dition for the production of perfect flowers. In March the plant
may be pruned, *but very little*: on the weak shoots, five or six eyes
should be left; on the strong ones, from six to nine eyes.

It is only by the recent introduction of the Persian Yellow Rose
that we have become, in some measure, indifferent to the possession
of the old double Yellow; the former, though not of equal beauty,
being yet a free and tolerably certain bloomer.

1. DOUBLE YELLOW, or SULPHUREA; flowers of the deepest and
    brightest yellow found among Roses; very large and
    full; rarely expand well; form, globular. Habit,
    branching; growth, moderate, or sometimes vigorous.

———

ROSA SPINOSISSIMA,

GROUP III.—THE SCOTCH ROSE.

WELL has this Rose been named " Spinosissima," for it is indeed the
most spiny of all Roses, and the spines are as sharp as they are
plentiful. They are far more so than they seem to be; and a word
of caution here may save the tyro an unpleasant greeting. The
Scotch Rose is a native species, growing plentifully in many parts
of Britain. I have somewhere read or heard it stated, that the first
double Scotch Roses were raised from seed by Mr. Brown, a Nurseryman at Perth. It is from that part many of our finest varieties
have issued, and varieties have been exceedingly numerous; for
they seed so abundantly, and the seed vegetates so freely, that
there is no difficulty in raising seedlings. But with English
amateurs they are not popular; why, I do not know, except it arise
from the short duration of their flowers.

They all form compact bushes, being usually grown as such, for
they are not well adapted for standards. They flower abundantly,
and early in the season. The flowers are small and globular; many
of them, as they hang on the bush, looking like little balls. I
recollect being much struck with a stand of these Roses brought to
one of the Horticultural exhibitions in May. The season was an
early and a genial one, and they were produced in great beauty.

Scotch Roses are in character planted as a hedge round a
Rosarium, where such may be required: a bank of Scotch Roses I
should also conceive to produce a good effect. They *like* a pure

air—and indeed what Roses do not?—but will grow almost anywhere.*

When plants of the Scotch Rose become established in the soil, the stems push laterally under ground, often rising to the surface at a considerable distance from the plant. These are called suckers, and are separated from the mother plant to form new plants ; and thus is the Scotch Rose propagated. It is not easy to confound this with any other group, the spines are so thickly set on the stems. The growth is dwarf. The flowers are mostly small, double, and globular in form, possessed of a peculiarly grateful fragrance. The plants resemble each other so nearly in every respect, that it seems only necessary to affix the colours.

There is one hybrid of this group well worthy of cultivation, the Stanwell Perpetual, which blooms both in summer and autumn.

1. AIMABLE ROSETTE ; flowers red or rose.
2. AMBUCHELET ; flowers rosy lilac.
3. ARTERRESEA ; flowers blush and purple marbled.
4. CELESTA ; flowers white.
5. COUNTESS OF GLASGOW ; flowers deep purple.
6. COUNTESS OF KINNOUL ; flowers purple.
7. GUY MANNERING ; flowers blush, large.
8. IRIS ; flowers white.
9. JAMES'S PURPLE ; flowers purple.
10. JOSEPHUS ; flowers light yellow.
11. KING OF SCOTS ; flowers rosy purple.
12. LADY BANKS ; flowers blush red.
13. LADY ROLLO ; flowers lilac.
14. MARY STUART ; flowers yellow.
15. MIDAS ; flowers dark red.
16. MRS. HAMILTON ; flowers blush purple.
17. MRS. M. STIRLING ; flowers dark velvety red, fine.
18. MOZART ; flowers blush.
19. NEPTUNE ; flowers fine dark red.
20. PRINCESS ; flowers blush white.
21. PRINCESS ELIZABETH ; flowers bright pink.
22. PYTHAGORAS ; flowers marbled red or rose.
23. VISCOUNTESS OF STRATHALLAN ; flowers blush.
24. WAVERLEY ; flowers red.

----

* I recollect once meeting with a plant at Garth Point, North Wales, which had fastened itself in the crevice of a bare rock, where it not only lived, but flourished. It was solitary : no plant disputed its position.

ROSA DAMASCENA.

GROUP IV.—THE DAMASK ROSE.

In common parlance, all dark Roses are termed Damask, probably from the first dark varieties having borne this name. But this is not literally correct. There are dark Roses belonging to almost every group ; and there are Damask Roses of various colours : some are white. The Damask are readily distinguished from others by a robustness of growth, in conjunction with rough, spinous shoots, and downy, coriaceous leaves of a light green colour. Owing to this latter feature, they present a striking contrast when introduced among other groups. The flowers are mostly of fair size ; some are large, and all are showy.

The Damask Rose is allowed to be of great antiquity. Some suppose it to be of this Virgil speaks in the Georgics and elsewhere. It is generally believed that it was first introduced from Syria, and brought to England in 1573. But Johnson, in " The History of Gardening," says, " The learned Linacre, who died in 1524, first introduced the Damask Rose from Italy." Who will fight the battle ? We must not pause to do so. Wherever the truth may lie, it is evident that it has been cultivated in England for a great length of time ; and it affords a singularly striking example of the treasures Nature's plants are capable of yielding beneath the hand of the industrious cultivator ; of the power given unto man to improve by his labour the races of the vegetable world. For two hundred years this Rose underwent but little change ; but modern Rose-growers have improved and varied it to such a degree, producing through it, first, Damask Perpetual, then Hybrid Perpetual, that the favourites of so long standing are threatened with oblivion.

The Damask Roses are very hardy, thriving well either as standards or dwarfs. They do not form compact-headed trees, but their growth is graceful ; rather more rambling than that of the French Roses. They flower abundantly : in some instances the flowers rest among the leaves and branches which surround them ; in others they are elevated above. It is chiefly from the petals of this species, in common with those of the Provence (R. CENTIFOLIA), that Rose-water is distilled. Acres of Roses are grown in some parts of the country expressly for the purpose.

1. BOUVET ; flowers purplish rose ; second rate.
2. COLUMELLA ; flowers rose, changing to flesh colour, slightly globular.
3. CARDINAL D'AMBOISE ; flowers pink, pale edges ; second rate.

4. DÉESEFLORE; flowers almost white, pink centres; small and full.
5. DUKE OF CAMBRIDGE; flowers deep purplish rose, large and full.
6. HARRIET MARTINEAU; white; second rate.
7. LA CHÉRIE; flowers flesh-colour, their centres salmon-pink; second rate.
8. LA VILLE DE BRUXELLES; flowers light vivid rose, the colour gradually receding from their centre, leaving the edges of a rosy blush; large and full; form, expanded. Habit, branching; growth, vigorous. A beautiful Rose.
9. LEDA; flowers blush, tinged with flesh, the petals often margined (*Painted Damask*) with lake; of medium size, full; form, expanded. Habit, branching; growth, robust; leaves, broad, short, and handsome. A beautiful Rose when the lake margin is perfect.
10. MADAME HARDY; flowers pure white, occasionally delicately tinged with flesh, large and full; form, cupped. Habit, erect; growth vigorous, frequently producing the flowers in large clusters. A beautiful Rose. Raised at the Jardin du Luxembourg in 1832.
11. MADAME SOETMANS; flowers delicate flesh, changing to white, glossy, large and full; form, cupped. Habit, branching; growth, vigorous. A beautiful Rose.
12. MADAME STOLTZ; flowers pale straw; form, cupped.
13. MARIQUITA; flowers white, tinged with flesh-colour.
14. POPE; flowers crimson and purple shaded; second rate.
15. PULCHERIE; flowers pure white; of medium size, very double; form, cupped. Habit, branching; growth, moderate.
16. SÉMIRAMIS; flowers fawn, shaded with pink; second rate.
17. TRIOMPHE DE ROUEN; flowers soft even pink, the tops of the petals slightly turning over soon after expansion, large and full; form, expanded.

———

ROSA CENTIFOLIA.

GROUP V.—THE PROVENCE ROSE, WITH ITS HYBRIDS.

WHO has not heard of the Provence, or, as it is more frequently called, the Cabbage Rose ? There are numerous varieties, though Nature has not been so lavish with her gifts here—has not answered so fully to the strivings of art to improve this group—as in some other instances. Perhaps the old favourite is so perfect that it cannot be surpassed. Be this as it may, the group has improved by the varying of the colours, if no individual variety has been raised to surpass the original.

The Provence Roses are deliciously fragrant ; their habit is for the most part branching, or pendulous ; and among them are some of the finest globular-shaped Roses grown.

The foliage is bold and handsome ; the leaflets broad and wrinkled, in many instances obtuse, the edges deeply serrated. The prickles on the branches are very unequal ; some are fine and straight, others large at their base, and falcate. These points, with the drooping habit, and usually globular flowers, serve as marks by which we distinguish them.

They thrive well either as dwarfs or standards; but some varieties require the fostering care of the cultivator to tempt them to produce their flowers in full beauty. To ensure complete success, plant them in a soil made rich, and water them occasionally in spring with liquid manure. All, except the vigorous growers, which are in many instances hybrids, should be subjected to close pruning.

1. ADÉLE DE SENANGE (hybrid) ; flowers blush pink, sometimes marbled, of medium size, full ; form, expanded ; blooming abundantly, and in clusters.
2. ADRIENNE DE CARDOVILLE ; flowers rosy crimson, large and full ; form, cupped, fine. Habit, branching ; growth, moderate. A good and distinct Rose. Raised in the neighbourhood of Paris. Introduced in 1845.
3. BLUSH PROVENCE ; flowers soft light pink, of medium size, double. Habit, branching ; growth, moderate.
4. COMMON or CABBAGE ROSE ; flowers rosy pink, their circumference changing paler soon after expansion ; the tops of the petals sometimes slightly reflexing, large and full ; form, globular. Habit, branching ; growth, vigorous.
5. CRISTATA ; flowers rose pink, their circumference changing paler,
   (*Crested Moss*) often assuming a lilac tint, very large and full; form, globular. The flower-buds beautifully crested, the crest sometimes extending to the leaves. Habit, branching ; growth, moderate. An extraordinary and beautiful Rose, first noticed growing on the walls of a convent near Berne, in Switzerland. Prune short; the more vigorous the growth, the more is the crest developed.
6. DOMETELLE BECAR ; flowers bright pink, large.
7. MADAME HENRIETTE (hybrid); flowers rosy lilac, outer petals blush, very large and full; form, cupped. Habit, branching ; growth, moderate.

8. MADAME L'ABBEY (hybrid); flowers brilliant rose, large and full; form, cupped. Draws closely towards the Hybrid French.

9. REINE DE PROVENCE; flowers glossy lilac blush, large and very double; form, globular. Habit, branching; growth, vigorous; shoots very spinous.

10. ROYAL; flowers blush, of medium size, full; form, globular.

11. SCARLET PROVENCE; flowers rosy lilac, their centre deep rose, (*Regent*) large and double; form, expanded. Habit, branching; growth, vigorous. A good seed-bearer.

12. UNIQUE; flowers paper white, large and full; form, deeply (*White Provence*) cupped. Habit, erect; growth, vigorous. A good white Rose, well suited for masses.

13. UNIQUE PANACHÈ SUPERB; flowers white striped with lake, but (*Superb Striped Unique*) sporting much, sometimes coming altogether white, and sometimes wholly red; large and full; form, cupped. Habit, erect; growth, vigorous, shoots very spinous. This is one of the most beautiful Striped Roses known; but there is some difficulty in keeping it in true character. To assist in this, avoid a rich soil; let it be planted in a mixture of good turfy loam, burnt earth, and old mortar or brick rubbish, two parts of the former to one of each of the latter.

WHITE PROVENCE; see Unique.

ROSA CENTIFOLIA.

GROUP VI.—THE MINIATURE PROVENCE, OR POMPON ROSE.

THE Roses in this group are remarkable for their diminutiveness. They are well adapted for edgings to the Rosarium, or Rose-clumps generally. They are sometimes planted in masses, in which manner they look well, as they are of neat growth, and bloom profusely; but they do not last long in flower: and for this reason we should hesitate to recommend them, except under particular circumstances. The Chinese and Bourbon Roses are usually preferred for dwarf masses, and no wonder, when it is considered that they produce their beautiful flowers during one half of the year.

1. DE MEAUX; flowers light rose, very small and full. Habit, (*Pompon*) erect; growth, dwarf.

2. DWARF BURGUNDY; flowers deep red, very small and double; form, cupped; growth, dwarf.

3. SPONG; flowers pale rose, small, and very double; form, cupped; growth, dwarf.

4. WHITE BURGUNDY ; flowers white, their centres pink, very small
and very double; form, cupped; growth, dwarf.

———

ROSA CENTIFOLIA.
GROUP VII.—THE MOSS ROSE.

The history of the Moss Rose is wrapped in obscurity. It was
first introduced to England from Holland; and it is generally
believed that it was a sport from the Provence Rose; that it was
not originated by seed, as most new varieties are, but by a branch
of the Provence Rose sporting, as it is termed,—that is, producing
flowers differing in character and habit from others of its own
nature,—flowers enveloped in moss. Some tribes of plants are
more disposed to sport than others; and the Provence and Moss
Roses possess this peculiar property to a remarkable degree. I
have seen the White Moss bearing at the same time, and
on the same plant, red, white, and variegated flowers. I have
also seen the Perpetual White Moss, whose flowers should be
white, produce pink flowers, entirely destitute of moss. I am informed, and think it probable, that the Moss Unique was first obtained in this manner : a branch of the White Provence Rose produced flowers enveloped in moss; the branch was propagated from;
and the plants so propagated produced flowers retaining their
mossy characteristic.

Like many others, the group now before us has been much improved of late years : many of the old varieties, formerly so much
esteemed, though possessed of but few petals, and almost destitute
of form and fragrance, are now quietly departing to give place
to more perfect kinds. A remarkable illustration of the effects of
hybridizing is met with here. There have been introduced lately
some Moss Roses of the most vigorous growth, with shining foliage;
and others bearing flowers in the autumn. The former have been
produced by crossing the Moss with the Hybrid Chinese Roses, or
vice versâ : the latter by bringing together the Moss and Perpetual.
(See Article *Hybridizing*.)

The Perpetual Moss we refer to a separate group (Class II.
Group XX. Autumnal Roses): the others we retain here. Besides
these, there are varieties possessing some of the characters of the
French Rose : such is Gloire des Mousseuses.

Moss Roses require high cultivation ; some are of delicate growth,
and will only flourish in a kindly soil; others are very hardy; but
all, whether hardy or delicate, delight in a rich soil. But few of
the Moss Roses are well adapted for Standards : it is true that
many will exist as such, but they merely suffer existence; they
cannot be said to flourish. The Moss should be grown either on

their own roots, or budded on short stems (the latter is preferable in most cases), and should be closely pruned. Exceptions may be made to this rule, which will be noticed in describing the varieties. If we except the common Moss, we do not consider this group well suited either for pot-culture or for forcing. Their distinctness, however, stands forth prominently in their favour; and in large collections it is worth while to introduce a few, for the sake of variety. The Flower Garden or the Rosarium is their proper place; and we think a greater space should be allotted them there than is usually done. No Roses can be more interesting; certainly none are sweeter or more beautiful.

On rich, warm, dryish soils, with an airy situation, the varieties termed "vigorous" may be fashioned into "Pillar Roses," and they are indeed unique when cultivated in this manner.

Could any thing be more beautiful than a collection of Moss Roses, formed into pillars varying in height from six to eight feet? There is an abundance of material with which to form such. All the kinds marked "vigorous" are suited for the purpose.

The moss-like substance which surrounds the flower-buds of these Roses is a sufficient mark of distinction; but they are altogether dissimilar to others. They vary much in character and vigour.

1. ADELE PAVIE; flowers blush, large; growth, vigorous.
2. ALICE LEROI; flowers lilac blush, shaded with rose, large and double, well mossed; form cupped; growth, vigorous. Should be pruned moderately close.
3. ANGÉLIQUE QUÉTIER; flowers rosy lilac, large and very double; well mossed; form, cupped; exquisite in the bud state; growth, vigorous, forming a bush densely clothed with foliage.
4. BARONNE DE WASSENAER; flowers bright red, of globular form, produced in clusters, large, but not very double. A good hardy free Rose; growth vigorous.
5. BLUSH; flowers blush, their centres pink, well mossed, large and full; form, cupped; habit, branching; growth, moderate; foliage, fine. A beautiful Rose.
6. CAPTAIN INGRAM; flowers dark velvety purple, exceedingly rich in colour, of medium size, full; growth, vigorous.
7. CELINA; flowers deep rosy crimson, shaded with dark purple, a streak of white occasionally tracing the centre of a petal; colour brilliant when newly opened; large and double; form, expanded; growth, moderate. A beautiful Rose. A good seed-bearer.
8. CLEMENCE BEAUGRAND; flowers bright pink, large and double; growth, vigorous.
9. COMMON, or OLD; flowers pale rose, very large and full, well

mossed; form. globular; growth. vigorous; foliage fine.
One of the most beautiful. Thrives as a Standard.

10. COMTESSE DE MURINAIS; flowers pale flesh when newly opened,
soon changing to white, large and very double; form,
cupped; growth vigorous. Raised from seed by M. Vibert
in 1843. Thrives as a Standard.

CRESTED MOSS; see Group V. Provence Rose. "Cristata."

11. CRIMSON; flowers rose, large and double; form, expanded, well
(Damask Moss) mossed; growth. vigorous; foliage large and fine.
Raised at Tinwell, in Rutlandshire; and hence sometimes
called the Tinwell Moss.

12. CRIMSON FRENCH; flowers rosy crimson, of medium size, full;
(Reverlata) form, expanded; habit, branching; growth, moderate.
The wood has a reddish appearance from being densely
covered with red spines.

DAMASK MOSS; see Crimson.

13. DANVILLE; flowers lilac, crimson centres; growth moderate.

14. DUCHESSE D'ABRANTES; flowers rosy blush, large and full;
growth vigorous.

15. DUCHESSE D'ISTRIE; flowers rosy pink; growth moderate.

ECARLATE; see Crimson French.

16. ECLATANTE; flowers deep even pink, large and double, well
mossed; form, expanded; growth, vigorous.

17. EMPEROR; flowers reddish crimson, of medium size, full; form,
compact; habit, branching; growth, vigorous; shoots
thickly covered with red spines. A very pretty Rose:
not unsuitable for a short pillar. Raised at Brenchley,
in Kent.

18. ETNA; flowers brilliant crimson with a purplish tinge, of large
size, and very double. A beautiful Rose. Raised at
Angers. Introduced in 1845.

FERRUGINEUSE; see Luxembourg.

19. FELICITÉ BOHAIN; flowers bright rose, large and full; growth,
vigorous.

20. FREDERIC SOULIÉ; flowers crimson and purple shaded, large,
full, and excellent; growth, moderate.

21. GLOIRE DES MOUSSEUSSES; flowers pale rose, margined with
blush, very large, full, and well mossed. One of the
handsomest of this group. Thrives as a Standard. Growth,
robust.

22. GRACILIS; flowers deep pink, large and full, well mossed; form,
(Minor) globular. An abundant blooming variety, with fine large
(Prolific) foliage; excellent for masses; growth moderate.

23. GRANDIFLORA; flowers deep rose, very large and double; form,
cupped.

24. JAMES MITCHELL ; flowers shaded rose ; growth, moderate.
25. JEANNE DE MONTFORT ; flowers flesh colour, large and full ; growth, vigorous.
26. JOHN CRANSTON ; flowers crimson and purple shaded, of medium size, full ; form, expanded ; growth, free but moderate. Thrives as a Standard.
27. JULIE DE MERSENT ; flowers rose shaded with blush. A good free-flowering sort, of moderate growth.
28. LANEII (hybrid) ; flowers rosy crimson, occasionally tinged with purple, large and full ; form, globular ; buds broad, bold, and well mossed ; foliage very large. Raised by M. Laffay of Bellevue.
29. LATONE ; flowers blush, large and full ; growth, vigorous.
30. L' EBLOUISSANTE ; flowers crimson.
31. LUXEMBOURG (hybrid) ; flowers deep crimson, often shaded with (*Ferrugineuse*) purple, of medium size, and double ; form, expanded ; growth, vigorous. A beautiful Rose, not unsuitable for a short pillar, or a standard ; requires but little pruning. A good seed-bearer.
32. MADAME DE LA ROCHELAMBERT ; flowers amaranth, large and full ; growth moderate.
33. MADAME HOCHE ; flowers white, very double.
34. MALVINA (hybrid) ; flowers rosy pink, large and full, well mossed ; form, cupped. Habit, branching ; growth, vigorous.
35. MADEMOISELLE ALBONI ; flowers blush, pink centres, large and double ; growth, moderate.
36. MADEMOISELLE ROSA BONHEUR ; flowers rose-colour, large and full ; growth, moderate.
37. MARIE DE BLOIS ; flowers bright rosy lilac, large and full, well mossed ; growth vigorous. One of the best.
MINOR ; see Gracilia.
38. MOUSSEUSE PRESQUE PARTOUT ; flowers rose-colour, large and very double ; growth, moderate.
39. NUITS D'YOUNG ; flowers dark velvety purple, very double ; growth, vigorous.
40. PANACHÉE PLEINE ; flowers white or flesh-colour, occasionally beautifully streaked with rose, of medium size, very double ; form, cupped ; growth, vigorous. Probably a sport from the White Bath Moss.
41. PARTOUT ; flowers light rose, large and full ; form, cupped ; (*Zoé*) habit, branching ; growth, vigorous ; shoots very spinous ; leaves mossed and curled.
PERPETUAL MAUGET ; see Group XX. Perpetual Moss.
PERPETUAL WHITE ; see Ditto.

42. POMPON ; flowers blush, their centre pale pink, small and full;
(*De Meaux*) form, cupped. Habit, dwarf. A very pretty and interesting Rose of delicate growth. Found growing in a
garden at Taunton, in Somersetshire, about forty years
ago. Prune closely.

43. PRESQUE PARTOUT ; flowers rose, of medium size, full ; form,
cupped ; growth, vigorous. Probably a sport from M.
Partout, which variety it resembles in some particulars,
but is a freer bloomer and a better Rose. Forms a fine
Standard. Prune moderately.

44. PRINCESS ALICE ; flowers blush, pink centres, large, full, and
well mossed ; growth vigorous.

45. PRINCESS ROYAL (Portemer) ; flowers rosy flesh, large and full ;
form, globular, beautiful, well mossed ; flower stalks very
erect. Raised at Gentilly. Introduced in 1846. Prune
closely.

46. PRINCESSE ADELAIDE (hybrid) ; flowers pale glossy rose, blooming in large clusters, large and full ; form, compact.
Habit, erect ; growth, vigorous. A fine Rose for a sunny
wall or pillar. Prune sparingly.

PROLIFIC ; see Gracilis.

47. PRINCESSE DE VAUDEMONT ; flowers pink.

48. PURPUREA RUBRA ; flowers dark purple, large and full. A good
and distinct variety ; growth vigorous.

49. REINE BLANCHE ; flowers pure white, large and full ; growth,
vigorous. Very good.

50. ROSE PALE ; flowers blush, their centre rose-colour, large and
full ; form, cupped.

51. SPLENDENS ; flowers pale glossy peach, large and double.

52. UNIQUE ; flowers pure white, occasionally tinted with lake, large
and full, well mossed ; form, cupped. Habit, erect ;
growth, moderate ; shoots, very spinous. Prune closely.

53. VANDAEL ; flowers rich purple, lilac edges, large and full ; growth,
robust. A good dark Moss Rose.

54. WHITE BATH ; flowers paper-white, occasionally producing
striped or pink petals, well mossed. exquisite in bud,
large and full ; form, globular. Habit, erect ; growth, moderate. A beautiful Rose, and still the best White Moss.
Prune closely.

ZOÉ ; see Partout.

55. WILLIAM LOBB ; flowers crimson, changing to slate, large ;
growth vigorous.

ROSA GALLICA.

GROUP VIII.—THE FRENCH ROSE.

THE French, or Garden Roses, as they are often termed, once formed the most extensive group belonging to the genus "Rosa." They have been long, very long, under cultivation, and many of the old varieties are prolific beyond measure in producing seed, which vegetates freely. Hence is accounted for the number of French Roses which have been introduced to our gardens; and some even of the oldest are still admired and cultivated. They are very hardy, thriving well in the commonest garden soil.

All hues are here, and some interesting striped, marbled, and spotted Roses, which are singularly beautiful. To see the latter in perfection, they should be viewed early in the morning, before a summer's sun has dimmed their beauty; for the colours of these Roses, in particular, fly at the Fire King's approach, when the contrast often becomes too feeble to please.

The French Roses approach nearer to the Provence than to any other group: they are distinguished from them by a more upright and compact growth; the prickles are also smaller and less numerous, and the flowers are more flat. The Hybrid Chinese are descended from these, but there is little fear of confounding the two.

In pruning French Roses, the heads should be well thinned out, as they are disposed to produce an abundance of shoots, far more than can be suffered to remain, if fine flowers, combined with the ultimate good of the tree, are the chief ends in view. Thin out the heads well; then, when pruning, shorten the shoots left, back to four, five, or six eyes, or to where the wood is firm and well ripened, and the eyes full and plump.

1. ADÈLE PREVOST; flowers beautiful blush, their centre pink; cupped, large and full; form, fine. Habit, erect; growth, vigorous.

2. ASSEMBLAGE DES BEAUTÉS; flowers crimson scarlet, shaded (*Rouge éblouissante*) with purplish crimson, of medium size, double; form, expanded. Habit, erect; growth, moderate.

3. BELLE ROSINE; flowers deep pink, their circumference of a paler hue, large and full; form, expanded. Habit, erect; growth, moderate.

4. BÉRÉNICE; flowers rose and crimson, shaded with slate, very rich and beautiful, large and full; form, globular. Habit, pendulous; growth, vigorous.

P 2

BIZARRE MARBRÉE ; see Cecile Boireau.

5. BOULA DE NANTEUIL ; flowers crimson purple, their centre sometimes fiery crimson, the largest shaded dark rose, very
large and full; form, compact. Habit, branching; growth,
moderate. A splendid Rose, which should be in every
collection.

6. CAMBRONNE ; flowers bright rose, shaded with dark slate, very
large and full; form, expanded. Habit, branching;
growth, robust.

7. CÉCILE BOIREAU ; flowers lively rose, marbled with blush, of
(*Bizarre Marbrée*)   medium size, full; form, compact. Habit, erect;
growth, moderate.

8. CÉLESTINE ; flowers rosy blush, of medium size, full; form,
compact. Habit, branching; growth, moderate.

9. CERISE SUPERBE ; flowers bright cherry, of a beautiful colour, of
medium size, very double. Habit, branching; growth,
moderate.

10. COLONEL COOMBES ; flowers light crimson, shaded with purple
and lilac, very large and full; form, expanded. Habit,
erect; growth vigorous.

11. COLUMELLA ; flowers rich rosy crimson, often shaded with
violet, of medium size, full; form, cupped, perfect. Habit,
branching; growth, moderate. Raised at Angers. Introduced in 1841.

12. CUPID ; flowers delicate pink, large and double ; form, cupped.

13. CYNTHIE: flowers pale rose, their circumference almost blush,
large and full; form, cupped. Habit, erect; growth,
moderate.

14 D'AGUESSEAU ; flowers fiery crimson, occasionally shaded with
dark purple, glowing, large, and full; form, compact.
Habit erect; growth, moderate.

15. DIDO ; flowers rose, their centre crimson, large and full; form,
cupped. Habit, erect; growth, moderate.

16. DOCTEUR DIELTHIM : flowers rose, often shaded with purple,
very large and full; form, compact. Habit, branching;
growth, robust.

17. DUC DE TRÉVISE ; flowers bright rosy crimson, mottled with
violet, glowing, large and full ; petals, thick ; form, compact. Habit, branching ; growth, moderate.

18. DUCHESSE D'ORLEANS flowers light vivid rose, large and full ;
form, cupped. Habit, branching ; growth, moderate.

19. DUCHESS OF BUCCLEUCH ; flowers lively crimson, their circumference inclining to lavender blush, very large and full ;
form, cupped. Habit, erect ; growth, vigorous.

20. EBLOUISSANTE DE LAQUEUE ; flowers dark velvety crimson, their centre almost scarlet, large and very double ; form, expanded. Habit, erect ; growth, small.

21. FEU BRILLANTE; flowers light vivid crimson, of a splendid colour when newly opened, very large and double ; form, expanded. Habit, erect; growth, robust. A very showy Rose.

22. FEU DE MOSKOWA ; flowers lively rose, shaded with purple, of medium size, full ; form, cupped. Growth, moderate.

23. GÉNÉRAL BERTRAND (Vibert) ; flowers white, striped with red and lilac, of medium size, very double. Introduced in 1845.

24. GÉNÉRAL FOY ; flowers purplish rose, their centre salmon rose, large and full ; form, cupped. Habit, pendulous ; growth, moderate.

25. GEORGES VIBERT ; flowers white, striped with rose.

26. GLOIRE DE COLMAR ; flowers rich crimson ; form, compact.

27. GRANDISSIMA ; flowers rosy crimson, sometimes purplish, very (Louis Philippe) large and full ; form, compact. Habit, branching ; growth, moderate.

28. GUILLAUME TELL ; flowers fresh rose, their circumference blush, (William Tell) very large and full ; form, compact. Habit, branching ; growth, robust.

29. HEUREUSE SURPRISE ; flowers vivid rose, mottled, and shaded with purple and crimson, large and, full ; form, compact. Habit, erect ; growth, vigorous.

30. JE ME MAINTIENDRAI ; flowers fine rosy pink, large and very double, the petals broad and thick ; form, expanded. Habit, branching ; growth, robust. A pleasing and distinct Rose.

31. JULIE D'ETANGES ; flowers rosy lilac, their circumference inclining to blush, large and full ; form, cupped. Habit, erect ; growth, vigorous.

32. KEAN ; flowers rich velvety purple, their centre crimson scarlet, large and full ; form, compact, perfect. Habit, branching ; growth, vigorous. A beautiful Rose, worthy of a place in the most limited collection.

33. LA CALAISIENNE ; flowers pink, distinct, large and full ; form, compact. Habit, erect ; growth, vigorous.

34. LA JEUNE REINE ; flowers bright rose ; form, cupped.
LA MAJESTEUSE ; see La Moskowa.

35. LA MOSKOWA ; flowers dark velvety brownish crimson, of me- (La Majesteuse) dium size, double. Habit, erect ; growth, moderate. One of the darkest of Roses, and a very desirable variety, though scarcely double enough.

36. LA VOLUPTÉ; flowers rose, slightly shaded with lilac, large and
(*Lætitia*) full; form, cupped, the petals exquisitely arranged.
Growth, moderate.

37. LATONE; flowers rose, slightly mottled with slate, the summits
of the petals reflexing, large and full; form, cupped.
Habit, erect; growth, vigorous; foliage, large and fine.

38. LATOUR D'AUVERGNE; flowers rosy crimson, sometimes inclining to purplish crimson, their centre vivid, large and full;
form, cupped. Habit, erect; growth, moderate; foliage,
dark and fine.

39. MATTHIEU MOLÉ; flowers rosy crimson, mottled with purple,
of medium size, full; form, compact. Habit, erect;
growth, moderate.

40. NAPOLEON; flowers bright rose, shaded with purple, very large
and double; the petals large and thick. Habit, erect;
growth, robust; foliage, bold and fine.

41. NELLY; flowers delicate flesh, wax-like, of medium size, full;
form, cupped. Habit, erect; growth, moderate.

42. NOUVELLE PROVINS; flowers crimson scarlet, vivid, sometimes
(*Nouvelle Bourbon*) shaded with purple, of medium size, full; form,
compact. Habit, branching; growth, moderate.

43. OHL; flowers violet purple, their centre brilliant red, large and
full. Habit, branching; growth, robust. A fine show Rose.

44. ŒILLET FLAMAND; flowers white, distinctly striped with rose
and rosy lilac, large and very double; form, expanded.
Habit, erect; growth, moderate.

45. ŒILLET PARFAIT; flowers pure white, distinctly striped with
rosy crimson, the latter colour shaded with purple, of medium size, double; form, cupped. Habit. erect; growth,
small. Beautiful when true, like a scarlet bizarre Carnation. Somewhat hybridised, partaking slightly of the
Damask, Group IV.

46. ORACLE DU SIÈCLE; flowers crimson purple, large and full;
form, cupped. Growth, moderate.

47. PASHOT; flowers light crimson, occasionally tinged with purple,
large and full; form, globular. Habit, erect; growth,
moderate.

48. PERLE DES PANACHÉES; flowers white, striped with rose-
colour, the marking very clear and distinct, of medium
size, full; form, expanded. Habit, erect; growth moderate. One of the best of the striped Roses.

49. PHARERICUS; flowers light lively rose, occasionally shaded with
(*Warivicus*) dove, of medium size, full; form, compact. Habit,
erect; growth, moderate.

50. PIERRE JAUSSENS; flowers fiery scarlet, their circumference shaded with crimson purple, large and full; form, compact. Habit, branching; growth, moderate.

51. PRINCE REGENT; flowers bright rose, large and very double: form, cupped. Habit, erect; growth, moderate.

52. QUEEN ADELAIDE; flowers dark velvety purple, large and full; form, compact. Habit, erect; growth, moderate.

53. REINE DES FRANÇAIS; flowers rich rosy crimson, shaded with slate, very large and full; form, cupped. Habit, pendulous; growth, vigorous.

54. ROSAMONDE; flowers pale rosy lilac, large and very double; form, compact.

55. ROSA MUNDI; flowers white, striped with carnation, large and semi-double; form, expanded. Habit, branching; growth, moderate. An abundant seed-bearer, and the parent of most of the striped French Roses.

56. ROUGE ADMIRABLE; flowers purplish red, large and very double; form, compact.

ROUGE 'EBLOUISSANTE; see Assemblage des Beautés.

57. SANCHETTE; flowers even rose, very large and full; form, cupped, exquisite. Habit, erect; growth, robust.

58. SCHISMAKER; flowers dark clouded purple, rich and velvety when newly opened, large and very double; form, globular. Habit, erect; growth, moderate.

59. SCIPIO; flowers deep crimson; form, cupped.

60. SOPHIE DUVAL; flowers rose, shaded with lilac and violet, very large and full; form, compact. Habit, erect; growth, robust.

61. SURPASSE TOUT; flowers rich rosy crimson, sometimes shaded with purple, large and full; form, cupped. Habit, erect; growth, moderate.

62. TÉLÉMAQUE; flowers light red, shaded with purple, large and full; form, expanded. Habit, erect; growth, vigorous.

63. TRANSON GOMBAULT; flowers red, clear and pale at their circumference, large and full.

64. TRICOLORE DE FLANDRE; flowers white, striped with crimson, lilac, and amaranth, of medium size, full. Raised at Gand in 1844. Introduced in 1846.

65. TRIOMPHE DE JAUSSENS; flowers vivid rosy crimson, shaded with purple, of medium size, full; form, cupped. Habit, branching; growth, moderate.

66. TRIOMPHE DE RENNES; flowers lively rose, marbled with slate, very large and full; form, expanded. Habit, erect; growth, robust.

67. TUSCANY; flowers blackish crimson, velvety, large and semi-double. Habit, erect, growth, vigorous.

68. VILLAGE MAID; flowers white, striped with rose and purple, (*La Rubanée*) the stripes varying in breadth, sometimes the one and sometimes the other colour preponderating, large and full; form, cupped. Habit, pendulous; growth, small.

WILLIAM TELL; see Guillaume Tell.

ROSA GALLICA.

GROUP IX.—HYBRID FRENCH, COMMONLY CALLED HYBRID PROVENCE.

THIS Group resembles the last more nearly than any other, and for that reason we term them Hybrid French. Their growth is less robust than that of the true French: the shoots are less knotty, and the wood is usually of a pale green. The eyes are in many cases formed on the shoots at very short distances from each other. The flowers are mostly light coloured, and are remarkable for their beauty and purity of appearance.

It has appeared to us advisable to place in this Group the names of all the varieties which other authorities view as Hydrid Provence; but we give *the names only* of such, referring the reader to the Group to which we consider them properly to belong for their descriptions. By this plan it will be shewn which are considered Hybrid Provence by other cultivators.

The varieties of this Group are hardy, requiring no particular treatment, and flourishing equally well whether grown as Standards or Dwarfs.

1. ALETTE; flowers of a pinkish blush, their circumference white wax-like, large and full; form, gobular. Habit, erect : growth, moderate,

ADÈLE DE SÉNANGE; see Group V. Provence.

ADÈLE PREVOST; see Group VIII. French.

2. ASPASIE; flowers flesh, changing to blush after expanding, of medium size, full; form, cupped. Habit, erect; growth moderate.

3. BLANCHEFLEUR; flowers white, slightly tinged with flesh, large and full; form, compact, perfect. Habit, erect; growth, moderate. An abundant and early bloomer; very beautiful on the tree.

4. BOTZARIS; flowers yellowish white, becoming purer in colour

soon after expansion, of medium size, full. Growth, moderate.

· COLONEL COOMBES ; see Group VIII. French.

5. COMTESSE DE SEGUR ; flowers flesh colour, buff centre, of medium size ; nicely cupped, full. Growth, moderate.

6. DEVIGNE ; flowers of a pinkish blush, of medium size, full ; form, compact. Habit, branching ; growth moderate.

7. DUBOIS DESSAUZAIS ; flowers soft pink, large and very double : (*Eugénie Dubois Dessauzais*) form, cupped. Habit, branching, growth, vigorous.

8. DUCHESSE D'ORLEANS ; flowers flesh, wax-like, large and full ; form cupped. Habit, erect ; growth, moderate.

9. EMÉRANCE ; flowers cream, their centre pale lemon, the petals smooth and of even form, of medium size, full ; form, cupped. Habit, erect ; growth, moderate. A beautiful and distinct Rose.

LA CALAISIENNE ; see Group VIII. French.

LATOUR D'AUVERGNE ; see Group VIII. French.

LA VOLUPTÉ ; see Group VIII. French.

LETITIA ; see La Volupté, Group VIII. French.

MADAME AUDOT ; see Group XIII. Alba.

10. MRS. RIVERS ; flowers deep blush, large and full ; form, cupped, Habit, branching ; growth, vigorous.

11. PAULINE GARCIA ; flowers creamy white, large and very double ; form, cupped. Habit, erect ; growth, moderate.

12. PRINCESSE CLEMENTINE ; flowers paper-white, of medium size, full ; form, compact. Habit, erect : growth moderate.

ROSA GALLICA.

GROUP X—HYBRID CHINESE.

THE Hybrid Chinese Roses have originated from the French and the Provence crossed with the Chinese ; or *vice versâ :* they are, therefore, Hybrids. Although called Hybrid Chinese, they partake more intimately of the nature of the French and Provence Roses than of that of their Chinese parent : we therefore arrange them under Rosa Gallica. One feature in particular has conduced to this : they bloom only in June and July ; whereas the Chinese are the most protracted bloomers, flowering constantly from June till November. But besides this, they resemble the French Roses more nearly than any other Group, and the unpractised eye might confound the two, were it not for certain marks in habit and flowering, which we will now endeavour to point out.

The Group "Hybrid Chinese" of some Catalogues includes more than the name seems to imply : it embraces those Varieties, also, whose parentage on the one side is of the Noisette and Bourbon. In our arrangement they stand divided into three Groups ; namely, Hybrid Chinese, Hybrid Noisette, and Hybrid Bourbon ; the first of which is the one now under consideration.

The Hybrid Chinese differ from the French Roses in their growth, which is more diffuse ; in their foliage, which is usually smooth, shining more or less, and retained on the tree later in the year ; in their thorns, which are larger, and usually more numerous ; and in their flowers, which are produced in larger clusters, whose petals are less flaccid, and which remain in a perfect state a longer time after expansion. These Hybrids are more vigorous in growth than either of their parents, and are in their nature very hardy. There are, therefore, none better for planting in unfavourable situations, or where the soil is poor.

They require but little pruning, especially the vigorous growers. The heads should be well thinned out in November, and the shoots shortened in to from six to twelve eyes in March. We here allude to the mass only. There are some few which require closer pruning : such are all those which are particularized in the descriptions as of moderate growth.

To the cultivator of Roses for exhibition the Hybrid Chinese are altogether indispensable, frequently concentrating in the same flower perfection in the desired points of size, form, and fulness. There is also found among them almost every shade of colour. To those who plant Roses chiefly with the view of ornamenting the flower-garden, or to produce effect by masses of flower, there are perhaps none so well adapted to ensure the perfecting of their design, as very many of them form large-headed trees of elegant growth, producing their brilliant-coloured flowers in gorgeous abundance. It is advisable to select these Roses on stems rather above the average height : they are mostly of a pendulous habit, and, when budded on tall stems, the flowers droop gracefully, and are displayed to great advantage.

The kinds denominated vigorous form the best of Summer-flowering Pillar Roses. They will grow from four to ten feet in the course of a year, they bloom freely when established, and are well clothed with handsome foliage.

1. AURORA ; flowers light lively crimson, sometimes shaded with
　　violet, a ray of white often tracing the centre of the

petals, large and double; form, cupped.   Habit, branching; growth, moderate.

2. BEAUTY OF BILLIARD; flowers vivid scarlet, of medium size, full; form, compact.   Habit, pendulous; growth, moderate; shoots slender.

3. BELLE MARIE; flowers fine rose colour, their circumference paler, large and full; form, cupped.   Habit, branching; growth, vigorous.

4. BELLE THURETTE; flowers crimson, shaded with purple, very velvety, small and full; form, expanded. Habit, branching; growth, vigorous.

5. BLAIRII, No. 2; flowers rosy blush, very large and double. Habit, branching; growth, vigorous; foliage, fine.   One of the largest of Roses, and one of the freest growers, often attaining to ten or twelve feet in one season.   A fine Wall Rose.

6. BRENNUS; flowers light carmine, large and full; form, cupped. Habit, branching; growth, vigorous; foliage, fine.

7. CARRÉ DE BOISJELOUP; flowers slate colour, of medium size, full; form, expanded.

8. CHARLES FOUCQUIER; flowers reddish crimson, their circumference inclining to lilac; form, globular. Habit, branching; growth, vigorous.

9. CHÉNÉDOLE; flowers light vermilion, very large and very double; form, cupped.   Habit, erect; growth, most vigorous; shoots, very spinous.   A superb Rose for a pillar; a good seed-bearer; and one of the most attractive Roses grown.

COCCINEA SUPERBA ; see Vingt-neuf Juillet.

10. COMTE COUTARD; flowers lilac rose, large and full; form, compact.   Habit, pendulous; growth, moderate.

11. COMTESSE DE LACÉPÈDE; flowers silvery blush, their centre sometimes rosy flesh, large and full; form, cupped, delicately beautiful.   Habit, branching; growth, moderate.

12. COUP D'AMOUR; flowers bright salmon rose, of medium size, full; form, cupped.   Habit, branching; growth, moderate.

13. DECANDOLLE; flowers crimson scarlet, vivid, large, and semi-double.

14. DUKE OF DEVONSHIRE; flowers rosy lilac, striped with white, large and double; form, cupped.   Habit, branching; growth, vigorous.

15. EMPEROR PROBUS; flowers deep lilac red, large and very double; form, cupped.

16. FIMBRIATA ; flowers vivid red, the petals serrated at their circumference.
17. FREDERICK THE SECOND ; flowers rich crimson purple, large and double ; growth, vigorous.
18. FULGENS ; flowers brilliant crimson, of medium size, full ; form, (*Malton*) cupped, fine. Habit, branching ; growth, vigorous. Requires but little pruning.
19. GÉNÉRAL ALLARD ; flowers rosy carmine, of medium size, very double ; form, globular. Habit, branching ; growth, small.
20. GÉNERAL CHANGARNIER ; flowers purplish red, large and full.
21. GENERAL JACQUEMINOT ; flowers deep purple, shaded with, brilliant crimson, large and full ; form, compact. Habit, erect ; growth, vigorous. Introduced in 1846.
22. GENERAL KLEBER; flowers rich purplish red, sometimes changing to violet, of medium size, full ; form, cupped. Habit, pendulous ; growth, vigorous.
23. GEORGE THE FOURTH ; flowers vivid crimson, shaded with dark purple, glowing, large and full ; form, cupped. Habit, branching ; growth, moderate.
24. GENERAL LAMORICIÈRE, alias GERVAIS ROUILLARD ; flowers rose-colour, large and full ; growth, moderate.
25. GLOIRE DE COULINE ; flowers carmine, shaded with crimson, large and full ; form, cupped. Habit, branching ; growth, moderate.
26. JENNY ; flowers rosy lilac, large and very double ; form, cupped. Habit, branching ; growth, vigorous.
27. LADY STUART ; flowers silvery blush, large and full ; form, cupped. Habit, erect ; growth, small.
28. L'ATTRAYANTE ; flowers flesh or nankeen, ranunculus-shaped, of medium size, full.
29. LAS CASAS D'ANGERS ; flowers carmine, shaded and marbled with crimson purple, of medium size, very double ; form, cupped.
LEOPOLD DE BAUFFREMONT ; see Group XI. Hybrid Noisette.
MADAME PLANTIER ; see Group XI. Hybrid Noisette.
30. MADAME RAMEAU ; flowers rich dark purple, very velvety, large and full. Habit, erect ; growth, vigorous.
31. MAGNA ROSEA ; flowers light rose, very large and very double ; form, cupped, fine. Habit, branching. One of the largest of Roses, and most vigorous in growth.
MALTON ; see Fulgens.
32. MARIE DE CHAMPLOUIS ; flowers deep red or crimson, marbled

with slate, large and full; form, cupped. Habit, branching; growth, moderate.

MARIE DE NERREA ; see Group XI. Hybrid Noisette.

33. MARJOLIN ; flowers purplish slate, very large and full; form, cupped. Habit, branching; growth, robust.

NATHALIE DANIEL ; see Group XI. Hybrid Noisette.

34. RICHELIEU (Verdier); flowers lilac rose, large and full; form, (*Duc de Richelieu*) compact. Habit, branching; growth, vigorous.

35. STADTHOLDER ; flowers blush, their centre light rose, large and full; form, compact. Habit, branching; growth, vigorous.

36. TRIOMPHE D'ANGERS ; flowers bright carmine, often striped with white, large and very double ; form, cupped. Habit, branching; growth, moderate.

37. TRIOMPHE DE LAQUEUE ; flowers rosy lilac, veined with slate, their centre sometimes vivid crimson, large and full; form, cupped. Habit, pendulous; growth, vigorous.

38. TRIOMPHE DE BAYEUX ; flowers creamy white.

39. VELOURS EPISCOPAL ; flowers bright red, shaded with violet purple, of medium size, full; form, globular. Habit, erect ; growth, moderate.

40. VINGT-NEUF JUILLET ; flowers dark crimson, their centre almost (*Coccinea superba*) scarlet, glowing, large and full ; form, compact. Habit, branching ; growth, vigorous; requires but little pruning.

41. VIVID ; flowers brilliant crimson, very showy. A fine pillar or climbing Rose.

WILLIAM JESSE ; see Group XXIII. Hybrid Perpetual.

ROSA GALLICA.

GROUP XI.—HYBRID NOISETTE.

THE Hybrid Noisette Roses form but a small group. They are, nevertheless, a distinct and interesting one. Their parentage on the one side is mostly of the French or of the Provence, and on the other of the Noisette Rose. They resemble the Hybrid Chinese more nearly than any other group : they differ from them in the flowers being of smaller dimensions, and formed in large corymbs or clusters ; owing to which there is a greater succession and longer duration of bloom. They are suitable for the same purposes, and require the same treatment as the Hybrid Chinese, Group X.

1. BELLE DE ROSNY ; flowers delicate peach, their centre often rosy, of medium size, very double ; form, globular.
2. LÉOPOLD DE BAUFFRÉMONT ; flowers pale rose, large and very double ; form, cupped. Habit, branching ; growth, vigorous.
3. MADAME PLANTIER : flowers creamy white when newly opened, changing to pure white, of medium size, full ; form, compact. Habit, branching ; growth, vigorous ; shoots, slender ; foliage light green. An immense bloomer, and a beautiful Rose, forming a large bush or tree, producing a sheet of white blossom, and lasting a long time in flower.
4. MADELINE ; flowers creamy white, or sometimes pale flesh, usually (*Emmeline*) margined with crimson, large and very double ; (*Double margined hip.*) form, compact. Habit, erect ; growth, vigorous. A beautiful Rose when produced true to character, and by no means an inconstant one.
5. MARIE DE NERREA ; flowers clear pale pink, dying off lively blush, large and double ; form, expanded. Habit, branching ; growth, moderate. A most abundant bloomer, producing a fine éffect on the tree.
6. NATHALIE DANIEL : flowers pale peach, of medium size, very double ; form, cupped, fine. Habit, branching ; growth, vigorous ; the foliage of a dull green.

ROSA GALLICA.

GROUP XII.—HYBRID BOURBON.

THE Hybrid Bourbon Roses are also, in greater part, descended from the French or the Provence crossed with the Bourbon, or *vice versâ*. They are less diffuse and more robust in growth than the Hybrid Chinese, being readily distinguished from them by their broad stout foliage, the leaflets of which are more obtuse. The *tout ensemble* of these Roses is particularly fine : some are compact growers, many are abundant bloomers, and the flowers are in general large and handsome. They are well suited for growing in pots, either for forcing or exhibition. In pruning, they may, with few exceptions, be treated as recommended for the Hybrid Chinese.

1. CELINE : flowers pale rose, very large and double ; form, cupped. Habit, branching ; growth vigorous ; the flowers produced in large clusters.
2. CHARLES DUVAL ; flowers deep pink, large and full ; form cupped.

Habit, erect; growth, vigorous; the shoots clothed with beautiful foliage. A good Rose, either for pot or pillar; forms also a very handsome tree.

2*. CIMABUE; flowers crimson; growth, vigorous.

CHÉNÉDOLÉ; see Group X. Hybrid Chinese.

3. COMTE BOUBERT; flowers rose-colour some of the petals occasionally blush, large and double; form, cupped. Habit branching; growth, robust.

4. COMTESSE MOLÉ; flowers bright rose-colour, tinted with purple, changing to flesh-colour, with a lilac tint, very large and full; form, cupped. Habit, erect; growth, robust.

5. COUPE D'HÉBÉ; flowers rich deep pink, exquisite in colour, large and very double; form, cupped, perfect. Habit, erect; growth, vigorous; foliage fine. Good either for a pot or a pillar, and a first-rate show Rose. Raised by M. Laffay of Bellevue. A good seed bearer.

DUKE OF DEVONSHIRE; see Group X. Hybrid Chinese.

6. ELIZA MERCŒUR; flowers rosy crimson, their circumference rosy blush, very large and very double; form, cupped. Habit, branching; growth, moderate.

6*. GARIBALDI; flowers light crimson.

7. GREAT WESTERN; flowers crimson scarlet, marbled with violet purple, varying exceedingly, sometimes brilliant, sometimes dark and beautiful, produced in great clusters, very large and double; form, globular. Habit, branching; growth, robust.

8. HENRI BARBET; flowers light carmine, beautiful in colour, large and double; form, cupped. Habit, branching; growth, robust.

9. JUNO; flowers pale rose, very large and full. Habit, branching; growth, robust. A good Pot-rose.

10. LA DAUPHINE; flowers clear pale flesh, slightly tinged with lavender, peculiar in colour, large and very double; form, cupped. Habit, branching; growth, robust.

11. LORD JOHN RUSSELL; flowers brilliant rose, changing paler when full blown, large and double; form, compact. Habit, branching; growth, robust.

MALTON; see Group X. Hybrid Chinese, " FULGENS."

12. PAUL PERRAS; flowers beautiful pale rose, large and very double; form, compact. Growth, vigorous. A first-rate Rose, either for a pot or pillar; forms also a fine tree, and is a good variety for exhibition. An abundant seed bearer.

13. PERFECTION; flowers delicate pink, fine form; growth, vigorous.

14. PRESIDENT PIERCE ; flowers rich deep crimson, large and full ; growth, robust.
15. SYLVAIN ; flowers bright crimson, large and very double ; form, cupped.
16. TRIOMPHE EN BEAUTÉ; flowers deep shaded rose, large and globular.
17. VICTOR HUGO ; flowers rosy lilac, shaded, large and full ; form, globular. Habit, erect ; growth, vigorous.
WILLIAM JESSE ; see Group XXIII., Hybrid Perpetual.

ROSA ALBA,

GROUP XIII.—THE ALBA, OR WHITE ROSE.

WHAT shall be said of the varieties of this Rose ? Their strongest claim to notice rests, perhaps, on their distinctness : they differ from all others. Although forming but a small group, the extreme delicacy and surpassing beauty of the flowers, which are chiefly of white, blush, flesh, and pink hues, make them a highly popular one. Great size they cannot boast of, but the flowers are neat and elegant, and produced in great abundance.

The upper surface of the leaves of the true Albas has a whitish appearance, beneath which is shewn an intense green : the shoots are, in many instances, spineless ; but the varieties are, as in most other groups, hybridized, and some are very spinous. They form handsome trees, both as standards and dwarfs : the strong growers require moderate pruning ; the others close pruning.

The Alba Rose ranges over the middle of Europe, and was introduced in 1597.

1. BELLE DE SEGUR ; flowers soft rosy flesh, edges blush, beautiful, of medium size, full ; form, cupped. Habit, erect ; growth, vigorous ; foliage, fine dark green.
2. BLUSH HIP, NEW ; flowers delicate blush, their centre flesh, of medium size, full ; form, compact. Habit, branching ; growth, vigorous.
3. CELESTIAL ; flowers flesh colour, beautifully tinted with the most delicate pink, of medium size, double ; form, cupped. Habit, erect ; growth, moderate.
4. ETOILE DE LA MALMAISON ; flowers flesh, fading to French white, large and full ; form, cupped. Habit, erect ; growth, vigorous.
5. FÉLICITÉ PARMENTIER ; flowers rosy flesh, their margin white,

exquisite in bud, of medium size, full; form, compact. Habit, erect; growth, robust. A very abundant bloomer, and indispensable even in a small collection.

6. LA REMARQUABLE; flowers white; form cupped. Growth, robust.
7. LA SÉDUISANTE; flowers rosy flesh, large and full; form, compact. Habit, erect; growth, robust. Shoots covered with small red spines.
8. LUCRÈCE; flowers pale rose, their centre deep rose, very large and double; form, globular.
9. MAIDEN'S BLUSH; flowers soft blush, colour of the buds exquisite, of medium size, double; form, globular. Habit, branching; growth, moderate.
10. MADAME AUDOT; flowers glossy flesh, edges creamy blush, large and full; form, cupped. Habit, branching; growth, moderate.
11. MADAME LEGRAS; flowers pure white, their centre sometimes creamy, large and full; form, expanded. Habit, branching; growth, moderate.
12. PRINCESSE LAMBALLE; flowers pure white, sometimes delicately tinted with flesh, of medium size, full; form, compact. Habit, branching; growth, vigorous in some places, in others shy and delicate. A lovely Rose.
13. QUEEN OF DENMARK; flowers rosy pink, their margin paler, of medium size, full; form, cupped. Habit, erect; growth, moderate. A beautiful Rose; a hybrid.
14. SOPHIE DE BAVIÈRE; flowers deep rosy pink, produced in clusters, of medium size, full; form, compact. Habit, branching; growth, moderate.
15. SOPHIE DE MARSILLY; flowers blush, their centre rose, large and full; form, globular. Habit, erect; growth, vigorous; more spinous than others of the group. A beautiful Rose when about half blown; but requires clear dry weather to produce its flowers in perfection.
16. VISCOMTE DE SCHRYMACKER; flowers pale carmine, their margin lighter, large.

———

ROSA LUTEA,

GROUP XIV.—THE AUSTRIAN BRIER.

THIS may be called a group of Yellow Roses, for the varieties which compose it are mostly of that colour. The Austrian Brier is a native of Germany and the south of France, and was introduced to England in 1596. It is distinguished by its small leaflets and solitary flowers, the bark of the wood being, for the most part, of a chocolate colour. The varieties are very hardy, but require a pure air and dry soil to flower them in perfection. Hence, they rarely succeed well near London : the Harrisonii is perhaps an exception. I have been told that the Persian Yellow grows wild in the hedges of Persia. If so, strange it is that a Rose of such rare beauty should only so recently have reached Europe. But probably it was the single kind which caught the eye of my informant.

The Harrisonii is capable of being formed into a perfect Weeping Rose. Select a plant on a four-feet stem, grow it vigorously, thinning out, but not shortening the shoots. Thus it will droop beautifully, producing its golden blossoms in gorgeous abundance. If a Weeping Rose is wanted every year, two plants should be grown, *that each may be cut in close every alternate year*, otherwise the tree becomes weak and shabby.

These Roses require very little pruning : the flowers are usually produced from the eyes at the middle or near the top of the shoots: the branches should, therefore, be well thinned out in ordinary pruning, the shoots left having their mere tips taken off.

1. COPPER ; flowers rich reddish copper, single ; form, cupped. Habit, branching ; growth, moderate.
2. DOUBLE YELLOW, (Williams') ; flowers bright yellow, of medium size, double ; form, cupped. Habit, branching ; growth, moderate. An abundant and early bloomer ; requiring but little pruning. A good seed-bearer. Raised by Mr. Williams of Pitmaston.
3. HARRISONII ; flowers fine golden yellow, of medium size, double : form, cupped. Habit, pendulous ; growth, moderate. An abundant and early bloomer, producing a splendid effect on the tree, but very transitory. Requires little pruning. Introduced from America about twenty-five years since.
4. PERSIAN YELLOW ; flowers of the deepest yellow, large and full ; form, globular. Habit, branching ; growth, varies, often vigorous. Requires but little pruning. Introduced from Persia by Sir H. Wilcock in 1837.
   PROVENCE ; see Rosa Sulphurea, Group II. "DOUBLE YELLOW."
5. SINGLE YELLOW ; flowers bright primrose, large and single ; form, cupped. Habit, branching ; growth, vigorous.

ROSA ARVENSIS.

GROUP XV.—THE AYRSHIRE ROSE.

THIS is a native species, abounding also throughout Europe, trailing over waste lands, and climbing the hedges and thickets, often completely hiding the undergrowth from view, producing its solitary blossoms in magnificent profusion in June and July. This is the hardiest of Climbing Roses, growing exceedingly rapid where others will scarcely exist. The shoots are slender, owing to which the varieties form admirable Weeping Roses when worked on tall stems ; they are also of the best description for planting to cover banks, and rough places in parks or shrubberies, soon converting the dreary waste into a flowery plain. "Ruga," one of the best of the Group, is apparently a Hybrid between the Ayrshire and Tea-scented. It was raised in Italy, and is hardy, notwithstanding the proverbial delicacy of the one parent.

As may be supposed from the names of these Roses, they are chiefly of British origin ; indeed, we scarcely find mention of them in foreign Catalogues.

1. ALICE GRAY ; flowers creamy salmon blush.
   (*Scandens*)
2. BENNETT'S SEEDLING ; flowers white, of medium size, double ; (*Thoresbyana*) form, expanded. A free bloomer.
3. COUNTESS OF LIEVEN ; flowers creamy white, of medium size, double ; form, cupped.
4. DUNDEE RAMBLER ; flowers white, of medium size, double ; form, compact.
5. LOVELY RAMBLER; flowers pink, large and single ; form, cupped.
6. MILLER'S CLIMBER ; flowers rosy pink, the buds cherry colour when young ; large and semi-double ; form, cupped.
   MYRRH-SCENTED ; see Splendens.
7. QUEEN OF THE BELGIANS ; flowers creamy white, thick petals, large and double ; form, expanded.
8. RUGA ; flowers flesh-colour, changing to creamy white, large and double ; form, cupped ; very sweet. A good seed-bearer.
   SCANDENS ; see Alice Gray.
9. SPLENDENS ; flowers pale flesh, buds crimson when young, presenting a pretty effect on the tree, large and double ; form, globular. One of the best of Weeping Roses. A good seed-bearer.
   THORESBYANA ; see Bennett's Seedling.

ROSA SEMPERVIRENS.

GROUP XVI.—THE EVERGREEN ROSE.

THE Sempervirens Rose abounds throughout the middle of Europe, and is supposed to have been introduced in 1629. It is suited for the same purposes as the Ayrshire, from which it differs by producing its flowers in corymbs, instead of singly, and by holding its beautiful dark green leaves till the depth of winter. On account of these properties, we think it more valuable than the last mentioned. It is not strictly evergreen, as its name would lead us to suppose. It is very hardy, of vigorous growth, and an abundant bloomer. As Pillar Roses some are very beautiful, rising quickly to the height of ten or twelve feet, their pretty ranunculus-shaped flowers drooping in graceful corymbs of from ten to fifty blooms each. In pruning they require much thinning, and the shoots left should be merely tipped.

1. ALBA PLENA ; flowers pure white, full.
2. ADELAIDE D'ORLEANS ; flowers creamy white, of medium size, (*Leopoldine d'Orleans*) full ; form, globular. Blooms in large handsome clusters. A superb Climbing or Weeping Rose.
3. BANKSIÆFLORA ; flowers cream, with yellowish centre, of medium size, very double ; form, cupped. A distinct and good Pillar or Climbing Rose ; the foliage of a fine light green. Requires very little pruning.
4. BRUNONII ; flowers rosy crimson, large ; form, expanded ; showy.
5. CARNEA GRANDIFLORA ; flowers flesh-colour, large and double ; form, cupped.
6. DONNA MARIA ; flowers pure white, of medium size, full ; form, cupped, fine. A beautiful Rose, blooming in large handsome trusses ; foliage, pale green ; growth less vigorous than others. Raised by M. Vibert.
7. FÉLICITÉ PERPÉTUE ; flowers flesh-colour, changing to white, produced in graceful trusses, drooping with their own weight, of medium size, full ; form, compact. A superb Pillar or Climbing Rose. Raised at the Chateau de Neuilly in 1828.
8. FLORA ; flowers fine bright rose, full.
LEOPOLDINE D'ORLEANS ; see Adelaide d'Orleans.
9. MÉLANIE DE MONTJOIE ; flowers creamy white, of medium size, full ; form, compact. A fine Rose, but rather a shy grower.
10. MYRIANTHES RÉNONCULE ; flowers pale peach, their centre white,

hanging in graceful trusses, of medium size, full; form, cupped, fine. A handsome Climbing or Pillar Rose.
ODORATA; see Triomphe de Bolwyller, Group XXX. "TEA-SCENTED.

11. PRINCESSE LOUISE; flowers creamy white, the back petals shaded with rose, large and double; form, cupped. Raised at the Chateau de Neuilly in 1829.

12. RAMPANT; flowers pure white; sometimes produced in autumn. A profuse bloomer.

13. ROSEA MAJOR or PLENA; flowers rosy flesh, changing to white, large and very double; form, cupped; foliage, glossy, fine. Raised by M. Laffay.

14. SPECTABILE; flowers rosy pink, of medium size, double; pro-
(*Noisette Ayez*) duced occasionally in the autumn; form, cupped, pretty and distinct.
TRIOMPHE DE BOLWYLLER; see Group XXX. "TEA-SCENTED."

———

ROSA MULTIFLORA.

GROUP XVII—THE MULTIFLORA ROSE.

To Japan and China we look for the habitats of the type of this Group. It was introduced to England in 1804. These are also Climbing Roses, producing their flowers in large corymbs, and consequently continuing a long time in bloom. The varieties marked with an asterisk are not hardy, and should be planted against a wall: the others may be grown as open Climbers. The foliage of this Group is particularly elegant, and the branches have but few spines. Lauré Davoust, a Hybrid, classed here, deserves a passing word. It forms a magnificent Weeping Rose, but requires a sheltered situation.

1. *ALBA; creamy white, small and very double; form, compact.
2. DE LA GRIFFERAIE; flowers deep rose in bud, changing to blush, large and full; form, compact. Extremely robust.
3. *ELEGANS; flowers reddish rose, small and full.
4. GRAULHIÉ; flowers pure white, outer petals tinged with rose, of medium size, full; form, cupped.
5. LAURÉ DAVOUST; flowers clear pink, changing to flesh, dying off white, small and full; form, cupped. The flowers are produced in large and elegant trusses, the three colours shewing on the truss at the same time.

6. RUSSELLIANA; flowers rich dark lake, gradually changing to
(*Scarlet Grevillei*) lilac, of medium size, very double; form, expanded. A good and distinct Pillar Rose.

ROSA BANKSIÆ.

GROUP XVIII.—THE BANKSIÆ ROSE.

THE Banksiæ Rose, so named in compliment to Lady Banks, is a
complete departure from the ordinary run of Roses: the flowers,
indeed, resemble more closely those of the double-blossomed Cherry.
The White variety, which is deliciously sweet, was introduced
from China in 1807, and about twenty years later our gardens
were enriched by the arrival of the Yellow one.

In "*La Rose*, &c., par Dr. Deslongchamps," we find mention of
a remarkable White Banksiæ Rose growing in the Jardin de la
Marine at Toulon. If still in existence, it is now about forty-four
years old. In 1842 the trunk was 2 feet 4 inches in circumference at its base. It divided into six branches at a little distance
from the ground, the thickest of which was 12 inches in girth.
Its branches covered a wall 75 feet broad and 15 to 18 feet high;
and were there greater space it could be covered, for the tree is
subjected to severe pruning every alternate year to keep it within
bounds; and the more it is pruned the faster does it seem to grow,
often producing shoots 15 feet long in a year, and as thick as the
thumb. The flowers are produced from the middle of April to the
middle of May; and at the time that it is in full blossom it is calculated that there cannot be less than from 50,000 to 60,000 flowers
on the tree. The effect is described as magnificent, almost magical.

In the same Work is mentioned a plant of the same variety,
growing at Caserta, in the kingdom of Naples, the branches of
which had climbed to the top of a large poplar tree 60 feet high.
The poplar was dead, killed probably by the embrace of its insi-
dious friend, whose branches almost exclude it from view, presenting, at the epoch of flowering, a most lovely spectacle.

There was growing at Goodrent, Reading, the seat of Sir Jasper
Nicholls, Bart., some ten years since, a Yellow Banksiæ Rose,
planted out in the conservatory border. It produced one year
above 2000 trusses of flowers, and there were from six to nine expanded Roses on each truss. It was trained up a wire to an horizontal wire fixed about three feet from the glass. There was a

plant of the White variety in the same house, but with very few flowers on it.

The Banksiæ Roses are of very rapid growth, but they are not hardy, and can only be grown successfully out of doors against a wall ; and if a dry warm border can also be secured for them it is all the better. They should be pruned in summer, immediately after they have flowered : the gross shoots, if any, should be cut out, and the plants well thinned, merely tipping the shoots that are left : these will then form new wood, which, cut back to three or four eyes in spring, will throw an abundance of flowers. There have arisen lately several new varieties, but they bloom indifferently in our climate, and we cannot say much in their favour. Unfortunately, these elegant Roses do not thrive well out of doors in the atmosphere of the metropolis.

1. ALBA GRANDIFLORA ; flowers white.
2. JAUNE SERIN ; flowers bright yellow, larger, deeper in colour, (*Lutescens spinosa*) and fuller than the old Yellow.
3. JAUNE VIF ; flowers bright yellow.
4. ODORATISSIMA ; flowers white, fragrant.
5. WHITE ; flowers pure white, small and full; form, compact. Neat and exceedingly pretty. Very fragrant.
6. YELLOW ; flowers bright yellow, small and full ; form, compact. Very pretty and distinct.

CLASS II.—AUTUMNAL ROSES.

ROSA SPINOSISSIMA.

GROUP XIX—THE PERPETUAL SCOTCH.

THESE are Scotch Roses, hybridized, probably, with the Damask Perpetual, and blooming in the autumn. The Stanwell is, perhaps, the only one worthy of the attention of the Amateur. It is among the first to unfold its delicate blossoms, flowering in May, and throughout the summer and autumn, till arrested by frost. It is deliciously sweet : some say it has the fragrance of the Attar of Roses ; but it appears to me more closely to resemble the Provence Rose in this particular.

1. SCOTCH ; flowers pale rosy blush, large and double ; form, expanded ; growth, moderate.
2. STANWELL ; flowers rosy blush, their centre often pink, large, and double ; form, cupped. Habit, branching ; growth, moderate. Raised at Stanwell ; hence its name.

ROSA CENTIFOLIA.

GROUP XX—THE PERPETUAL MOSS.

HERE we have a group of Moss Roses blooming in the autumn. The flowers are not oppressed with moss, although they have sufficient to denote their origin. They require the same treatment as the summer-blooming Moss, (Group VII.)

1. ABELE CARBIERE ; flowers deep rose, changing to red, of medium size ; very sweet. Growth, moderate.
2. ALFRED DE DALMAS ; buds rose-colour, flowers light pink, blush edges ; produced in clusters ; distinct and good. Growth, robust.
3. EMILE DE GIRARDIN ; flowers delicate rose-colour ; form good. Growth, moderate.
4. EMPRESS EUGENIE ; flowers rose, not large, but of exquisite form. Growth, dwarf. The prettiest of the group, but perhaps the most delicate.

5. EUGÈNE DE SAVOIE; flowers bright red, shaded, of good form, average size, and full. Growth, moderate.

6. FORNARINA; flowers deep rose, small, growth dwarf.

7. GENERAL DRUOT; flowers purple and crimson shaded, of fair size, but not very double. A good hardy free-flowering sort, of robust growth.

8. HERMAN KEGEL; flowers purplish crimson shaded, very double. Growth, moderate. Similar and scarcely equal to No. 7.

9. HORTENSE VERNET; flowers white shaded with rose, of good average size, and very double. Growth, moderate.

10. JOHN FRASER; flowers bright red, shaded with crimson and purple, large, full, and of fine form. One of the finest as a flower, but apparently of shy growth.

11. MADAME EDOUARD ORY; flowers bright rosy crimson, large and full. Growth, vigorous. One of the freest and best.

12. MADAME LARIVIERE; flowers rose-colour, spotted. Growth, moderate.

13. MADAME DE STAEL; flowers blush, well mossed. Growth, moderate.

14. MA PONCTUÉE; flowers rose-colour, spotted with white. Growth, dwarf.

15. OSCAR LECLERC; flowers rose-colour, spotted. Growth, moderate.

16. PERPETUAL White; flowers white, produced in large clusters, buds plentifully and beautifully mossed. Growth, vigorous.

17. Pompon; flowers lilac-rose small, full and produced abundantly. Growth, dwarf.

18. RAPHAEL; flowers flesh-colour, produced in clusters. Growth, vigorous.

19. REINE D'ANJOU; flowers rosy-pink. Growth, moderate.

20. SALET; flowers bright rose, blush edges, large and full. Growth, vigorous. One of the best.

21. VALIDE; flowers lilac-rose, with deeper centres; of average size and full. Growth, moderate.

ROSA BRACTEATA.

GROUP. XXI—THE MACARTNEY ROSE.

THE original Bractreata Rose was introduced from China by Lord Macartney in 1795. It is a shy seed-bearer, and consequently few varieties have been obtained from it. Perhaps the only one the

Amateur will care for is the Maria Leonida, but the single is also beautiful. Both are of vigorous growth, but not very hardy. The best situation for them is a south or east wall, where they form most interesting objects, flowering during summer and autumn.

The plants are evergreen; the foliage dark, and shining as if varnished; which feature, in contrast with the milk-white apricot-scented flowers, is striking and beautiful.

The Berberiifolia Hardii, according to previous arrangements, finds place by the side of this species. We think it distinct enough to stand alone; but, as there is only one variety, we retain it in its accustomed place. This pretty plant, differing from all its congeners, was raised from seed by M. Hardy, of the Jardin du Luxembourg, from between R. INVOLUCRATA and R. BERBERIIFOLIA. The latter species has always been extremely delicate in Britain, baffling the skill of the ablest cultivators, although in its native habitats, in the north of Persia, it grows so freely that it is used for fire-wood.

1. ALBA SIMPLEX; flowers white, large and single; form, cupped; (Grandiflora) free bloomer when trained against a wall. Very showy.

GRANDIFLORA; see Alba simplex.

2. MARIA LEONIDA; flowers white, centre rosy, and sometimes creamy, large and full; form, cupped.

3. BERBERIIFOLIA HARDII; flowers bright yellow, with a deep chocolate spot at the bottom of each petal, small and single; form, cupped. Habit, branching; growth, vigorous; shoots, slender.

ROSA MICROPHYLLA.

GROUP XXII.—THE MICROPHYLLA, OR SMALL-LEAVED ROSE.

THIS Rose is a native of the Himalaya Mountains, and also of China, and was introduced to England about thirty years since. It is a decided curiosity. The leaves are composed of numerous small leaflets, sometimes as many as fifteen ranging on the sides of the petiole; the branches are of a whitish brown, the outer bark often peeling off in autumn: they are almost destitute of prickles, but the broad sepals of the calyx are densely covered with them, owing to which the flower-buds are as rough as a hedgehog. The Micro-phylla appears to delight in a warm sandy soil: it is rather tender, and requires a wall to ensure the production of its flowers in full beauty. It requires very little pruning. No varieties have yet been raised to surpass the original.

1. Du Luxembourg; flowers deep pink, shaded with blush, large and full; form, cupped. Habit, branching; growth, moderate.
2. Rubra, old or common; flowers rosy carmine, margined with blush, large and full; form, globular. Habit, branching; growth, moderate.
3. Rugosa; flowers violet and crimson, expanded; very large hardly double; very free and showy. Growth, vigorous.

ROSA DAMASCENA.

Group XXIII.—HYBRID PERPETUAL.

How came we in possession of these lovely Roses which have so suddenly delighted us with their presence, forming, as they do, the most valuable Group among Autumnals? Their origin is various; doubtless, in many instances unknown. The first varieties were raised by M. Laffay from between the *Hybrid Bourbon* or *Hybrid Chinese* and *Damask Perpetual*. Princesse Hélène, which was introduced in 1837, was the first *striking* variety that was obtained; Queen Victoria followed next; and in 1840 there were above twenty varieties enumerated in the Rose Catalogues. Several of these, however, were drawn from other Groups: one-fourth were Bourbon Perpetuals.

If we analyze this Group we shall find several races or strains of flowers, which, in some cases, may be traced very near to their first source. Other varieties are so intermixed that it is difficult to say which race preponderates. After maturely weighing all the circumstances, I have cast these Roses into three groups:—Hybrid Perpetual, which is intended to contain those varieties in which the Damask Perpetual or Hybrid Chinese are distinctly traceable; —Bourbon Perpetual, embracing those in which the Bourbon Rose preponderates; and Rose de Rosomène, to which certain kinds resembling the Gloire de Rosomène seem naturally referrible. There are also many minor distinctions: for instance, there is the Géant des Batailles race, the General Jacqueminot race, and others, but such divisions are less strongly marked than those above given.

I remember when the first Hybrid Perpetual Roses were introduced, it was generally asked, " Will they bloom freely in autumn?" The question now is, " Will they grow?" the perpetual blooming propensity having been developed to such a degree as to produce in some cases feebleness of constitution. Kinds of the latter nature, which bloom very freely, should be planted in a rich soil, pruned closely, and have some of the flower-buds cut away when just forming, at any time of the year when they can be best spared.

The Group before us, spoken of in reference to their external characters, might be called Hybrid Chinese blooming in the autumn. They are indeed fine Roses, quite hardy, and very sweet. They thrive under common treatment, and are generally suited alike for standards and dwarfs, for pot-culture and forcing. Indeed, nowhere are they out of place : they grow and flower well in the vicinity of London, and in the northern parts of England and Scotland.

1. ABBÉ FEYTEL ; rose, shaded with lilac, second-rate.
2. ABD-EL-KADER ; flowers scarlet and purple shaded, very velvety, large and double; form, cupped. Beautiful in colour, but rather a loose flower and hardly double enough.
3. ADELAIDE FONTAINE ; flowers deep pink, large and full. A superior flower, but does not always expand wide; the growth is any thing but free.
4. ADMIRAL NELSON ; flowers brilliant crimson, of exquisite colour and fine cupped form. Resembles Chénédolé in habit and flowers. Growth, vigorous. Not a full Rose.
5. ADOLPHE NOBLET ; flowers brilliant red, large, full, and constant ; form, cupped. Growth, vigorous.
6. AGATOIDE, flowers rose tinted with pink, large, full, and showy. Growth, vigorous.
7. ALBERT DE STELLA ; flowers dark red. Second-rate.
8. ALCIDE VIGNERON ; flowers light pink, large and full, petals rather twisted.
9. ALEXANDRE DUMAS ; flowers dark blackish purple, small and cupped ; full enough, with good outline in the early and medium stages of the flower. Growth, dwarf.
10. ALEXANDRE FONTAINE ; flowers reddish cerise, fine form, blooms freely. Growth, moderate. Very good.
11. ALEXANDRINE BACHMETEFF ; flowers fine bright red, large and full. Growth, vigorous. A good hardy free-growing sort.
12. ALEXANDRINE BELFROY ; flowers peach-colour, shaded with white. A large, full, and handsome Rose, of vigorous growth.
13. ALEXANDRE BRETON ; flowers cherry red. Second-rate.
ALFRED DE ROUGEMONT ; see p. 165.
14. ALPHONSE DAMAIZIN ; flowers brilliant shaded crimson, blooming in clusters, showy, but not a Show Rose. Growth, vigorous.

15. ALPHONSE KARR; flowers bright rosy pink, of medium size, full. Quite a model in form. Growth, robust.
16. ALPHONSE DE LAMARTINE; flowers rosy blush, of medium size, full; form, good. Growth, moderate.
17. ALTESSE IMPERIALE; flowers crimson and purple shaded, petals of great substance. Growth, moderate; foliage fine; blooms freely.
18. AMANDINE; flowers pale rose, pretty and distinct. Growth, moderate.
19. AMIRAL GRAVINA; flowers blackish purple, shaded with scarlet, large and very double. Growth, vigorous.
20. ANNA ALEXIEFF; flowers rose, tinted with pink, large, full, and produced in great abundance; form, cupped. Growth, vigorous. A first-rate bedding Rose.
21. ANNA DE DIESBACH; flowers clear rose, unusually large; petals also large and thick; deeply cupped. Growth, vigorous. One of the finest.
22. ANDRÉ DESPORTES; flowers rose-colour, large and full. A seedling from Lord Raglan. Growth vigorous.
23. ARCHEVEQUE DE PARIS; flowers crimson and purple shaded; petals of good form, and of a substance giving to the flower a metallic appearance; of medium size, double. Growth, moderate; habit, good and hardy.
24. ARDOISÈE DE LYON; flowers purple, very large, opens indifferently. Second-rate.
25. ARMIDE; flowers rosy salmon, paler edges, expanded, large and full. Growth, vigorous; foliage and habit, good.
26. ARTHUR DE SANSAL; flowers rich crimson purple, very dark and velvety; of medium size, full; form, cupped, fine. Growth, moderate.
27. AUGUSTE GUINOISSEAU; deep red, shaded; large and full, but a little coarse.
28. AUGUSTE MIE; flowers light glossy pink; large, full, and globular; blooms late. Growth, vigorous. One of the best.
29. AUGUSTINE MOUCHELET; flowers rose, shaded with purple. Second-rate.
30. BACCHUS; flowers crimson scarlet, changing to rosy crimson; of medium size, full; form, cupped. Growth, dwarf.
31. BARLOW; flowers purplish maroon, velvety, produced in clusters.
BARON ADOLPHE ROTHSCHILD; see p. 165.
BARON ATHALIN; see p. 165.
32. BARONNE DE HECKEREN; flowers rosy pink, petals large, cupped very large and double. A fine showy Rose, of beautiful

33. BARONNE HALLEZ; flowers dark red, of medium size, full. A good useful Rose, of fine form and moderate growth.

BARONNE DE KERMONT; see Bourbon Perpetual, Group XXIV.

BARONNE DE LASSUS DE SAINT GENIES; see p. 165.

34. BARONNE PREVOST; flowers clear pale rose, glossy, very large and full; form, compact. Habit, erect; growth robust. A superb kind. Raised by M. Desprez of Yèbles. One of the largest and best.

35. BEAUTÈ DE ROYHEM; flowers rose, edged with white and carmine; large and full. Pretty and distinct. Growth, moderate.

BEAUTÉ FRANÇAISE; see p. 165.

36. BEAUTY OF WALTHAM; flowers rosy crimson, cupped, large, full, and very sweet; petals, of good substance. Blooms abundantly. Raised by me from Jules Margottin. Growth, moderate.

BELLE ANGLAISE; see Bourbon Perpetual.

37. BELLE BRUNE; flowers violet shaded.

38. BELLE DE BOURG LA REINE; flowers satin-like rose, large and full, and sometimes fine; form, cupped. Growth, moderate.

BELLE DES MASSIFS; see p. 166.

39. BELLE JARDINIERE; flowers blush, pink centres.

BELLOTTE; see p. 166.

40. BERCEAU IMPERIAL; flowers rosy flesh, distinct, large and full. Growth, moderate.

41. BICOLOR INCOMPARABLE; flowers rose-colour, dark centre, distinct.

42. BOUQUET DE MARIE, flowers white, pink centres, small, produced in clusters like the Noisettes. Pretty and distinct. Growth, moderate.

43. BUFFON; brilliant red, shaded with crimson, cupped, of medium size, full. Good and distinct. Growth, moderate.

CARAVANE DE NISMES; see p. 166.

44. CARDINAL PATRIZZI; flowers brilliant red, shaded with purple, very velvety; of medium size, full; form, cupped; growth, moderate. A beautiful Rose: best under glass.

45. CAPTAIN JOHN FRANKLIN; flowers rosy crimson; hardy. Second-rate.

46. CAROLINE DE SANSAL; flowers clear flesh-colour, edges blush, very large and fine; form, cupped; growth, vigorous. One of the best in fine weather, but soon soils.

CHARLES LEFEBVRE; see p. 163.

47. CHARLES ROBIN ; flowers peach-colour, of medium size, full ; petals of good form and great substance, slightly reflexing at the summit ; growth, vigorous.

CHARLES BOISSIERE ; see Rose de Rosomène, Group XXV.

48. CHATEAUBRIAND ; flowers rosy flesh, large ; second-rate.

49. CHRISTIAN PUTTNER ; flowers purple, shaded with crimson, large and full ; growth, moderate.

50. CLEMENCE JOIGNEAUX ; flowers red, shaded with lilac, cupped ; of fine form, large and very double ; growth, vigorous.

51. CLEMENT MAROT ; flowers clear rosy lilac, globular, large and very double ; growth, vigorous. Good and distinct.

52. COLONEL CAMBRIELS ; flowers crimson, shaded ; growth, vigorous.

53. COLONEL DE ROUGEMONT ; flowers pale rose, shaded with carmine, expanded, large and full ; growth, robust. Very fine.

COLONEL SOUFFLOT ; see p. 166.

54. COMTE CAVOUR ; flowers shaded rose. Second-rate.

COMTE BOBRINSKY ; see Rose de Rosomène, Group XXV.

COMTE D'EU ; see Rose de Rosomène.

COMTE DE BEAUFORT ; see Rose de Rosomène.

COMTE DE FALLOUX ; see Rose de Rosomène.

55. COMTE DE NANTEUIL ; flowers rose, darker edges, large and full ; form, cupped, perfect ; growth, vigorous. One of the best.

56. COMTE ODART ; flowers crimson. Second-rate.

57. COMTESSE BATTHIANY ; flowers blush. Second-rate.

58. COMTESSE DE CHABRILLANT ; flowers pink, large and full ; form, cupped, perfect ; growth, vigorous ; foliage and habit fine. One of the best.

COMTESSE DE COURCY ; see p. 166.

59. COMTESSE DE KERGORLAY ; flowers rosy purple, cupped, large and full ; growth, moderate.

COMTESSE DE POLIGNAC ; see p. 166.

60. COMTESSE DE SEGUIER ; flowers crimson, large and full ; form, expanded ; something in the way of Triomphe d'Avranches ; growth, vigorous.

61. COMTESSE D'ORLEANS ; flowers blush. Second-rate.

62. CORNET ; flowers rose, tinted with purple. Second-rate.

63. COQUETTE DE LYONS ; flowers rose, shaded with carmine. Second-rate.

64. COURONNE DES PARTERRES ; flowers bright crimson, suffused with purple, large and very double ; growth, vigorous.

65. CRIMSON PERPETUAL, or Rose du Roi ; flowers crimson, cupped ; growth, moderate.

66. DARZENS; flowers rosy pink, very large and double; growth, robust.
67. DELAMOTHE; flowers rosy crimson, large and full; growth, vigorous.
DESGACHES; see Rose de Rosomène, Group XXV.
DEUIL DE PRINCE ALBERT; see p. 166.
68. DOCTEUR BRETONNEAU; flowers dark rose, shaded with crimson, large and full; form, expanded; growth, moderate.
69. DOCTEUR BRIERE; flowers cherry-red, large and full; growth, robust.
70. DOCTEUR HENON; flowers white, large, full, and fine; form, globular. A first-rate flower, but habit delicate.
DOCTEUR JUILLARD; see Bourbon Perpetual, Group XXIV.
71. DOCTEUR MARX; flowers rosy crimson; second-rate.
72. DOCTEUR RUSHPLER; flowers rose-colour, large, full, and fragrant; form, globular; growth, vigorous.
73. DOMINIQUE DARAN; flowers dark crimson purple, large and very double; growth, moderate.
DUC D'ANJOU; see p. 166.
DUC DE BASSANO; see p. 166.
74. DUC DE CAZES; flowers crimson, shaded with blackish velvety purple, large and full; form, globular; growth, vigorous. One of the best.
75. DUC DE MALAKOFF; flowers red; growth, moderate.
76. DUC D'OSSUNA; flowers crimson, changing to rose, of medium size and good form; growth, moderate.
77. DUC DE ROHAN; see p. 163.
DUC DE RUSHPLER; see Dr. Rushpler.
78. DUKE OF CAMBRIDGE; flowers dark red, of medium size; full, fine form; growth, moderate.
79. DUCHESS OF NORFOLK; flowers rich purplish crimson, of medium size, full; fine form; growth, moderate.
80. DUCHESS OF SUTHERLAND; flowers fresh rosy pink, very large and very double; form, cupped. Habit, erect; growth, vigorous. Raised by M. Laffay. Introduced in 1839.
81. DUCHESSE D'ALENÇON; flowers cerise, shaded, large and full; growth, moderate.
82. DUCHESSE DE MAGENTA; flowers flesh-colour, changing to white, large and very double; form, cupped; exquisite in the bud state; growth, moderate; rather delicate.
83. DUCHESSE DE MONTPENSIER; flowers delicate rose, edged with blush; second-rate.
84. DUCHESSE D'ORLEANS; flowers lavender blush, very large and full; growth, vigorous. One of the best.

85. DUCHESSE DE POLIGNAC; flowers scarlet crimson; growth, dwarf.
86. DUNANT; flowers crimson, shaded with violet; growth, moderate.
EMILE DULAC; see p. 163.
88. EMPEREUR DE MAROC; flowers rich velvety maroon, of medium size and good substance. An intensely dark Rose of free growth; very distinct.
89. EMPEREUR NAPOLEON; flowers velvety scarlet, shaded with crimson; colours splendid; form, irregular; growth, dwarf.
90. ENFANT DU MONT CARMEL; flowers crimson, large and full; growth, vigorous.
91. ERNEST BERGMANN; flowers pink. Second-rate.
92. ETENDARD DU GRAND HOMME; flowers shaded rose. Second-rate.
93. ETIENNE LECROSNIER; flowers slate, shaded with rose; petals large and smooth; growth, vigorous.
94. EUGÉNE APPERT; flowers scarlet and crimson shaded, very velvety; petals thick; colours splendid; form, irregular; growth, vigorous; foliage, fine.
95. EUGÉNE BOURCIER; flowers crimson and purple shaded, cupped, large, and almost full; growth, vigorous.
96. EUGENIE LEBRUN; flowers dark crimson, of medium size, very double; form, cupped; growth, moderate.
97. EVÊQUE DE NISMES; flowers bright purplish red, sometimes scarlet crimson, large and full; form, expanded. A distinct and beautiful Rose, of rather shy growth.
98. FRANÇOIS ARAGO; flowers rich velvety purple, large and full; form, good; growth, vigorous. A good and distinct Rose.
FRANÇOIS LACHARME; see p. 163.
100. FRANÇOIS LOUVAT; flowers red, shaded with lilac, large and full; growth, vigorous.
101. FRANÇOIS PREMIER; flowers brilliant red, often shaded with crimson and purple, of medium size, full; form, expanded; growth, moderate. One of the best.
102. FRANÇOIS ROUGIER; flowers pale rose. Second rate.
103. GÉANT DES BATAILLES; flowers brilliant crimson, shaded with purple, large, full, and sweet; growth, moderate.
104. GENERAL BEDEAU; flowers carmine.
105. GENERAL BISSON; flowers bright rosy blush, very large and full; form, globular; growth, vigorous.
106. GENERAL BREA; flowers bright rose, large, full, and of good form; growth, dwarf.

R

107. GENERAL CASTELLANE ; flowers brilliant crimson, large, full, and of exquisite form ; growth, moderate.
108. GENERAL CAVAIGNAC ; flowers rosy pink ; too small.
109. GENERAL FOREY ; flowers red, large and full ; growth, vigorous.
110. GENERAL JACQUEMINOT ; flowers brilliant red, large and very double ; form, cupped ; growth, vigorous. One of the best.
111. GENERAL MACMAHON ; flowers rose, large. Second-rate.
112. GENERAL NEGRIER ; flowers pale rose, fine shape, but of too shy growth.
113. GENERAL PELLISSIER ; flowers delicate rose, very large and full ; form, globular. Uncertain.
114. GENERAL SIMPSON ; flowers bright carmine, fine shape, but too small.
115. GENERAL WASHINGTON ; flowers bright crimson, very large and full ; form, expanded ; occasionally splendid, but a little uncertain ; growth, vigorous.
116. GENERAL ZACHARGERSKY ; flowers pale satin-like rose, of medium size, good form, and very double ; growth, moderate.
GLOIRE DE CHATILLON ; see p. 163.
118. GLOIRE DE FRANCE ; flowers deep red, large and full ; form, compact ; growth, moderate.
119. GLOIRE DE LYON ; flowers crimson, shaded with violet, large and full ; form, cupped ; growth, vigorous. Occasionally very fine.
120. GLOIRE DE PARTHENAY ; flowers rose ; growth, moderate.
GLOIRE DE ROSOMÈNE ; see Rose de Rosomène, Group XXV.
121. GLOIRE DE SANTENAY ; flowers scarlety crimson, often shaded with violet ; large, full, and of fine form ; growth, vigorous. Somewhat uncertain, but usually first-rate.
122. GLOIRE DE VITRY ; flowers bright rosy carmine, large and full ; form, globular ; growth, moderate. One of the best.
GRANDIFLORA ; see p. 166.
123. GREGOIRE BOURDILLON ; flowers bright scarlet crimson, large and full ; growth, vigorous.
124. GUSTAVE CORAUX ; flowers purple. Showy.
GUSTAVE ROUSSEAU ; see p. 166.
125. HENDERSON ; flowers purplish rose, very large and showy ; growth, moderate.
HENRI IV. ; see p. 166.
HENRIETTE DUBUS ; see Mademoiselle Henriette Dubus.

HORTENSE BLACHETTE ; see p. 166.
127. INERMIS ; flowers shaded rose. Second-rate.
128. IMPERATRICE DES FRANÇAIS ; flowers blush. Too small.
129. IMPERATRICE EUGENIE ; flowers white, tinted with rose, of medium size, full. Growth, moderate. Rather shy.
IMPERATRICE MARIA ALEXANDRINA ; see p. 166.
130. JAMES DICKSON ; flowers scarlet crimson, colour splendid, but hardly double enough.
131. JEAN BAPTISTE GUILLOT ; flowers rich purple, shaded with reddish purple, of medium size, small and good. Growth, moderate.
132. JEAN BART ; flowers red and violet shaded, large and very double ; colours brilliant ; very effective. Growth, vigorous.
JEAN GOUJON ; see p. 166.
133. JOAN OF ARC ; flowers white, with rosy centres, large, full, and of exquisite form. Unsurpassed as a flower, but of shy growth.
134. JOHN HOPPER ; flowers lilac rose, their centres rosy crimson, cupped, large and full. Growth, vigorous. An effective rose in the garden.
135. JOHN STANDISH ; flowers violet crimson ; very dark ; form, expanded ; produced in clusters. Growth, vigorous.
136. JOHN WATERER ; flowers brilliant red, almost scarlet, of medium size, full ; form, cupped.
137. JOSEPH VERNET ; flowers bright rose. Second-rate.
138. JULES MARGOTTIN ; flowers bright cherry-colour, large and full ; form, cupped. Growth, vigorous. One of the best.
139. JULIE GUINOISSEAU ; flowers pale rose. Second-rate.
140. LA BELLE EGARÉE, or MADAME DAMET ; flowers rosy lilac. Second-rate.
LA BRILLANTE ; see p. 163.
LA ESMERALDA ; see p. 167.
142. LA FONTAINE ; flowers purplish rose, very large and full. Growth, vigorous. A good show Rose although sometimes a little coarse.
LA GLOBULEUSE ; see p. 167.
143. LA REINE ; flowers rose, often shaded with lilac, sometimes with crimson, very large and full ; form, cupped. Habit, erect ; growth, moderate. A magnificent Rose, but varies much as to quality. Raised by M. Laffay. Introduced in 1843.
LA TOUR DE CROUY ; see p. 167.
144. LA VALLOISE ; flowers lilac. Second-rate.

R 2

145. LA VILLE DE ST. DENIS; flowers rosy-carmine, large and full; form, cupped, fine. Growth moderate. One of the best.

146. LADY ALICE PEEL; flowers rosy pink; originally good, but now surpassed.

LADY EMILY PEEL; see p. 167.

147. LADY STUART; flowers delicate flesh-colour. Second-rate.

148. LANE; flowers rose colour. Second-rate.

149. LAURE RAMAND; flowers pale rose, hardly first-rate.

LAURENT DESCOURS; see p. 167.

LE BARON DE ROTHSCHILD; see p. 165.

150. L'EBLOUISSANTE; flowers brilliant red large full; and of good habit. Growth, vigorous.

L'ECLETANTE; see p. 167.

L'ELEGANTE; see Bourbon Perpetual, Group XXIV.

151. L'ETENDARD DES AMATEURS; flowers rich velvety scarlet; of medium size, and great substance. Growth, moderate.

LE JUIF ERRANT; see p. 167.

152. LE MONT VESUVE; dark purplish crimson. Second-rate.

LE RHONE; see p. 167.

154. LE ROYAL EPOUX; flowers rosy pink. Second-rate.

155. LION DES COMBATS; flowers reddish violet, sometimes shaded with crimson scarlet, large and full. Growth robust.

156. LÆLIA; flowers rose shaded with lilac, very large and very fine. Growth, robust. Closely resembles Louise Peyronny, but the flowers appear larger and the growth freer.

LÉONCE MOISE; see Rose de Rosomène. Group XXV.

LORD CLYDE; see p. 167.

158. LORD. ELGIN; flowers crimson and purple shaded, of medium size, full. Growth, moderate.

LORD HERBERT; see p. 167.

Lord MAUCAULAY; see p. 167.

LORD PALMERSTON; see Bourbon Perpetual, Group XXIV.

161. LORD RAGLAN; flowers scarlet crimson edged with violet crimson; form, expanded. Growth, vigorous. One of the best.

162. LOUIS BUONAPARTE; flowers vermilion. Second-rate.

163. LOUIS CHAIX; flowers bright red shaded with crimson, of medium size, full. A beautiful Rose but of rather shy growth.

164. LOUIS D'AUTRICHE; flowers rose colour, large and full. Growth, vigorous.

LOUIS XIV.; see Rose de Rosomène, Group XXV.

165. LOUIS GULINO; flowers crimson and purple shaded.

Louise Darzins ; see p. 163.
166. Louise Magnan ; flowers white tinged with flesh-colour, large and full. Growth, vigorous. A beautiful Rose but uncertain.
Louise Margottin ; see p. 167.
Louise Odier ; see Bourbon Perpetual, Group XXIV.
167. Louise Peyronny ; flowers rose shaded with lilac, large and full ; form, globular. Growth, robust.
Madame Alfred de Rougemont ; see p. 167.
168. Madame Boll ; flowers rose colour, sometimes edged with blush ; a very large, full, and handsome Rose, with some of the blood of the Rosa Gallica in it. Growth, robust.
169. Madame Boutin ; flowers cherry crimson, large full, and of good form. Growth, vigorous.
Madame Brianson ; see p. 167.
171. Madame Bruni ; see Bourbon Perpetual, Group XXIV.
172. Madame Caillat ; flowers bright even rose, large and double, very smooth ; shape good. Growth, vigorous.
173. Madame Campbell ; flowers pale rose, sometimes striped with red.
174. Madame Charles Crapelet ; flowers rosy scarlet, often veined with lilac, large and full ; form, cupped. Growth, vigorous. One of the best.
Madame Charles Roy ; see p. 168.
Madame Charles Wood ; see p. 163.
Madame Crespin ; see p. 168.
178. Madame de Cambaceres ; flowers rosy crimson, large and full ; habit free, foliage fine. Growth, vigorous.
179. Madame Desirè Giraud ; flowers white striped with lilac, large and full. Growth, vigorous. Pretty and distinct.
180. Madame de Trotter ; flowers rosy carmine, distinct and good. Growth, vigorous.
181. Madame Domage ; flowers bright rose, very large and double. Growth, robust. A fine showy Rose.
182. Madame Duchère ; flowers rosy white, delicate tint ; of medium size, full Growth, moderate.
Madame Emain ; see p. 168.
Madame Ernest Dreol ; see p. 163.
185. Madame Eugene Verdier ; flowers deep pink, large and full ; form, finely cupped. Growth, vigorous.
Madame Freeman ; see p. 168.
186. Madame Faugel ; flowers rose mottled. Growth, moderate.
188. Madame Furtado ; flowers rosy crimson, very large and full ; form, globular. Growth, moderate. One of the best.

189. MADAME GUINOISSEAU; flowers rosy crimson. Growth, moderate.
190. MADAME HECTOR JACQUIN; flowers clear rose shaded with lilac, very large and full; form, globular. Growth, vigorous.
MADAME HELYE; see p. 168.
192. MADAME HERAUD; flowers bright rose, fine form. Growth moderate.
193. MADAME HILAIRE; flowers blush. Second-rate.
MADAME JULIE DARAN; see p. 163.
195. MADAME KNORR; flowers bright rose, pale edges, large and full; form, cupped. Growth, moderate.
196. MADANE LABASTIDE; flowers rosy pink. Growth, moderate.
197. MADAME LAFFAY; flowers rosy crimson, large and double. Growth, vigorous.
198. MADAME LAMON; flowers reddish cerise, shaded with violet, large and full. Growth, moderate.
199. MADAME LEVEAU; flowers clear lilac, free and good. Growth, moderate.
200. MADAME LOUISE CARIQUE; flowers bright rosy carmine, large and full : form, cupped, fine. Growth vigorous ; foliage, handsome.
201. MADAME MARTEL; flowers flesh-colour, pretty, but not large enough.
202. MADAME MASSON; flowers reddish crimson, changing to violet, very large and full. Growth, vigorous. A splendid Rose.
203. MADAME MELANIE; flowers crimson and purple shaded, of medium size, very double. Growth, moderate.
204. MADAME OCTAVIE DEPYRE; flowers rosy carmine.
205. MADAME PAULINE VILLOT; flowers crimson purple, large and produced freely; form, fine. Growth, moderate.
206. MADAME PHELIP; flowers rose shaded; too small.
207. MADAME PIERSON; flowers rosy pink, large and full; form, globular. Growth, vigorous. A bold showy Rose.
208. MADAME PLACE; flowers rosy carmine, fine shape, but too small.
209. MADAME RIVERS; flowers clear flesh, changing to blush, large and full; form, cupped, fine. Growth, vigorous.
210. MADAME SCHMIDT; flowers rose-colour, changing to pink, very large and full. Growth, vigorous.
211. MADAME STANDISH; flowers clear pale pink, of medium size and perfect form. Growth, vigorous.
212. MADAME SYLVAIN CAUBERT; flowers flesh colour. Second-rate.
213. MADAME TRUDEAUX; flowers red. Growth, robust.
MADAME VALEMBOURG. see p. 168.

215. MADAME VAN GEERT; flowers rose, striped with white, small. Growth, vigorous.

216. MADAME VAN HOUTTE; flowers rosy blush, of medium size; full, form, fine. Growth, moderate.

MADAME VARIN; see Mdlle. Jenny Varin.

217. MADAME VIDOT; flowers transparent flesh-colour, shaded with rose, large and full; form, cupped, exquisite. Very fragrant. Growth, robust. One of the best.

218. MADAME VIGNERON; flowers rose-colour, large, full, and very fragrant; form, cupped. Growth, vigorous. Good and distinct.

219. MADEMOISELLE ALICE LEROY; flowers delicate rose shaded, large and full; form, cupped, fine. Growth, moderate. A pretty and distinct Rose, flowering in clusters.

220. MADEMOISELLE AUGUSTE; flowers deep pink, large and full; form, globular, fine. Growth, robust.

221. MADEMOISELLE BONNAIRE; flowers pure white, with rosy centres, of medium size, full; form, exquisitely cupped. Growth, moderate. One of the best.

222. MADEMOISELLE CLAUDINE D' OFFAY; flowers brilliant red, large and full; form, cupped. Growth, vigorous. A good, free, hardy Rose.

223. MADEMOISELLE EUGÈNE VERDIER; flowers white, tinted with rose, of medium size, full; form, cupped. A beautiful Rose of rather shy growth.

224. MADEMOISELLE GODARD; flowers rose, large and full. Growth, moderate.

225. MADEMOISELLE HENRIETTE DUBUS; flowers red, shaded with violet; of medium size, full; form, cupped. Growth, moderate. A good useful Rose, blooming freely in Autumn.

226. MADEMOISELLE JENNY VARIN; flowers rose-colour, hardly first-rate.

MADEMOISELLE HAIMAN; see Rose de Rosomène, Group XXV.

227. MADAME THERESE APPERT; see Bourbon Perpetual, Group XXIV.

228. MARECHAL DE LA BRUNERIE; flowers rose mottled. Growth, moderate.

MARECHAL VAILLANT; see p. 163.

MARGUERITE APPERT; see Bourbon Perpetual, Group XXIV.

230. MARIA PORTEMER; flowers purplish red, large and full; form, globular. Growth, moderate. Occasionally fine, but rather uncertain, best in autumn.

231. MARIE DAUVESSE; flowers rose-colour, smooth petals; form, cupped. Growth moderate.

232 MARIE THIERRY; flowers bright rosy carmine, large and full; form, expanded. Growth, moderate.

MARQUIS OF AILSA; see Dr. Marx

233. MARQUISA BOCCELLA; flowers delicate pink, edges blush. Second-rate.

234. MARQUISE DE MURAT; flowers pink, edges paler. Growth, dwarf.

235. MARQUISE DE PARIS; flowers deep red, large and full; form, globular. Growth, vigorous.

236. MATHURIN REGNIER; flowers pale rose, large and full; form, expanded. Growth, robust. A good hardy Rose.

MAURICE BERNARDIN; see p. 163.

238. MAXIME; flowers violet rose, large and full. Growth, moderate.

MAXIMILLIAN II.; see Rose de Rosomène. Group XXV.

239. MÈRE DE ST. LOUIS; flowers rosy white, large and double, colour exquisite. Growth, vigorous. Hardly full enough.

240. MIGNARD; flowers rosy crimson, white edges, large and showy. Growth, moderate.

241. MONSIEUR DE MONTIGNY; flowers rosy carmine, very large and full; form, globular. Growth, vigorous.

MONSIEUR DUNANT; see DUNANT.

MONSIEUR EUGENE PETIT; see p. 168.

243. MONSIEUR JOIGNEAUX; flowers purplish crimson, of medium size; form, cupped. Growth, moderate.

MONSIEUR RAVEL; see RAVEL.

244. MONTEBELLO; flowers violet crimson, of shy growth.

MONTE CHRISTO; see p. 164.

246. MRS. ELLIOT; flowers purplish rose, very large and very double; form, cupped. Habit, erect; growth, vigorous. A beautiful Rose, with fine large petals, and handsome foliage. Raised by M. Laffay. Introduced in 1840.

247. MRS. STANDISH; flowers rosy lilac, large and showy. Growth, vigorous.

MRS. WM. PAUL; see p. 168.

MURILLO; see p. 168.

250. NOEMI; flowers blush, pretty, but too small.

251. NOTRE DAME DE FOURVIERES; flowers glossy pink, very large and full. Growth, vigorous.

OLIVIER DELHOMME; see p. 164.

253. ORDERIC VITAL; flowers silvery rose, very large and full; form, expanded. Growth, robust. Good and distinct.

254. ORIFLAMME DE ST. LOUIS; see Rose de Rosomène. Group XXV.

255. ORNEMÈNT DES JARDINS ; flowers brilliant crimson, velvety, of medium size, full ; form, cupped. Growth, moderate.

256. PÆONIA ; flowers carmine. Second-rate.

257. PALESTRO ; flowers rosy lilac ; large, full, and globular. Growth, moderate.

258. PANACHÉ D'ORLEANS ; flowers flesh-colour, striped with rose and purple, large and full ; form, cupped. Growth, moderate. A pretty and distinct variety.

259. PARMENTIER ; flowers rosy pink, very pretty, blooms freely, but rather small.

PAUL DESGRAND ; see p. 168.

261. PAUL DUPUY ; flowers bright velvety crimson, shaded, large and full ; form, expanded. Growth, moderate.

262. PAUL FEVAL ; flowers cherry-colour, large and very double ; form. cupped ; outline good. Growth, vigorous.

263. PAULINE LANSEZEUR ; flowers bright crimson, changing to violet.

PETER LAWSON ; see p. 168.

265. PHILOMÈNE ; flowers rosy pink, large and double ; form, cupped.

266. PIUS THE NINTH ; flowers crimson purple, large and full ; form, cupped. Growth, vigorous.

267. POURPRE D'ORLEANS ; flowers velvety purple, large and full.

268. PRAIRE DE TERRE NOIRE ; flowers velvety purple, large and full ; form, cupped ; colour, rich and distinct. Growth, vigorous.

PRESIDENT LINCOLN ; see p. 168.

PRINCE CAMILLE DE ROHAN ; see p. 164.

271. PRINCE CHIPETOUZIKOFF ; flowers red. Second-rate.

272. PRINCE DE LA MOSKOWA ; flowers dark maroon, shaded with crimson, large. Growth, vigorous.

PRINCE HENRI DES PAYS BAS ; see p. 168.

274. PRINCE IMPERIAL ; flowers rosy carmine, very large and full ; form, globular. Growth, moderate.

275. PRINCE LEON ; flowers bright crimson, large and very double ; form, compact, perfect. Growth, moderate. One of the best.

276. PRINCE NOIR ; flowers dark crimson purple, velvety, colour exquisite, but not double enough. Growth, moderate.

PRINCESSE ALICE ; see p. 168.

278. PRINCESSE CLOTHILDE ; flowers brilliant rose, large and full. Growth, vigorous.

279. PRINCESSE IMPERIALE CLOTHILDE ; flowers white, rosy centres, of medium size, full ; form, cupped. An exquisitely beautiful Rose of shy growth.

PRINCESSE MATHILDE; see Rose de Rosomène, Group XXV.
PROFESSOR KOCH; see p. 164.
281. PRUDENCE RŒSER; flowers rosy-lilac. Second-rate.
282. QUEEN OF DENMARK; flowers lilac flesh, transparent, large
and full; form, cupped. Growth, moderate.
283. QUEEN VICTORIA; flowers white, shaded with pink colour of
the old Celestial Rose, very large and full; form, globular.
Growth, vigorous.
284. RAPHAEL; flowers lively rose, large and very double. Growth,
robust.
285. RAVEL; flowers brilliant crimson; fine form. Growth, moderate.
286. REBECCA; flowers violet red, fine form, but too small.
RED ROVER; see p. 168.
288. REINE DE LA CITÉ; flowers blush pink, centres large and full.
A good Rose of robust growth.
289. REINE DES FLEURS; flowers light pink, of medium size; form,
globular. Growth, moderate.
290. REINE DES VIOLETTES; flowers dove and violet shaded, large
and full; form, cupped, outline good. Growth, vigorous.
Occasionally fine in autumn.
291. REINE MATHILDE; flowers pale rose. Second-rate.
REYNOLDS HOLE; see Bourbon Perpetual, Group XXIV.
292. RICHARD SMITH; flowers purple and crimson shaded. Growth,
vigorous.
293. RICHESSE DE COULEUR; flowers bright velvety purple, deeper
centres.
294. ROBERT DE BRIE; flowers rosy salmon, distinct. Growth,
robust.
ROBERT FORTUNE; see p. 164.
296. ROBIN HOOD; flowers red. Second-rate.
297. ROI DAVID; flowers dark purplish red, large and full; form,
globular. Growth, moderate.
298. ROSINE PARRON; flowers rose; second-rate.
ROUGE MARBRÉE; see p. 169.
300. SALOMON; flowers rose; second-rate.
301. SALVATOR ROSA; flowers red, large and very double; form,
cupped. Growth, vigorous.
302. SENATEUR VAISSE; flowers brilliant red, large and full; form,
cupped. Growth, vigorous. Perhaps the finest of this
Group.
303. SIMON ST. JEAN; flowers crimson purple, very dark.
SŒUR DES ANGES; see p. 169.
305. SOPHIE DE COQUERELLE; flowers blush, rosy centres, large and

full, colours clear and pleasing. Sometimes good, but uncertain. Growth, vigorous.

306. SOUVENIR DE BERANGER; flowers rose colour, very large and full. Growth, moderate. A fine variety.

SOUVENIR DE CHARLES MONTAULT; see Rose de Rosomène, Group XXV.

SOUVENIR DE COMTE CAVOUR; (Margottin) see p. 164.

SOUVENIR DE LADY EARDLEY; see p. 164.

309. SOUVENIR DE LEVESON GOWER; flowers dark red, changing to ruby, very large and full; form, cupped. Growth, vigorous. One of the best.

310. SOUVENIR DE LA REINE D'ANGLETERRE; flowers bright glossy rose, very large and full; petals of great substance; form, cupped. Growth, vigorous. A fine hardy Rose.

SOUVENIR DE MONTCEAU; see Rose de Rosomène, Group XXV.

SOUVENIR DE M. ROUSSEAU; see Rose de Rosomène, Group XXV.

311. SOUVENIR DE LA REINE DES BELGES; flowers bright red. Second-rate.

312. STANDARD OF MARENGO; flowers bright red. Second-rate.

313. STEPHANIE BEAUHARNAIS; flowers rose. Second-rate.

314. SYDONIE; flowers pink, large and full.

315. THERESE DE ST. REMY; flowers red. Second-rate.

THOMAS RIVERS; see Bourbon Perpetual, Group XXIV.

316. TOUJOURS FLEURI; flowers purplish crimson, of medium size, full; form, cupped, exquisite. A free blooming Rose of good quality, but shy growth.

317. TRIOMPHE D'ALENÇON; flowers bright red, shaded, very large and full; form, cupped. Growth robust. One of the best.

318. TRIOMPHE D'AMIENS; flowers vivid crimson, sometimes striped with lake, large and double. Growth, moderate.

TRIOMPHE D'ANGERS; see p. 169, also Group XXV.

319. TRIOMPHE D'AVRANCHES; flowers bright red, large and full. Growth, dwarf.

320. TRIOMPHE DE BAGATELLE; flowers rosy carmine. Growth, dwarf.

321. TRIOMPHE DE CAEN; flowers brilliant scarlet, shaded with purple, large and full. Growth, vigorous

322. TRIOMPHE DE L'EXPOSITION; flowers reddish crimson, large and full. A good free hardy Rose, of vigorous growth.

323. TRIOMPHE DE LYON; flowers dark crimson, shaded with blackish purple, large and full. Growth, moderate. A fine Rose, rather uncertain, sometimes splendid.

TRIOMPHE DE NANCY; see p. 169.

325. TRIOMPHE DE PARIS ; flowers dark velvety crimson, very large and full ; form, cupped. Growth, vigorous. One of the best.

326. TRIOMPHE DES BEAUX ARTS; flowers crimson and purple shaded, velvety ; form, cupped. Growth, moderate. A pretty and distinct Rose, but hardly full enough.

TURENNE; see p. 164.

VAINQUEUR DE GOLIATH ; see p. 169.

329. VAINQUEUR DE SOLFERINO ; flowers dark red, brighter centres, large and full ; form, cupped. Growth, moderate.

VELONTÉE D' ORLEANS ; see p. 169.

331. VICOMTE VIGIER ; flowers crimson maroon, large and very double ; form, cupped. Growth vigorous.

VICOMTESSE DE MONTESQUIEU ; see Bourbon Perpetual, Group XXIV.

VICTORIA ; see Queen Victoria.

333. VICTOIRE DE MAGENTA ; flowers red, shaded with purple, of medium size ; form, cupped. Growth, moderate.

334. VICTOR TROUILLARD ; flowers brilliant crimson and purple shaded, large and full. Colours beautiful ; form, irregular. Growth, moderate.

335. VICTOR VERDIER ; flowers rosy carmine, purplish edges, very large and full ; form, cupped. Growth, robust. One of the best.

336. VIRGINAL ; flowers pure white, delicately tinted with flesh, large and very double ; form, cupped, exquisite. Growth, moderate. A lovely Rose, of rather shy growth.

337. VULCAIN ; flowers bright purplish violet, shaded with black, of medium size, very double ; form, cupped. Growth, moderate. Good and distinct.

338. WILLIAM GRIFFITHS ; flowers pale satin-like rose, large and full ; form, expanded. Growth, robust. One of the best.

339. WILLIAM JESSE ; flowers crimson, tinged with lilac, very large and double ; form, globular. Growth, moderate. Very sweet.

WILLIAM PAUL ; see p. 169.

WILHELM PFITZER ; see p. 164.

ROSA INDICA.

GROUP XXIV.—THE BOURBON PERPETUAL.

THIS Group embraces the " Hybrid Perpetuals " of some Catalogues in which the characters of the Bourbon Rose are strikingly developed. They are generally of dwarf and compact growth, with roundish shining leaflets. They form beautiful objects grown as Dwarfs or Dwarf Standards; and, if planted in a rich soil, are certain autumnal bloomers. It is only necessary to keep them growing, for every new shoot will bear bloom. The flowers are not large, but they are well formed, and usually produced in clusters. They thrive best when closely pruned.

1. BARON GONELLA; flowers pink and lilac, shaded, large and full; form, cupped, fine; growth, moderate.
2. BARONNE DE KERMONT; flowers bright rose, form, cupped, fine; growth, moderate.
3.* BARONNE DE NOIRMONT; flowers rose, large, full, and very sweet; form, cupped, fine; growth, moderate.
4. BELLE ANGLAISE; flowers bright pink; form, cupped, perfect; growth, moderate.
5. CATHERINE GUILLOT; flowers pink; of moderate size, full; form, cupped, fine; growth, moderate. A superb Rose.
6. COMTESSE BARBANTANNE; flowers flesh-colour, large and full; form, cupped; growth, vigorous. A good, useful Rose.
7. DOCTEUR JUILLARD; flowers rosy purple, shaded with carmine; large and very double; form, cupped; growth, vigorous.
8. L'AVENIR; flowers glossy pink; large and full; form, cupped, fine; growth, vigorous.
9. L'ELEGANTE; buds pink, flowers flesh-colour, large and full; form, cupped, fine; growth, moderate. A good Rose.
10. LORD PALMERSTON; flowers cherry-red, of medium size, full; form, cupped, fine; growth, moderate. A very sweet and distinct free-flowering Rose.
    LOUISE MARGOTTIN; see p. 167.
12. LOUISE ODIER; flowers bright rose, of medium size and full; growth, vigorous. A good hardy Rose.
13. MADAME BRUNI; flowers peach-colour, Provence-scented, large and full; growth, vigorous.
14. MADAME COMTESSE; flowers flesh-colour, of medium size, full.
15. MADEMOISELLE EMAIN; flowers white, with rosy centres, of medium size, full; growth, moderate.
16. MADEMOISELLE THERESE APPERT; flowers peach-colour, large and full; shape, cupped, perfect. A free and constant blooming Rose of moderate growth.
17. MARGUERITE APPERT; flowers lavender blush, large and full; form, cupped; growth, moderate. A pretty and distinct Rose.
18. MODÈLE DE PERFECTION; flowers lively pink; large and full;

form, globular, exquisite ; growth, moderate. A beautiful Rose.

19. REYNOLDS HOLE ; flowers lively pink, increasing in brilliancy as the flowers advance in age, large, not very full ; growth, vigorous.

20. THOMAS RIVERS ; flowers rosy lilac, large and double ; form, cupped ; growth, moderate.

21. VICOMTESSE DE MONTESQUIEU ; flowers delicate flesh-colour, of medium size, full ; form cupped.

———

ROSA INDICA.

GROUP XXV.—THE ROSE DE ROSOMENE.

WHENCE arose the Gloire de Rosomène, the type of this Group, it is difficult even to conjecture, so distinct is it in appearance from all its congeners.   It was raised by M. Vibert, of Angers ; but I believe he does not know from what source.   The brilliancy of the flowers caused some stir among lovers of Roses when it was first introduced, and cultivators have long been striving to obtain full Roses to vie with it in colour.   This is now accomplished, and in this small group are some of the richest and most beautiful of high-coloured Roses. I have classed here only such kinds as have the features of the Gloire de Rosomène plainly visible ; although it is pretty evident that Géant des Batailles, Lord Raglan, and others of like aspect, are of the same blood.   But in these there is more of the Hybrid Chinese.   The kinds of moderate and dwarf growth require close pruning : the others, which, with the Tea-scented, are the very finest of Wall-roses, should be pruned sparingly.

1. CHARLES BOISSIÈRE ; flowers crimson, large and full ; form, compact ; growth, robust.

2. COMTE BOBRINSKY ; flowers crimson scarlet, large and full ; form, irregular ; colour splendid ; growth, moderate.

3. COMTE D'EU ; flowers brilliant carmine, large and very double ; form, cupped ; growth, moderate.   A very pretty free-flowering Rose.

4. COMTE DE BEAUFORT ; flowers blackish purple, centre fiery crimson ; large and full ; form, cupped.   A rich-looking handsome Rose of moderate growth.

5. COMTE DE FALLOUX ; flowers scarlety crimson, shaded with purple, large and full : form, cupped, fine. A free-blooming hardy Rose.
6. DESGACHES ; flowers rosy carmine, large and double ; growth, vigorous.
7. ECLAIR DE JUPITER ; flowers rosy crimson, large and showy ; growth, vigorous.
8. GLOIRE DE ROSOMÈNE ; flowers brilliant carmine, large and semi-double. A good autumn-blooming Climbing Rose, of vigorous growth.
9. LEONCE MOISE ; flowers scarlet crimson, shot with maroon, large and full ; brilliant and beautiful in colour, but irregular in form ; growth, moderate.
10. LOUIS XIV. ; flowers rich blood-colour, large and full ; form, globular ; growth, moderate. A distinct and beautiful variety.
11. MADEMOISELLE HAIMAN ; flowers brilliant cerise, large and double ; finely cupped ; growth, vigorous. Colour particularly lovely.
12. MAXIMILIAN II. ; flowers crimson, shaded with blackish purple, of medium size, full ; form, cupped ; growth, dwarf.
13. ORIFLAMME DE ST. LOUIS ; flowers brilliant carmine, large and very double ; growth, vigorous. A superior Pillar Rose.
14. PRINCESSE MATHILDE ; flowers crimson maroon and purple shaded, of medium size, double ; form, expanded ; growth, vigorous. A good hardy variety, colours exquisite.
SOUVENIR DE CHARLES MONTAULT ; see p. 169.
16. SOUVENIR DE MONTCEAU ; flowers scarlet crimson, shaded with maroon, of medium size, full ; form, cupped ; growth, vigorous. Colours exquisite.
SOUVENIR DE M. ROUSSEAU ; see p. 164.
TRIOMPHE D'ANGERS ; see p. 169.

ROSA INDICA.

GROUP XXVI.—THE BOURBON ROSE.

THE type of this group, which has furnished us with some of the most lovely roses of autumn, was discovered by M. Breon, in the Isle of Bourbon, in 1817. He noticed it growing among a lot of seedlings of a different cast, raised for forming a hedge. He took charge of and flowered it; and, in 1819, sent seeds to M. Jacques, gardener at the Chateau de Neuilly, near Paris. A little later it found its way to England. Its origin is unknown; but it is supposed to be a hybrid between the Chinese and Four-seasons. What a numerous progeny has it given birth to, and what a lovely assemblage they form, graduating from pure white to the darkest tints! The brilliancy and clearness of the colours, the large smooth petals of the flowers, their circular outline, and the beauty of the foliage, has rendered them especial favourites. The tardy growth of spring seldom produces them in full beauty; but the more rapid growth of summer provides us with an ample supply of perfect flowers during the autumn months.

There are certain kinds here partaking slightly of the Chinese : these are marked thus† : there are others, marked thus ‡, approaching to the Noisette : the flowers arguing in favour of the one group, and the foliage in favour of the other.

The Bourbon Roses have been recommended for planting against walls; but they are hardy, and thrive well under ordinary culture. Surely, then, this extra care is unnecessary : we would rather choose the Rose de Rosomène and Tea-scented for that purpose, for the former are improved by wall-culture, and the latter need protection.

The kinds of vigorous growth form handsome standards; they also look chaste and elegant trained up pillars or poles. The moderate growers are very pretty as Dwarf Standards : the Dwarf form striking and beautiful objects when grown on their own roots. A great many are excellent for Pot-culture, and are beautiful in the Forcing-house. All prefer and delight in a rich soil, requiring (with the exception of the vigorous kinds) close pruning.

1. ACIDALIA; flowers pure white, their centre blush, large and full; form, globular. Growth, vigorous. A beautiful Rose in fine weather. An excellent kind for forcing. Very sweet.
2. ADELAIDE BOUGÈRE; flowers dark velvety purple, changing to dove, large and full. Growth, moderate.
3. AGAR; flowers rose-colour.
4. ALINE PIERRON; flowers black, white flowers freely.
5. ANGELINA BUCELLE; flowers rosy carmine, of medium size, double; form, cupped. Growth, moderate.
6. APOLLINE; flowers light pink, large and full; form, cupped, fine. Growth, vigorous.
7 †ARMOSA flowers deep pink, of medium size, full. Growth, mo-

derate. A most abundant bloomer, partaking somewhat of the Chinese. A good variety for planting in masses; good also for a Standard or Pot-Rose.

8. AURORE DU GUIDE; flowers purplish violet, sometimes crimson scarlet, large and full; form, globular. Growth, robust; foliage magnificent.

BARON GONELLA; see Group XXIV. Bourbon Perpetual.

BARONNE DE NOIRMONT; see Group XXIV. Bourbon Perpetual.

9. BEAUTE SÉDUISANTE; flowers purplish pink, large and full. Growth, vigorous.

10. BLANCHE LAFITTE; flowers white, shaded with flesh-colour of medium size, full. Growth, moderate.

11. BOUQUET DE FLORE: flowers light glossy carmine, very large and double; form, cupped, exquisite. Growth, vigorous. Foliage and petals particularly elegant. Flowers, sweet. Forms a fine Standard or Pillar; good also for Pot-culture. A good seed-bearer.

12. CAMILLE DE CHATEAUBOURG; flowers purple and crimson shaded, large and double; form, cupped. A distinct and good variety, of vigorous growth.

13. CARDINAL FESCH; flowers cherry crimson, changing to purple, of medium size, very double; form, compact. Growth, vigorous.

14. CAROLINE RIGUET; flowers pure white, centres blush. A free-blowing Rose of vigorous growth, with handsome foliage.

CATHERINE GUILLOT; see Group XXIV. Bourbon Perpetual.

15. CHARLES SOUCHET; flowers dark crimson, sometimes finely shaded with purple, of medium size, full; form, compact, fine. Growth, dwarf. Uncertain, but occasionally fine.

16. ‡COMICE DE SEINE ET MARNE; flowers crimson scarlet, changing to rosy purple, produced in clusters, of medium size, very double; form, cupped. Growth, moderate.

17. COMICE DE TARNE ET GARONNE; flowers lilac rose, large and full; form, cupped. Growth, moderate.

COMTE D'EU; see Group XXV. Rose de Rosomène.

18. COMTE DE MONTIJO; flowers rich reddish crimson, sometimes shaded with purple, of medium size, full. Growth, moderate.

COMTESSE DE BARBANTANNE; see Group XXIV. Bourbon Perpetual.

19. ‡COMTE DE RAMBUTEAU; flowers dark rose, tinted with lilac, large and full; form, compact. Growth, dwarf. A good seed-bearer.

57. MADAME DESPREZ; flowers rose and lilac shaded, produced in large clusters, large and full; form, cupped. Growth, vigorous. A fine Standard or Pillar Rose.

58. †MADAME ELISE CHENIER; flowers bright rose, blooms freely. Growth, vigorous.

59. MADAME HELFENBIEN; flowers pale rose, large and full. Growth, vigorous.

60. MADAME LACHARME; flowers white, tinted with flesh, large and very double; form, cupped. Growth, robust.

61. MADAME MARECHAL; flowers flesh-colour, edges white, of medium size, full. Growth, moderate.

MADEMOISELLE EMAIN; see Group XXIV. Bourbon Perpetual.

62. MADAME NERARD; flowers delicate pink, shaded with blush, large and double, sweet; form, cupped, fine. A beautiful Rose, of moderate growth.

63. ‡MADAME TRIPET; flowers dark rose, their circumference whitish, large and very double; form, cupped.

64. MADEMOISELLE FELICITE TRUILLOT; flowers clear soft pink, of medium size, with large smooth petals, very elegantly arranged. Growth, moderate, and blooms freely.

65. MADEMOISELLE PIERRON; flowers creamy white, produced abundantly. Growth, moderate.

66. MANTEAU DE JEANNE D'ARC; flowers clear flesh colour, changing to white, of medium size, very double; form, cupped. camellia-like. Growth, dwarf.

67. MARIE JOLY; flowers rose-colour. Growth, vigorous.

68. MARQUIS BALBIANO; flowers rose-colour, tinged with lilac, large and full; form, cupped, fine. Growth, vigorous, well furnished with handsome foliage.

69. MARQUIS DE BUISSON; flowers white. Growth, vigorous.

MODÈLE DE PERFECTION; see Group XXIV. Bourbon Perpetual.

70. MARQUISE D'IVRY; flowers bright rosy pink, changing to lilac; form, cupped. Growth, vigorous.

71. MARQUISE DE MOYRIA; flowers bright carmine, large and full.

72. MENOUX; flowers carmine, large and full; form, cupped. Superb.

73. MOLIERE; flowers rose shaded with lilac. Growth, vigorous.

74. MONSIEUR JARD; flowers cherry-red, large and full. Growth, vigorous.

75. †MRS. BOSANQUET; flowers white, their centre delicate flesh, large and full; form, cupped. Growth, vigorous. A beautiful Rose, sweet, and an abundant bloomer. Good either for Bedding, Pot-culture, or a Standard.

76. OCTAVIE FONTAINE; flowers white tinted with flesh colour, of

medium size, full; form, compact good. Growth, moderate.

77. OMAR PACHA; flowers brillant red, large and full; form, compact. Growth, moderate.

78. PAUL ET VIRGINIE; flowers blush.

79. PAUL JOSEPH; flowers rich purplish crimson, often shaded with fiery crimson large, and full; form, compact. Growth, moderate. Thrives best as a Dwarf, or Dwarf-standard.

80. PHŒNIX; flowers bright purplish crimson, large and very double; form, cupped. Growth, moderate.

81. PIERRE DE ST. CYR; flowers pale glossy pink, large and very double; form, cupped Growth, vigorous. A good Weeping-Rose.

82. PIGERON; flowers purplish red. Second-rate.

83. PRINCE ALBERT; flowers scarlet crimson, of medium size; very double; form, compact. Growth, moderate. A beautiful Rose, flowering in clusters.

84. PRINCE DE CHIMAY; flowers purplish crimson, large and very double. Flowers freely. Growth, moderate.

85. PRINCE IMPERIAL; flowers white, shaded with rose. Growth, moderate.

86. QUEEN; flowers delicate salmon flesh, often tinged with buff, large and very double; form, cupped, fine. Growth, moderate. An abundant bloomer, sweet, and of fine habit; excellent for bedding.

87. REVEIL; flowers cherry-crimson richly shaded with violet-purple, large and full. Growth, moderate. A fine hardy dark Bourbon rose.

88. SCIPION; flowers crimson shaded with scarlet, large and very showy, the colours splendid. Growth, moderate.

89. SIR JOSEPH PAXTON; flowers bright rose shaded with crimson, large and full; form, expanded. Growth, vigorous. A fine hardy Rose, with handsome foliage, good for a wall or pillar.

90. SOUCHET; flowers bright rosy purple, sometimes brilliant crimson, glossy, very large and full; form, compact. Growth, moderate. A good Rose, and sweet.

91. SOUVENIR DE DUMONT D'URVILLE; flowers rosy crimson, large and full. Growth, moderate.

92. SOUVENIR DE L'ARQUEBUSE; flowers crimson and purple shaded, produced abundantly.

93. SOUVENIR DE L'EXPOSITION; flowers dark crimson, of medium size, full. Growth, moderate.

94. SOUVENIR DE MALMAISON; flowers flesh colour, their margin

almost white; very large and full; form, compact.
Growth, vigorous. A magnificent Rose, with large thick
petals. Forms a fine sort for a Standard or Pot-culture.

95. SOUVENIR DE MALMAISON À FLEURS ROUGE; flowers rose colour,
    very large.

96. SOUVENIR D'UN FRÈRE; flowers brilliant crimson, of medium
    size, very double. Growth, moderate.

97. SPLENDENS; flowers rosy lilac to rosy crimson, variable, large
    and full, sweet; form, compact. Growth, moderate.

98. THERESIA MARGAT; flowers fresh rose-pink, their circumference
    paler, of medium size, very double; form, cupped.
    Growth, moderate.

TRIOMPHE DE LA DUCHÈRE : see Group XXXII. Noisette.

99. TRIOMPHE DE LA GUILLOTIÈRE; flowers rosy lilac, of medium
    size, full; form, cupped.

100. TRIOMPHE D'OUILLINS ; flowers rosy crimson.

101. VICOMTE DE CUSSY : flowers cherry colour, tinged with purple,
     large and very double ; form, compact. Growth, mode-
     rate.

102. VICTOR EMMANUEL ; flowers purple and purplish maroon
     shaded, large and double ; form, cupped. A good Rose,
     of moderate growth.

103. VORACE; dark crimson purple, large and full ; form, cupped.
     Growth, moderate. Sometimes fine, but rather uncertain.

ROSA SEMPERFLORENS.

GROUP XXVII.—THE CRIMSON CHINESE ROSE.

THE original of this group was introduced from China in 1789.
There are perhaps no Roses more beautiful late in the year, when
the autumn is mild. I was particularly struck with this in the
autumn of 1846. A few cold misty days had obscured their bright-
ness, when warm weather succeeded, and the buds, which the wet
and cold had sealed, suddenly expanded, producing a brilliant show
in November. There are some very handsome blood-coloured
Roses here. All are of a branching habit, and of moderate growth.
Some do not thrive well as Standards ; but all luxuriate on their
own roots, and form pretty and interesting objects budded on
dwarf stocks. They thrive best in a rich soil, with close pruning :
there are none better for planting in clumps on lawns or in the

flower-garden, for they produce a great number and regular succession of flowers throughout the summer and autumn.

1. ABBÉ MIOLAND ; flowers reddish purple, often streaked with
   white, large and very double ;. form, globular.
2. ALBA ; flowers white, tinged with straw-colour, of medium size,
   (*White*) double ; form cupped.   A good Rose for planting in
   masses.
3. BEAU CARMIN ; flowers crimson, suffused with purple, velvety,
   of medium size, very double.
4. BELLE DE FLORENCE ; flowers pale cherry, produced in elegant
   clusters, of medium size, semi-double ; form, cupped.   A
   showy Rose.
5. BELLE EMILIE ; flowers blush, their centre flesh, large and
   (*Theresia Stravius*) double ; form, expanded.   Excellent for planting in masses.
6. CITOYEN DES DEUX MONDES ; flowers deep blackish crimson, of
   medium size, full ; form expanded.
7. CRAMOISIE EBLOUISSANTE ; flowers vivid crimson, small and
   (*L' Eblouissante*) full.
8. CRAMOISIE SUPÉRIEURE ; flowers velvety crimson, of medium
   size, very double ; form cupped ; exquisite in bud.   A
   good Pot-Rose.
9. DUCHESS OF KENT ; flowers creamy white, sometimes beautifully edged with rose, then very pretty and distinct,
   small and full ; form, cupped.
10. EUGÈNE BEAUHARNAIS : flowers amaranth, the buds beautiful
    (*Prince Eugène*) when first unfolding, sometimes dying off
    blackish crimson, large and very double ; form, cupped.
11. FABVIER ; flowers crimson scarlet, of medium size, semi-double ;
    form, expanded.   One of the most brilliant of Roses, very
    showy, and a superb kind for planting in masses.
12. GLOIRE D'ÉTAMPS ; flowers crimson.   Growth moderate.
13. HENRY THE FIFTH ; flowers crimson scarlet, often striped with
    white, large and very double ; form, cupped.
14. LADY OF THE LAKE ; flowers pure white.
15. LUCULLUS ; flowers dark purplish crimson.
16. LOUIS PHILIPPE ; flowers dark crimson, the edges of the centre
    petals almost white, of medium size, full ; form, globular.
    Raised at Angers.
17. MARJOLIN ; flowers rosy crimson to deep crimson, variable,
    large and full ; form, cupped.   Raised at the Jardin du
    Luxembourg.
18. PRESIDENT D'OLBECQUE ; flowers cherry red ; form, cupped.
    Free and good.

19. PRINCE CHARLES ; flowers brilliant crimson, often suffused with
    light purple, of medium size, full ; form, cupped.
20. SANGUINEA ; flowers crimson, small and very double.
    THERESIA STRAVIUS ; see Belle Emilie.

ROSA INDICA.

GROUP XXVIII—THE CHINESE OR MONTHLY ROSE.

THE varieties of this and the preceding species are included in one
group by many cultivators; and in some of the hybrids the balance is so nicely adjusted, that it is hard to say to which species
they belong.   But the majority are well marked in character.
Compare, for instance, Alba, Cramoisie Supérieure, Fabvier, &c., of
the former group, with Archduke Charles, Joseph Deschiens, and
Napoleon of the present.   Archduke Charles, and many others
classed here, are distinct and beautiful as variegated Roses : they
expand rose and white, soon becoming mottled with, then changing
wholly to, crimson, from the action of the sun's rays.   Strange
that he who bids the colours of other roses fly at his approach
should lend these a deeper and more brilliant tint !
    The varieties of this group are also of even growth, although
more robust than the Crimson Chinese : they are suited for the
same purposes, and, in addition, form fine Standards, thriving under
common treatment.   It has been said that the Bourbon Roses are
hardier than the Chinese, which has led many to suppose that
they are easier of culture ; but nothing could be more contrary to
fact.   The Bourbons *are less susceptible of frost;* but if we except
the varieties hydridized with the Tea-scented, *which are marked
thus**, the Chinese are of the freest growth.   The first Chinese
Rose was introduced from China in 1789.   The varieties which
have sprung from it are too numerous to be described, and withal
resemble each other so closely, that we content ourselves with making
a selection of the best.
    1. *ANTEROS ; flowers white, with creamy centre, large and full ;
        form, cupped.   A capital Forcing Rose.
    2. ARCHDUKE CHARLES; flowers rose, their margin almost white
        when newly expanded, gradually changing to rich crimson,
        from which peculiarity the plant bears flowers of various
        tints at the same time ; very large and full ; form, ex-
        panded.

3. *CAMELLIA BLANC; flowers white, large and double; form, globular. A free bloomer, but rather loose.
4. *CELS MULTIFLORA; flowers white, their centre flesh, large and full; form, cupped. A good forcing Rose; flowers very freely.
5. *CLARA SYLVAIN; flowers pure white, large and full; form, (*Lady Warrender*) cupped. A very fine Rose, suitable either for the borders or the greenhouse.
6. ELISE FLORY; flowers rose-colour, large and full. Growth, vigorous.
7. *EUGÈNE HARDY; flowers white, their centre flesh-colour, of medium size, full; form, cupped.
8. FANNY DUVAL; flowers white, their centre flesh, large and full; form, cupped.
9. JOSEPH DESCHIENS; flowers dark crimson, their centre rosy purple, of medium size, full; form, cupped.
10. LE CAMÉLÉON; flowers whitish pink, often changing to blackish crimson before decaying, of medium size, double; form, expanded.
11. LA FRAICHEUR; flowers rosy white, centre yellowish. Growth, moderate.
12. LORRAINII; flowers French white; form, cupped.
13. MADAME BRÉON; flowers rich rose-colour, sometimes a little tinged with salmon, very large and full; form, compact. A beautiful Rose, with handsome foliage.
14. MADAME BUREAU; flowers white, their centre inclining to straw, (*Infidélité de Lisette*) large and very double; form, cupped. One (*Madame de Rohan*) of the finest White Autumnal Roses.
15. *MADAME DESPREZ; flowers white tinged with lemon, large and very double; form, cupped.
MADAME DE ROHAN: see Madame Bureau.
MADAME LACHARME; see Virginale.
16. MIELLEZ; flowers pale lemon, changing to white, of medium size, double; form, cupped.
MRS. BOSANQUET; see Group XXVI. Bourbon.
17. NAPOLEON; flowers blush, mottled with pink, large and double; form, cupped.
18. SULLY; flowers pale rose, shaded with fawn; form, cupped.
19. TANCREDI; flowers light purple, suffused with crimson, variable, large and full; form, cupped. A distinct and desirable variety.
20. TRIOMPHE DE GAND; flowers rose, mottled, large and double.

21. *VIRGINALE ; flowers flesh-colour, of medium size, full ; form,
(*La Séduisante*)　　　globular. A fine Forcing Rose, but seldom
(*Madame Lacharme*)　opens clean and good out of doors.
22.*VIRGINIE ; flowers rose shaded, large and full ; form, cupped.
23. VIRIDIFLORA ; flowers green, curious.

ROSA INDICA.

GROUP XXIX.—THE LAWRENCEANA, OR FAIRY ROSE.

THE first of these interesting Roses was introduced from China in
1810. The varieties form pretty objects cultivated in pots, rarely
exceeding a foot in height. Thousands of them are sold in our
markets every year, and beautiful they are when covered with their
tiny blossoms. In dry soils the Fairy Roses may be planted in
masses, also as edgings for beds in the Rosarium : for the latter
purpose the hardiest kinds should be chosen. They require the
same treatment as the varieties of the succeeding group.
1. ALBA, or BLANC; flowers white, delicate.
　BLUSH ; see Fairy.
2. FAIRY ; flowers pale pink
　(*Blush*)
3. GLOIRE DES LAWRENCEANAS ; flowers dark crimson.
4. JENNY ; flowers bright crimson.
　(*Rubra*)
5. LA DESIRÉE ; flowers crimson.
6. NEMESIS ; flowers crimson, changing blackish, larger and more
　　robust in habit than the others.
7. NIGRA ; flowers very dark crimson.
8. RETOUR DU PRINTEMPS ; flowers bright rose.
　RUBRA ; see Jenny.

ROSA INDICA.

GROUP XXX.—THE TEA-SCENTED ROSE.

IN 1810 the Blush Tea-scented Rose was introduced from China,
and fourteen years later the Yellow variety was received from the
same country. They have given birth to a very numerous family,
some remarkable for their large thick petals ; others for possessing
a strong tea-like scent ; and others for the delicacy and bewitching
tints of the flowers. It has been said, both by French and English

writers on this subject, that the Yellow, although a fertile seed-bearer, never produces varieties worthy of notice. As if to redeem its character from this aspersion, a few years ago it produced, *in this country*, the Devoniensis, one of the handsomest of the group, raised by Mr. Foster of Plymouth, with others from the same parent, one of which was a Noisette of a yellow cast.

It must be admitted that this beautiful group is somewhat difficult of culture. (See p. 159) They require a rich well-drained soil, close pruning, and, *if grown out of doors*, a dry warm border and protection from frost. The practice of removing them from the ground for protection during winter, and again transferring them to their places in the Rosarium in spring, is not altogether satisfactory. To remove a plant once endangers its growth and perfect flowering the first year, and to remove it twice more than doubles the risk of failure. Tea-Roses may be divided into two classes; "Ligneous*," represented by the Comte de Paris; and "Herbaceous," of which we may instance the Yellow. The former, which are marked †, are far hardier than the others, and form good Standards. If the latter are grown as such, they must be thoroughly protected during winter.—See p. 145.

If trained to a wall with a south or east aspect the Tea-Roses grow vigorously, and flower in great beauty, much earlier and finer than in the open ground, producing a constant succession of flowers for one half of the year. They also flower well grown in pots and plunged in the open ground, if removed to a cold frame for protection during winter. But for Pot-culture under glass, for Forcing, and for planting out in the Conservatory, they are unsurpassed.

There are some fine specimens at the Royal Horticultural Society's Gardens at Chiswick, growing in a house devoted entirely to their culture.

1. ABRICOTÉ; flowers apricot colour, their margin flesh, large and (*Fanny Dupuis*) double; form, cupped. Growth, vigorous. A beautiful Rose.
2. ADAM; flowers rich rosy salmon, very large and full; form, globular. Growth, vigorous. A superb Rose, and very sweet.
   ALBA ROSA; see p. 165.
3. †AMABILIS; flowers flesh-colour, buff centres, thick petals, large and full; form, expanded; habit, branching. Growth, vigorous. A good hardy free sort.
4. ARCHIMÈDE; flowers rosy fawn, darker centres, large and full; form, expanded. Growth, moderate.

---

* The words "Ligneous" and "Herbaceous" are not used here in their strict *botanical* sense, but to distinguish the two races.

5. AUGUSTE OGER; flowers rose-colour, centres copper colour, large and full; form, cupped fine. Growth, moderate. One of the best.

6. AUGUSTE VACHER; flowers golden fawn, shaded with copper colour, large and full; form, cupped. Growth, moderate.

7. BARBOT; flowers cream, suffused with rose and salmon, large and full; form, globular. A good Forcing Rose, but uncertain out of doors.

BARILLET DESCHAMPS; see Madame Barillet Deschamps.

8. BELLE ALLEMANDE; flowers delicate pink, often tinged with fawn, variable, very large and double; form, expanded. A free bloomer, and very sweet.

9. BELLE CHARTRONNAISE; flowers bright red, shaded with rosy crimson, large and full. Growth, vigorous.

10. †BELLE DE BORDEAUX; flowers pink, centres crimson, large and full. Growth, vigorous.

11. †BELLE MARIE; flowers white, shaded with rose, large and full. Growth, moderate.

12. †BELLE MARGUERITE; flowers rose, shaded with crimson, large and very double; form, expanded. Growth, robust.

13. BOUGÈRE; flowers deep salmon colour, very large and full; form, cupped. Growth, vigorous. A superb Pot or Forcing Rose, with thick petals.

14. †BURET; flowers crimson, tinged with light purple, of medium size, full; form, globular. A free bloomer. A distinct Rose, of vigorous growth.

15. CANARY; flowers bright canary colour, beautiful in the bud, of average size, hardly double. Growth, moderate.

16. †CAROLINE; flowers blush, suffused with deep pink, large and full; form, cupped. Grows and flowers freely.

17. CERISE POURPRE; flowers rosy crimson marbled. Second-rate.

COMTESSE DE BROSSARD; see p. 166.

18. CHARLES REYBAUD; flowers pink, large and double; form, expanded.

19. †COMTE DE PARIS; flowers flesh colour, shaded with rose, very large and full; form, cupped. A noble Rose. Raised at the Jardin du Luxembourg.

20. COMTESSE DE LABARTHE; flowers salmon pink. Second-rate.

21. COMTESSE OUVAROFF; flowers rose-colour, shaded with pink and fawn; large and full. Growth, moderate. Beautiful in bud.

22. COMTESSE DE WORONZOW; flowers rose and crimson, large and full. Growth, vigorous.

23. DAVID PRADEL; flowers rose-colour mottled, large and full. Growth, vigorous.

24. DELPHINE (GAUDÔT); flowers pure white; form, cupped.
25. DEVONIENSIS; flowers creamy white, their centre sometimes buff, sometimes yellowish, very large and full; form, cupped. A splendid Rose, of robust growth.
26. DUC DE MAGENTA; flowers bright rosy salmon, shaded with flesh-colour and fawn, very large and full. Growth, moderate. A fine Rose, with large thick petals.
27. DUCHESSE DE LAVALLIERE; flowers pink. Second-rate.
28. DUCHESSE D'ORLEANS; flowers flesh-colour. Second-rate.
29. ELISE SAUVAGE; flowers pale yellow, their centre sometimes inclining to buff, sometimes to orange, large and full; form, globular. One of the most beautiful, but of a rather delicate habit.
30. ENFANT DE LYON; flowers pale yellow, large and full; form, cupped, fine. Growth, moderate. A beautiful Rose, similar to, but paler than Narcisse.
31. †EUGÉNIE DESGACHES; flowers rose, large and full; form, cupped. Growth, vigorous. One of the best.
32. †FRAGOLETTA; flowers rosy blush to crimson, variable, large and double; form, cupped. Foliage, fine.
33. †FRAGRANS; flowers rosy to bright crimson; form, cupped.
34. GENERAL TARTAS; flowers flesh-colour, shaded with rose, large and full. Growth, moderate.
35. GEORGES DE FRANCE; flowers flesh-colour, large and double. Growth, moderate.
36. GERARD DESBOIS; flowers bright rosy red, large and full. Growth, vigorous.
37. GLOIRE DE BORDEAUX; flowers silvery white, the back of the petals rosy pink, very large and full. Growth, vigorous. A fine Wall-Rose.
38†.GLOIRE DE DIJON; flowers yellow, buff, orange, and salmon shaded, large and full; form, globular. Growth, vigorous. One of the best. A splendid wall or pillar Rose.
39†. GOUBAULT; flowers bright rose, very large and double; form, expanded. The young buds of this Rose are of the most elegant form, shewing of a rich deep crimson as the sepals part. Very sweet.
40. GRANDIFLORA; flowers shaded rose, very large and double. Growth, vigorous.
41.†HOMER; flowers blush rose and salmon,, very variable, form, cupped. Growth, vigorous. A good hardy free blooming sort.
42. JOSEPHINE MALTON; flowers rich cream colour, their centres often inclining to buff, the tops of the petals sometimes

tinged with lake, large and very double; form, cupped, exquisite. A beautiful Rose. Very susceptible of frost.

43. JULIE MANSAIS; flowers straw colour, their margin almost white, large and full; form, cupped. Very sweet. The buds long and very beautiful. Rather delicate.

44. LA BOULE D'OR; flowers fine golden yellow, petals broad and smooth, large and full; form, globular. Growth, moderate. A fine Rose under glass only.

LADY WARRENDER; see Group XXVIII. Chinese "Clara Sylvain."

45†.LA SYLPHIDE; flowers blush, very large and double.

46. LAURETTE; flowers rosy blush shaded with salmon, large and very double. Growth, vigorous.

47. L'ENFANT TROUVÉ; closely resembles, if not identical with, Elise Sauvage.

48. LEONTINE DE LAPORTE; flowers sulphur and fawn, large and full; form, cupped. Growth, robust.

49. LE CAMÉLEON; flowers French-white, with salmon centre, large and double.

50. LEVESON GOWER; flowers pale yellow, distinct.

51. LOUISE CLÉMENT; flowers creamy yellow. Growth, dwarf.

52. LOUISE DE SAVOIE; flowers fine pale yellow, large and full. Growth, moderate. Very sweet. One of the best.

53. †LYONNAIS; flowers rosy pink, changing to flesh-colour, very large and double; form, cupped. Growth, vigorous. A noble Rose, but rather loose.

54. MADAME BARILLET DESCHAMPS; flowers white, creamy centre, large and full. Growth, moderate. A good free sort.

55. MADAME BLACHET; flowers rose and fawn, very variable, and very sweet, large and full. Growth, dwarf.

56.†MADAME BRAVY; flowers cream, large and full; form, cupped, good.

57. MADAME DAMAIZIN; flowers buff, cream, and salmon, variously shaded, large and full; form, cupped. Growth, moderate. A good, distinct, and hardy sort.

58. MADAME DARRU; flowers rose shaded. Growth, moderate.

59.†MADAME DE SALVANDY; flowers yellowish buff, large and double. Growth, moderate. A free-flowering hardy sort.

60†.MADAME DE ST. JOSEPH; flowers pink, with deeper centre, sometimes dying off apricot colour, very large and double; form, expanded. Growth, vigorous. A splendid Pot-Rose.

61. MADAME DE TARTAS; flowers bright rose, large, full, and produced abundantly. Growth, moderate.

62. MADAME DE VATRY; flowers deep rosy salmon, paler edges, large and full. Growth, moderate.

63. MADAME FALCOT; flowers rich saffron yellow, large and very double; petals, large and thick. Growth, moderate. In the way of Safrano, but of a higher colour.

64. MADAME HALPHIN; flowers French-white, tinted with salmon, pink, and fawn, large and very double; form, cupped. Growth, moderate. A most beautiful Rose.

65. MADAME JACQUEMINOT; flowers white, their centre yellow, large and full; form, cupped.

66. MADAME LAFITTE; flowers salmon flesh, large and full. Growth, moderate.

67.†MADAME LARTAY; flowers yellow, shaded with salmon, large and full. Growth, moderate. A good hardy free growing sort.

68. †MADAME MAURIN; flowers creamy white, shaded with salmon, large and full. Growth, moderate. Good and distinct.

69. †MADAME PAULINE LABONTÉ; flowers salmon, circumference creamy buff, very large and full; form, expanded. Growth, moderate. A good hardy sort.

70.†MADAME ROUSSELL; flowers white, shaded and sometimes edged (*Eugénie Jovian*) with rosy-flesh, large and full; form, compact. A free grower and free bloomer, but not very sweet.

71. MADAME SYVESTRE; flowers creamy white, yellowish centres. large and full. Growth, moderate.

72.†MADAME VILLERMOZ; flowers white, centres fawn and salmon, large and full; form, cupped. Growth, vigorous. A splendid Rose, and very hardy.

73. MADAME WILLIAM; flowers rich yellow, orange centre, large and full; form, globular, fine. Growth, moderate. Closely resembles Elise Sauvage.

MADEMOISELLE ADÈLE JOUGANT; see p. 168.

74. MADEMOISELLE AMANDA; flowers red, shaded with rose, small and sweet.

75. †MANSAIS; flowers rose, shaded with buff, very large and full; form, cupped. Very sweet.

76†.MARÉCHAL BUGEAUD; flowers bright rose, large and very double; form, cupped.

77. MARIE; flowers white. Growth, dwarf.

78. MARIE DE MEDICIS; flowers flesh colour, tinged with rose and carmine, large and full; form, globular. Growth, robust. Sometimes splendid, but does not always open well.

79. MARQUISE DE FOUCAULT; flowers white, fawn, and yellow, variable, large but not very double; form, globular. Growth, moderate, but free. Good and distinct.

80. MELANIE OGER; flowers creamy white, centre yellow.

81.†MIRABILE ; flowers apricot yellow, edged and shaded with rose, variable, of medium size, full ; form, cupped. A very pretty Rose when in true character.

82.†MOIRET ; flowers fawn, sometimes yellowish, exquisitely tinted with rose, variable, very large and full ; form, cupped, fine. Growth, vigorous. A superb Rose, and very sweet.

83.†NARCISSE ; flowers pale yellow, large and full ; form, cupped, fine. Growth, moderate. One of the best.

84.†NINA ; flowers white, delicately tinted with pink, large and very double ; form, globular. A free grower, and blooms freely.

85.†NIPHETOS ; flowers white, their centre pale lemon, magnolia-like, very large and full ; form, globular. A distinct and beautiful Rose, of vigorous growth.

86.†NISIDA ; flowers rose and fawn, variously shaded, of medium size, very double ; form, cupped. Habit and foliage fine ; flowers deliciously sweet.

87. OLYMPE FRECINAY ; flowers yellow, produced abundantly.

88. OPHELIA ; flowers pale yellow, deeper centre. Growth, moderate.

89. †ORIGINALE ; flowerscreamy white, their centre salmon buff, large and full ; form, expanded. Growth, vigorous.

PAULINE LABONTE ; see Madame Pauline Labonte.

PACTOLUS ; see Group XXXII. Noisette, " Le Pactole."

91. †PAULINE PLANTIER ; flowers white, tinged with lemon, of medium size, full ; form, globular.

92. PELLONIA ; flowers pale yellow, their centre flesh, large and very double ; form, globular. Very sweet.

93. POLONIE BOURDIN ; flowers creamy yellow, yellowish centre, of medium size, full. Growth, moderate.

94. PRESIDENT ; flowers rose shaded with salmon, very large and full ; form, globular. Growth, moderate, One of the sweetest and best under glass.

95. PRINCE ESTERHAZY ; flowers flesh colour, their centre rose, very large and very double ; form, globular. Deliciously sweet.

96. PRINCESSE ADELAIDE ; flowers straw colour, their margin of a paler hue, large and full ; form, cupped. Very sweet.

97. PRINCESSE MARIE ; flowers rosy pink, large and full ; form, globular. Uncertain out of doors, but forces well.

98. QUEEN VICTORIA ; flowers pale yellow, large and full ; form, globular. Closely resembles Princesse Adelaide.

99. REGULUS ; flowers bright rose shaded with copper, irregular in shape. Growth, vigorous.

100. REINE DES PAYS BAS ; flowers pale sulphur, deeper centre, large and full ; form, cupped. Growth, moderate. A free blooming variety, of delicate beauty.

101. †RUBENS ; flowers white shaded with rose, centres bronzy yellow, large and full ; form, cupped, fine. Growth, vigorous. A good and distinct sort.

102. †SAFRANO ; flowers saffron to apricot in the bud, changing to pale buff, large and very double ; form, cupped. A pretty and hardy variety, worthy of place in every collection.

103. SÉMÉLÉ ; flowers pale flesh, their centre yellowish, of medium size.

104. SMITH'S YELLOW ; flowers pale straw-colour, large and full ; (*Yellow Noisette*) form, globular. A fine forcing Rose, but seldom opens well out of doors.

105. SOCRATES ; flowers deep rose, centres apricot, large and full. Growth, vigorous.

106.†SOMBREUIL ; flowers white tinged with rose, very large and full ; form, cupped. Growth, vigorous. A good hardy free flowering sort.

107. SOUVENIR DE DAVID ; flowers cherry-colour, very large and double. Growth, moderate. Very distinct.

108. SOUVENIR D'ELISE VARDON ; flowers creamy white, centre yellowish, very large and full ; form, globular, fine. Growth robust. A splendid Rose.

TRIOMPHE DE GUILLOT FILS ; see p. 164.

109. SOUVENIR DU 30 MAI ; flowers rose and yellow, their centre copper-colour, large and full ; form, cupped.

110.†SOUVENIR D'UN AMI ; flowers salmon and rose, shaded, large full ; form, cupped. Very fine.

111.†TAGLIONI ; flowers creamy white, their centre tinted with flesh and lemon, large and full ; form, cupped.

112.†TRIOMPHE D'ORLEANS ; flowers white, large and full.

113. TRIOMPHE DU LUXEMBOURG ; flowers flesh-colour, tinged with fawn and rose, very large and full ; form, globular. Growth, vigorous. A beautiful Rose, and very sweet. Raised at the Jardin du Luxembourg

114. VICOMTESSE DE CAZES ; flowers bright orange yellow, often tinged with copper-colour, large and very double ; form, cupped. One of the most beautiful.

VICTORIA ; see Queen Victoria.

VIRGINALE ; see Group XXVIII. Chinese.

115. YELLOW ; flowers sulphur-coloured, large and double ; form, (*Flavescens*) globular. The petals of this Rose are very large, (*Jaune*) the buds long and beautiful in a half-expanded state.

T

ROSA MOSCHATA.

GROUP XXXI.—THE MUSK ROSE.

THE Musk Rose is supposed to have been introduced to England about the year 1596, and by reason of its long residence among us, has become widely spread throughout the country. The original Musk Rose is a rambling shrub, abounding in Madeira and the North of Africa, also in Persia: indeed, it is generally supposed that the attar of Roses is made from the species now under consideration. The flowers, which form in large clusters, seldom appear till late in summer: their peculiar musk-like scent is a point of distinction, although not so powerful as some authors would lead us to believe: it is one of the fine things of nature, which requires the existence of special circumstances—a still moist atmosphere—to be readily appreciable. These Roses are of rapid growth, best adapted for Climbers : they are not sufficiently hardy to bear exposure in bleak unsheltered situations. They require long-pruning.

1. BLUSH, or FRASER'S ; flowers pale red, small and semi-double ; form, cupped.
2. DOUBLE WHITE ; flowers yellowish white, of medium size, double ; form, cupped.
3. EPONINE ; flowers white ; form cupped.
4. FRINGED ; flowers white, the petals serrated ; form, cupped.
5. NIVEA ; flowers white, shaded with rose, large and single ; form, cupped. Growth, robust.
6. PRINCESSE DE NASSAU ; flowers yellowish straw ; form cupped ; very sweet.

ROSA MOSCHATA.

GROUP. XXXII—THE NOISETTE ROSE.

THE original Noisette, due probably to the accidental fertilization of the Chinese with the Musk Rose, was obtained by M. Philippe Noisette, in North America, and sent to Paris in 1817. The peculiar features recommended to notice were, its hardy nature, free growth, and large clusters of flowers, produced very late in the year, which were indeed recommendations of no common order. Its appearance was hailed with delight, and it soon spread throughout Europe. But we are losing the old style of Noisette, and multiplying kinds hybridized with the Tea-scented. This is a matter of regret ; for however much we may extend the range, or improve the delicacy of the colours, by this process, we are rendering a hardy group of Roses tender, and blotting out the prettiest feature of the group—flowers produced in large and elegant trusses.

The kinds partaking of the nature of the Tea-scented require a wall, and the treatment advanced for Tea Roses : they are marked thus § that they may be distinguished from the others. Among the true Noisettes the kinds of vigorous growth form handsome, late-flowering Weeping or Pillar-Roses : the others thrive equally well either as Dwarfs or Standards. Rather less pruning is required here than is recommended for the Chinese and Tea-scented : a common soil suffices. I have seen these Roses blooming unchecked amid the early storms of winter.

1. ADELAIDE PAVIE ; flowers pale lemon, large and double, flowering in clusters. Growth, vigorous.

2. AIMÉE VIBERT ; flowers pure white, produced in large clusters, of medium size, full ; form, compact. Growth, moderate. Forms a noble Standard, the foliage of a dark green, and shining ; good also for bedding. Raised by M. Vibert, at Angers.

3. AIMÉE VIBERT SCANDENS ; resembles Aimée Vibert, but of more vigorous growth.

4. §AMERICA ; flowers creamy white, centres fawn, very large and full ; form, cupped. Growth, vigorous. A fine Climbing Rose under glass, but good out of doors in fine weather only.

5. BEAUTY OF GREENMOUNT ; flowers bright rose, changing to pale rose, small and double, produced in clusters, in the way of, but scarcely equal to, Fellenberg.

6. §BLANCHE DE SOLVILLE ; flowers creamy white, with pink centre, large and double ; form, cupped. Growth, vigorous.
BOUQUET DE MARIE ; see Hybrid Perpetual. Group XXIII.

7. CAMELLIA ROUGE; flowers rosy pink.

8. CAROLINE MARNIESSE ; flowers creamy white, produced in large clusters, small and full ; form, compact. Growth, vigorous.

9. §CELINE FORESTIER ; flowers pale yellow, deeper centres, large (*Liesis*) and full ; form, cupped. Growth, vigorous. An excellent and hardy Rose.

10. CERISE; flowers purplish rose, large and double ; form, cupped. (*Mayflower*) (*Rothanger*) Growth, vigorous.

11. CLAUDIA AUGUSTIN ; flowers white, yellow centres. Growth, vigorous,

12. §CLOTH OF GOLD ; flowers creamy white, their centre yellow,

(*Chromatella*) varies as to colour and fulness, usually very large and very double; form, globular. Growth, vigorous. A beautiful Rose, and sweet, but a shy bloomer. The best mode of treatment is to plant it against a south or an east wall, pruning it very little : when thoroughly established it will flower. Raised from Noisette Lamarque. Introduced in 1843.

13. §CORNELIA KOCH ; flowers straw-colour, large and full ; form, globular, fine. Growth, robust.

14. CORNELIE ; flowers rose-colour, shaded with lilac, produced in clusters. Growth, vigorous.

15. D'ESPALAIS ; flowers rose. Growth, vigorous.

16. §DESPREZ A FLEUR JAUNE ; flowers red, buff, flesh, and sulphur, (*Jaune Desprez*) very large and full; form, cupped. Growth, (*New French Yellow*) vigorous, making shoots three or four feet long, the flowers forming in clusters at their points, the foliage large and fine. Very sweet. A most desirable kind for a wall.

17. DU LUXEMBOURG ; flowers lilac rose, their centre deep red, large, and very double ; form, cupped. Growth, vigorous, ECLAIR DE JUPITER ; see Group XXV. Rose de Rosomène.

18. §EUPHROSYNE ; flowers pale rose, fawn, and yellow, variable, large and very double ; form, cupped. Growth, moderate. A pretty Rose, with pale green shining foliage. Very sweet.

19. FELLENBERG; flowers bright crimson, of medium size, double ; form, cupped. Growth, robust. An abundant bloomer, with dark foliage, showy, but rather loose. Desirable for bedding : fine late in the year.

20. §ISABELLA GRAY, or MISS GRAY ; flowers deep yellow, large and full ; form, globular. Growth, vigorous. A splendid Climbing Rose under glass, but worthless out of doors.

21. JACQUES ORMYOTT ; flowers rose-colour.

22. §JANE HARDY ; flowers golden yellow, large and full. Growth, vigorous. Like ISABELLA GRAY, best under glass.

23. JEANNE D'ARC ; flowers pure white ; form cupped. Growth, vigorous.

24. LA BICHE ; flowers white, their centre flesh, very large and very double ; form, cupped. Growth, vigorous. A fine Pillar-Rose.

25. LAIS ; flowers French white, large. LIESIS ; see Celine Forestier.

26. §LAMARQUE ; flowers white, their centre deep straw-colour, very large and full ; form, cupped. Growth, vigorous.

A splendid kind for a wall with a sunny aspect, producing its elegant flowers in large clusters.

27. §Le Pactole ; flowers cream, their centre yellow, large and (*Pactolus*) full ; form, cupped. Growth, moderate. A beautiful Rose.

28. Madame Deslongchamps ; flowers pale flesh, tinged with pink, large and double.

Madame Lartay ; see Tea-scented Group XXX.

29. Madame Massot ; flowers pure white, flesh-coloured centres, small, full, and produced in clusters ; form, cupped, fine. Growth, vigorous. Good, free, and distinct.

30. §Madame Schultz ; flowers pale yellow, deeper centres, of medium size, full, and very sweet. Growth, vigorous.

31. Mademoiselle Aristide ; flowers pale yellow, centres salmon colour. Growth vigorous.

32. §Marie Chargè ; flowers yellow, shaded with fawn, sometimes tinged with crimson. Growth, moderate.

33. Miss Glegg ; flowers white, their centre sometimes flesh-colour, produced in large clusters, small and full ; form, cupped. Growth, dwarf. Much in the style of Aimée Vibert, but the flowers are smaller and more regularly formed. A pretty Rose. Raised by M. Vibert.

34. §Mrs. Siddons ; flowers bright yellow ; form, cupped. Growth, dwarf.

35. Octavie ; flowers bright rose.

Polonie Bourdin ; see Tea-scented. Group XXX.

36. §Ophirie ; flowers reddish copper, the outer petals rosy and fawn, of medium size, very double ; form, cupped. Growth, vigorous. Distinct and sweet. Foliage handsome. An excellent Wall or Weeping Rose.

37. §Phaloé ; flowers cream, delicately tinted with carmine, large and full ; form, compact. Growth, moderate.

38. Pumila alba ; flowers white, small and double ; form, cupped. A free bloomer of small growth, good for bedding.

39. Sir Walter Scott ; flowers rosy lilac, large and double ; form, cupped. Growth, vigorous.

Smith's Yellow ; see Group XXX. Tea-scented.

40. §Solfaterre ; flowers creamy white, their centre bright sulphur, very large and full ; form, cupped. Growth, vigorous. A fine Rose, with handsome foliage, and very sweet. Excellent for a wall. Raised from Noisette Lamarque. Introduced in 1843.

41. §Triomphe de Bolwyller ; flowers cream, shaded ; form, cupped.

42. Triomphe de la Duchere ; flowers pale rose, produced in

large clusters, of medium size, full ; form, cupped. Raised
by M. Beluze, of Lyons.   Introduced in 1846.

43. §Tromphe de Rennes ; flowers canary, cream edges, large and
full ; form, cupped, fine.   Growth, vigorous.   A good
hardy Rose, and very sweet.

44. Vicomtesse d' Avesne ; flowers rosy lilac, produced in clusters,
small and full.   Growth, vigorous.

End of Division II.

APPENDIX.

THE BOTANY OF THE ROSE.*

BOTANICALLY considered, the family of Roses is as difficult as it is beautiful. In this view the Wild forms only are comprehended, the botanist having nothing to do with the varieties originated by the Florist. These Wild forms, notwithstanding their simplicity, are the very impersonations of elegance and beauty. We are not about to discuss the general question, whether the Single Wild Roses, or the Double Garden Roses, are the most beautiful; but, whatever opinion may be formed on that point, it is believed that no one will deny to the Wild Roses of our woods and hedges, all that has just been claimed for them.

Perhaps, indeed, at the present day, the number of cultivators may be limited who would care to collect, in their prim gardens, the aboriginal species of Roses, whether native or exotic; but, amongst those who are most interested in Rose-culture, some may desire to know the extent of materials which the genus affords, especially in reference to the working out, by hybridization, of characters differing from those which predominate in our present cultivated races. Those who may wish to do this, especially amateurs, may find some useful hints in the few particulars which follow.

We by no means, however, assent to the broad and sweeping conclusion, at which perhaps the genuine Florist would arrive, that the original forms or species of Roses are unworthy a place in our gardens. We maintain that many of them are very beautiful objects. There is among them a much greater diversity of elegance than the cultivated varieties, with all their richness and splendour, are found to possess. It is therefore assumed at the outset, that there are many Wild Roses which are quite admissible into select Rose-gardens ; and many more which the hybridist might turn to his advantage. Moreover, a plea might be urged on behalf of Single Roses, though they are often, indeed generally, set aside as inferior to those having double blossoms. Even if only for the sake of variety, a Single Rose, highly coloured and finely formed—that is, floriculturally modelled, or improved, as it is called—is a thing not to be despised. It is less enduring than a double blossom, no doubt ; nevertheless, who scouts the Austrian Brier ?

Before proceeding to sketch the various groups of Wild Roses, it may be useful to the uninitiated to explain the application of some of the terms which are employed in referring to the different parts of the plant.

Rootshoots, or *surculi*, are the strong one-year old shoots produced from the base of the plant; these do not usually bear any blossoms, except on their lateral branches, which are most commonly produced during the second season. The habit of these rootshoots is different, and this helps to distinguish some of the species.

---

* For this chapter on Wild Roses I am indebted to my friend, Mr. Thomas Moore.

Branches are the ramifications of the rootshoots or principal stems.

Branchlets are the small lateral shoots produced in some instances from the stronger shoots of the same season's growth.

Prickles of various kinds.   Setæ.

Arms indicate the armature of the stems and branches, that is to say, the rigid processes borne on their surface. The term *armed* is used when prickles and setæ are borne indiscriminately; while *unarmed* is used to denote smoothness, or the absence of prickles and setæ.

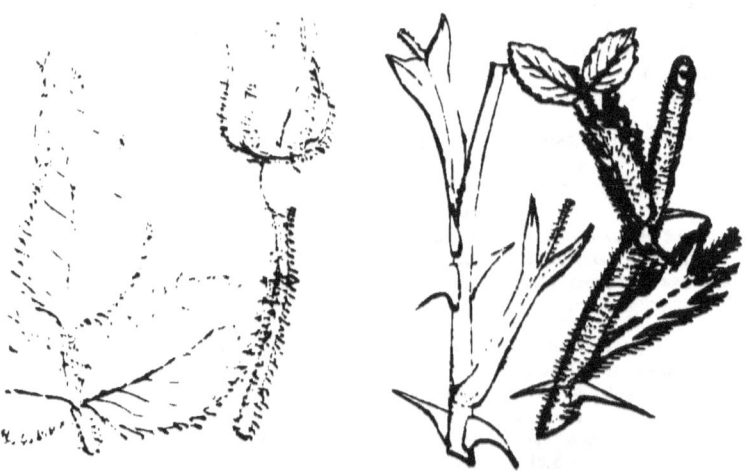

Glands.   Stipules.

Prickles or *aculei* are the sharp rigid processes which occur on most of the species: in some they are straight, and in others more or less hooked: they vary much in size.

Setæ are small straight prickles or aculei, tipped with a gland, and are known from true glands by their rigidity: they are believed to exist upon the root-shoots, at some period, in all the species, becoming soon changed into bristle-like aculei by the loss of the gland. In general they are deciduous.

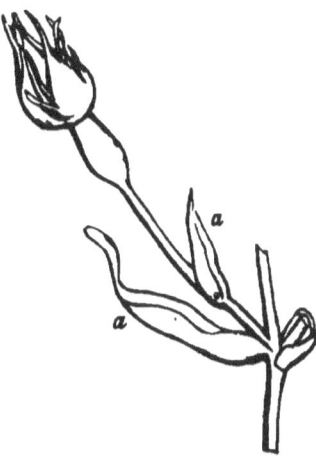

Glands are secretory bodies, for the most part attached to leaves on their under surface, and better distinguished from setæ by their scent than by any thing else. The well-known appearance of the Moss Rose is caused by glands in a peculiar condition.

Pubescence is applied to a kind of downiness caused by the presence of short fine hairs. When found on the branches, peduncles. or the tube of the calyx, pubescence offers a useful discriminative character.

Stipules are little leaf-like appendages growing one on each side of the leaf stalk at its base, to which they always in some degree adhere: sometimes they are much developed, sometimes they are deciduous.

Bracts are small leafy bodies produced in some species, and always situated between the true leaves and the flowers.

Bracts indicated at *a*).

Disk is a term applied to a projecting part of the flower which occurs between the base of the stamens and the ovary.

Fruit is a common term for the hip or fleshy tube of the calyx, grown on to maturity, and enclosing the pericarps, or true fruits.

The Rose constitutes the genus ROSA of Linnæus. This name *Rosa*, by

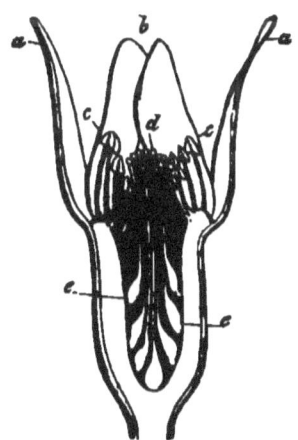

Perpendicular section of a Rose flower:
a, sepals; *b*, petals; *c*, stamens; *d*, pistils; *e*, pericarps.

which the plants are known to botanists, is derived from the Celtic *rhos*, red, whence come the Greek 'Ροδον, and the Latin *Rosa*. The plants form a very extensive and well-marked family, easily recognised as a whole, but in many cases its members are by no means easily distinguished the one from the other. The peculiar characteristics of Roses, from a botanical point of view, are, the presence of an urn-shaped calyx, which has a limb of five segments, and a fleshy tube the apex of which is constricted into a ring or glandular disk; numerous stamens, inserted with the petals on the rim of the tube of the calyx; and numerous dry bony pericarps, which are enclosed in the fleshy calyx-tube. The foregoing diagrammatic section of a Rose-flower will make these peculiarities more intelligible. The segments of the calyx are usually divided in a pinnate manner, but not in all cases, and they are sometimes deciduous. The petals are normally five in number, the five-petaled flowers being represented by the Wild Roses of our hedge-rows. The ovaries, which are numerous, and enclosed in the calyx-tube, are distinct, bristly, and tipped by the style, which passes up to the orifice of the tube: these styles are usually separate, but in some few species they are joined together into an elongated column. The leaves of Roses are what are called impari-pinnate, and stipules grow to the sides of their stalks.

The Rose family is classified by botanists into several distinct groups, for the purpose of facilitating the discrimination of its numerous and often closely-similar species. The groups most generally adopted, which bear the names of *Feroces*, *Bracteatæ*, *Cinnamomeæ*, *Pimpinellifoliæ*, *Centifoliæ*, *Villosæ*, *Rubiginosæ*, *Caninæ*, *Systylæ*, and *Banksianæ*, we now propose to pass briefly in review.

Rosa ferox.

The FEROCES consist of deciduous bushes, whose branches are clothed with permanent down. The leaves fall early in autumn, after which the branches are remarkable for their hoary bristly appearance; the sepals are usually toothed; and the fruit is perfectly smooth.

This group is represented by *R. ferox*, a shrub of 3 to 4 feet high, introduced to our gardens from the Caucasus, before the close of the last century. Its branches are densely covered with prickles, which are all of the same shape; the leaves consist of from five to nine elliptic retuse leaflets; the flowers are large and red; and the globose fruit is scarlet. One of its forms, called *nitens*, has smoother leaves, and paler crimson flowers. Another species is *R. kamtschatica*, which bears solitary flowers of a very deep red. This group does not appear to have influenced our Garden Roses.

The BRACTEATÆ form evergreen and sub-evergreen bushes, the branches and fruit of which are clothed with permanent tomentum. The leaves are dense and usually shining; and the prickles of the stem are placed under the stipules in pairs. The sepals are nearly or quite simple.

The type of this group is *R. bracteata*, the parent of the Macartney Roses. It is a shrub of 3 to 4 feet in length, with erect branches, strong hooked prickles, and leaves consisting of from five to nine obovate shining leaflets. The flowers are pure white, solitary, and nearly sessile within the appressed pectinated downy bracts. The fruit is woolly and spherical, of an orange red colour. This plant was introduced from China in 1795. Maria Leonida, which is one of the varieties, and which bears double white flowers tinged in the centre with pink, is one of the finest of Autumnal Roses.

R. involucrata, from Nepal and China, which has white nearly solitary flowers surrounded by three or four approximate leaves, whence the name of involucrated, belongs here also. Another species referred to this group

Rosa bracteata.

by some, but by others to the Caninæ, is *R. microphylla*, a small compact shrub, with slender branches, furnished beneath the stipules with straight prickles, and having small shining roundish-ovate leaflets, and solitary double full red flowers, whose calyx is covered with close-set straight prickles. It resembles the Macartney Rose in its general appearance, and has given rise to the garden group of Microphylla Roses.

The CINNAMOMEÆ are deciduous Roses, the stems being unarmed or setigerous towards the base, and bearing bracts upwards. The leaflets are lanceolate, without glands; the disk of the calyx-tube is never thickened; and the sepals are long and narrow, and fall immediately after the ripening of the small round fruit.

This group is chiefly one of botanical interest, not having yielded, at least directly, any of the choice races which are prized in gardens. It contains a good many North-American species, and some of our common English ones; and hence, being a very hardy race, might be employed to impart the desirable quality of hardihood to some of the fine tender breeds so much prized. Among them are:—*R. nitida*, a bush of 2 feet high, with crowded slender straight red

prickles, dark-green leaves consisting of from three to seven narrow lanceolate shining leaflets, and deep red flowers, succeeded by bright scarlet depressed
spherical fruit. *R. lucida*, the Single Burnet Rose, a compact shrub of from
4 to 6 feet high, with erect branches, nearly solitary prickles under the stipules,

and a few scattered setæ; the
leaves consisting of nine oblong imbricated flat shining
leaflets ; and the flowers red,
overtopped by the leaves and
young branches. *R. Lindleyi*,
a diffuse shrub, of 3 to 4 feet
high, with twiggy almost unarmed branchlets ; leaves consisting of from seven to nine
opaque glaucescent oblong
leaflets; and rose-coloured
flowers, usually growing in
pairs. *R. parviflora*, a dwarf
shrub of a couple of feet in
height, with slender branches,
linear stipules, needle-shaped
prickles, leaves of about five
lance-shaped finely-toothed
shining leaflets, and pale blush
flowers usually growing in
pairs. *R. carolina*, a shrub
of from 3 to 6 feet high,
with erect branches, twin or
solitary straight prickles under the stipules, which are
convoluta, opaque leaves of
seven lance-shaped leaflets,
and crimson flowers with

, Rosa cinnamomea.

spreading sepals. *R. gemella*, a low shrub, armed with short hooked prickles
growing in pairs beneath the axils of the leaves, which have oblong acute leaflets ; the flowers being large and red. *R. Lyonii*, a shrub of 3 to 4 feet high
with glabrous stems, armed with straight scattered prickles; leaves formed of
from three to five small ovate-oblong leaflets, which are smooth above and
tomentose beneath ; the flowers usually ternate, and pale red. All these are
North American. *R. cinnamomea*, the Cinnamon Rose, which is the type of the
group, is an erect grey shrub, of 5 to 6 feet high, the branches armed with a
pair of straightish prickles under the stipules: the leaves dense, made up of
five rarely seven lanceolate leaflets, grey and smooth above, downy beneath;
the flowers small pale or bright red, and the fruit round naked crimson. It is a
native of England, and is found also in the Middle and South of Europe.
R. Dicksoniana, a shrub of 5 to 6 feet high, with flexuous setigerous branches,
oval leaflets, white flowers, and ovate urceolate naked fruit, is said to be a
native of Ireland. *R. majalis*, the Dwarf Cinnamon or May Rose, is a small
grey shrub of 3 or 4 feet high ; it has straight branches, scattered nearly equal
prickles, and leaves of about seven oblong glaucous leaflets; the flowers are
solitary, pale red ; the fruit orange-red, spherical, and naked. This last is
indigenous in Sweden and Denmark, and is also found in England, being the
R. cinnamomea of some English Botanists.

The PIMPINELLIFOLIÆ consist of deciduous bushes, whose stems and branches either bear crowded nearly equal prickles, or are unarmed, being also sometimes bractless, more rarely bracteate. The leaflets are ovate or oblong, varying in number from seven to fifteen. The sepals are connivent and permanent, and the disk is almost wanting.

This section is represented in two or three groups of our Garden Roses. Thus *R. alpina*, the Alpine Rose, a free-habited unarmed shrub of 5 to 8 feet high, with erect branches, is the original of the group of Boursault Roses. The leaves of the typal form of this Rose consist of from five to nine leaflets; it has solitary erect blush flowers, and orange-red pendulous elongated fruit. It was introduced in 1683 from the Alps of Europe. *R. rubella*, a small erect shrub, 2 or 3 feet high, having the branches covered with nearly equal weak setæ and prickles, and bearing deep red flowers, is a native of England. *R. sulphurea*, the Double Yellow, or Sulphur-coloured Rose, has become familiar in gardens for its beauty and its—intractability. It forms a shrub of 4 or 5 feet high, having its branches beset with unequal scattered falcate or nearly straight prickles and setæ; while the leaves are glaucous, and consist of seven obovate leaflets. The flowers are large, transparent yellow, and only known in the double form. This species is recorded to have been introduced from the Levant in 1629. *R. lutescens*, a North American and Siberian yellow Rose, forms a stout erect shrub of 4 to 6 feet high; the leaves dense, perfectly free from pubescence; the flowers solitary pale yellow, followed by large ovate black fruit.

R. Wilsoni.

The Scotch Rose, *R. spinosissima*, is another example of the section under notice. It has given us the group which bears the name of Scotch Roses—very distinct and very pretty little plants. The species itself, which is one of our native plants, forms a dwarf compact bush, with creeping roots, and short stiff branches, the latter beset with very dense unequal, sometimes falcate, prickles and setæ. The leaves are close, free from pubescence, and consist of about seven flat nearly orbicular leaflets. The flowers are small, solitary, white or blush; the fruit ovate or roundish, purple or blackish, crowned by the connivent sepals. The varieties are numerous: some have the peduncles glandular or bristly, while some have them naked; certain of them are dwarf with slender prickles, the lower ones deflexed; others are taller, with unequal crowded prickles; and others, again, have the leaflets clothed with white down on the under side. It is an early flowering species, which must be regarded as a recommendation. The group of Perpetual Scotch Roses may also be referred to this origin. *R. myriacantha* is like a stunted Scotch Rose, its almost simple erect shoots being defended by dense slender unequal straight prickles and setæ, the largest of the prickles being dagger-formed. *R. hibernica, involuta, Sabini, Doniana, gracilis,* and *Wilsoni,* are further examples of Wild British Roses belonging to this group. The latter, which is shown in the accompanying figure, is a slender shrub of 2 to 4 feet high, the branches furnished with very unequal straight prickles and glandular setæ; the leaves consisting of from five to nine ovate hairy leaflets; the flowers of a beautiful dark pink colour, usually three together; and the fruit nearly globular, scarlet.

The CENTIFOLIÆ are all setigerous deciduous shrubs, the stems bearing bristles and prickles, and being furnished with bracts. The leaflets are oblong or ovate, and wrinkled; the disk of the calyx tube is thickened, so as to close in the throat; and the sepals are compound, that is, divided.

This is, for Rosarians, one of the most important of the groups, yielding him, under the hands of the cultivator, the following distinct races, namely, the Damask, the Four Seasons, the Rose de Trianon, the Damask Perpetual, the Hybrid Perpetual, the Bourbon Perpetual, all referrible to *R. damascena;* the Provence or Provins, the Pompon or Miniature Provence, the Moss, and the Perpetual Moss, all sprung from *R. centifolia;* and the French, the Hybrid French, the Hybrid Chinese, the Hybrid Bourbon, and the Hybrid Noisette, all traceable to *R. gallica,* though, of course, in each case, this parentage has been modified by the influence of surrounding races. The Centifoliæ undoubtedly comprise a majority of the finest and choicest of Garden Roses.

R. damascena, the Damask Rose, of which mention has just been made, is a compact shrub of 2 to 4 feet high, bearing on its branches unequal prickles, the larger of which are falcate. The flowers are large, and either white or red, single or double, the sepals being reflexed, and the fruit elongate. It is of Syrian origin. The French or officinal Rose, *R. gallica,* forms a compact shrub of 2 to 3 feet high. Its branches are armed with weak nearly equal uniform prickles; its leaflets are elliptic, coriaceous, and rigid; its flowers are erect, red crimson or white, single or double; and its fruit coriaceous, and nearly globose. This comes from central Europe.

R. centifolia, the Hundred-leaved, Provence, or Cabbage Rose, is the type of the group. It forms a shrub of 3 to 5 feet high, the branches of which

Rosa centifolia; *a* fruit of R. damascena sub-alba.

are armed with unequal prickles, the larger ones being falcate. The leaflets are ciliated with glands. The flowers are cernuous or nodding, white or red, single or (most commonly) double; the sepals not being reflexed, and the fruit being oblong or roundish, not elongated. This species comes from the Eastern Caucasus, and yields us also the Moss Rose, which differs in having the glands of the surface of the calyx and peduncles developed into a moss-like covering: it forms the var. *muscosa* of botanists. The Pompon Rose (var. *Pomponia*) is smaller in every part. The Celery-leaved Rose, which has the leaves bipinnate, is the var. *bipinnata*.

The VILLOSÆ comprise a set of deciduous shrubs, producing straight erectish surculi (rootshoots), and furnished with straightish prickles. The leaflets are ovate or oblong, with diverging serratures; and the sepals are connivent and persistent, while the disk is thickened so as to close the throat of the calyx-tube.

Rosa villosa.

R. villosa, the type of this section, is a native Rose. It forms a large shrub, sometimes a small tree, the branches being very glaucous, and armed with strong straight or somewhat falcate equal prickles, the branchlets sometimes bearing a few setæ. The leaves are large, grey, of five unequal elliptic rugose leaflets, downy all over, and coarsely serrated. The flowers often grow in pairs, and are red or pink, succeeded by elliptical or globose, purplish-red or crimson bristly fruit, having a grey bloom. There are several varieties.

Here also belong:—*R. turbinata*, the Frankfort Rose, which has the habit of *R. damascena*, and is remarkable for its large, red, very double flowers, the tube of the calyx being turbinate. *R. tomentosa*, a common British Rose, forming a spreading grey-looking shrub of 7 or 8 feet high, the branches armed with straight rarely falcate equal scattered prickles, and without setæ; its leaves are hoary, consisting of about five oblong or ovate obtuse leaflets; the flowers reddish, white at the base; and the fruit purplish, elliptical, and usually hispid. *R. alba*, the type of the garden group of Alba Roses, a spreading greyish shrub of 6 or 7 feet high, the branches of which are armed with straightish slender scattered prickles, and have no setæ. The leaves consist of 5 or 7 oblong glaucous leaflets. The flowers are large, numerous, white or delicate blush, and gratefully fragrant; and the fruit is oblong, deep scarlet. It is an European species, and has been cultivated since 1597.

The RUBIGINOSÆ are deciduous erectish shrubs with arching surculi, distinguished by the lower surface of the leaves being glandular. Their stems are armed with unequal prickles, which are sometimes bristle-formed, rarely wanting; the leaflets are ovate or oblong, glandular, with diverging serratures; the sepals are permanent, and the disk thickened.

Rosa rubiginosa.

The Sweet Brier or Eglantine, *R. rubiginosa*, is a very favourite form of Rose, from the pleasant scent of its glandular foliage. It grows into a much branched shrub of 4 to 6 feet high; the flexuose branches armed with numerous strong hooked unequal prickles; the dull green, rugose, sweet-scented leaves consisting of from five to seven roundish-ovate leaflets, which are covered with numerous glands beneath; the flowers pale blush or pink, two or three together, their peduncles and calyxes hispid with weak setæ; and the fruit orange-red, roundish or obovate, hispid or smooth, crowned by the ascending sepals. The varieties are numerous:—*micrantha* has the prickles nearly equal, the calyx deciduous, and the fruit small, elliptic or obovate; *umbellata* has the branches very prickly, the flowers several in a fascicle, and the fruit globose, nearly smooth; *grandiflora* has large flowers and purple fruit; *flexuosa* has very flexuose branches, and nearly orbicular leaflets; *rotundifolia* has flail-like branches, and roundish leaflets; *sepium* has slender flexuose branches, shining leaflets, subsolitary flowers, and polished fruit; *inodora* has much hooked, nearly equal prickles, nearly scentless oblong leaflets, deciduous sepals, and smooth oblong fruit; and *aculeatissima* has very prickly branches, usually solitary flowers, and ovate fruit. These forms are scattered throughout Europe, some of them being found in Britain. *R. rubiginosa*, the American Sweet Brier, is a shrub of 3 to 6 feet high, the branches furnished with straight scattered prickles; the leaflets scented, ovate, and sparingly glandular beneath; the flowers usually solitary, pink, with entire sepals; and the fruit ovate.

R. lutea is the Yellow Eglantine Rose, a naked-looking bush of about 4 feet high, with erect dark-brown shining branches, armed with pale straight nearly equal prickles, and no setæ. The leaves are shining, and consist of five to seven elliptic leaflets, more or less hoary beneath. The flowers are solitary, deep yellow, large, and cup-shaped. There are some varieties known:—*punicea*, the Austrian Brier, has the petals scarlet above and yellow beneath; *Harrysonya*, Williams's Double Yellow, is a handsome double-flowered yellow Rose; as also is *Harrysoni*, an American variety. The species is native in Germany and the South of France; it gives us the roses known as Austrian Briers. There are many other Roses of this section, but they are little known, or lost to our gardens.

The CANINÆ consist of deciduous or sub-evergreen shrubs, which are in some instances sarmentose, the larger surculi arched, and the branches furnished with equal hooked prickles. The leaflets are ovate, glandless or glandular, with connivent serratures. The sepals are deciduous; and the disk is thickened so as to close the throat.

This group of the Dog Roses shares with the Centifoliæ the highest position in respect to the value of its varieties as ornamental Garden Roses. Here we find the Chinese, the Tea-scented, the Bourbon, and the Rose de Rosomène, all owing parentage to *R. indica;* the crimson Chinese, descendants of *R. semperflorens;* and the Fairy, which come from *R. Lawrenceana.* These comprise some of the sweetest of all Roses, and deservedly hold a prominent place in popular estimation.

Rosa canina.

R. caucasica, the Caucasian Dog Rose, is a very robust shrub of 10 or 12 feet high, nearly allied to *R. canina;* it has remarkably soft ovate leaflets, and the large pale red or white flowers grow in bunches. *R. canina,* the Wild Dog Rose, a straggling bush of 6 to 8 feet high, is one of the commonest of Wild Roses, growing in almost every hedge-row of our own country, and extending throughout Europe and Northern Asia. The branches are armed with strong scattered hooked nearly equal prickles, and are without setæ. The leaves are quite smooth, of five to seven ovate or oblong leaflets; the flowers large, pale red; the fruit ovate or oblong, shining scarlet. The pulp of these fruits, divested of the seeds, forms a very grateful conserve with sugar, and contains, besides saccharine matter, citric acid. The varieties of this common

Rose are exceedingly numerous. Some of the most striking are:—*aciphylla,* dwarf, with smooth leaves and smaller flowers; *obtusifolia,* with the petioles glandular, the leaflets ovate-roundish, and rather pilose beneath; *pilosiuscula,* with the petioles tomentose and hispid, and the leaflets ovate acute puberulous beneath, and smoothish above; *microcarpa,* with smaller fruit, and oblong-lanceolate leaflets, velvety beneath; *ambigua,* with straight prickles, solitary or ternate flowers, and ovate-globose fruit; *rubiflora,* with the prickles strong and rather puberulous, the leaflets large and smooth, and the flowers usually solitary, about the size of those of *Rubus Idæus;* *dumetorum,* with the leaflets flat and more or less hairy on both surfaces; *Fosteri,* with the leaflets more or less hairy, and not flat; *cæsia,* with very glaucous leaflets, hairy beneath. Several of them are to be found in Britain. Though scarcely ornamental as a garden plant, the Dog Rose is very useful, as it furnishes one of the most extensively used and most desirable of stocks for working other Roses upon. Doubtless, on the other hand, it is answerable for a large proportion of the mop-headed plants, which can scarcely be called ornaments of our gardens.

R. indica, the Monthly or Common China Rose, a stout shrub, with glaucous branches, armed with scattered compressed equal hooked brown spines, is the original source of the Chinese, Bourbon, Tea-scented, and Rosomène groups. In this the leaves are shining, without pubescence, and consist of from three to five elliptic leaflets. The flowers are pink, usually semi-double, and growing in panicles. The fruit is obovate, scarlet. There are numerous varieties, of which the most distinct are :—*odoratissima*, with most deliciously-scented flowers; *ochroleuca*, with large double cream-coloured scentless flowers ; and *flavescens*, the true Tea-scented Yellow China Rose. The race of Noisette Roses is also sometimes attributed to a hybrid descendant from this species. *R. indica* comes from China, and was introduced in 1789. *R. semperflorens*, the Ever-flowering China Rose, is a smaller and more elegant shrub, with slender branches armed with scattered compressed hooked prickles and few glands; the leaves are shining, deeply stained with purple, and formed of from three to five ovate-lanceolate leaflets ; the flowers are solitary, deep crimson, and the fruit is spherical. This, also introduced from China in 1789, gives us the Crimson Chinese Roses. *R. Lawrenceana*, a compact-habited shrub of about a foot high, whose branches are armed with large nearly straight prickles, whose leaflets are ovate, and whose flowers are small, semi-double, pale blush, is also of Chinese origin, and is the parent of the Fairy Roses. This little gem blossoms nearly all the year round.

Rosa systyla.

The SYSTYLÆ are deciduous or sub-evergreen shrubs, resembling the Caninæ in habit, but differing in the styles cohering into an elongated column. Though not equalling either the Centifolia, or the Caninæ in the number and value of the garden varieties it has originated, the present group affords some interesting subjects, as the Ayrshires, which come from *R. arvensis*; the Evergreens, which come from *R. sempervirens*; the Multifloras, which come from a species bearing that name; the Musks, the Hybrid Musks, and the Noisettes, which are referred to the *R. moschata*; and the Prairies, which spring from *R. rubifolia*. Some of the most valuable of Climbing Roses are comprised in this series.

R. systyla, an European species, also found in Britain, is a rambling slender shrub of 8 to 10 feet high, with much the character of *R. canina*; the surculi are ascendant; the prickles strong, and hooked; the leaflets ovate; the flowers fragrant, pinkish; and the fruit ovate-oblong. *R. arvensis* is a rambling or trailing, sometimes sub-evergreen, shrub, with stems 20 or 40 feet long, the slender branches armed with scattered equal either falcate or straightish prickles. The leaves are dark green, distant, formed of five or seven ovate somewhat waved leaflets. The flowers are white with a yellow base, slightly scented, solitary on the branchlets, numerous on the rootshoots, and they are followed by round or oblong scarlet fruit. A variety called *hybrida* has semi-double delicate flesh-coloured flowers; it is called in nurseries the Double-hip Rose. The sub-evergreen Ayrshire Roses appear to have originated from a variety called *ayreshirea* or *capreolata*. The species, which is European, is found in hedge-rows and thickets.

R. sempervirens, the Evergreen Rose, from the North of Europe, is a climbing shrub, with long slender shoots, armed with slender somewhat hooked prickles; its leaves are shining, evergreen, formed of five or seven oval or ovate-lanceolate leaflets; its flowers are numerous, white, fragrant; and its fruit small, round, and orange-coloured. There are some cultivated varieties, among which are *Russelliana* and *Clarei*, the former with blush, the latter with deep red flowers.

R. multiflora, from China and Japan, is a sub-climbing shrub, with long naked flexuose branches furnished beneath the stipules with a pair of hooked prickles. The leaves consist of from five to seven approximate soft dull lanceolate leaflets, hairy on both sides; and the flowers are small, numerous, single or double, white or red, succeeded by bright red turbinate fruit,. There are some interesting varieties:—*Thunbergiana*, with small white double clustered flowers; *carnea*, with small pink double clustered flowers; *Grevillei*, the Seven Sisters' Rose, a beautiful plant, with large double clustered flowers, purple, changing colour as they fade; and *Boursaultii*, an early free-flowering Rose, with small double pink flowers, the petals of which have a reticulated appearance. *R. Brunonii*, a rambling shrub, with branches 10 to 12 feet long, and white or pale red flowers in terminal bunches, comes from Nepal. *R. anemonæflora*, is a moderate-sized shrub, with smooth branching stems, the leaves usually ternate, and the flowers in globular clusters, small, pale blush, the outer petals broad, forming a kind of cup, filled up with narrow petals, resulting from the deformation of the stamens; this is a Chinese plant, found in the gardens of Shanghae.

R. moschata, the Musk Rose is said to be the species which yields the precious Persian Attar of Roses. It is a rambling shrub of 10 to 12 feet high, the branches glandular, armed with nearly equal strong hooked scattered prickles. The leaves are naked above, glaucous beneath, made up of five or seven unpolished ovate-lanceolate leaflets. The flowers grow in very numerous many-flowered cymes; they are pure white, with a scent of musk, and are followed by small red fruit. One variety of this, called *nivea*, has large white or pale rose-coloured very handsome flowers; while *multiplex* has double white flowers. The species comes from the North of Africa and Madeira. Some refer the Noisette Roses to this species, others to a cross-bred form of *R. indica*.

The Prairie Rose, *R. rubifolia*, found in North America, is a shrub of 3 to 4 feet high, with straight ascending rootshoots, glabrous branches armed sparingly with scattered falcate prickles, and distant leaves of about five ovate leaflets shining above and downy beneath. The flowers are small pale red, and grow about three together. The fruit is small, round, naked. It blooms in August and September.

The BANKSIANÆ comprise rambling deciduous or sub-evergreen shrubs, somewhat tender in their constitution, having trailing stems, and usually ternate shining leaves, the stipules of which are nearly free, subulate or very narrow, and usually deciduous.

The most important Rose in this group is that known as the Bankaian, of which yellow and white-flowered varieties exist. This plant, *R. Banksiæ*, Lady Banks's Rose, forms a climbing and rambling shrub, the branches of which are unarmed, weak, and of a dull green colour. The leaves are entirely free from pubescence, except at the base of the centre nerve where they are very hairy, and they consist of three or five flat oblong lanceolate obtuse leaflets. The flowers are numerous, arranged in corymbs, nodding, small, white, and very double, with a weak but pleasant scent. The fruit is small, globose, black, unarmed. The variety called *lutea* differs in having the blossoms of a nankeen yellow. This Rose, which flowers in June and July, and was introduced in 1807, comes to us from China.

Rosa sinica.

It is a remarkably fine conservatory plant. *R. sinica*, the Three-leaved China Rose, is also a rambling sub-evergreen shrub, the branches of which are covered with equal scattered red falcate prickles. The leaves are very shining, composed of three ovate-lanceolate leaflets, pale beneath, with a prickly rib. The flowers are large white solitary, succeeded by elliptic orange-red muricate fruit, crowned with the spreading rigid undivided sepals.

With this group of Banksians we complete our Garland of Wild Roses—which we especially commend to the notice of those who are busy at the fountain head of that flood of sweets which pour in upon our gardens in the shape of New Roses each revolving year. Perchance a spray, culled here and there, may not be without its use to them.

INDEX.

FRUIT TREES : including Grape Vines, Strawberry Plants, &c.
> *∗* *No pains or expense is spared to obtain the best sorts, and to keep them healthy, vigorous, and true to name.*

FOREST TREES of all descriptions, which are kept constantly transplanted, in order that they may succeed well after removal.

SEAKAIL, ASPARAGUS, RHUBARB, &c. &c., for forcing and planting out.

II. GREEN HOUSE AND FLORIST DEPARTMENT.

> Azaleas.
> Camellias.
> Cinerarias.
> Chrysanthemums.
> Dahlias.
> Fuchsias.
> Geraniums.
> Greenhouse Plants generally.
> Hollyhocks.
> Pentstemons.
> Phloxes.
> Verbenas.

A selection of the choicest and most distinct varieties of the above are always on sale. Every novelty of merit is added, in order to keep the establishment on a level with the times.

III. SEED DEPARTMENT.

VEGETABLE SEEDS.
> *∗* *The collection of Vegetables recently commended by the Royal Horticultural Society were grown from seeds furnished by him.*

Flower Seeds, including Asters, Stocks, Primulas, &c. of the best races.

Farm Seeds, including Turnips, Mangold Wurtzel, Grasses, &c.

This, which has always appeared to me one of the most important branches of the business, receives a large share of my personal superintendence. Every effort is made to secure for my customers the best races, by growing and saving the more critical crops, and buying others from inspected stocks. Free and strong vegetative powers are secured by furnishing new seeds only, and by keeping them in a dry, cool, and airy warehouse, built on the most approved principles expressly for the purpose.

In this department

Mushroom Spawn.
Russian Mats.
Garden Tools.
Tobacco Paper.

and sundry miscellaneous articles for garden use, are kept.

IV. BULB DEPARTMENT.

HYACINTHS, for which he has obtained several PRIZES at the leading Metropolitan Shows.

TULIPS; all the best early kinds, for spring-gardening and pot-culture.

GLADIOLI, one of the first Collections in Europe, of this most beautiful of Autumn flowers.

Such of these as are better matured in foreign soils and climates, are annually imported thence from the very first sources. These, and sundry garden requisites, it has ever been, and will continue to be, his aim to furnish at the lowest rates compatible with the supply of a first-rate article.

PAUL'S NURSERIES & SEED WAREHOUSE,

WALTHAM CROSS, N.

WORKS OF GARDENING.

BY WILLIAM PAUL, F. R. H. S.

	s.	d.
THE ROSE GARDEN. Second Edition, with numerous wood-cuts	6	6
THE ROSE ANNUAL, 4 Coloured Plates. 1858-59	5	0
Do. 4 Do. 1859-60	5	0
Do. 4 Do. 1860-61	4	0
Do. 4 Do. 1861-62	4	0
ROSES IN POTS. Second Edition	1	6
MORNING RAMBLES IN THE ROSE GARDENS OF HERTFORD-SHIRE	1	0
AMERICAN PLANTS, THEIR HISTORY AND CULTURE	2	6
AN HOUR WITH THE HOLLYHOCK. Second Edition	1	0
THE HANDBOOK OF VILLA GARDENING	2	6

"Well adapted to the end, being of a plain, practical character."—*Spectator.*

"We anticipate it will become, as it deserves, a general authority in suburban cultivation."—*Gardeners' Chronicle.*

NURSERY CATALOGUES.

The following Priced Descriptive Catalogues may be obtained free by post :—

A.—ROSES. New Edition published annually.

B.—EVERGREENS, ORNAMENTAL TREES, FLOWERING SHRUBS, &c.

C.—FRUIT TREES.

D.—HYACINTHS, &c. New Edition published annually.

E.—FOREST TREES.

F.—NEW ROSES, HOLLYHOCKS, GLADIOLI, PELARGONIUMS, DAHLIAS, VERBENAS, &c. New Edition published annually.

G.—SEEDS : Vegetable, Flower, and Agricultural.

EXPERIENCED GARDENERS RECOMMENDED.

W. M. Watts, Crown Court, Temple Bar.